Praise for *House of Coates*

"Transfixing. . . . A haunting change of pace." —*The New York Times*

"An enigmatic, innovative, and deadpan novel. . . . What [Zellar and Soth have] mined here falls somewhere in between W. G. Sebald's photograph-strewn novels and Carson McCullers's small-town freaks and loners: the result is an unaccountably strange and liberating narrative." —*Vogue*

"A kind of case study of human drift." —*Star Tribune*

"This collaboration between writer Brad Zellar and photographer Alec Soth . . . captures in 133 pages the essence of those who live on the edges of society." —*Pioneer Press*

"Gentle and unsparing in equal measure." —*Bustle*

"A standout. . . . Exquisitely written." —*Book Riot*

"An interesting, well-executed book. Ultimately, it's less a narrative about Lester than it is a prose poem about loners and losers, the many Lesters who 'never entirely disappear as adults, even if you still persist in not seeing them.'" —*Publishers Weekly*

"A poetic attempt not to fully form a life but only to capture moments of memory and objects of counterintuitive beauty. . . . The prose is crisp and thoughtful and well-matched to the photos that show the side of America to which even most Americans never give a second thought." —*Kirkus*

Till the Wheels Fall Off

Also by Brad Zellar
House of Coates

Till the Wheels Fall Off
BRAD ZELLAR

COFFEE HOUSE PRESS

Minneapolis

2022

Definition of daytime parahypnagogia quoted from E. B. Gurstelle
and J. L. de Oliveira, "Daytime Parahypnagogia: A State of Consciousness That Occurs When We Almost Fall Asleep," *Medical Hypotheses* 62,
no. 2 (200402): 166–68.

Coffee House Press books are available to the trade through our primary distributor, Consortium Book Sales & Distribution, cbsd.com
or (800) 283-3572. For personal orders, catalogs, or other information, write to info@coffeehousepress.org.

Coffee House Press is a nonprofit literary publishing house. Support
from private foundations, corporate giving programs, government
programs, and generous individuals helps make the publication
of our books possible. We gratefully acknowledge their support in
detail in the back of this book.

LIBRARY OF CONGRESS CATALOGING-IN-PUBLICATION DATA

Names: Zellar, Brad, author.
Title: Till the wheels fall off / Brad Zellar.
Description: Minneapolis : Coffee House Press, 2022.
Identifiers: LCCN 2021062605 (print) | LCCN 2021062606 (ebook) |
    ISBN 9781566896399 (paperback) | ISBN 9781566896474 (epub)
Classification: LCC PS3626.E3626 T55 2022 (print) |
    LCC PS3626.E3626 (ebook) | DDC 813/.6—dc23
LC record available at https://lccn.loc.gov/2021062605
LC ebook record available at https://lccn.loc.gov/2021062606

PRINTED IN THE UNITED STATES OF AMERICA

29 28 27 26 25 24 23 22   1 2 3 4 5 6 7 8

Till the Wheels Fall Off

I.

The past deceives in every direction. The memory plays a game of Telephone with itself and with the present.

Every day at noon, for reasons that have never been clear to me, the bell rings out from the tower at St. Augustine, the huge old Catholic church right in the middle of Prentice. The orbit of my father's family was centered on that church for most of my childhood, and the ringing comforted and oriented me when I was growing up. At some point in the recent past, however, the bell apparently sustained some damage, and you could no longer refer to its sound as ringing. In the brief time I've been back in Prentice, I'm inevitably startled when I hear the bell at noon. It sounds like someone striking a steel girder with a sledgehammer. There's nothing at all sonorous or sustained or remotely lovely about the sound, which, frankly, is already getting on my nerves. It's a small town, though, and there's no way to hide from that cracked bell, no drowning it out. Every day the Catholics insist on calling me to attention at noon and reminding me that here I am.

Two parallel one-ways cut straight through the south side of town—one runs east to west, the other west to east, and both tie in with the interstate highway that skirts Prentice to the north. Once darkness falls, most of the bored teenagers still left in town troll aimlessly up and down the one-ways, the windows of their late-model cars rolled down and the music from their stereos drifting into the humid summer nights. Sound carries in a flat, prairie town, and this summer there's no escaping Ricky Martin's "Livin' la Vida Loca" and Smash Mouth's "All Star." I can expect to hear both songs at least a dozen times every night. A bit later, when the streets are taken over by bored stoners who never left, I'll hear strains of older, more familiar music, songs by the sorts of bands who never go out of style in a town like Prentice: Yes, for instance, and ZZ Top, Black Sabbath, Journey, Kiss, even Foghat.

Then, an hour or so after the downtown bars close, this little town will grow eerily quiet. There's an almost otherworldly silence you just can't experience in a bigger city. It's still, after all these years, the time I love and the thing I love most about Prentice. It's an illusion, I know, but it's thrilling: everyone's gone to bed, I'm the last man standing, and my music is the only music for miles around.

Last Saturday I drove to Floyd Valley to check out Sergeant Floyd's, a record store that opened during the years I was gone. It's a small, decent store run by young zealots I'd probably discover I have things in common with if either they or I had the social skills to start a proper conversation. There weren't any other customers while I was there, and as a result this awkward tension hung in the air, and I felt self-conscious and furtively scrutinized. I also felt obligated to buy *something*. I browsed for maybe a half hour and ended up buying Outkast's *Aquemini* and Billy Bragg and Wilco's *Mermaid Avenue*.

I've since listened to both discs repeatedly, and though it's always a thrill to discover new music, sitting alone and studying the liner notes I was reminded of a quote from Randall Jarrell's *Animal Family*, a quote that shattered me when I first encountered it while reading in a motel room somewhere in North Dakota:

> In spring the meadow that ran down from the cliff to the beach was all foam-white and sea-blue with flowers; the hunter looked at it and it was beautiful. But when he came home there was no one to tell what he had seen—and if he picked the flowers and brought them home in his hands, there was no one to give them to. And when at evening, past the dark blue shape of a far-off island, the sun sank under the edge of the sea like a red world vanishing, the hunter saw it all, but there was no one to tell what he had seen.

I'm sure I have other, earlier memories, but the one that returns to me again and again is waking to loud music and making my way into a still-unfamiliar apartment. This would've been no more than a few days after my mother's marriage to my stepfather, and after we moved from my grandmother's house to our new apartment downtown. The music was coming from across the hall, from the big, high-ceilinged room, formerly a ballroom owned by Freemasons. Our apartment was connected to this room by a short dogleg hallway—a dark and narrow corridor accessible from the back of our kitchen, next to the refrigerator; you walked maybe seven feet down this hall, took a ninety-degree turn into an identical passage, also dark, parted a heavy velvet curtain, and entered the old ballroom, which was ringed by high transom windows (the only source of natural light) way up near the ceilings. It was early, probably before seven, a Saturday (I'm pretty sure), winter in a small Midwestern town where the winters were merciless and long. The light in that room was dream light, the kind of light I associate in my memory or imagination with ancient cathedrals and temples and other holy places similar to those I saw in the pictures in my father's old confirmation Bible, which my mother kept on her nightstand.

It *was*, it turns out, a holy place, or at least one of the few places that occupies a sacred place in my memory.

Perhaps a dozen globes of colored light dangled from the ceiling, purely ambient, or at least ineffectual for anything but establishing a mood. Pastels. Easter egg colors. Also up there, hanging in the middle of the room, was a giant disco ball, the first I'd ever seen, turning slowly and showering the room—the carpeted walls and gleaming hardwood floors—with shimmering polka dots of light. From the high windows on the east end of the room, beams of winter sunlight loaded with tumbling dust motes carved through the murk at precise and startling angles.

My stepfather, Russ, wearing roller skates, was gliding around the hardwood oval that dominated the room, making graceful stirring motions with a long, flat mop he held in his hands. The music seemed to come from all over. The song, I later learned, was Sly and the Family Stone's "I Want to Take You Higher."

I stood at the back of the room, just outside the entrance to our apartment. I watched my new stepfather, seemingly in a trance, go around and around, oblivious to my presence. I marveled at the light, the shadows, the music. I was pretty sure that what I felt in that moment—awe and pure wonder that I'd stepped into a world beyond my then-limited imagination—I'd never felt before. I was nine, my stepfather had turned an old ballroom into a roller-skating rink, and I was about to become the person I helplessly am.

Russ's rink was called Vargo's Screaming Wheels, and it was above the fire department and armory in Prentice. My father had been killed in Vietnam before I was born, and my mother and I had spent the intervening years living with various family members (or in houses my father's family owned) before we moved into the cramped apartment adjoining the rink. Russ was socially awkward and music obsessed, to the exclusion, really, of everything else, and from the moment we moved our stuff to that apartment, I was his shadow and loyal disciple. It was possible, I sometimes thought, that I was his only real friend.

I listened to a lot of Russ's monologues over the years; if I hadn't been around, I'm pretty sure he would've just talked to himself. But as I got older, his monologues became long, rambling conversations between the two of us, and I learned about the Grip, which Russ defined as a claiming desire you discovered at some young age, an obsession or fascination—sometimes kink, sometimes compulsion—that put down roots in your skull and staked a permanent camp, some ceaselessly hectoring preoccupation that wouldn't leave you alone and ultimately defined you and determined how you spent (or squandered) your time and what you did with your life.

What I'm talking about, I suppose, is sort of the earliest experience with the Crossroads. It's the thing that grabs you, that gets you in a grip from which it has no intention of releasing you. A brand you get stamped with in childhood or adolescence, something that makes it clear you've either been found, fucked, or saved: *You will love me always. You will follow me forever and wherever I lead. You will serve me until the end of your days.*

There are, of course, a million tiny and ridiculous ways a person can get sidetracked and carried away off the main trail. But in the end, always, you become a hostage to who you are, to what you want or what you can't say, to what fascinates you, what breaks you down and holds you under; the sense (or nonsense) you feel compelled to build, the truth or meaning you try so desperately to find.

II.

I still remember the way the wheels would sound when Russ would skate alone out in the rink in the early mornings or late at night, and I'd sit awake in my little bedroom next door. Or when the rink was crowded with skaters, and the hundreds of polyurethane wheels going around and around created a steady hum—equal parts highway traffic, gully washer, or heavy surf. You could feel it even beneath or beyond the music pulsing from the ceiling speakers.

When Russ was alone in the rink, he kept the stereo volume at a respectful level as a courtesy to my mother and me. And because he had lined all the walls dividing the apartment from the rink with burlap bags stuffed with cotton batting or foam rubber, when I was in my bedroom, I mostly just heard the wheels—or felt their vibration in the floorboards. The music was more distant, unless Russ had the bass cranked up, which he usually did during open hours. The bass was a pulse in the floor and walls, an atmospheric phenomenon, something you felt like a gently pummeling presence rippling up through the soles of your shoes.

I'm thinking, though, of the mornings in particular, when Russ skated alone, pushing a mop or floor buffer around the rink. I'm thinking of the sound I heard virtually every day as I got ready for school. At that hour Russ would skate to records he'd likely never play during public hours—maybe Lou Reed's *Transformer*, Van Morrison's *Veedon Fleece*, or anything by The Band. When he was alone and listening to music without a strict skating groove, he was a loud, percussive skater. He liked to pick his skates up and slap them down with the beat, or, often, a hard stomp on the downbeat and a subtler toe-tap on the upbeat. Even when he was just gliding there was something aggressive and turbulent about his skating; he rolled hard, pushing big waves up against rock cliffs, or he sometimes whooped, "Balling the jack!" *Boom . . . swoosh. Boom . . . swoosh.*

More freight train than automobile. Late at night his skating was steadier, languid, a lullaby almost indistinguishable from the hum of distant freeway traffic.

Actually, it reminded me—or reminds me in the remembering—of being sprawled in the far back seat of one of my uncles' station wagons, returning late at night from some family outing, the surf of darkness and the thrum of the tires on the pavement murmuring at the slightly open windows; streetlamps and headlights strobing the car's interior, disorienting, and the faint strains of some pop hit or baseball game drifting from the dashboard radio. Everyone else in the car was so quiet, and I was so tired I wobbled back and forth at the edge of sleep. I had the comforting and unquestioned knowledge that I was on my way home, and I felt the earliest shivers of the wonder I would later experience in the dazzling crepuscule of that roller rink.

A long-standing Prentice custom involved the high school senior class taking a poll during the last weeks before graduation. The question: How many seniors had any intention of hanging around Prentice for the rest of their lives?

On graduation day a delegation would go to the edge of town with reflective stickers to adjust the population number on the "Welcome to Prentice" sign; during the early years of this tradition, if I remember correctly, this involved a subtraction of anywhere from forty to sixty every year, depending on the size of the graduating class (which had been diminishing for the last couple decades before the high school was closed and the remaining kids bused to a multihyphenated school over in Floyd Valley).

There was no way I could've imagined that in the last year of the twentieth century and seven months away from my thirtieth birthday, I would be back in Prentice. Yet here I am, already getting used to the idea. Earlier today I had a weirdly serendipitous grocery store encounter with my junior high English teacher, Miss Aldine, one of the few teachers who made any real impression on me. I didn't immediately recognize her at the grocery store, and she had to introduce herself. When I told her I was surprised she remembered me, she said, "You were my captive for two years. Of course I remember you. You were absolutely bored to tears, poor thing."

In the classroom this woman had had a jittery, birdlike presence, with a disconcertingly deep voice she had trouble modulating—it was the voice, actually, of an adolescent boy struggling through the humiliating changes of puberty. One day in class she said, "Some of you will soon discover, if you haven't already, that this is a town of rather smothering conformity. If that bothers you at all, I'd encourage you to spend some time over the next several years contemplating what I consider one of the loveliest and most consoling phrases in the English language." She turned and, in her elegant, looping cursive, wrote on the blackboard REARVIEW MIRROR. "Think of those words as a poem, or even a useful mantra, if you know what that is. Tattoo them on your hearts. Two words, four syllables. *Rear. View. Mir. Ror.* They positively unfurl themselves from your tongue, don't they? I trust you'll have plenty of time to decide if you'll find those words crushing or hopeful."

I guess I'm finally confronting that decision, poised as I am at a point in my life when I seem to stare into a rearview mirror everywhere I turn. I've now maintained an official residence here in Prentice for almost a month. Like Russ before me, I tried to make my escape, tried to make a go of it in Minneapolis, and failed. Even before the weekly paper where I'd landed a job folded, I knew I'd never master the logistical and time management challenges of living in a big city. I'd also had a series of relationships that proved frustrating and heartbreaking to varying degrees; I was generally the primary source of the frustration, and the heartbreak was almost always inflicted on me. By the time everything started to unravel up there, the harbingers of the new century had been grimly trending for much of the last decade. In the Twin Cities I'd found myself learning—or trying to learn—the language of technology and machines. None of that stuff seemed useful or at all intuitive to me, and by the time I started to contemplate my retreat, I already knew I was the wrong sort of man for the twenty-first century. I can't even straddle the divide with any grace; I am, helplessly and resolutely, a product of the late twentieth century. I can't get the hang of computers, don't want a mobile phone, and have absolutely no appreciation for or understanding of gizmos of any kind.

When I ran into Miss Aldine I was coming from having coffee with my old friend, the Cowboy. I hadn't seen him in a couple years, and he admitted to being startled to learn I was back in Prentice.

"And here I thought you'd finally broken out of the past," he'd said.

"So did I," I said. "But I still can't get the hang of the present, and the future is starting to spook me."

"*Present tense*," he said, and laughed. "That's an uncomfortable anteroom for you, isn't it? It's both a purgatory and a crucible. You're still trying to find your way into the big room of the present—you any closer to figuring out what you hope to find once the doors swing open?"

I shrugged. "I don't know. I think I have to find Russ, though. One way or another, I need that closure."

"Right," the Cowboy said. "So try harder."

The Cowboy is the therapist I started seeing about fifteen years ago: a leathery, older fellow, stooped, with a wild head of white hair and turquoise rings on most of his fingers. The first time I met him, he wore a big leather-tooled belt with a buckle as large as a teacup saucer. Cowboy boots, for which some kind of snake or alligator or lizard had been sacrificed, rounded out his look. For such a little man he had huge feet. Next to the desk in his office over in Floyd Valley stood a framed drawing of a woman tied to railroad tracks. Above this drawing were the words "Trouble? See the Cowboy."

As I said good-bye to the Cowboy outside Cuppa Joe, he said, "I'm starting to believe a happy and enchanted childhood can be as disabling as a childhood marked by sadness and neglect. Remember that wild-eyed kid who grew up in the roller rink and spent all those years driving around the Midwest in a car packed with condoms and quarters? Maybe you're never going to shake him. And maybe this is his home."

Is that the truth that's sat across the room from me every night, engaged in a staring contest for the last twenty years? Have I been a hostage to the impossibly happy ten-year-old boy I once was? Maybe I need to learn to be mostly fine with that, because I love that kid, and I love his dreams.

This is an American story, or a story of America in the late twentieth century, and things happened. And by "things happened," I mean things fell apart. This town, for instance, which was prone to historic floods and tornadoes throughout most of its history. The factory where for many, many decades hundreds of local employees made blenders and toasters and microwave ovens was sold to pirates; almost fifty percent of the workforce was laid off. Then, five years later, the whole kit and kaboodle was shut down. Other, smaller industries—a box factory and a shipping company—that depended on the appliance factory also shut down. And with alarming rapidity the entire downtown and most of the major businesses in the retail development just outside town were evacuated, or it felt as if they'd been evacuated; block after block went dark.

If you've ever spent time in any of the towns that have been similarly obliterated all over the world, you might know what I mean when I say that Prentice now has a positively apocalyptic vibe, the feel of a futuristic Western or a postnuclear horror movie. Pretty much everything I remembered and loved about the place is gone. I have some photo books that depict the ostensibly different ruins of Chernobyl and Detroit—you could swap scenes from present-day Prentice for pictures in any of those books and nobody would notice.

The trajectory of my life—or, really, whatever the opposite of a trajectory is—is in too many ways similar to that of my hometown. From my birth until my mother married Russ, we were essentially wards of my father's Catholic family. My father, the surprise child, was sixteen years younger than his next oldest sibling, Rollie. Big Leonard (II) was the eldest Carnap child, and he had always struck me as almost as old as my grandfather. In the half dozen years between Rollie and Big Leonard, my grandmother—married and pregnant at seventeen—produced three other children, my aunts Helen and Elaine and my uncle Mooze. Of my father's five siblings, only Mooze and Elaine ever married, and—mysteriously, improbably—none of them ever had children.

For almost five years after I graduated from high school I worked for my uncles, servicing bathroom condom machines in gas stations, truck stops, and bars all over the Midwest. My mother and Russ had been divorced for four years by that point, and it was during my time on the Rubber Route that Russ disappeared from Prentice and my life. Things between us had been awkward after the divorce—my mother and I had moved to Floyd Valley—but I'd tried to stay in touch. When the rink closed, though, he'd drifted away from me, and then he just seemed to vanish.

Throughout my twenties, death kept drawing me back to Prentice. My mother died of breast cancer a month before my twenty-fifth birthday. My grandmother, the Carnap matriarch, went a few years before my mother (she'd had dementia and was bedridden with one thing or another for as long as I could remember). Aunt Tina was next; her husband, my uncle Mooze, was inconsolable and seemingly intent on drinking himself to death when, four months later (and on his deceased wife's birthday), he had a heart attack and fell over dead on a golf course. My aunt Helen, who'd lived with my grandmother and never left the house she grew up in, died the next year, allegedly of cancer, but she'd been a pretty serious stay-at-home alcoholic for decades. I was living in Minneapolis right around the time all this death commenced in earnest.

I remember walking to the library from my mother's hospital room in Floyd Valley at least once a day to dial up the internet in the computer room. That was my first experience with computers. I don't remember what models they were or how I learned to use them, but I remember monkeying around and thinking I might find some trace of Russ in that mystifying web. I had no idea if Russ would want to know my mother was dying, or how he would respond if he knew, but I felt at the time a real sense of urgency to be in touch with him and let him know what was going on. We'd had a life together, the three of us.

After she left Russ and we moved to Floyd Valley, she never asked about him or my relationship with him. But during her final stay in the hospital she and I talked a lot about those years, for the first time, really. I think by then she had enough distance and perspective to look back with a bit more clarity and even fondness.

She told me she'd assumed Russ and I had continued to talk to and see each other. She had hoped, she said, that that was the case. "You were so close to him," she said. "And I was envious, but I'm not such a horrible person that I wanted to tear you apart. You were probably the best thing that ever happened to him, and he had more energy and enthusiasm for his relationship with you than he ever had for me. Somehow you understood him in a way I never could. You had a real connection. He once, in his typically clumsy and bashful way, brought up the possibility of adopting you—so you could have a dad, he said—and I reacted horribly. Really, I was awful, and I've felt terrible about that ever since. His heart was in the right place, but I was so young, and I still wasn't over the shock of your dad's death. I was already afraid of losing you, afraid you were choosing sides, and I couldn't begin to understand the things you both cared about. I tried, but I just couldn't get it. I was too lost, and that rink and that town and that obscure little world you two lived in felt claustrophobic to me. I wanted to escape all that, and I wanted to get you out of there too, because I thought it was just a phase and it was unhealthy for you. But I realize now how selfish that was of me. And I'm sorry, Matthew. It wasn't easy for me to recognize how much more you were Russ's child than mine. It made me sad. I could see your dad in you when you were young—

you were so obviously a Carnap, and it bothered me that I could see nothing of myself in you. And then you just became a little Russ right before my eyes. It was heartbreaking."

When I told her I hadn't seen or heard from Russ in years she cried. She turned her head from me, but I could hear the quiet sobs, could see them spasming up her spine and shaking the whole bed.

After a time, she pulled herself together and asked, "Where is he?"

"I have no idea," I said. And that just made her cry more.

"I'm so sorry, Matt," she said. "Shame on both of you. If ever two people needed each other. How could either of you let that happen?"

"We just drifted apart," I said. "I think he couldn't handle it after we left the rink, and then the rink folded. I tried to stay in touch with him, but it was hard for both of us after we moved. I knew you and Baron didn't like him, and it didn't seem like anyone else in the family liked him either. He left Prentice to work at the radio station in Iowa, and then he just sort of disappeared."

"You really should find him," she said.

"I've tried," I said. "Nobody seems to know where he is. I've started to think maybe he doesn't want to be found."

After my mom died, there wasn't anybody left in Prentice except my uncle Rollie, the youngest of the Carnap siblings.

Rollie had always been the ebullient engine of the family, but he was sixty-five at that point and understandably diminished by the staggering collapse of the once indomitable Carnaps. I'd never known Rollie to appear beleaguered, but with all the economic calamity already baring its teeth in Prentice and the myriad loose ends involved with the family businesses, he seemed like a man crossing off his own days on a jailhouse calendar. He kept going, though, and after a few years he was seemingly attacking all the challenges in Prentice with renewed determination. We talked on the phone all the time; I was the only family he had left.

"Don't ever let anyone bad-mouth all these new immigrants," he said one day. "The Mexicans are going to save this town. I've never seen a bunch of people willing to work so fucking hard to build a new life from the ground up."

And then, a year or two later: "The Mexicans aren't going to save us, Matty. Too many other idiots are willing to watch the town die, or they're fleeing like rats from a sinking ship. You wouldn't believe how many houses are on the market. Everybody's trying to sell out—good luck with that—and move to Florida or Arizona."

When the plant finally closed, and then the high school was dissolved in the consolidation, I asked Rollie what he was going to do. "I'm going down with the ship," he said. "This is my fucking home. My whole family is buried out there in Calvary, and our name is all over this stinking town. This is personal, Matty. I can't leave. Your grandfather is rolling in his grave."

When my life started to fall apart a couple years ago, Rollie started agitating for me to move back to Prentice.

"Come home and get some wind back in your sails," he said.

"In Prentice?"

"Stranger things have happened, Matty," he said. "Maybe it'll clear your head and give you a little perspective."

It took a few months to get my head around the idea. On a number of occasions over the last five years—as my mother was dying and I was floundering in Minneapolis—I'd spent some long stretches in Prentice that were, it turned out, trial runs for the eventual move. I'd usually stay in my grandmother's old house—which still had the smell and the feel of a recently abandoned hospice—or at Big Leonard's midcentury modern split-level out by the golf course. Big Leonard's house had a lot of promise and was somewhat up my alley in terms of style, but it was also a depressing museum of a bachelor lifestyle that had gone out of style decades earlier (Rollie's house was even more over the top in that regard, but he was fussy, a little more concerned about contemporary style points, and didn't smoke). Big Leonard had smoked cigarettes and cigars for his entire adult life, and everything in the place—the wall-to-wall shag carpeting, the textured wallpaper, the nubby matching living room furniture—reeked like a flophouse motel. His house was also low-slung with lots of dark wood and murky lighting and, after a couple days, tended to get a bit too noirish for my comfort. It didn't help that no one had apparently set foot in the place since he died, and I was depressed to find his cupboards still full of canned soup and beef stew. I was even more depressed when I found his stash of seventies-era porn heaped in boxes in his bedroom closet. This was the type of cheap and superskeezy stuff I knew my uncles had peddled for years, one of several unsavory sidelines they'd stumbled into during their years in the liquor business.

A year or so ago I was visiting and hanging around for a few days when Rollie and I went to the Carnap athletic complex to take stock. The high school had been gone for years, and the city was riding Rollie's ass about the property. The complex was built on land belonging to the family, and Rollie and his brothers had bankrolled much of the project. The actual football field and track—officially the Roland Carnap Athletic Field—were inside a locked fence and surrounded by practice fields, baseball diamonds, and tennis courts that were now used, if they were used at all, by whatever kids were still around. A number of immigrant communities were settling in Prentice—many of them, actually, had arrived to work in the appliance and box factories near the end—and some of them used the fields to play soccer or as picnic grounds for family gatherings and birthday parties.

The grass was now unmarked and clearly hadn't been mowed for a long time. There were a handful of mostly modest small-town graffiti tags here and there along the base of the bleachers and on the facing of the press boxes, but otherwise it seemed that most of the facilities were in remarkable shape and just waiting for the next football game or track meet.

Rollie, though, was depressed by the whole sad spectacle. "All that fucking money down the toilet," he said. "We didn't cut a single corner, and the team won a total of twenty games in the seven years they played here."

"It's an amazing place for a high school football team," I said.

We climbed the steps of the home-team bleachers to the press box, and Rollie fiddled with a huge ring of keys, found the right one, and took us inside. There were two levels: upper and lower. The lower level had a series of long tables or workstations, each of which had power outlets. On the back side of the lower level were a trio of separate office-like spaces, slightly elevated; one of these offices had a small refrigerator and freezer, a microwave, and a wall of cupboards and counters. The entire length of the press box was lined with huge transom windows that could be cranked open to provide an unobstructed view of the field. We climbed a short flight of stairs to the upper level, which served as a private party room. Both levels had bathrooms.

"The whole damn thing is heated and air conditioned," Rollie said.

"I could live here," I said.

"Sure, you could," Rollie said. "You could shower in the locker room, and this place has more toilets than any house in town."

There was a stairway at the back of the press box that took you down to the locker room, which was huge and had an attached weight room, medical office, and suite of other offices for the coaches and trainers. "It's surprisingly tidy," I said.

"I have someone come in and clean the place every month or so," Rollie said.

"Why?" I asked.

Rollie shrugged. "Maybe wishful thinking?"

"Does everything work?"

"To the best of my knowledge."

There was also a tunnel down there that took you all the way around the stadium to the visitor's locker room. Beneath one of the end zones was a full kitchen with stainless-steel industrial appliances.

"What's this for?" I asked Rollie.

Rollie shrugged again. "We went wild," he said. "I guess we were thinking banquets, retirement parties, weddings, that sort of thing. There's a big party room under the other end zone, and the second level of both press boxes was designed for private groups, company events, stuff like that."

He stared around the kitchen with a haunted look on his face. "I don't think this fucking thing has ever been used."

"It's ridiculous," I said. "But it's also incredible."

"I thought so. I haven't been so proud of anything in my life."

We went back into the tunnel and wandered down to a room that held all the fuse boxes and mechanical contraptions that made the place run. Rollie pointed out the heating and air conditioning, the sprinkler system, and the control panel for the field lights and scoreboard. "The PA system is all run from the press box," he said, "and you can monkey with the scoreboard from up there too." He flipped a bunch of switches and we walked down the hallway and up some stairs to the field level.

When we emerged onto the track, the whole place was lit up like a giant spacecraft that had been plopped down in the middle of that dying town.

"Holy shit," I said.

Rollie stared across the field at the blazing scoreboard towering above the home end zone. "That thing has all sorts of bells and whistles," he said. "I don't think anybody ever figured out how the hell to use it."

"I could live here," I said again.

He looked at me and smiled. It was his old, familiar smile, huge, slightly lopsided, all his teeth and upper gums exposed. "You *should* live here, Matt. What a kick that would be. What a story."

"I'm serious," I said.

"So am I. I wouldn't want you living in any of them other haunted houses. This place doesn't have any ghosts yet. Seriously, we could set you up in the locker room. You'd have everything you need."

"It's too dark down there," I said. I pointed up at the press box. "I'd prefer *that.* The penthouse. I can shower downstairs."

Rollie let out a whoop and clapped his hands. "Shit, Matt. That's beautiful. We should make it happen."

"We should." I looked around the stadium and tried to take it all in, tried to get my head around the idea. Was I actually serious? I decided I was. I had more than $100,000 in my bank account in Minneapolis. I'd also come into money and property after the deaths of my mother, grandmother, and uncles. That money was in a bank account in Prentice, and I'd never touched it.

Rollie slapped me on the head and let out a whoop. "Your uncle Mooze would laugh so hard he'd fall over," he said. "He gave me endless shit about this whole thing, thought I was out of my mind. 'For Chrissakes, Rollie, it's a Class A football team,' he said. 'They haven't won a conference championship or been to state since Mikey was still strapping on shoulder pads.'"

Mikey was my dad. Nobody ever talked about him. I'd once asked Russ if he'd known him and he said, "Sure. It's a small town."

"What was he like?" I'd asked.

Russ had thought for a moment, as if he was trying to decide how much to say or how willing he was to violate the family's compact of silence on the subject. Then he'd said. "He was a jock. Tough guy. Didn't say much."

As I stood there on the track with Rollie, I decided to press my luck since he had raised the subject. "Was my dad any good?"

"At football?" Rollie said. "He was a monster, smaller than the rest of us but tougher than all of us combined. That team he was on ran the table in the conference and went all the way to the finals of the state tournament, where they got pounded by a Catholic school from up in the Cities."

"What position did he play?"

"He was a running back and linebacker. Played pretty much every down and returned punts and kickoffs." Rollie was silent for a time, his eyes roaming the stadium. "What a shit I am," he finally said. "I should've named this after Mikey." He slapped me on the back and started to walk away down the track. As he started up the bleacher steps he turned and stared at me as if taking me in for the first time. "We called him Mystery Meat," he said. "Your uncles and me. He hated it."

And with that he plopped down in a row of bleachers and stared out at the empty field. I made an entire lap of the track, and when I came back around Rollie was standing there waiting for me. He pulled me into a bear hug and cupped the back of my head in one of his big hands. We were having a moment, I knew; this was how the Carnaps communicated both great sadness and great joy. They yanked each other into tight embraces, patted each other on the back, then went back to the business of life. "We aren't big talkers or deep thinkers," Uncle Mooze once told me. "But we're yappers, every one of us. Nobody likes that woe-is-me crap."

Rollie eventually pushed me away from him, gripped me by the shoulders, looked me right in the eyes, and shook his head. "We're the last of the Mohicans, Matty," he said. "Can you believe it?"

"It breaks my heart," I said.

"No, it doesn't," he said. "You know whose hearts are broken? All those people we buried. Those hearts are broken. Yours and mine still work just fine."

"I'm not sure about that," I said. "Russ used to tell me that you just keep rolling until the wheels fall off. The wheels have fallen off."

"Shut the fuck up, Matty. Look at us and listen to you." He spread his arms wide and grinned. "We own this dead-ass town, kid. Or what's left of it. You wanna know what pisses me off?"

"What's that?"

"All those fuckers like the Vargos spent decades buying up properties downtown and out in the neighborhoods, never put a fucking dime into any of them, milked decent people dry, and the minute the plant was in trouble and the shit hit the fan, they started selling them off to the city and the county, and the city and the county started pulling them all down and replacing them with nothing. Art Vargo owned all those houses over in the floodplain, and every time the waters would recede, he'd find some poor fucks to move right back into the pieces of shit, and the instant the state and federal government started to throw around money to clear out the whole kit and kaboodle, he—or that kid of his, or whoever—cut bait and got the fuck out. You've been over there. You've been downtown. Those are the fuckers who killed this town, not us. Not the Carnaps. We're still here, and I'll be damned if we don't still have plenty of money in the fucking bank. This is our town."

Rollie was trying to put it on Russ. I knew Rollie despised the Vargo clan and felt Russ had led me astray, away from the grip of the Carnaps and into a driftless life he couldn't begin to understand. I wasn't, though, ready to talk about Russ.

"I'd like to get it all back," I said.

"What, the town?" Rollie said. "Me too, kid."

"All of it," I said. "The past."

III.

Rollie is still the best-connected guy in Prentice. Whenever new people move to town to take advantage of the cheap housing, Rollie gets to know them. He helps them find houses, furniture, jobs. You could transport Rollie to any small town or big city in America and he'd find a way to become one of those little kings of everything that exist everywhere. My uncle Mooze was the same way. I'm sure there was some self-interest involved—they both knew how to keep money moving into the places and institutions that needed money to survive—but I also think it was just the way they were. They loved to get people connected and understood that those connections, when constantly nourished and expanded, were how people and communities stayed alive, and though they both made a lot of money in their lives, they were the most instinctively generous people I've ever known. And they were dreamers, proponents of a fierce, old-school patriotism that embraced immigrants as a lifeline for all things they believed in and thought were still possible in Prentice. And so, when Rollie became convinced that I really was desperate and crazy enough to move into the football stadium, he went right to work.

I was taken with the idea, but it was initially pure fantasy. I didn't believe I would ever go through with it. After that day I toured the place with Rollie, I went back to Minneapolis and probably would've eventually forgotten about the whole thing if Rollie hadn't kept calling me a couple days a week with "project updates."

"I've been working with this really terrific Bosnian who I just found out is an architect," he told me one day. "We need to get together to talk about how you're picturing the setup over at the football field."

"Wait," I said. *"What?"*

"Come on, fella," he said. "Let's get this thing done. I already had some guys over there cutting the grass and doing some painting, and I've got a shitload of furniture stashed all over this town. I was going to have some shelves built for all your fucking books and records, but I need you to draw up a little plan of where you want shit to be."

"Man, Rollie, you don't fuck around," I said, "You're really serious about this?"

"You should know damn well I don't fuck around, Matty. I hate the idea of you sitting up there feeling sorry for yourself. Come on down and we'll find some stuff for you to do here. Or I'll leave you the hell alone. Whatever you want."

For several months an army of immigrants worked feverishly to not only convert the press box into a sort of penthouse apartment but to also spruce up the entire stadium. Rollie came up to Minneapolis one day with the Bosnian architect, and they took pictures of every nook and cranny of my apartment and measured the stacks and piles and racks and shelves of my records, CDs, and books. At that point in my life my shelves and record racks were a hodgepodge of thrift-store castoffs, flimsy garbage from IKEA, and cinder blocks and boards. I was living like a college freshman.

When I made a trip down a few months ago and first saw the press box post-conversion, I was speechless. A giant master bedroom and a cozy office space and den occupied much of the upper level, and the main level was a giant and very stylish penthouse library, living room, and music lounge, highlighted by the long unbroken wall of high windows with eastern exposure. All the other wall space was filled with floor-to-ceiling shelves made of some decent wood and stained a rich amber. Rollie had even rustled up some old and expensive-looking Oriental rugs.

The place was gorgeous and full of light and leather furniture. Rollie also had his crew install a guest apartment down in the locker room. A set of lockers just outside the door to this apartment was full of towels and toiletries, and I had my choice of thirty-five showers. There was a small kitchenette off the living room level of the press box, as well as the giant commercial kitchen down in the tunnel, should I decide at some point to host a party or a convention. The only off note was a giant TV on the back wall.

I told Rollie the television would be a terrible distraction and asked if there was any way to return it.

He looked at me as if I was out of my mind. "Seriously?" he said. "It's theater quality. What's not to like?"

"It's just that I don't watch TV," I said. "Never have. It depresses me."

"That's a better TV than I have."

"I'm sorry, Rollie, but I wouldn't watch it. Or I couldn't. It's the ADD. Put me in front of a television and hand me a remote and I'd still be sitting there ten hours later."

"That's sort of the point," Rollie said. "What the hell else are you going to do in this town?"

"Everything else is perfect. It's incredible. I just don't want the TV."

Rollie rolled his eyes. "The place has a fucking dish. You could get like two thousand channels. But fine; I'll eighty-six the TV. You want some plants?"

"I don't need any plants. Trust me, they'd be dead in two months."

"How about some stuff for the walls?"

"They're pretty much all covered with shelves," I said. "What kind of stuff are you talking about?"

"Art, I guess," Rollie said. "I've got a bunch of paintings from the old Best Western. Probably not classy enough for you, but they're looking for a home."

"Thanks, Rollie, but I have some stuff of my own I can throw up on the walls."

"Okey dokey, Matty," Rollie said, clapping his hands. "You're not going to back out on me, right? I spent some serious coin on this."

I assured him I wouldn't back out and was beyond pleased, beyond impressed, and beyond grateful.

"So, when do you want to make the move?" he asked. "It's ready when you are."

"I didn't expect you to pull it together so quickly," I said. "I'll have to give my landlord notice, and then I'll have to pack all my shit and figure out how to get it down here."

"Don't worry about that. Just let me know when you're ready to roll and I'll send some guys with a truck. Also, I've got some Mexican pals who'll be coming by here to haul away the trash and keep the grass cut. Good guys. If there's anything else you need, just let me know and they'll take care of it."

As I sat in the bleachers beneath the press box windows a couple hours ago, Rollie's crew of "Mexican pals" came to cut the grass. They arrive every few weeks like a small army—three trucks pulling trailers loaded with machinery and gas cans, and one old Econoline van still bearing a faded CarnapCo logo on the side. Eighteen guys piled out of those vehicles, fired up the various contraptions—push mowers, giant mowers operated by a guy standing on a metal lip with hand controls similar to a motorcycle's, weed whips, and an assortment of push brooms and other lawn tools. The giant mowers reach incredible speeds and move in swift, circular motions; five of them roar around out there at the same time, barely avoiding collisions with each other, along with a handful of more conventional mowers whose presence seems superfluous. The scene is straight from a Dr. Seuss book, or maybe a Brueghel painting, and it takes about fifteen minutes for the crew to dispatch with the entire field.

The vantage from the press box is spectacular. Prentice is a flat prairie town and, standing at the high windows, I can see clear down the straight, tree-lined avenues toward downtown. The view faces east, but because of the length of the press box—130 feet, I think Rollie told me—and its perch high above the bleachers and the field, I can also see all the way across the town to the north, out to the interstate highway that choked off traffic to downtown in the seventies. There used to be, starting in my early adolescence, a bunch of convenience stores, chain restaurants, grocery stores, a pathetic shopping mall, and a Fleet Farm out there. The Fleet Farm eventually gave way to a Wal-Mart, and these days there's not much left on that strip but the Wal-Mart, a combination gas station/convenience store/McDonald's, and a handful of ragtag businesses: Vietnamese nail salon, Subway franchise, dollar store, laundromat.

Looking south, beyond the goal posts in the home end zone, I see the moldering facade of Prentice's original strip mall, which thrived throughout my childhood; among its tenants were a bank, barber shop, movie theater, Woolworth's, Ben Franklin, Lansing Drug, Trowbridge's Grocery, and a hardware store.

The old Lansing Drug is long gone. It closed when I was still in high school, as did the movie theater and most of the original tenants of the strip mall, which was called Lansing Shopping Center. Much of the strip still stands, but the only extant business is the Floyd Valley Credit Union on the western end. Over the years other small businesses—a video store, an insurance office, a dry cleaner, and a check-cashing place—came and went, but to the best of my knowledge there hasn't been, with the exception of the bank, any business operating there for at least five years.

When you're young the past is yesterday, a small and relatively manageable compartment of memories, most of which still have living corollaries or prompts you spend your days living with and moving among. You have all these people who share at least some portion of your memories and your past, and your orbit is often so compact and reliable that every day you move in and out of familiar places that are concrete repositories of memories. They contain you and all your stories and history.

Prentice in my childhood was a sprawling town of around twelve thousand people and rather neatly divided by a railroad yard and a river into east and west sections. The distinctions have mostly blurred now, but once upon a time the east and west sides had radically different identities and felt in most ways like completely different towns. We were a west-side family, and there was clear segregation in those days. Downtown was on the eastern edge of the west side, and no one in my family ever had much reason to venture farther east than downtown. Each side had its own elementary schools, churches, markets, and bars, and residents of both sides lived in relatively equidistant proximity to downtown and its stores, restaurants, bakeries, bars, social clubs, and other businesses. It was possible when I was a kid to not so much as lay eyes on a kid from the east side until you were in junior high (there was one junior high school and one high school for all the kids in town, and kids from either side didn't generally venture downtown on their own until they were teenagers).

For years I've been monkeying around in a sketchbook trying to recreate a block-by-block map of downtown Prentice as it existed in my childhood. A couple days after I moved into the press box, I took the sketchbook and set out to take a present-day inventory. Main Street is an eight-block walk east from the football field, right down Third Avenue through quiet blocks of solid, middle-class houses that date from the 1920s and '30s. Big family homes, for the most part. The original Carnap family home—or at least the home I remember, where my mother and I lived with my grandmother and my aunt Helen for a time—is in this neighborhood, and my aunt Elaine and uncle Eugene's old house is right on Third Avenue just a couple blocks from the football field. At one time early in my childhood, all six of the Carnap siblings lived within five blocks of each other. The earliest rationale for settling in that particular neighborhood was its proximity to St. Augustine Catholic Church. My grandmother didn't drive, and I never knew Aunt Helen to drive either. Both made the three-block walk to St. Augustine every morning and often several times a day.

I had once known people up and down every street in that neighborhood, but now it seems like half the houses have *For Sale* signs in the front yard. I have no idea if any holdovers from my childhood still live over there, but in all the years I've been coming back to Prentice, I've encountered fewer and fewer familiar faces. I walked past Aunt Elaine's house and, a few blocks later, my grandmother's. They both still looked exactly as I remember them; the grass was cut, and my grandmother's house appeared to have been recently painted. Rollie—or his army of immigrant laborers—was keeping them up, along with Big Leonard's house in a more recent development on the south side and Mooze and Tina's place out by the golf course northeast of town. St. Augustine still dominated the middle of town. Dating from the late nineteenth century, the church is an awe-inspiring work of architecture; the spire is visible from roads outside of town in every direction, and the entire compound—which includes several houses, a parish school, and a hulking limestone convent that had already been converted to a retirement home for nuns when I was a kid—occupies three square blocks on the edge of downtown. It seemed like more church than necessary for a town of Prentice's size especially with two other Catholic churches to choose from: Queen of Angels, which is almost as impressive as St. Augustine, is on the east side and has waged a nearly one-hundred-year battle with floodwaters, and St. Edward's, a more modern and modest competitor in one of the newer—late sixties or early seventies—neighborhoods on the western edge of town.

The old high school sits kitty-corner from St. Augustine, a couple blocks west of Main Street and downtown proper. It was unsettling to walk past it. I'd hated virtually every minute I spent in the place, but seeing it sitting there empty—a monument to how far and how swiftly the town had collapsed—was difficult to process. I asked Rollie why they didn't just tear it down, and he said there was still some small hope that the town would make a comeback. They'd appropriated money—all sorts of desperate incentives, land grabs, and tax breaks—to lure new industry and business to town; so far, Rollie said, there hadn't even been any nibbles.

Screaming Wheels was a few blocks south and east from the high school, directly across the street from the old courthouse. The whole block had been razed and replaced with a giant building that was a virtual twin to the county complex across the street and connected to it by a skyway over First Avenue. The entire area around the former site of the rink—and the apartment where my mother and I lived with Russ—was so wholly transformed that it was difficult to remember it as it was in those days.

One of the things I've wrestled with in remembering my years at the rink is the actual size of the physical space. The entrance on the First Avenue side was through a door on the eastern end of the fire department, right next to the three garage bays, which were deep enough for two trucks each. The door to the actual fire department—the office, equipment room, dispatcher's and living quarters—was on the opposite side of the garages, and the old armory occupied the entire block at the rear of the building.

The entrance to the rink took you into a small vestibule at the bottom of a long and narrow flight of stairs, three flights, actually, broken up by two landings in the middle. The most fascinating characteristic of these stairs, though (at least to a pre-adolescent boy), was what Russ called the Geezer Lift, a one-chair funicular that was a remnant from the old Masons' ballroom. I can sit for hours remembering the profound peace I felt whenever I strapped myself into the Geezer Lift and just glided up and down those stairs in the middle of the night. Even then it felt like a form of dreaming.

My question now—and this has perplexed me for years—is whether or not it is possible that the rink occupied the entire second floor of the block, or whether it was merely carved out of the space above the fire station. My childhood memories are so intensely focused on and dominated by the rink itself that I often see the place standing alone in the middle of town, abstracted from everything around it.

I wandered a block over to Main Street—which on a weekday afternoon had the desolate vibe of a city operating under a state of emergency—and tried to record a running list, street address by street address, of the buildings, operating businesses, and storefronts that were shuttered or had *For Lease* signs in the windows. The Town House Café had been at the corner of First and Main.

Next to that, butted up against the fire department, used to be the Eggleston Market. Opposite the entrance to the rink there had been a cluttered little space where an ancient Italian made keys and repaired shoes, and at the eastern end of the block had been Misto's Tap Room, a sort of clubhouse for local wise guys like my uncles that provided some of my first intimations that even a gloomy little nowhere town like Prentice held reservoirs of mystery and magic. It was all gone now. With the possible exceptions of a bank, a title company, and a couple insurance or real estate offices, there wasn't one business that was familiar from my childhood. Not a trace of that old world remained.

There are now a handful of Mexican restaurants, bakeries, and markets, a dollar store, a Sudanese community center with a barber shop and a small grocery, the Chamber of Commerce office, and a coffee shop so sparsely furnished and devoid of signs of life (or business) that I didn't go in. In one block, directly across from the courthouse, is a business that advertised itself as a health-food store, but it wasn't open when I passed, and I couldn't tell whether it was still in business. A couple doors down from the health-food store I wandered into a skateboard-and-bike shop and tried to engage the clearly stoned teenager behind the counter in conversation; after a few monosyllabic answers, he went back to playing his Game Boy. I did learn, however, that the store had been there for "maybe five years," and business was "pretty good."

I stood for a time in front of one particularly large and abandoned storefront, trying to remember what had occupied the space when I was a kid. I couldn't come up with anything, so I called Rollie from a phone booth on the corner and asked him.

"That was the Jupiter Department Store," he said. "Remember? They had those big ceiling fans and the open balcony over the floor where the salespeople sat at their desks all day? The place always smelled like mothballs. Old Man Carnap owned that building."

Across the street from the abandoned Jupiter store was the newish (now probably at least ten years old) county courthouse complex, which included the police department, the sheriff's office, city offices, and the county jail. There had been a classic limestone courthouse with a cast-iron dome on that same block when I was a kid, and the land surrounding it had been a sort of town square and downtown park, complete with a little band shell and lots of benches. The new complex was a typically uninspired piece of bureaucratic architecture. It could've been a corporate office, university building, or medical clinic. On the front lawn—which was really just a small crescent of grass shoehorned into one corner and garnished with some paving bricks and a bench—was the Prentice Vietnam War Memorial, a gleaming marble obelisk. At the top of this memorial was an engraved flag and the words THEY GAVE THEIR ALL. Beneath this were three columns of names—twenty-five, twenty-six, and twenty-five names in each alphabetized list. My father's name— Michael Leonard Carnap—was the eighth name down in the first column. I had no idea how long that memorial had been there, but I'd never seen it or had it called to my attention before.

Later, at dinner with Rollie, I said, "It was really kind of surreal walking around downtown. There's almost nothing left from when I was a kid."

"It's a completely different place," Rollie said. "We just have to roll with it. Most of these immigrants and all these other new people still see opportunities here. I try to make sure they get money in their pockets, because they turn right around and put the money back into the town, and a lot of the money that goes back into Prentice at this point eventually ends up back in my pocket. *Symbiotic*, I think that's the word for it."

I miss most of the places and people that are gone, but in many ways, I find this new, hardscrabble Prentice more fascinating than the homogenous town of my childhood. The random clash of all these different cultures gives the place a whole new vibe. As with many other small American towns that are being transformed by economic calamity and waves of immigrant labor, there is apparently a lot of frustration and anger among the mostly aging and dwindling population of locals, who have spent their entire lives and careers in Prentice. Views are equally divided between those who feel the town is being rapidly destroyed and those who, like Rollie, believe the only way the place can be saved is by embracing the new arrivals and encouraging them to make Prentice their home. Every week the *Prentice Dispatch* is full of letters, usually rancorous and fueled by bigotry, complaining about all the changes and calling for an impossible return to the way things were.

Things are so bad that the city has a program through which residents, businesses, and organizations can adopt abandoned or neglected properties and do what they can to keep them from descending further into worthless eyesores.

"The city no longer has the money to tear shit down," Rollie told me. "It's expensive, and they finally figured out that all those empty lots weren't doing them any favors."

My residence at the football field is, at least unofficially, made possible through this adopt-a-property program. Since Rollie is still paying down the debt on the complex and taking care of the maintenance, he told me that if anybody comes nosing around, I'm to identify myself as the caretaker and live-in security. People must wonder; you can see the lights blazing in the press box at night from all around town. It only took a week or so for someone to write to the *Dispatch*. "Why is someone living at the football field?" a Baptist minister wrote. "And shouldn't we have full disclosure of who this person is and what their plans are for what I believe is a publicly subsidized facility? I realize that Roland Carnap is the de facto overlord of what is left of this town, and the Carnaps have historically done exactly what they please, but surely we as a community could find creative ways to use that facility and provide a benefit to the taxpayers of Prentice."

For the most part, though, I seem to be living on an island, surrounded as I am by the fences and locked gates of the stadium itself, and the acres of practice fields, softball and baseball diamonds, and tennis courts on all sides. Even the Prentice police cruisers seem either oblivious or indifferent to my presence.

It's lonely out here much of the time, but it's a fairy tale kind of loneliness, a feeling of dreamy and otherworldly solitude, or romantic desolation of exactly the sort I've secretly courted all my life.

IV.

I've learned over the years that roller rinks tend to occupy a particularly nostalgic hot spot in the memories of small-town kids who grew up in the 1970s and '80s. Birthday parties and other special occasions were celebrated there. In later childhood and early adolescence, rinks became some of the first independent free zones, places where kids could congregate without adults and sort out the inevitable pecking orders and cliques that would be crucial to navigating the often-perilous emotional terrain of junior high and high school. Rinks were frequently the staging ground for the first clumsy attempts at romance, for all sorts of amorous firsts—first dates, first time holding hands, first furtive kiss.

For me—an only child who spent his early years almost exclusively in the company of adults and whose childhood was so insular he didn't even know he was lonely—the rink was the primary laboratory where I learned how other kids lived and behaved and how they got along with each other and in the world. Mostly, though, it was where I studied Russ, the way he talked and moved and carried himself, and the things he loved and the fierce, deliberate, and unyielding way he loved them. I would spend my truly formative years as Russ's sidekick and shadow at the rink, and I acquired most of my obsessions, passions (if a passion differs in some significant way from an obsession), and pretty much all my habits, attitudes, and general inclinations from him. My mother used to wonder about the whole nature-versus-nurture question, especially as it applied to my relationship with Russ, but I've long thought there must be something like adaptive genetics: the things you learn and the things you learn to love, your acquired habits and behaviors, become in time so hardwired that they're as much a part of who you are—if not more so—than your genetic makeup, and can be passed along just as helplessly and unknowingly.

At any rate, through Russ, and through living in the middle of his world, the rink quickly became a hothouse incubator for the person I became. From those first wondrous days there was almost no other place I'd rather be. Even now, all I have to do is close my eyes and I'm transported back there; it seemed like I lived much of my young life with wheels on my feet, moving in that cozy and permanent twilight, swept along by Russ's incomparable soundtrack, and, beneath it all, that sussura, almost oceanic, almost tidal, of wheels on wood.

At the time he came into my life Russ was twenty-six years old, a year younger than my mother. Like so many other Prentice kids he had gone off to college after high school. He'd briefly attended the University of Minnesota, worked at the college radio station, protested the war that killed my father, and hung out in coffee shops, bars, and record stores. School, he always told me, wasn't his thing; the rest of the stuff was why he'd gone, and he'd gotten what he needed. "In college everybody's supposed to be figuring out 'something' they want to be, and I was trying to figure out what sort of 'someone' I was going to be. If you don't first learn what it takes to live in your own skin, you're gonna have a tough time living in the world. That was a fucked-up time, and I decided I wanted to create a refuge."

My mother's contention was that Russ was simply lazy and didn't have any ambitions. And because his dad was wealthy and owned a lot of real estate in Prentice, he had opportunities there that he never would've had in Minneapolis or anywhere else.

"Prentice is a jerkwater burg, but it's relatively easy," he'd said. "It's boring, and the people are mostly sloths and rubes, but it's cheap to get around, and failure and futility don't have the same consequences or price tags that they do in a big city."

A snob believes in and defends his taste. Russ was more than happy to admit he was a snob. What he wasn't, though, was a smarty-pants. A smarty-pants pretended to know about everything but wasn't passionate about anything. Russ knew what he loved, he loved it with a sometimes irrational zeal, and he was prepared to defend it against any and all dissenting opinions. A conversation—and these were usually arguments—with an equally passionate and knowledgeable dissenter (however misguided) was welcome, but he had no patience with people whose taste he despised or who didn't care enough or weren't sufficiently informed.

Compared with a lot of other rinks I've visited over the years, Screaming Wheels was tiny. The fire station downstairs occupied maybe half a city block and was almost as deep as it was long. The old ballroom that had been converted into the rink took up most of the space upstairs, but our tiny apartment was also crammed in there, as were the skate rental and concession stands. The DJ tower (which Russ called the High Tower) and a strip of carpeted lounge area where people could hang out and change into and out of skates ran along the southern length of the rink. I wish I had the exact dimensions, and it's probably bigger in my memory, but I'm guessing the rink was seventy-five feet long and maybe fifty feet wide.

I never acquired Russ's technical know-how or sophistication, let alone his obsession with gear. I'm not smart enough and apparently don't have sharp enough ears to be a fussy audiophile. I do know how proud Russ was of the rink's PA setup. I heard him recite the details so many times I can still recall them with near accuracy: he had two Audio-Technica turntables in the High Tower, as well as ten fifteen-inch speakers and a pair of five-hundred-watt subwoofers mounted to the ceiling throughout the rink. The system was routed through a crossover and powered by a couple three-thousand-watt amplifiers. Maybe some of those details are wrong, but I know I was in awe of the sound in that room and of the incredible volume the system could sustain without breaking up into distortion.

There was a birthday party one afternoon, maybe a dozen kids a couple years younger than I was. I was ten years old, old enough to be aware of the grousing among the small gaggle of mothers and fathers. "What is this?" I heard one of the mothers say. "What kid wants to roller-skate to this music?"

I skated to the High Tower and asked my stepfather what record we were listening to.

"It's Charlie Parker's birthday," Russ said. "So, we're going to listen to some Charlie Parker."

"Some of the grown-ups are complaining again," I said.

Russ shrugged. "If they can't skate to Charlie Parker, they've got no business strapping on skates. Tell them to go home and play pin the tail on the donkey. If Charlie Parker were still around, he'd only be sixty years old. Imagine that."

One of the fathers staggered partway up the tower steps and asked Russ to play "The Devil Went Down to Georgia."

"Coming right up," Russ said.

When the man skated away, I said, "Do you really have that record?"

"Of course not," Russ said.

In all the years we lived at the rink, we had a handful of emergency situations—a few broken bones, a couple concussions, a fire in the garbage can in the boy's bathroom—but only one time that Russ ever called the police.

It was a Saturday afternoon and, as with most Saturdays, there were a couple of groups of birthday party kids. At some point another one of the fathers came over to the tower, where I was sitting with Russ, and said, "Come on, fella, play some songs the kids want to hear."

"I'll see what I can find," Russ said, and, as always, kept right on playing the records he wanted to play. He probably jacked the volume.

After maybe half an hour, the father approached the tower again. "Come on," he said. "Play something else, anything else."

"Really?" Russ said. "Anything else? Like what? Do you have a specific request?"

"Anything but this jigaboo music," the guy said, making a dismissive gesture with his hands.

Russ jabbed the power button and cut the sound. He stood up in the tower and started down the steps. "You're done," he said. "You and everybody with you has to go or nobody skates."

"We're not going anywhere," the guy said. "We paid to come in here. It wouldn't kill you to play songs the kids want to hear. They're trying to have a good time."

"They look like they're having a good time to me," Russ said. "And not one of them has complained about the music. I've got one asshole with a problem in here, and it's you. And you gotta go."

"Don't give me this garbage," the guy said, "and watch your mouth. There are kids in here."

Everybody in the rink had stopped what they were doing to watch.

"You gotta go," Russ said again. "Now."

"Shut up and do your job," the guy said. "Get up there and play some music the kids might actually want to hear."

With that, Russ walked to the phone by the skate rental counter and called the police. The guy instructed the kids to keep skating, and he sat back down with the other parents.

Everyone sat in awkward silence while we waited for the police to arrive. When the two officers came up the stairs and into the rink, they seemed puzzled by the scene.

"What's the problem here?" one of the cops asked, addressing the crowd at the end of the rink.

"We came here for a birthday party," the guy who'd started the thing said, "and the dope who runs this place has been doing everything in his power to make sure the kids have a lousy time."

Russ had come out from behind the skate rental counter. I was amazed by how calm he was.

"I asked that guy and his party to leave and they've refused," he said. "This is my business, and they're not welcome here anymore."

"What exactly happened?" one of the cops asked.

"He tried to tell me how to do my job," Russ said, "and in doing so revealed himself to be a racist dick. I want him out of here."

The other cop had been talking to the adults on the benches, and he came over and said they'd agree to leave if they got their money back.

"They're not getting their money back," Russ said. "They've been skating for two hours. If you throw a drunk out of a bar, you're not expected to reimburse him for his drinks." He shrugged. "Look, it's my place and my party, and they have to go. I'm sorry for the kids, but there are other people here who want to skate, and nobody's skating until you get these others out of here."

"Last I checked Prentice was a small town, Vargo," the cop said. "This sort of thing isn't exactly good for business."

Russ shrugged again. "So be it," he said.

"All right, folks," the cop said. "Let's go. You're going to have to take your party somewhere else."

By this time everybody in the rink was trying to figure out what was going on. The people who were with the guy who'd made the remark packed up their stuff and headed down the stairs. One woman who was with the party—there were maybe a dozen kids and five adults—argued with Russ briefly; I was still sitting in the High Tower and couldn't hear most of what they said, but I did hear her say, "This is inexcusable."

"I have my own ideas about what qualifies as inexcusable," Russ said.

As the last members of the party made their way out the door, one of them said, "I'm not setting foot in this place again."

"You're breaking my heart," Russ said.

As you get older, music acquires associations, connections with your past and your memories; it has a way of dragging you into a fierce undertow. Music also has its own specific history, its place on a continuum and within a genre or tradition, and that's how you get caught up and swept away; you follow the forks and the tangents, scour the liner notes and credits like an atlas, and in this way every new record you discover and love can lead you in a host of new directions. A record store clerk tells you that if you love James Brown, you should check out Fela, and Fela in turn sends you off on a long country-by-country tour of African music. "The Girl from

Ipanema" takes you into Brazil, and more than a decade later you're still fascinated and winding your way through the histories of bossa nova, samba, and Tropicália. Jimmy Smith leads you to Jimmy McGriff—or maybe Jimmy McGriff leads you to Jimmy Smith—and one or both of those guys point you in the direction of John Patton, Brother Jack McDuff, Larry Young, Lonnie Smith, Shirley Scott, Baby Face Willette, and Don Patterson, and for months at a time you don't want to hear anything but the glorious sound of a Hammond B3. Every single record is a crossroads that can shove you in a hundred new and different directions.

Russ had a wood-burned sign above his record racks: *The Garden of Forking Paths*. His record collection was both his chemistry set and his pharmacy. If he was in a lousy mood, or if we fell hostage to my mother's moods, or if we were pinned down by ceaseless rain, or if it was twenty below zero, he would say, "Let's change the weather in here," then he'd hunker down in front of his racks and emerge with an armful of records designed to shake things up and turn our weird little planet upside down. I never ceased to be amazed by how effective this was and how good he was at it. I could come home from school and gauge his mood by the music he was playing.

I don't recall my mother ever listening to records; I don't even think we owned a stereo. Before she married Russ, she occasionally listened to the radio in my grandmother's kitchen. I remember her sitting at the little Formica table late at night, smoking and playing solitaire while the radio played in the background. In those days there was one local AM station, which exists in my memory as an insufferable and stereotypical yokel operation. There was a lot of talk about farm prices and local high school sports and a daily program my grandmother liked to listen to called "Swap Shop," where people would call in and offer to sell or trade stuff they no longer wanted or needed. The show's theme song was Roger Miller's "King of the Road" ("Trailers for sale or rent . . ."), and as a result, that song was the first one to ever make an impression on me, or the first one whose lyrics I ever learned to sing from memory, even if I didn't then regard it as music in any meaningful way.

That show ran through all the years of my childhood, and my mother still tuned in occasionally after we moved to the rink. Someone would call in and offer to trade a used prom dress for a children's bicycle or something ridiculous like that, and my mother would look across the table at me and say, "This is so pathetic and sad." I have precious few memories of my mother really laughing, but one time I remember Russ came into the kitchen as we sat there listening, and he shook his head and left the room. A moment later we heard his voice on the air. "Yeah, hi, this is Rusty," he said. "I've got a few boxes of Kraft macaroni and cheese and a deck of cards I'm willing to trade for a copy of the Beatles' *White Album*. Or a pork chop." My mother's eyes got big, then she folded up at the kitchen table and laughed so quietly that if you didn't know her you might think she was grieving.

The original Big Leonard was my grandfather, a man who worked for the state patrol for more than forty years. Once upon a time he'd married into a large Roman Catholic family in Prentice, a small-town Irish mob that owned one of the oldest construction companies in town as well as, through various uncles, brothers, and the brothers-in-law who married into the family, all sorts of other properties and businesses. Big Leonard—the oldest of his three sons would also, in time, become Big Leonard—built his own empire within the original Murphy empire.

The tangled genealogy confused me throughout my childhood, particularly the question of which of the family enterprises were originally Murphy businesses and which were unique to the Carnaps. It was hard to sort out even before my mother married Russ, whose own family was the closest thing to business rivals the Murphy/Carnap clan had around Prentice.

I was nine when my mother married Russ, and by that time his family fortunes were in decline. His grandfather, August Vargo, was responsible for developing most of the postwar neighborhoods on the town's north side. Before August got his hands on all that land in the 1930s, everything directly west and just north of the football field was wooded countryside. He built or acquired numerous holdings, mostly office buildings, small apartment complexes, and a number of mixed-use properties downtown. When August died in 1970, his son Art Vargo, Russ's dad, was ostensibly in charge, but during the preceding decade, while August languished in a nursing home that he owned, Art pretty much ran his old man's legacy into the ground. He neglected most of the properties entirely and sold them off to support his lifestyle, such as it was. August Vargo had been a beloved character in town; he had a park named after him and was generally regarded as a reliable local patron. Art—August's sole surviving heir—was despised as widely as his father had been revered.

My grandfather, Big Leonard, was one of those small-town operators whose tentacles reached well beyond the little community he lived in. Largely owing to his decades with the state patrol, I'm guessing, he had big city connections—state legislators, cops, and other people engaged in similar sorts of business—that allowed the Carnaps a certain leeway and provided distinct advantages.

When he finally retired from the state patrol, he was on a first-name basis with the governor and a solid majority of the state senators and representatives, or so my uncles claimed. He died of a heart attack shortly before my mother took up with Russ, and in fitting tribute to a small-town big man, the state named a new overpass on 35W in his honor. The whole family drove there one Sunday afternoon for the dedication ceremony; the overpass was actually a half-hour drive from Prentice, just outside Floyd Valley. The plaque—bearing my grandfather's image, a nearly unrecognizable rendering of his face in what looked like copper—mentioned his long service to the state and his devotion to his community, family, and faith. Phil Buechner, who was nearing the end of a decades-long stint as Prentice's state senator (and who was a longtime crony of my grandfather and uncles), made a few remarks, the plaque was unveiled, and my uncle Rollie spoke on behalf of the family. The plaque itself was affixed to a support strut in the median strip, just off the shoulder of the freeway's northbound lanes. It wasn't accessible to pedestrians, and no one driving along the freeway at sixty-five miles an hour was ever likely to notice it. Afterward we all went to Big Sammy's, a supper club Rollie owned with a friend, and over drinks and steaks it quickly became apparent the family was none too pleased with such a dubious tribute to my grandfather. I remember my uncles ganging up on Phil Buechner at the table. Buechner, it seemed, had convinced enough of his senate colleagues to pass a resolution calling for the overpass to be named after my grandfather, but my uncles insisted he find a way to arrange a more conspicuous honor of some sort.

"Forty-two years with the freaking state patrol," Mooze said. "He saved how many lives? Who didn't he know? Put his name somewhere people are going to see it."

"Like where?" Buechner said.

Rollie suggested an office building, or maybe a courthouse.

"Most of those decisions are at the county or municipal levels," Buechner said. "The big state expenditures for buildings are usually named after people who operated at the federal level—senators and judges, people like that. The other stuff—sports complexes, hospitals, university buildings—are usually paid for by individuals and families. I thought this was a nice deal. Big Leonard drove up and down that road a million times."

"Sure," Mooze said. "And if he drove along that road today, he'd never know that stinking plaque was there. He wouldn't even see the damn thing, and neither would anyone else."

"I don't know what to tell you," Buechner said. "I thought this was a nice deal. It wasn't cheap."

"I know exactly what you can tell us," Rollie said. "'Okay, fellas. Your father was a great man. He deserves better. I'll find something else.' That's what you can tell us."

"I'll see what I can do," Buechner said.

A year or so later, the whole family once again got dressed up and drove down I-35, near Clarks Grove, where a big rest stop—the Leonard Carnap Memorial Roadside Park—was dedicated with a ribbon cutting and ceremony presided over by the governor.

I didn't dream in my childhood, or if I did, I wasn't aware of it. I didn't truly sleep, and I still don't. Sleep studies conducted at various points in my late teens and midtwenties corroborated this. The polysomnography tests showed I spent my hours in bed bouncing between the first and second phases of sleep, in what one doctor referred to as "the foothills of sleep." I never descended into the third or fourth phases, never experienced the rolling delta waves of deep sleep or the dream territory of REM sleep. The needle on the polysomnography test jerked like an erratic heart monitor, and every time I began the descent into phase three, my brain would be ambushed by apparent surges of dopamine and bursts of random thoughts—snippets of overheard conversation or music, fragments of memory, frissons of typical anxiety or anticipation, and just generally one synaptic brush fire after another.

I had nothing, obviously, to compare my version of sleep to; this was just the way it was. But as a result, I drifted into a state of almost perpetual hypnagogia, never properly asleep or awake. In the words of one of the specialists I visited in search of an answer, "The carnival never shuts down," and for much of my waking and (ostensibly) sleeping life, what goes on in my head—and what passes for consciousness or thought—is like nothing so much as channel surfing on a compulsive and manic scale.

People often ask me what I did all night as a kid. For a long time I couldn't answer this question with any concrete certainty. I would, though, at some point in every sleepless night, find myself sitting cross-legged on the floor beside my window and watching intently as shadows and light played games across the rooftops of downtown Prentice. I learned early on to think of that floor as the destiny of every day, or the bottom, the place where I could sit still and feel the memories rise and pool in me again. All the memories I could pin down. I would start, when I was very young, with an attempt to reconstruct, moment by moment, the day behind me, the day *beyond* me (*beyond* is, to me, a word or a concept that belongs exclusively to the past, to the backward glance and all the territory it encompasses). There's a vague horizon-like quality to the way I think about the future, but it's unfocused, blank, a pure flat line of landscape presided over by a pulsing mirage from which nothing clear ever emerges. It isn't beyond anything, and it holds no promises. It's just out there, not yet, and I've always had a blind faith—*faith* probably isn't an entirely accurate word—that it was where I was going, like it or not. Once I had created what felt like a reasonably accurate and orderly accounting of the day, I would step further into the past, working back in my memory, day by day, as far as I could go. Inevitably, of course, I would reach a point where such specific remembering or chronology was no longer possible; I was interested in discovering where—or how far back—this breakdown occurred. When I was younger and did not, of course, have such a deep reservoir of memories, it was much easier to travel to what would now be unthinkable distances in the past. In many ways this remembering is similar to listening to music—just as one record or artist can take you in new and unexpected directions, a specific memory might be loaded or fraught with potential snags that move you suddenly to other places, other times. My brain would change the channels on me, and it might take hours or even days to work my way back to the original programming, as it were. As it is.

So, anyway, I eventually arrived at an answer to the question of what I was up to in the middle of the night while others slept: I was on the floor. I was in the dark. I was remembering.

The world sits still. The phone doesn't ring. You are, in every essential way, alone, and in the middle of the night, you come to believe you're only and exactly who you are. Those moments, I know, are the closest I can come to anything resembling meditation. As the night stretches on, and the streets of your memory grow dark, and the past you're chasing becomes a tiny and distant light (I would think, *Now even my memories are sleeping*), the lights go down in your head and your mind begins to resemble (or so I thought, so I think) an aquarium—infused with soft, colored light, smeared, confused light, impossible to say precisely what color you're seeing from one moment to the next—in a dark room. When the aquarium appeared each night—reliably, and generally between 3:00 and 4:00 a.m.—I, or the observing I, the hypnagogic I, would recede, would pull back so it felt exactly as if I were sitting on a couch in a dark room watching strange, beautiful fish make almost calligraphic (if that's a word) orbits in the tank. The fish were stray sentences, words, snippets of songs, voices, or images, appearing and disappearing one after another, languid and generally hanging around long enough that I could study them with some intent and puzzle over where they had come from and what they might mean.

I once received one of those Magic-8 Balls as a birthday present— in the event you're unfamiliar, these toys were softball-sized black plastic orbs, supposed to resemble a pool ball, I think, that were marketed as oracular. You posed some question, shook the thing, and a luminescent answer to your question would appear in a quarter-sized peephole, bobbing up and suspended in some murky liquid. There were a limited number of possible answers, however many could be imprinted on the faces of a single die. Anyway, the way those answers appeared, and the dreamlike efflorescence of the words themselves, felt utterly familiar to me. The Magic-8 Ball was a simplified version of the way my brain worked in the middle of the night, except there were no limits, no simple question-and-answer relationship between my mind and what transpired in the aquarium at 4:00 a.m. Things appeared there unbidden, and I had absolutely no control over them.

There eventually came a point in every night when the aquarium went dark. I would be floating above the foothills by then, and I don't think I was ever precisely aware of the moment when even the aquarium in my skull gave up and left me alone in the darkness. In such times, however, I'm certain I was still awake, still sitting on the floor and staring into the static screen of my bedroom window. This was generally the time when things would get locked down: everything outside the window—the roofs of downtown stretching away to the north, the courthouse lawn just on the western edge of the window screen, the empty streets—would freeze, poised, *posed*, vogueing. I was accustomed to regarding that view as fluid and impressionistic—my personal version of Monet's paintings of the Rouen Cathedral—and it was altered from one moment to the next by the shifting shadows and light, drastically different depending on cloud cover, moon phases, the weather, seasons, and time of night. Around four or five o'clock each morning, though, even the light would stop moving and the shadows would freeze, creating a scene that felt as fixed and permanent as a photograph. The streetlights just stood there, their light carving precise lines in the darkness; those angles of light would almost appear to have been snipped out of paper and pasted down. I would stare, impassive, almost transcendentally muddled, at all the familiar objects in their place, every glint and shadow and line pinned down, the reflection of the moon etched on the windshield of a parked car. These moments, I felt sure, represented the longest time that the world could hold a pose, dioramas in real time.

Eventually some kind of snap would bring it all back to life. A police car, for instance, would round a corner somewhere downtown, its headlights sweeping across the storefronts and stirring up fresh shadows and light all the way to the courthouse. Russ had a record of radio transmissions from the first few Apollo space missions, and in the earliest days of my relative independence—when I felt emboldened to leave my place on the floor and explore the rink and eventually the town, and when I had received permission to use the High Tower stereo by myself—I used to take that record into the rink, put it on the turntable with the volume turned way down, and sit in the darkness listening to those voices breaking up in the static of space, sounding like the last fragmented transmissions of doomed explorers who'd been blown clean off the planet. *If the aquarium had a soundtrack,* I thought, *it would be that record.*

My mother's sadness made her essentially unknowable. Or, rather, the extent of what you could know about her was that she was sad. She was also pathologically shy, but I had no way of knowing whether that shyness was hardwired, or whether she had withdrawn so far into her sadness over time that she could no longer really engage with the world.

Often when I tried to draw her out or probe for explanations, she would shake her head or shrug and say, "I don't know, Matty. Something happened." I heard her say the exact same words dozens of times to Russ.

"That's not an answer," Russ would say. "Or it's an answer everybody in the world could give. At some point, though, you have to define what that 'something' is or was."

My mother—coiled into herself and wrapped in a blanket in a corner of the couch, which is where she spent much of her time, smoking and watching TV—said, "A whole bunch of somethings, then. Let's just leave it at that."

My father had been killed before she'd had a chance to push me out into the world, and probably before she'd even really gotten to know him. She was nineteen when he died and I was born. It was impossible to get her to talk about him, but he and his death in a place on the other side of the world was definitely one of the somethings that happened. I sensed, though, there were, as she said, "a whole bunch of somethings" that happened long before my father came into her life.

Her family was from someplace in Wisconsin, near Green Bay, but she'd left home when she was in junior high school and moved to Prentice to live with her grandmother, who had emphysema and died shortly before my mother and father married. The subject of her family was even more off-limits than the subject of my father.

As far as I knew she had nothing to do with any of them, zero contact, and had never gone back. Even now, all these years later, I couldn't with any certainty tell you much about her family. The full extent of what I know I learned from Russ or from eavesdropping on their conversations. One day I remember Russ confronting her about some mail she'd received bearing a return address from a women's prison in Fond du Lac. The gist of what I could understand was that this letter either concerned, or was from, her mother, who was an inmate there.

"What did she do?" Russ said.

"She's done lots of things," my mother said. "I hope they never let her out of there."

I once asked Russ if he'd ever met my mother's family. "Nope," he said. "And I'm pretty sure I don't want to. From what I gather they're Neanderthals, a bunch of savage drunks and petty criminals. Maybe not so petty."

My mother got pregnant with me while my father was home on leave after his first tour in Vietnam. I was apparently conceived at some point between Christmas and New Year's Eve, and my father flew back to Vietnam on January 3 and was killed on January 21. At his family's insistence he was buried at Fort Snelling, a huge military cemetery in the Twin Cities. I understandably had questions about all this, but it was difficult to get anyone in my family to talk about it, or to talk much about my father at all. I know, though, that I never visited my father's grave with my mother or with any of my aunts and uncles. It's possible, I suppose, that my grandmother and some or all of my aunts and uncles occasionally made the trip—it was a two-hour drive from Prentice—but if so, I wasn't aware of it. I made my own way up to that cemetery at some point shortly after I graduated from high school, but it was a cold and windy day, and the place was immense, row after row of the same uniform and anonymous gravestones arranged neatly and stretching as far as you could see in every direction. Here and there I encountered little floral displays, but the place was otherwise so

Spartan and quiet that it was spooky. I had the sensation I'd wandered into an immense and sterile institution crowded with people I would never see, one of whom was my father. The only sound was the wind and the rattling of flags—there were hundreds of them strung up on poles that lined every road of the cemetery. In the distance, I saw a small funeral party making its way along one of the roads. They were so far away that no sound carried to where I stood—there were six cars and a hearse, but I couldn't hear the slamming of doors or a single voice. I watched the people pile out of the cars and trudge through the grass to the grave site, all of them hunched into the wind, clinging to each other and moving like scattering gaggles of geese. They all seemed older, or perhaps the posture of grief made them appear old from a distance. The service didn't last long; I stood still through the whole thing. Out of respect, I suppose, or at least what I imagined was respect, some vague notion of the expected protocol for such a situation. Then I saw the honor guard—a slow-moving procession of clearly elderly men, windbreakers ballooning in the wind—raise their guns and fire. I heard almost no other sound the entire time I was in the cemetery, but I heard the guns.

I don't know how long I wandered around there, but I didn't find my father. And even if I'd managed to locate a stone with his name on it, I still wouldn't have found my father. He was—and remains—as unknowable as my mother. Even today, whenever I stumble across anything about Vietnam, I'm briefly curious, but something closes in me in a hurry, or a curtain goes down, and I don't want to know what's behind it. Once, in high school, I checked out a book of Vietnam War photographs from the library, and when my mother discovered the book in my bedroom, she was distraught. I don't know, actually, if that's the right word, but I remember her standing in the doorway and zeroing in on the book—it was a big book, full of pictures—lying on the bed. She had crossed her arms and hugged herself to the point where she was leaning slightly forward—I'd seen this a thousand times and knew what it meant—and she said, "No, Matty. You can't have that here. You need to take it back right now."

"I haven't even looked at it," I said.

"I don't want you to look at it," she said. "Take it back. Now."

I did as I was told. I knew that if I had refused or tried to take a stand, I would be subjected to the only punishment she had in her emotional arsenal: she would stay in her room for a week, or camp out on the couch, wrapped in a blanket and lost in an impenetrable fog. She would smoke cigarettes and cry, drink can after can of Tab, and stare at the television.

So, I took the book back. Even without my mother's disapproval, the book felt pornographic. And something in me, even as boy, instinctively recoiled from looking at it, and I couldn't bring myself to think about that place and the things that happened there.

I rode my bike back to the library—it was only a few blocks from the rink—and when I arrived, I sat quietly at one of the long white tables with the unopened book sitting in front of me. I finally opened the book to a random page, where I stared with an unnamable terror at a photograph of a soldier wading in a dark river, almost up to his armpits, a baby in his arms. It appeared to be raining on that river and that soldier and that baby, and a gray bundle dangled from a helicopter in the air above them. I closed the book, returned it to the cart, and rode my bicycle home.

At some point during those years I remember asking my mother, "How come Russ didn't have to go to Vietnam?"

She stared at me for a moment, then said, "Because he had a hole in his heart."

To this day I'm not at all sure if she was telling the truth, and I never again raised the subject with her or Russ.

V.

One of my favorite things in the world was watching Russ as he skated alone in the mornings before I went to school or late at night after the rink closed.

Russ was kind of ungainly, tall, or tallish—we were a short family, or shortish, and I'm pretty sure Russ was at least six feet tall—and skinny other than a slight paunch that was exaggerated by his lousy posture. He carried his head at a forty-five-degree angle from his shoulders, leaning forward, and he walked with exaggerated strides that incorporated a lot of drift and corrections. He'd throw one leg out in one direction and then the other leg would reverse the angle, lazy, meandering, preoccupied—with one step he was headed northeast, say, and with the next he was seemingly headed back northwest. It was a walk full of swerve and—at least from the looks of it—entirely lacking in purpose. When you walked beside him on a sidewalk you pretty much had to follow his lead or keep a healthy distance to avoid catching a lot of sharp elbows. His arms would swing with each stride, the only purposeful component of his gait: very compact and rhythmic, almost as if he were swinging ski poles.

Russ's gait was probably influenced by all the years he spent on roller skates. He glided, swaying from foot to foot, transferring his weight almost exactly as he did when he skated. As a skater, though, he was clearly in his own world, his element. When he skated alone, his movements were slow and elegant; his more polished moves (the Mix It Up, the Whole Thing, the Coffin, the Iceberg, the Grapevine, and the Snake Walk are some I remember him trying to teach me) were influenced by styles that had—or so he claimed—originated in the big industrial cities of the Rust Belt: Detroit, Cleveland, Chicago, and Gary, Indiana. I know Russ didn't see himself as effeminate and would've been mortified to be seen as effeminate in any way, but he understood that the rink was a place—a safe zone—where any such considerations went out the window.

There's something distinctly androgynous about great skaters, and Russ was a great skater. Alone, his skating moves suggested an NFL cheerleader or figure skater one moment, a dancer in a high-end strip club the next. He would roll his shoulders, shake his hips, throw his head back, and sway from side to side. He would clap his hands and let out whoops and moans. Much of the time he moved in what seemed like slow motion. He could skate much faster when he wanted to and was capable of all sorts of more aggressive spins, leaps, and balletic moves, but I like to think that in the mornings and late at night, he was engaging in his own version of private dancing. And there was an unmistakably erotic quality about this particular style of roller-skating.

I also have memories of my mother skating. She claimed she'd never skated before taking up with Russ, and I remember her earliest attempts, when she was more or less walking on skates the way a toddler might, arms extended and paddling the air, her face frozen with a combination of terror and concentration as she proceeded around the rink in unsteady Frankenstein-monster steps and Russ howled with laughter from the High Tower. There wasn't anybody else in the rink at the time, so this must've been in the later evening. "Fuck you," she'd shout with seemingly every step. "Fuck you, fuck you, fuck you." She did eventually get the hang of it, and became in time a reasonably graceful skater.

I tried at various times to get both Russ and my mother to explain their relationship to me or to tell me how they'd started dating. They both occasionally gave it a shot, but the only thing that sticks in my memory was the time Russ told me, "You'll probably learn this soon enough, but here's the story of the world: Eleanor Rigby spends her whole life pining for Nowhere Man, but somehow they don't cross paths. When they actually do—surprise, surprise—they're still Eleanor Rigby and Nowhere Man. There's not enough magic in the world for some people."

I remember one of Russ's favorite T-shirts was adorned with the words *new dope in town*. I puzzled over that shirt, and those words, every time he wore it. I must not have ever asked him what it meant, or at least I have no recollection of it, and the only reason I remembered it now is because this morning I was going through a bunch of records I recently picked up at a thrift store and I stumbled across a record from 1969 by the band Spirit that includes a song called "New Dope in Town." I put the record on the turntable right away. It was exactly the sort of turgid hippie rock that Russ used to regularly disparage, but I nonetheless have to conclude that the T-shirt was a deliberate, if ironic, reference.

Pretty much Russ's entire wardrobe was made up of T-shirts. I don't think I ever saw him in anything else but straight-leg Levi's and low-cut Converse All Stars. There was a print shop in Prentice where he used to silk-screen his own shirts. I just went into my closet and dug through a box of T-shirts Russ passed along to me when he grew tired of them—most of them are (I think) supposed to be funny, jokes to amuse no one but himself. He always seemed like such a culturally marooned character in Prentice that I have a hard time imagining anyone else making sense of his attempts at humor. One of the shirts in my possession features a photograph of a young Ricky Nelson with the name Sex Pistols—in the font from the *Never Mind the Bollocks* album cover—superimposed over it. Another has an album cover from the band Bread with the original band photo swapped for a picture of the Grateful Dead.

When I was in the closet, I stumbled across a shoebox—Converse All Stars—filled with notes on index cards and scraps of paper, all in either Russ's or my mother's handwriting. Some of them I fished out of books—music guides, mostly—that Russ passed on to me over the years, but many of them are notes Russ or my mother left for each other or for me.

Have you looked at my hair lately? Russ once wrote on a bank deposit slip he left on the counter. *Jesus. I look like Paul Anka.* PLEASE CUT MY HAIR! Some of the notes were straightforward (*Doesn't anyone around here ever get hungry?*), but many of them were inscrutable: *I killed a guy with a tambourine once. Do NOT mess with me.* Or, *Some bully was always throwing something at my head in gym class. For years I lived in fear of the cage ball. And you wonder what's wrong with me?*

One of my favorites, in my mother's hand: *That was yesterday, Russell.*

The saddest one was written on an old thank-you card. Russ had scratched out the original message and written, *How come you don't skate with me anymore, Jeannie?*

None of my aunts or uncles liked Russ. There was a lot of old animosity between the Carnaps and the Vargos, and I'm sure that was part of it, but their dislike of Russ was more personal. They thought he was a bum and a punk and that my mother—and I—deserved better. Russ certainly didn't do himself any favors; he made no attempt to ingratiate himself to my uncles (the prime engines of the animus) or, really, to anyone else.

Before he came along, my mother and I had essentially been wards of my father's family. We lived in houses or apartments they owned. My mother's jobs were exclusively in one of the many Carnap business interests. And in my earliest memories my aunts were constantly dropping by with groceries, and they'd often hang around cooking for my mother and me as if we were a couple of invalids, or children, which I suppose in a very real sense we were.

For many of my formative years of exploration and discovery, I had access to Russ's knowledge and his records, library, and collection of music guides and magazines. Russ was fanatical about the stuff he loved, but he wasn't particularly broad or encyclopedic, and for much of our life together, we both dealt with the same basic handicaps: Prentice was a small town and, in the days before cable TV and computers, mostly a cultural void. There wasn't a single dedicated book or record store in town, and you had to drive ninety miles to the Twin Cities to access the sorts of things that interested us. I'm also pretty sure neither of us had many people in Prentice who shared our precise inventory of interests. My education in almost all of this stuff proceeded like archaeology: I acquired most of my early knowledge forensically, and I was proud—and remain proud—that from the time I was fourteen or fifteen, I ranged more widely and investigated more doggedly than Russ, who didn't have the time or energy. He encouraged this doggedness and regularly rewarded me by taking an interest in my latest discoveries and even embracing with genuine enthusiasm some of the music I discovered on my own.

One of my favorite discoveries, for instance, was Harry Smith's *Anthology of American Folk Music*, which I checked out from the public library on some whim. The packaging and booklet were gone, and each of the two-record sets was packaged in heavy vinyl sleeves with distressed black-and-white Xeroxes of what I assumed were the original covers.

I listened to those records constantly for at least a year, checked them out over and over and recorded them on cassettes. I'd never heard anything like the music on those records, and neither, apparently, had Russ. We used to sit in the High Tower at night playing one record after another, trying to figure out what the hell we were listening to. I can't overstate how radically different and more satisfying that experience was compared to hearing those records today, with all the information I now have at my disposal. I love that music as much as ever, but it's been demystified.

When I first heard those records, I had no idea who Harry Smith was or that there was any historical interest attached to the music at all. The pleasure was private, a wholly personal thrill (shared with Russ) that was as weird, wonderful, and otherworldly as listening to that record of the Apollo transmissions had been. It would be almost fifteen years before I owned the records on anything but dubbed cassettes, and in those intervening years I never met another person who knew *The Anthology of American Folk Music*, much less responded to it in the same way that Russ and I did in those long-ago sessions at the rink. I was stunned—and overjoyed—when the entire package was released to huge fanfare a couple years ago, but selfishly I was also a little disappointed to learn that what I thought was my secret library discovery was in fact regarded—and had long been regarded—as a hugely influential monument beloved by a large and apparently international cult, of which I (and people like Bob Dylan) was just another gobsmacked member. I was especially startled to read that so many others had had essentially the same reaction as I'd had upon first hearing the music.

There were obviously all sorts of challenges and frustrations involved with living in a cultural vacuum like Prentice, and the lack of diversity was stunting in many ways. I know, based on my own family and many of the people I grew up with, that such an environment could—and often did—make you narrow and insular. If, however, you were curious and suspected the world was full of other options, attitudes, and kinds of people, you had to put in some real work and effort to make your own world a little more interesting and diverse.

From the time I came into Russ's life, the rink really was his world. He was there all the time, and, with rare exceptions when the rink was open, he was in the High Tower spinning records. He hired a couple high school kids to run the skate rental and concessions stands, and a legendary local drunk—Prentice's only real street alcoholic, who lived in a transient hotel by the railroad yard—usually came in the early afternoons to do basic janitorial chores. Russ, though, maintained the rink floor—dry mop, wet mop, buffer. Every morning. During the years my mother and I lived with Russ, he didn't have time for record-scrounging trips to the Twin Cities. Such trips, though, had been a regular part of his routine before he took over the rink; he told me that he used to drive up to Minneapolis at least once a month on a Friday afternoon, make the rounds to as many record stores as he could, spend the night in a motel and see some live music, then hit some more record stores and bookstores before driving back to Prentice on Saturday night.

Once the rink took over his life, he constantly worried he was losing touch. He subscribed to a bunch of music magazines—old issues of *Creem, Circus, Crawdaddy, New York Rocker,* and *Rolling Stone* were stacked around our apartment—and I think it drove him nuts that there was no place he could access all the new music he read about.

"I used to think my record collection was pretty solid," he said. "Five lousy years of falling down on the job and it's already full of holes; there are probably, at minimum, three hundred records I absolutely should have. That's the kind of shit that keeps me awake at night. I'm counting the days until you can get your driver's license, Matty, so you can pick up the slack. You're going to be my courier and my procurer."

Russ did have a couple mail-order sources, in New York and Chicago, I think, and at least once a month a big stack of records would get delivered to the rink. When Russ received these packages, I would study the postmarks and stamps, the handwriting on the packing carton, and imagine those faraway places, the people who had pulled and packed those records, all the other people who had handled the package en route from Chicago or New York to the rink in Prentice. Somehow—through an unimaginable journey of unimaginable steps—our little town was connected to all those other bigger places in the world.

And when later—or sometimes immediately—Russ opened one of his new records, put it on the turntable, and dropped the needle on the record, and when he gave the volume knob a twist and music filled the rink, I would, every single time, experience a thrill of indescribable wonder. It was impossible that all that sound was crammed in those tiny grooves, and that the sliver of the stylus could extract all that sound, and that that sound could be amplified to such an extent I could feel it in my spine, feel it vibrating and humming through the wheels of my skates. It was impossible, and it would never be explicable to me. It was more incredible and far-fetched than anything I'd encountered in the science-fiction books

I read so avidly as a boy. Then—as now, still—the wonder of a phonograph record was all the evidence I needed that I lived in an age of miracles.

I remember the first time Russ played a Robert Johnson record for me. "Listen closely to this," he said. "This is the voice of a man who's been dead for more than forty years. Those are a dead man's fingers plucking the guitar strings. There are almost no photographs of the dead man and very little information about his life, but we have this music, and we can endlessly reproduce it. It's fucking amazing."

It really was. It really is.

On the wall above the turntables Russ had an ever-evolving list.

Russ's Screaming Wheels Gold Standard mix:
Prince, "Delirious"
Michael Jackson, "Wanna Be Startin' Somethin'"
Rufus/Chaka Khan, "Do You Love What You Feel"
Marvin Gaye, "Got to Give It Up"
Stevie Wonder, "Superstition"
Gap Band, "You Dropped a Bomb on Me"
Sister Sledge, "He's the Greatest Dancer"
Rick James, "Super Freak"
James Brown, "The Payback"
Earth, Wind & Fire, "Shining Star"
Parliament, "Tear the Roof Off the Sucker (Give Up the Funk)"
Blackbyrds, "Happy Music"
The Brothers Johnson, "Stomp!"
Jimmy Bo Horne, "Spank"
Heatwave, "The Groove Line"
Billy Preston, "Outa Space"
Sugar Hill Gang, "Rapper's Delight"
Hamilton Bohannon, "Let's Start the Dance"
George Clinton, "Atomic Dog"

Chic, "Good Times"
Isley Brothers, "That Lady"
Kool & the Gang, "Hollywood Swinging"
Sly & the Family Stone, "I Want to Take You Higher"
Aretha Franklin, "Rock Steady"
Johnny Williams, "Slow Motion"
George McCrae, "I Get Lifted"
The O'Jays, "Love Train"
Zapp, "More Bounce to the Ounce"
Ernie K. Doe, "Here Come the Girls"
Brick, "Dazz"
Eddy Senay, "Cameo"
Manu Dibango, "Salt Pop-Corn"
The Beginning of the End, "Funky Nassau (Part II)"
Lunar Funk, "Slip the Drummer One"
The Chakachas, "Jungle Fever"
Slave, "Slide"
Teena Marie, "Behind the Groove"

Most of this was old-school funk, and though Russ's tastes were wildly eclectic and pretty much anything he loved was fair game at the rink, he considered these songs an essential part of any skating mix. "Until eternity, or until the wheels fall off," he said, "this is music people will be skating to," and these were the records he kept in a box in the High Tower. I heard every one of them for the first time at Screaming Wheels.

There are two songs I've heard many, many times at pretty much every roller rink I've ever visited, and I know from conversations with friends and coworkers over the years that these two songs—which were officially banned at Screaming Wheels—were staples at rinks across the country. The two songs—I've never heard them outside of a rink, or at least don't think I have—were "Bunny Hop" and "Hokey Pokey." They're essentially the same song, and whenever

I've encountered them at other rinks, they've been part of what Russ called "the dreaded group skate." Everything grinds to a halt, the skaters gather in a big circle or line, and everyone engages in these simple, corny dances. Like the songs, the dances are more or less the same—little kids could do them—and really don't involve much skating at all.

Russ hated "Bunny Hop" and "Hokey Pokey" with a passion, and his hatred was only exacerbated by the constant requests he got to play them. There was another, much bigger rink—a classic, freestanding Quonset rink—in Hollandale, which was fifteen miles from Prentice. On Saturdays and Sundays that rink, Gene's United Skates, would run free buses back and forth from the parking lot of the JCPenny in Prentice, a practice that of course pissed Russ off. The buses were usually packed. Gene's United Skates was clearly a much more successful operation than Screaming Wheels, and Russ insisted this was because Gene's was "a Hokey Pokey rink," and the hallmark of a Hokey Pokey rink—besides the fact it played "Hokey Pokey" and "Bunny Hop"—was "shit music all around."

When I was a little older, Russ occasionally sent me to Gene's on the free shuttle bus; my job was to come back with a comprehensive scouting report. He wanted to know how many people were there, what kind of concessions they offered, my opinion of the sound system quality as it compared to his, and a list of the songs they played. "And be honest," he would tell me. "If you actually have a good time, I want to know."

I sometimes had an okay time at United Skates, but I honestly had a lot more fun listening to Russ critique the playlist. "Tony Orlando and Dawn?" he'd shriek. "*Styx?* You have got to be fucking kidding me. *Shaun Cassidy? Leif Garrett?* Please tell me you didn't skate to this shit, Matt. *Little River Band's 'Reminiscing'?*"

"That was a couples' skate," I said. "They turn out most of the lights."

One time I came back with a list that included three songs—"Rubberband Man," "Werewolves of London," and "Le Freak"—that

Russ played with some regularity at Screaming Wheels. This news distressed him, especially since these songs had been part of one of Gene's mixes that also included Captain & Tennille, John Travolta and Olivia Newton-John, and Kansas.

"It's bad enough they play all that garbage," he said, "but now they're contaminating perfectly good songs. I have to scrub those records."

"You can't scrub 'Rubberband Man,'" I said. "Or 'Werewolves of London.' I love those songs."

"There are plenty of other great songs," Russ said. "My conscience won't allow me to play a single record on a United Skates playlist. I used to say I didn't want to play anything that any kid in this town had ever heard anywhere else, which was perfectly doable but a dumb policy all the same. Great songs can sneak onto the Top 40, and I try very hard, believe it or not, not to be a snob. But I'll be damned if I'm going to play the same songs United Skates plays."

Somewhere down in a storage room under the bleachers, I have a box with a bunch of Russ's Screaming Wheels logbooks. I could, from memory, re-create all sorts of reasonably accurate Russ playlists—for many, many years most of the mixtapes I made were in fact attempts to re-create those playlists. But I've been curious in recent years about two things: how much Russ's playlists overlapped with the Top 40 at any given time and what the Screaming Wheels breakdown was between Black and White artists. I sometimes waste time trying to recall White musicians who cracked the heavy rotation at Screaming Wheels, at least before the explosion of punk, new wave, and indie rock. It's surprisingly difficult to do. "Werewolves of London" is the first song that comes to mind, but that's probably owing to the anecdote above and because it was so strange initially and I loved it so much. Sweet's "Ballroom Blitz" was another case where I think Russ yielded to my adoration of a particular song.

I do remember the two of us skating after hours to *Exile on Main St.*, and Russ would often play *Blonde on Blonde* or *Highway 61 Revisited* when he mopped or buffed the rink floor, but I don't think he ever played Bob Dylan during open hours. He for sure played Johnny Cash's "Ring of Fire" regularly, and it was often the first song of the evening skate.

I am susceptible—I think this is the right term—and highly suggestible. I've spent my entire life avoiding television, so certain was I—and am I—that it would be the end of me. I saw what it did to my mother, saw the way she gradually disappeared into the television in our little living room and how she could sit for hours and days at a time staring at the screen. Part of me envied her the ability to sit still for so long, to give her undivided attention to whatever was on the TV, but I had no idea what the hell she was doing or thinking, or even what she was *seeing*.

The loneliest and most desolate sound in the world to me is the sound of a television in an otherwise dark and silent house. It was such a different experience to be in my bedroom and hear music playing in the rink in the early mornings or late at night. I knew Russ was out there, moving around on skates behind a mop or the buffer, or hunched intently in the High Tower, shuttling records on and off the turntable, playing air guitar and making mental notes for playlists. Often, I would get up and join him; I'd strap on my skates and make ferocious laps as he went about his business. Other times, though, I would lie in bed and listen to the music, playing Name That Tune. If I heard a new or unfamiliar song—it didn't matter how late or early it was—I'd make my way down the hallway, part the heavy curtain, and call out to Russ.

I'm sure I asked Russ "What is this?" on a thousand occasions. And for all my lifelong problems with memory and attention, I have incredibly precise recollections of the first time I heard hundreds of songs.

VI.

For a few years after I graduated from high school, the Rubber Route filled the huge hole the disappearance of Russ and the rink left in my life. It was a job that allowed me to spend weeks on the road listening to music, staying in motels, and scrounging in record and thrift stores. I always traveled with a duffel bag full of carefully curated cassettes. I had a notebook in which I kept a list of what I considered essential albums for the road. The list—and the criteria for selection—was constantly changing or expanding. I was learning that certain landscapes and stretches of road lent themselves to particular records, and other factors—weather, season, time of day—also influenced my choices. After a couple years of driving the Rubber Route, my list of road music stretched across a half dozen notebook pages and was broken down into all the different categories I'd come up with. I spent time in my motel room every morning, organizing the cassettes and pulling together a playlist for the day.

The Rubber Route was my first real taste of independence and freedom. I drove it for almost five years, chose it—sort of inadvertently—over a college education, and it really did feel at the time like an extension, or a natural progression, of the years I'd spent in the rink with Russ and the things I'd learned (and learned to love) there. I kept two of Russ's favorite mantras firmly in mind: Norman Mailer's "A man in motion has a chance," and "The spirit of the living creatures was in the wheels," which was from Ezekiel in the Bible and was on a sign above the doorway at the top of the stairs in the rink. I drove, listened to music, and had casual, hit-and-run encounters with people in the bars, gas stations, and truck stops where I serviced condom machines. I missed the rink, but I got to know all sorts of small-town rinks all over the Midwest and skated whenever I had a chance.

The Rubber Route was Big Leonard's baby. I don't quite understand how my uncles got into the business in the first place, but there was obviously some larger industry and network behind it. At the liquor warehouse in Prentice, there were piles of catalogs and manuals for the operation and maintenance of the machines. There were dozens of machine models and hundreds of plastic- and foil-wrapped condoms to choose from. There was even an industry newsletter, a handmade affair produced by some guy in New Jersey that featured typewritten text and poorly Xeroxed illustrations. It was Big Leonard who initially carved out the original route and gradually expanded it over the years. By the time I took it over from a guy named Beryl Osman, there were almost seven hundred (679, to be exact) condom dispensers spread over six states (six and a half, if you counted the thirty-one machines we had in eastern Montana).

As a labor-intensive sideline to my uncles' more compact and legitimate businesses, the Rubber Route initially seemed like pure nickel-and-dime folly. But it was, I would learn, a ridiculously profitable racket and, once the machines were paid off, almost pure profit. The machines were relatively inexpensive to buy and maintain, built to withstand abuse, and seemed to last forever. Big Leonard was forever buying up used models and stashing them away in the warehouse as replacements or for installation in prospective new accounts. He took the Rubber Route seriously, and I quickly understood why.

During my time on the Rubber Route, I averaged twenty-five trips a year, usually spending two and a half weeks on the road every month. On each leg of the route I serviced anywhere from seventy-five to a hundred machines, and I tried to get to every one of our machines three times a year. Most of the machines were either four-slotters or six-slotters, and each of the chutes held a hundred condoms. Usually, by the time I got back to one of the accounts, the machines would be empty, or close to empty. In my early years on the Route, the condoms were seventy-five cents apiece.

I had a trunk full of heavy canvas bank bags, and I generally walked away from a stop with, at minimum, $200 to $250 in quarters, and often, if the machine was a six-slotter, substantially more.

There were, as I said, different arrangements with every bar, gas station, and truck stop that had one of our condom machines. My uncles had built the business over many years and had acquired most of the existing accounts—along with their financial arrangements—from other smaller operators. Many accounts received an annual check, often for surprisingly paltry amounts, from Big Leonard. Others had some sort of tit-for-tat arrangement with my uncles that I never quite understood. I was unaware of any money changing hands in these cases; most of these places tended to be closer to Prentice and within the constantly expanding range of my uncles' liquor distribution business. Some of the accounts that were further afield involved a flat fee or percentage I often had to settle on the spot. Generally, there was some honor system in place, and we'd just work out the math on a calculator. Sometimes, however, I had to sit in the office or back room of some bar or truck stop and actually count out the change in front of a manager.

However you cut it, though, the bottom line was staggering. I would return from each leg of the Rubber Route with $20,000 to $30,000 in quarters. Those condom machines were netting at least $250,000 a year.

When Beryl Osman had driven the Rubber Route, he would just haul all those canvas bags of quarters around in the back of his station wagon and deliver them to the warehouse at the end of each trip. I quickly developed a more efficient system and stopped at a Wells Fargo every few days, ran the change through the automated machines, deposited the money in my uncles' business account, and tucked the deposit slip in my Rubber Route ledger, where I kept a running tally of each condom machine's inventory and gross. It was mindless work, and my uncles paid me fifteen percent of the gross plus my expenses, which meant that most years, as an uneducated twentysomething, I was clearing somewhere in the ballpark of $45,000. For the first few years I loved the Rubber Route, loved driving around and listening to music and seeing the country.

By the time I started driving the Rubber Route, Russ was taking classes at the vocational school just outside town, studying radio and television broadcasting. His dad had an old friend and business partner who owned a bunch of small AM radio stations in southern Minnesota and Iowa, and Russ had decided he wanted to take a crack at being a disc jockey. In typical Russ fashion, he set his sights low; the perfect scenario, he said, would be to hold down the graveyard shift at some jerkwater station where he could play whatever records he wanted.

In my early days on the Rubber Route, I used to talk to him on the phone pretty regularly, usually late at night from some roadside motel room. Those were the days of truck stop calling cards, and, though neither of us was ever much comfortable talking on the phone, I'd often burn through a hundred minutes in a single awkward and meandering conversation with Russ. At some point during this time I came home from the road and called his old family house, and his dad told me Russ was living in Mason City, Iowa. He gave me a phone number, but I called it several dozen times over the next month or so and never got an answer. Eventually I managed to track him down to a radio station there, where he was, in fact, doing an overnight show. Several times over the next couple years I managed to catch Russ's show when I was down that way on the Rubber Route. I'd check into a motel, dial up the station on a radio I'd bought for the purpose, and sit up all night listening. It was exactly as I imagined it would be, absolutely uncompromising and uncompromised. He was clearly playing whatever he wanted: a lot of songs I recognized from the Screaming Wheels days but also all sorts of stuff he would never have played at the rink, including records I was hearing for the first time. His banter between records was funny and deadpan and managed to be both educational and entertaining. He had a request line and often put callers—most of whom seemed to be stoned teenagers or drowsy third-shift workers—on the air and interrogate them about their requests, which were usually laughable and appalling. It reminded me of all the times people at the rink tried to get Russ to play some terrible oldie or current hit. I would pick up the phone a dozen times a night, screwing up the courage to call, but I never did, and to this day I can't understand or explain my reluctance.

I also can't explain why I didn't try to see him after he left Prentice. I passed through or near Mason City at least a half dozen times a year on the Rubber Route. I suppose maybe I was wary of his depression and bitterness; the last couple times I'd talked to him were exceedingly awkward. It was almost as if he had run out of enthusiasm or things to say. I remember asking him once if there were any new records I should check out, and he'd replied in his withering monotone, "Look at the *Village Voice* poll. They're all there. You don't need me to spoon-feed you anymore."

It's also possible I had run out of things to say. The years on the Rubber Route were interior years, even by my old standards. I spent every day on the road interacting with people who were mostly strangers. In a sense, it was a kind of assertiveness training.

I started driving the Rubber Route in the summer of 1988 and stayed on the road until the spring of 1993, when I was twenty-three. At some point during that time, I called the phone number I had for Russ—he was still living in northern Iowa and working at another radio station—and discovered it had been disconnected. I then sent a postcard to the last address I had for him, and found it waiting for me, stamped "address unknown," when I picked up my mail at the Prentice post office.

It was hard to stay in touch when I was on the road all the time—and even when I wasn't—and my only real options were the telephone (which neither of us had ever really liked) and the United States Postal Service. I made inquiries around Prentice and stopped by Art Vargo's place a few times to see if he had heard from Russ, but even then he was losing his marbles and didn't seem to have any idea where his son was. Art did give me a phone number for Russ's sister in Arizona, who I knew a little bit from her annual visits to Prentice. One night I finally screwed up the nerve to call her and we ended up having a touching conversation. She'd had the same experience I had.

"I have a handful of phone numbers for him that are all no longer in service," she said. "Or whoever answers hasn't heard of Russell. I tried the last radio station he was working at when I talked to him a year or so ago, but they would only tell me he no longer works there. It worries me. He's been so sad for such a long time, and, I'm sure you know as well as anybody, he's never been good at talking about whatever's going on in his life. I know, though, that he loved you so much. Those years he spent with you were really good for him."

I told her they were good for me as well, and I had fond memories of her infrequent visits to Prentice and the times she spent with us at the rink. We promised each other that if we heard from Russ or came up with any new information, we would be in touch.

VII.

When I was a teenager, before I took over the Rubber Route, I'd helped my uncles out at the warehouse now and then, and for a year and a half after I graduated from high school, whenever I wasn't on the road, I worked at their liquor store downtown. The liquor store was the original family business; my grandfather had started it back in the early 1950s, and the distribution business was a natural offshoot.

I can't imagine many worse jobs than working in a liquor store. I'd been around booze all my life. My father's family were all pretty big drinkers, but none of them—with the possible exception of my aunt Tina—were unhappy or out-of-control drinkers. They all, I think, prided themselves on being able to hold their liquor. When you work in a liquor store in a small town, you learn more than you ever wanted to know about your fellow townspeople. The job was depressing, and I often felt guilty about the whole racket. I wrestled with how my uncles could sell liquor for a living and have a clean conscience.

It didn't take me long to learn who all the really sad alcoholics in town were, and it was shocking to find out just how many there were. Heartbreaking encounters and incidents happened every day. The store opened at 10:00 a.m., and there were usually people waiting in the parking lot for the doors to open, mostly the same cast of pathetic characters. One guy, a retired farmer who lived way out in the country, would be so anxious that he'd be waiting at the door every morning or pacing on the sidewalk out front.

Some of the regulars came pretty much every day; others, perhaps hoping to avoid the embarrassment of the everyday visit, made weekly visits and bought in quantity. One woman, the wife of one of my high school teachers, would show up at noon already so drunk she could barely walk. These regulars, these people I'd grown up with, whose children and grandchildren I'd gone to school with, would come in and practically get lost in the store. They couldn't find what they were looking for, they didn't have enough money, or they'd count change out of their pockets or purses; they'd bounce checks; they'd drop glass bottles of vodka or bourbon or gin— happened all the time. Their hands would shake; they'd develop the vein-blown noses or cheeks; they'd lock their keys in their cars, sometimes while the vehicle was running. They'd fall asleep in their cars out in the parking lot. They'd work so hard to maintain their composure, to appear sober and normal, that they would comport themselves with the stiff and exaggerated bearing of the worst amateur actors. You'd see some of them coming across the parking lot, even in summer, and they'd be mincing along like they were trying to navigate an ice rink in penny loafers. I hated that job. I felt like I was killing those people every time I took their money.

And of course, every once in a while, one of the regulars would go to the hospital and never come out. And occasionally—maybe once a year—somebody who spent too much time and money at Big Leonard's Liquor Mart would crack up a car and kill themselves or somebody else. Nobody ever pointed fingers at us, though, and I don't think my uncles ever had any regrets or reservations about what they did for a living. "Liquor is a good provider," Uncle Mooze always said. Everybody in the family pitched in in some capacity, and everybody got a slice of the pie.

At one point the Carnaps owned two other liquor stores in town, but they sold those off when they opened the distribution business. Technically, my uncles owned and ran the liquor operation, but my grandfather was unquestionably involved in every decision. Through his Highway Patrol connections and his years of doing business in Prentice, my grandfather had a clear inside track with most of the beer and liquor reps, and by the time I was a kid, CarnapCo was a huge business with a sprawling delivery territory. I never knew for sure there was anything crooked going on, but I imagined there was. My uncles' world was full of suspicious characters and I suppose, truth be told, my uncles were sort of suspicious characters as well. They were always whispering among themselves in the warehouse office or going outside to huddle in the parking lot. I was also aware that people in town seemed to regard our family differently, with a kind of deference that had a nervous edge. Part of that, I'm sure, was that they were wealthy and powerful by Prentice standards, yet you wouldn't know that from the way they lived; they didn't believe in ostentatious displays of wealth or status—unlike Art Vargo, who was also presumably wealthy and certainly behaved as if he were. The Carnaps were modest, frugal people; they gave a lot of money to the community and their church, and all of them lived in solid, middle-class homes in solid, middle-class neighborhoods. They weren't fancy and looked down on people who were. The culture in their lives was strictly lowbrow. None of them had gone to college, and they seemed to have no real curiosity about the world beyond Prentice. What they really had, and what fueled them, was a fierce work ethic and an even fiercer, almost tribal, sense of family. They kept their secrets—and whatever sorrows they had—strictly within the family.

I didn't even know about the Rubber Route until I was in high school, and it was clear they'd scrupulously hidden that part of the family business from me. At the warehouse they also had a storage room—always locked and never spoken of—full of pornographic magazines and what my Uncle Mooze called "spicy paperbacks." They distributed these items to mostly interstate truck stops and the occasional small-town bookstore, where they would be sequestered behind the counter or in a secret room in the back. This part of the business was Mooze's baby, and I think even Rollie and Big Leonard felt sheepish about it. "It's just a little sideline," Rollie said to me, almost apologetically, when I finally became aware of its presence. "It's not my cup of tea, but there are lots of lonely people out in the sticks. Who am I to judge?"

During my years on the road, I started producing a little zine called *Rubber Route*. It was nothing, really, but a bunch of attitude, alternately manic and deadpan; music and book reviews; ruminations on the people and places I encountered; and an assortment of arcana about the condom racket. I printed copies at my uncles' warehouse and left them in various coffeehouses, record stores, and libraries along the road, and in similar places whenever I got up to the Twin Cities. An editor at one of the Minneapolis weeklies saw a copy somewhere and got in touch with me about doing some freelance writing. A year after I moved to Minneapolis, the same paper offered me a staff position as a music writer—which of course seemed like a dream job at the time—and I jumped at it. It didn't take me long, though, to get tired of going out to crowded bars at night to see music, and I was having increasing difficulty writing about music in a way that didn't feel formulaic and riddled with clichés. That difficulty was compounded by the fact that much of the music I was expected to write about was formulaic and riddled with clichés; I'd missed the glory days of the Twin Cities music scene— the days when Prince, the Replacements, Hüsker Dü, and tons of other great bands were still active in the local clubs—by maybe five years. Most of the time when I was grinding away at the office or out seeing a band, I couldn't wait to get home to listen to records by those artists, and all the other records I still loved to listen to, the older, tried-and-true stuff that was an unshakable part of me and had already passed the test of time. I was writing about music during the age of CDs, and I wanted to go home to listen to my *records*.

And increasingly, once I was home in my crammed little apartment in Uptown, I didn't want to go anywhere. The handful of women I dated—all of whom I met through the music scene or my job—wanted to go out and do stuff, and I couldn't blame them for not enjoying sitting around my apartment night after night listening to records and watching movies. More than one of them eventually accused me of becoming a stereotype.

I'm very aware, believe me, that the whole culture of record collecting is appalling pathology. I remember going to a record show with Russ during a particularly depressing time in his life. At some point he said to me, "You need to promise me you'll get away from this bullshit, Matt."

"Why?" I asked.

He waved his hand dismissively. "Look at these people. What do you see?"

I shrugged.

"Losers," he said. "A bunch of fat loners wearing identical costumes and speaking the same stupid secret language, talking about matrix numbers and trail-off grooves and imports and test pressings and promo copies. Every one of them goes home to their shitty apartment or their mom's basement and sits alone listening to their records. It's fucking pathetic."

"What's wrong with listening to records?" I asked.

"At this level?" he said. "When it comes to this? Everything. It's shameful. It's subhuman. I feel like I've spent my whole life making pointless small talk with attic bachelors. You run into these same desperate characters in every record store in the world. It's fine to love music and listen to records, but it should be something you share with other people, that connects you to the world. You should skate to it, dance to it, fuck to it, and drive around or sit with your friends listening to it and talking about other stuff. It's getting to the point where you won't have to leave your house, never even have to interact with another lonely geek in a record store; you'll be able to find out whatever you want, hear whatever you want, and buy whatever you want without having even the most meaningless human connection. It makes me want to get rid of everything. You should get a life. I should feel guilty for even bringing you to this fucking thing. Hell, I do feel guilty. This is a small half step removed from a pornography trade show."

I tried to get a life, and I've never felt any kind of real kinship with other music geeks and record collectors, other than Russ. I'm happy talking about music with friends or scrounging used record stores, but I've always been steadfast in my refusal to believe I'm part of any such community, and subcultures of any kind usually bore me to tears.

So why, then, do I cling to the obsession? And why do I still get so thrilled when I make a new discovery or finally get my hands on a record I've coveted for years? Because. It's who I am. It's what I want. I've become an even more disconnected version of the types of characters Russ railed about, in that I can't even bring myself to join their community or take solace in their company, in that I shy away from conversations in record stores and avoid going out on a limb to defend or champion my tastes, in that every single thing about my obsession is tied up with the years I spent with Russ and all the thousands of days and nights I spent in that rink, rolling around and around and falling in love with that music and those feelings. And every single time I put a record on the turntable, all I'm really looking for is to become, if only for a few transporting moments at a time, that wild-eyed boy again.

I was awkward and virtually friendless as a child and adolescent. Maybe that's why my memories and imagination became so tightly bound up in a virulent form of magical thinking: I process *all* the memories I cling to and constantly embellish them so they become even more comforting with each passing year. I was lonely as a kid—I must've been, surrounded as I was by inscrutable adults—and so unconsciously starved for the actual experiences of childhood that I tried (again, unconsciously) to make a fairy tale of my life.

There were only three kids I ever engaged with in any meaningful way as a child: two brothers I'm pretty sure I was actually friends with for maybe two years and a girl with whom I shared a brief incredible experience shortly after she moved to town when I was in junior high. But these engagements were so intense and personally extraordinary that I viewed them (and still view them) through the prism of a fairy tale. I don't even know for sure what I mean by "the prism of a fairy tale," but I sat here for a long time trying to figure out a way to say what I mean, and that's what I came up with. I wasn't much exposed to the sorts of commercial enchantments— Disney movies, fairy tales, or even many of the children's books I now understand are regarded as classics by people my age—that were so pervasive during my own childhood. Yet I nonetheless arrived at my own notions of magic and wonder, most of which were spawned by my loneliness and the unsupervised boundlessness of my childhood in Prentice and then fully incubated in the otherworldly hothouse atmosphere of the rink. Even now, I have a difficult time distinguishing between dreams and memories. I used to hate the *Popular Science* magazines Rollie found so fascinating. I hated their fixation on a version of futurism that struck me as pure nightmares from science fiction. These visions of the future seemed to promise nothing but ridiculous and homogenous outfits, human Habitrails, and all manner of contraptions apparently designed to eliminate any sort of inconvenience or difficulty. It all seemed either stupidly utopic or terrifyingly dystopic. And I didn't want any of it—whatever it was. I wanted life as it was to go on forever. I suppose some people—most people—dream of the future, but my dreams are almost exclusively of the past. I dream of going back, of reclaiming a life and a world that's either lost or rapidly disappearing.

VIII.

For a brief time in junior high, I'd see this girl around who lived with her mother in a trailer on the edge of town. They were recent arrivals; the girl started attending classes after the Christmas break. She was a loner at school and held herself close, a new kid trying to be hard enough to survive. The girl interested me, probably for those very reasons. She was at a terrible age to be thrown into the unfamiliar cliques and currents of a small-town school.

One night in the summer after her first year, I was walking along the railroad tracks just outside town. As I kicked rocks down the tracks, I encountered this girl along the creek, at the edge of a field grown over with grass and prairie flowers. She was catching fireflies.

I watched her for a time from the railroad trestle I liked to sit on. I was fascinated by her stillness, then by the grace with which she suddenly pounced. I walked down the bank below the trestle and approached her in the gloaming. If she was at all startled to see me there, she didn't let on. We'd shared a couple classes at school, and I'd said hello to her on occasion, but we'd never had an actual conversation. She glanced at me, then turned away and pounced again into the grass.

When she came back up, she looked me right in the eyes and said, "Do you remember your first memory?"

This was an interesting question. It hadn't occurred to me before. "I think it has to do with teething," I told her. "I just remember being miserable and rubbing my gums with my fingers, and one of my aunts put something on my gums with a Q-tip and it felt so good."

"Wow," she said. "That seems like a really early memory. How old were you?"

I shrugged. "It doesn't seem like that long ago, really."

"I guess not," she said. She held her Mason jar, clutched in both hands, right up to my face. "These," she said. "That's what I remember. Sitting at my bedroom window at night and listening to the strange sounds outside and seeing the fireflies floating in the darkness. I thought it was a dream." She studied the jar and smiled. "Maybe it was a dream. Maybe it is. But I love it all the same."

I asked her what she was going to do with the jar.

"I can show you," she said. "But I won't unless you tell me your full name and promise not to be a creep about anything."

I told her my name and said I would try not to be a creep about anything.

"I guess that's good enough," she said. "If you think it's weird, though, that's your problem."

We walked along the creek, back toward the lights of town. The yard light outside her trailer was the first light in the distance. It was a double-wide, one of those trailers with fake shutters and flower boxes and siding that tried hard to look like a real house. There was no car in the driveway. I asked where her parents were.

"My mom works the night shift at Tyson over in Fountain Lake," she said. "Chickens are wrecking her hands."

The girl led me into the dark trailer and down a short, narrow hallway to her bedroom. "I'm not trying anything," she said. "But we can't have any lights."

I stood in the doorway of her bedroom until I felt her hand gently push me between my shoulder blades and heard her voice behind me: "Go on in. I'm not going to kill you."

I went in and shut the door. She told me to sit on the bed, and I did as I was told. Light from outside crept in through the window curtains. The curtains had an embroidered heart in the middle, right at the part, and inside the heart a girl and a boy faced each other and bowed at the waist, awkwardly, leaning their heads in for a kiss. The real girl noticed me studying the curtains, laughed, and glided to the window.

"*Loves me*," she said, then she pulled the curtains apart. Just like that, the girl and boy were separated, the heart divided, the kiss interrupted. "*Loves me not.* My mom found these at a garage sale and thought they were funny."

She turned away from the window and crouched next to a doll-house in the corner. "My grandpa made this for me for Christmas one year," she said. "But I've never put dolls in there. It would just seem too sad. They would be trapped, and I would feel stupid trying to pretend they were alive."

I watched as she lowered the jar through the open side of the dollhouse roof. She removed the lid and shook the jar and then, in one lunging motion, sat next to me on the bed, the empty jar cradled in her arms.

"Just wait and watch," she said. "And be very quiet."

Nothing seemed to happen for several moments, but then I saw the first firefly flicker in the living room of the dollhouse, and then another, and another in an upstairs bedroom. Soon they started to float lazily out the windows and up through the roof opening and into the air around us, spark after spark flaring in the dark bedroom.

I looked at the girl. She was bent over, the jar gripped between her knees; her eyes were darting around, and she had a look of pure joy on her face. It was almost as if I wasn't there.

The girl's name was Veronica, and when I returned to school in the fall, she was gone. Yet when I remember that night, I'm four-teen years old again and breathless and trapped in one liminal moment of a past that seemed to promise nothing but enchant-ment and dreams.

The gossamer logic of that particular fairy tale, and its neat story-book parameters, in time became the lens through which I chose, or tried to choose, to view the real world, or at least the "and then" or "later" world. Eventually disenchantment closed in like a heavy curtain—a curtain, in fact, much like the one in Veronica's bed-room, or the one that separated our drab and generally glum apartment (an apartment whose soundtrack was the almost sub-liminal sound of the television and its insidious laugh track and artificial applause) from the energy of the rink, from the music and the dreamlike sweep of light and shadows and the steady hum of wheels on wood, as comforting to me as moving water. I found myself trapped between abject boredom and a despair that felt like permanent static, because the world suddenly wasn't as full of mystical, transformative power and possibility as the world of my selective memories was.

"It happens in one way or another to everyone," the Cowboy told me when I presented him with some scrambled lament about my slide into disenchantment.

"I can't stand that it happened to me," I told him. "I can't accept it."

"And why do you think that is?"

"Because that was me, and that's the only way I know how to think of my life. That's all there is. I can't live without fairy tales and magic. And lies, I guess."

The Cowboy gave me a sad smile and showed me his upturned hands. The turquoise rings on his fingers looked dead. Somehow they couldn't manage to catch even a single spark from all the artificial light sources in the room.

IX.

When I was a kid, the only place you could buy records in town was Lansing Drug, and the Woolworth's downtown. The selection of new records was severely limited, but the drug store had a bunch of cutout bins full of $1.99 records, and the majority of my earliest, purely private discoveries came from that bin, records I bought based on nothing but the album covers, titles, or the artists' names. Among the records I bought at that drug store, and which I still have today, were Dr. *John's Gumbo*, Thelonious Monk's *Underground*, Ornette Coleman's *Skies of America*, the Byrds's *Sweetheart of the Rodeo*, and Sun Ra's *Space Is the Place*. Dr. John, Thelonious Monk, Ornette Coleman, Sun Ra—what fourteen-year-old kid could resist names like that? The Monk record featured a photograph of a Black man seated at a piano with a machine gun slung over his shoulder. It was thrilling. And the music on every one of those records was unlike anything I'd ever heard and for the most part unlike anything in Russ's collection. All of them, though, were apparently cool enough to be met with his immediate approval. So much so, in fact, that though he'd never previously bought a record at Lansing Drug (it hadn't, he said, ever occurred to him), we started to make regular trips there to raid the cutout bin. I remember the day he found a bunch of Funkadelic and Bootsy's Rubber Band records, and that might've been the most demonstrably joyous I ever saw him.

"In Prentice!" he shouted as we made our way to the parking lot. "This might be the most unbelievable thing that's ever happened to me in this town."

Russ had gone to school with the guy who managed the store, the son of the owner, and one day Russ asked him, "Who orders this stuff?"

"We don't really order the cutouts," the guy said. "We just get random boxes. The distributor practically gives them away."

"Who buys them?" Russ asked.

"You guys," he said. "And a guy from the library comes in every once in a while and hauls out a hundred or so at a time."

That was how Russ and I discovered the record room in the basement of the public library. We drove right over there from the drug store, asked someone at the desk who bought the records, and were pointed in the direction of the director's office. The man's name was Robert Carle, and he was a short, skinny guy wearing a rumpled suit and tie and a pair of thick black glasses. His office was heaped with piles of books, magazines, newspapers, and records. He probably wasn't much older than Russ, and he seemed to have a lot of the same manic energy.

Russ asked him about the records from Lansing Drug, and he smiled bashfully and sprang from his chair behind the desk. "It's crazy good stuff!" he said. "I have such a small budget, but I've been able to build a really nice collection in a hurry."

Carle had hundreds of records in his office that hadn't been processed yet, and we all crouched down on the floor and flipped through them incredulously. I didn't yet have enough knowledge or experience to recognize most of the records, but I could tell by the wildly enthusiastic reaction from Russ and the giddy back-and-forth between him and Carle that it was a treasure trove. He eventually led us downstairs into the cramped record room.

"This is a seriously underutilized part of our collection," Carle said. "It's depressing, really. You can see from the cards that a lot of these records have never been checked out." All the records were enclosed in thick plastic sleeves, and in those days, before computers started to take over, each record had an index card enclosed in a pouch on the back cover; these index cards had a typed catalog number and the basic information about the album, and when you checked out a record, you signed and dated the index card, handed it to a librarian, and were given another card with the date the record had to be returned.

I ended up having a long and fruitful relationship with Robert Carle. He took an interest in me and steered me toward books and records he thought I would like, and as I got older we had frequent long and rambling conversations in his cramped office or down in the record room. In many ways, apart from Russ, he was the biggest adult influence on me during those years. And I was always secretly thrilled to check out a record that hadn't been checked out before. I took home records that had been in the library's collection for more than ten years and had never been checked out. A Son House record, for instance, I checked out a half dozen times, each time signing my name on the index card beneath a growing collection of my own signatures. For a period of six or seven years I watched the evolution of my handwriting from the awkward cursive of my early years to the more unintelligible scrawl of my late adolescence.

Russ envied the library's collection, but he couldn't stand borrowing records; it tormented him. I was happy to haul stuff home and record it to cassette, but if Russ loved a record, he had to own it, had to have the physical copy. I used to routinely find records in his collection that he'd taken from the library and never returned. I once pointed out a library copy of a Sir Douglas Quintet record—almost two years past its due date—and he merely shrugged and said, "That one can't go back."

The old library is long gone, as is Robert Carle. He took a job at a library in Milwaukee when I was a senior in high school, and a couple years later the city built a big and antiseptic new library on the other side of town and tore down the beautiful old Carnegie library of my dreams. That building had been a necessary refuge throughout my childhood, and books broke my heart in a way that felt different from the way I've learned hearts are broken in the real world. And I suppose those books, even more than the music, were what ultimately took me away and what broke my heart. But it was a beautiful heartache that didn't surrender longing.

The new library is little more than a glorified monument to new technology, a place crammed with blocky new computers and flooded with queasy fluorescent lights. They have a small collection of CDs—almost entirely garbage—but Carle's glorious record stash has disappeared. For most of my life libraries have been sacred spaces to me, sanctuaries where I could hide out and explore the world, but the Prentice Public Library is now one of the most depressing places on the planet, reduced to a sort of holding pen for the legion of indigent solitaries who now make up much of the town's population—senior citizens, alcoholics, unemployed middle-aged men, single mothers, and immigrants who come there to use the computers. The books now feel like an afterthought, and the collection is deplorable: ancient best sellers, romance novels, genre fiction that all seem to have a vaguely (or explicitly) apocalyptic vibe, and all manner of self-help, celebrity bios, and automobile and home repair manuals.

Yesterday I accompanied Rollie to a small, glum funeral for one of his buddies from the old days. I thought I'd see lots of familiar faces, but the maybe two dozen attendees were mostly elderly Greeks.

"Where is everybody?" I asked Rollie.

"Dead," he whispered.

Michael Papadoul, the deceased, was the Misto of Misto's Tap Room, the bar just up the block from Screaming Wheels. The Tap was the kind of place I associate with old New York or with smaller, hard-boiled industrial towns and cities of the northeast. Misto was a magic enthusiast, and in the front room of the Tap was a cluttered magic and novelty shop that felt more like a museum than an actual functioning business. He had magic props, theatrical accessories, and all sorts of classic gags (whoopie cushions, squirting rings, rubber chickens, a rack of glasses with goggle eyes or fake noses and mustaches) and inappropriate greeting cards. My uncles used to take me in there in the years before my mother met Russ and we moved into the rink, and Misto would show me sleight-of-hand tricks or give me plastic fangs and tubes of fake blood while my uncles played cards in the back room, where there was a 3.2 bar and a bunch of beat-up tables. A guy named Arno "Chick" Ruckert ran a one-chair barber shop out of Misto's, in the back corner of the bar, and also sold cigarettes, cigars, and a small selection of newspapers and magazines. (Years later, I would learn that Misto's was the only place in Prentice where you could buy pornographic magazines.) A partition separated the bar at Misto's from the novelty and magic shop, and I don't think the shop itself generated any revenue; I don't remember ever encountering any other customers in there. I regarded the place as my own little curiosity shop, and most of the inventory was dusty and seemed to have been there since the 1950s. The action was obviously in the back room, at the card tables.

At some point early in my time driving the Rubber Route, Misto was indicted for gambling and tax evasion, and in the ensuing investigation Chick Ruckert was also indicted for bookmaking. A lot of the guys who played cards at Misto's were members of the booster club for the powerhouse basketball team at the junior college over in Floyd Valley, a team whose coach was legendary for recruiting excellent big-city basketball players who couldn't pass academic muster at Division One schools. I knew my uncles and their pals took good care of many of these guys who came to play basketball for a junior college in the middle of nowhere. Floyd Valley was twenty-five miles from Prentice, and a lot of the basketball players drove loaner cars from a dealership in Prentice, drew paychecks from local businesses for which they seldom did any actual work, and generally raised hell around the county. A number of them, it turned out, lived in apartments owned by Chick Ruckert, and during Chick's trial it was alleged that some of these players who rented—or "rented"—from Chick had been persuaded to throw games over a couple different seasons. An assistant coach apparently ratted out the scheme, and along with Chick Ruckert, my uncle Rollie and his best friend and longtime business partner, Big Sammy, were named in the allegations. No games had been thrown, Rollie would insist; points might've been shaved, he'd allow, but that was a different kettle of fish and unprovable. He also, officially and under oath, denied having anything to do with it or possessing any direct knowledge of the scheme. The whole thing was a pretty major scandal for these parts and took more than a year to play out. Only Misto and Chick ended up being indicted; Chick wasn't ultimately convicted, but I think Misto did a little time on the tax evasion charges.

It was an awkward time for my uncles and my entire family. My grandmother refused to speak to Rollie for six months, and Uncle Mooze was furious with him over the ridiculous embarrassment of the thing: For Chrissakes, he wanted to know, what kind of idiot got himself mixed up with fixing a fucking *junior college basketball game*.

X.

I haven't provided a fair or even an accurate portrait of my mother. There was more to her than just sadness and lethargy, even if that sadness, particularly, obscured or even sometimes eclipsed many of her most interesting or compelling qualities. I have a hard time writing physical descriptions of people, partly, I think, because I tend to distrust a lot of what qualifies as physical description in literature. Or perhaps *distrust* isn't quite the right word; I can't think of a single character from a book I've read whose physical description was vivid enough that I could form a clear mental impression of an actual person. When I do picture characters from books I've read and loved, I suspect I've conjured their physical appearance from my imagination or that they're composites of people in the real world. I tend to cast books the way one might a movie. I can't for some reason picture the people in my life the same way I can conjure imaginary characters.

My mother could never be anyone but my mother. But my mother, I think pretty much everyone would agree, was beautiful. My uncles, I know, believed she was the most beautiful woman in Prentice. That she herself didn't believe this and thus made so little effort to stress or cultivate her beauty, and that, in fact, she almost seemed to go out of her way to obscure her beauty, makes it hard for me to remember how truly beautiful she was.

She was as tall as I am—five ten—and had long legs and long, thick hair that was wavy enough to be unruly and the sort of deep brown that could be mistaken for black in certain lights and took on reddish highlights in the summer. Her eyes, I think, were hazel technically, but they often appeared green, like the eyes of a cat, striated like certain marbles that used to fascinate me as a child. She also had long eyelashes, and on the rare occasion she would dress up, she could apply mascara to devastating effect.

Early in my childhood, my mother used to go out pretty regularly and leave me at home with my grandmother and aunts. She would've been in her early or midtwenties at the time, and I have no real idea where she might've gone or who she was going out with. There wasn't, though, a whole lot to do in Prentice at night other than to go to the bars, of which there were many. In those days, and through all the years we lived at the rink, in the thick of many Main Street neighborhood bars, downtown was hopping most nights with drinkers from the appliance factory and other still-functioning industries.

I would usually still be awake and muddling around the house when my mother came home. I was never a kid anyone nagged to go to bed; I honestly don't recall having any wrestling matches with my mother, or my grandmother, aunts, uncles, or Russ, about the fact that I was up and wandering around all night. By the time my mother would come home my grandmother and my aunt Helen would be in bed, and my mother used to pull me onto her lap on the couch and hug me like a stuffed animal, holding on tight and rocking gently and seldom saying much of anything, and I think I instinctively understood that these moments were really for her rather than me. At a certain point I started pulling away. Later, after we'd moved to the rink, I remember sitting around alone in the apartment after school, often paging through one of the trashy magazines my mother bought at one of the convenience stores where she worked part time for many years, and she would come in the door and say, "Oh, Matt," and those might be the last words she'd speak for hours.

I don't remember my mother ever having a boyfriend before Russ came along, or even going on any dates. By the time she met Russ, I was just old enough—nine, I'm pretty sure—to recognize how her behavior and personality changed whenever men roughly her own age were around. Russ was friends with two guys who lived next door to a duplex we lived in at the time, a house with upstairs and downstairs units. My uncle Mooze owned the house, and my mother and I lived briefly in the upstairs apartment after we moved out of my grandmother's house when she had a stroke and had to be transferred from her bedroom into a hospital bed in the living room. The guys next door were always working on motorcycles in the front yard or hanging around on the big front porch, drinking beer and listening to music. When Russ started hanging around over there, I noticed a change in my mother's behavior. She started ingratiating herself into their company and conversations much as a stray cat might, drifting in and out, going up and down the stairs of our apartment and busying herself with obviously bogus errands and projects around the house and yard. My uncles had always mowed the lawn and taken care of the property, but suddenly my mother was out there every week mowing and puttering around. We had a clothes dryer in the basement, but she started to use the clothesline in the backyard, most noticeably when Russ was visiting and the guys were all hanging around on the front porch.

She and Russ clearly gravitated toward each other but with the odd, almost calculated indifference so characteristic of both of them. They were two of the most naturally cool people you'd ever meet. Over the years I would glimpse occasional playful moments between them but precious little of what I'd describe as intimacy. As I grew older, I suspected they'd found in each other a reasonably comfortable hiding place, and I imagined—and I guess I still imagine—that they had discovered ways of communicating I was unaware of, that each knew what the other was thinking and feeling and hiding, and that they were relieved to not have to directly express much of anything.

I have to imagine my mother dated or at least saw other men during those years we lived with my grandmother. I suppose now that if she did see anyone, she snuck around so as not to offend my father's family. I do remember too many late nights when she'd be curled up on the couch and talking on the phone—and often crying—for what seemed like hours at a time. I could never figure out who she was talking to or what she was crying about.

I have one early memory that creeps me out to this day. My mother used to occasionally take me to a lake in the summer. This lake was maybe a dozen or so miles from Prentice, which just happened to be in the only county in the entire state that didn't have a lake of its own. One day we were hanging out at the crowded public beach, and there was a group of guys seated near us who seemed to me to be quite a bit younger than my mother. I was maybe six or seven at the time, and I remember being aware that my mother seemed distracted by the presence of these guys. She would've been twenty-four or twenty-five years old. She was wearing a bright red two-piece swimsuit, and at that point she was still very conscious of her appearance and spent a lot of time in the backyard working on her tan. I kept trying to get her to go in the water with me, but she refused.

At some point she sat up on her towel, straightened her swimsuit, and said, "Okay, Matt, I'm going to go to the concession stand to get us some snow cones. I want you to sit right here and watch to see if those guys over there turn and look at me when I walk past them. And tell me if you hear them say anything, okay?"

I did as she asked, and after the guys all turned and watched her almost all the way across the beach to the concession stand, one of them turned to me and said, "Hey, kid, is that your mom?"

"Yes," I said.

I noticed they were all smiling at me.

"Nice ass," one of them said, and they all howled with laughter.

I find myself thinking about that day, or that moment, often, and I'm not quite sure why, other than that I suppose it provided a brief glimpse into the woman my mother once was, or how she might've once regarded herself, and in the years to come the woman she was that day at the beach would make a rapid disappearance, and I'm not sure I remember ever seeing her in a swimsuit again.

I wonder now if my little-boy self completely misunderstood my mother's request at the beach that day or was confused about what was expected of me and what sort of response she wanted. I certainly couldn't have understood the moment the way I now think I understand the memory, and when my mother returned, handed me my snow cone, and asked if the boys had looked or had said anything, I responded with what I thought was a protective lie. "No," I said.

For much of her life my mother seemed to work hard to not reveal anything of herself to me, even as much of what she said and did revealed certain obvious things. There wasn't, however, a thing I could do about it, and I figured—wrongly, I'm sure—I had nothing to gain from knowing specific details about her life or the sources of her sadness. She didn't talk about what she'd been through, where she came from, or how she felt. When she did talk—and she could be alarmingly effusive in certain social settings—it felt like a filibuster or chatty subterfuge designed to avoid anything resembling real memories, feelings, or thoughts. Besides the fact that she had no contact with whatever family she had and never spoke about the subject, she also had no apparent photographs from her childhood or her years in Wisconsin—the first sixteen years of her life—and never, to the best of my knowledge, took or kept a single photograph of me, my father, or Russ. She seemed most accomplished at not remembering, and I'm sure my own obsession with memory and the past is somehow bound up with the frustration I felt every time I attempted to extract even a modest accounting of her past and the time she spent with my father. For the most part, though, I learned very early on to be respectful of her privacy, which extended to much of our shared life. Surrounded as I was on all sides by closed doors and apparently taboo subjects, I learned there wasn't much point in asking a lot of questions or trying to get to the bottom of much of anything.

I do remember, though, one time when we had a school assignment where we had to write a short report on the day of our birth, reconstructed as a newspaper story after interviewing our parents and other family members. My mother seemed genuinely puzzled by this assignment. She swore she couldn't remember the time of day, the weather, or any of the other circumstances.

"Did my father drive you to the hospital?" I asked.

"Your father was already dead, Matt."

Had anyone else been there or come to see me on the day I was born? I wondered. She said she didn't remember. "I don't know," she kept saying in response to my questions. "I just don't recall."

I asked her if she'd been happy. "Of course," she said, and then added, "at some point."

The teacher had sent us home with a mimeographed sheet with a bunch of questions printed in that blurry blue ink the color of the veins in your wrist. My mother had a difficult time answering even the most seemingly innocuous questions and quickly got frustrated, then angry with me.

"Jesus, Matthew," she finally snapped. "Don't interrogate me like I'm some kind of criminal. I won't have it. You can tell your teacher that none of this is his goddamn business."

At this point Russ got involved, which was always a big mistake. "I don't see what the issue is, Jean," he said. "It's a silly little school project, for crying out loud. Nobody's accusing you of anything."

"It was a long time ago," my mother said.

"It wasn't a long time ago," Russ said, raising his voice. "How old is Matt?"

My mother fled to her bedroom and slammed the door behind her. Russ then sat down with me at the kitchen table and said, "This is easy. You ask the questions one more time, and I'll be your mother." We went down the whole list and he invented beautiful answers to every question.

I think that around that point I began to understand that whatever my mother didn't want to tell me I probably didn't want to know, or at least wouldn't be satisfied with, and I learned not to push when I ran up against her obvious reluctance to talk.

I can't recall a single instance of her speaking about my father without being prompted. "You can't know your dad from anything I could ever tell you," she once said to me, and I'm still not sure if she meant that she'd never really known or understood him herself, or if she was just misguided about the natural curiosity of a child and couldn't grasp how important it was to me to have some idea of who my father was, in general but also specifically to her—how she had seen him and whether she saw anything of him in me.

I seldom asked Russ about my father, but I think he understood I was curious, and he would occasionally offer up some random memory. One time we were walking to the Sinclair station to get some pop, and as we passed the playground at Tower Park, we saw some high school guys doing chin-ups.

"Your dad used to be able to do a lot of those in gym class," he said. "I couldn't do any, but he seemed to be able to do dozens of them. I was in awe."

"What does it matter how many chin-ups somebody can do?" I asked.

"It mattered," Russ said. "It still matters. It's a big deal. You'll find out soon enough. In a town like this, it's always a big deal if you can run fast or jump high or lift a lot of weight. And it's a big deal if you can't."

"What happens if you can't do anything like that?" I asked.

Russ shrugged and smiled. "Then you better find something else you can do, or you're in trouble. Actually, it's probably better if you find something else that you *like* to do. At some point when you grow up, what you do is kind of meaningless if it isn't what you like to do. Still, when you're a kid, if you can run fast and do a bunch of chin-ups, it makes the other stuff a whole lot easier."

Russ wasn't a sports fan, but he also wasn't the type of guy who was bitter or disdainful of sports, and he seemed to genuinely admire the sorts of physical accomplishments of which he was incapable. Most of the little things he told me about my father were related to sports or athletic prowess.

"Your dad was always one of the best in all the physical fitness tests in school," he told me. "But he was never a loudmouth or a bully like some of the other jocks. He never said much at all, but he seemed like a decent guy. He had faraway eyes, like his mind was somewhere else. He was nothing like your uncles."

Much of what I know about my mother I also learned from Russ. He was never expansive on the subject, or on any subject, really, other than music, but I got information from him in bits and pieces whenever I could. Building anything resembling a coherent history or pathology from these fragments was a slow and often maddening process, much, I suppose, like reconstructing some lost civilization from nothing but pottery shards.

One day when Russ and I were driving around town he pointed out a small, run-down house set well back from the street on a big lot with several old elm trees. "There's the house where your ma lived with her grandmother when she moved to town," Russ said. I took bits of information like that, mulled them, and let them settle, and if I asked a follow-up question it was often several days later.

"Did you know my mother in high school?" I eventually got around to asking.

"No," Russ said. "But I noticed her."

"Did you ever talk to her?" I asked.

"No," Russ said. "But I didn't talk to much of anybody."

I asked him what he'd done in high school.

"Nothing much," he said. "I wasn't a popular kid, but I also tried hard not to do anything conspicuous so as not to be branded a troublemaker or a loser. I went out of my way not to be noticed. I was a nobody."

"What was my mother like?"

"She was from someplace else," he said, "and acted like she was from someplace else and wished she was someplace else. She was good-looking and mysterious, and that worked for her in Prentice. That works anywhere, in fact."

"I noticed her"—that was, I think, about as wild-eyed a romantic proclamation as you were likely to get from either Russ or my mother. When I asked her as she was dying what she'd seen in Russ, she had said, after a long hesitation during which she was clearly thinking about the question, "He was interesting."

Nobody around our house talked about falling in love or being in love or anything like that. Both of them were unsentimental and seemed to avoid public displays of affection. I of course assume, and hope, that there was some genuine affection that escaped my attention or went on behind closed doors.

Years later my mother would tell me from her hospital bed, almost like some kind of warning, "If you wanted to know what Russell was feeling or what he thought, good or bad, you had to listen closely to the music he played. He'd say as much. He talked to you through his records. Those songs had to say all the things he couldn't find it in himself to say, and I'm still not sure if he ever really felt those things or only wished he did. It was almost as if the songs did his feeling *for* him, and those stupid records were the only cards he ever sent to me. I don't listen to music like that, so most of the time we were together I didn't know what the hell he was 'talking' about or trying to tell me. He heard things I just could never hear. You know how one person might think a cloud looks like Abraham Lincoln but no matter how hard you try, you can't see anything but a cloud? It was like that. All those records just seemed to make him increasingly lost and speechless. Poor Russell."

I tried to defend Russ and said that the music was inseparable from the rink; the goal, I said, was to inspire transcendent motion.

"No, it wasn't," my mother said. "Matty, you know damn well that rink was just an excuse to hide out and play records."

XI.

Confabulation. **Is that** the word I'm thinking of? The tricks memory plays, or that imagination plays with your memory. The inventions of memory. Or maybe just the way you choose to remember so your memories in time become better than your actual life.

As a kid I had about as little knowledge of a world beyond the one I lived in as it was possible to have. Or, rather, direct knowledge. Through books and music, I was forming romantic ideas about the world, the elsewhere world I hoped to one day explore and experience. It turns out most of those old romantic notions were exactly that, and now, after almost thirty years, this little town feels as strange and exotic as anyplace I've ever been.

Earlier tonight I walked downtown to Louie's Bar to see a band whose Xeroxed gig poster caught my eye at Cuppa Joe. The band, Monica's Dress, appeared to be teenagers. They were a trio—guitar, bass, drums—and all of them wore button-down dress shirts and ties. From the poster and the name I'd expected some variety of punk rock, or at least some indie rock attitude, but as near as I could tell they were playing it straight. They were thoroughly incompetent but wildly entertaining. The set list was so anachronistic and schizoid as to be genius—in the short time I was there, they played Talking Heads's "Psycho Killer," R.E.M.'s "Don't Go Back to Rockville," and Creedence Clearwater Revival's "Run through the Jungle"—and they delivered lumbering, flat-footed, off-key, nearly unrecognizable versions of every song.

There weren't more than a couple dozen other people in attendance, all of them at least my age or older, and they were all in the back of the bar, as far away from the little stage as they could get, drinking, playing pool, and completely ignoring Monica's Dress. The band seemed oblivious to the indifference and slogged along loudly and heroically. The whole spectacle was funny, sad, and inspiring all at the same time, and as I walked back to the press box I actually got weirdly emotional. I've thought about it for a while now, and I'm pretty sure I was feeling some really complicated form of joy.

Before Russ, there was just time and waiting. Not even looking but biding my time. Then Russ came along, and I know I watched him and studied him endlessly. He gave me names, dates, connections, and cross-references. He showed me the way one type of music, or one specific artist or record, evolved naturally from another (Howlin' Wolf to Screamin' Jay Hawkins to Captain Beefheart to Tom Waits), and the ways obvious influences could be absorbed or incorporated to make something wholly original (Phil Spector plus Bob Dylan plus the Rascals plus Creedence Clearwater Revival equals Bruce Springsteen).

I also credit Russ with teaching me how to push my ears, how to get them in shape for music I hadn't yet heard, music he knew I wasn't yet ready to hear, so that when I did finally hear, say, Pere Ubu or Ornette Coleman (or even freer jazz I grew to genuinely love more than Russ ever could), it sounded to me as natural and purely intoxicating as the cleanest, most undiluted pop music.

We never, however, really talked about anything else. Russ loved books and always seemed to be reading something interesting, but when he recommended books to me, he usually just handed them to me and said, "Check this one out." I would read the books he gave me without fail, and if he saw me reading a book he'd recommended, he might say, "What do you think?" And I would invariably say something like, "It's great," and he would nod and that would be that.

I don't remember him, though, asking me how things were going in school or what I was up to when I wasn't hanging around the rink. He might—and in fact regularly did—say, "What's going on?" but it never felt like an invitation to open up or unburden myself, and he certainly didn't push or pry. He was the same way with my mother, and I assume with everyone else. There was an almost Socratic purity to the way he interacted with me (and with the world), as well as the way he engaged, educated, and indoctrinated me to the ins and outs of his record collection. "Who does this sound like?" he might ask. Or, "What does this remind you of?" If I didn't have a ready answer he would say, "Think about it for a bit and let me know. I'm curious to hear what you come up with."

Soul to Russ was just another category in his record collection, another bunch of chemicals in his chemistry set. Everything was physical. Funkadelic's *Free Your Mind . . . and Your Ass Will Follow* was, I think, Russ's central credo. Or creed. Or philosophy. Or whatever.

All I know, or at least what I believe, is that the music seemed to rewire me, and it transformed the whole world, made it seem a bigger, more exciting place. Even Prentice felt wholly changed, or at least I suddenly had the feeling doors were opening all around me. The music was coming from somewhere else, after all, and that knowledge was a huge, fascinating comfort to me and tickled the lazy wonder for which I had such great, slack-jawed capacity.

I think most of my first real, clear, and vivid memories came when I was nine and we moved to the rink, and though I'm probably mistaken, it seems to me I didn't start remembering, or at least forming detailed memories, until around that time. Maybe, of course, it's simply that those early experiences at the rink, and that time of radical change in my life and my routines, were so wonderfully strange and powerful that they penetrated my buffer of oblivion in a way nothing else ever had. It was as if I'd finally been awakened. The oblivion, though, was a comforting old habit, a protective shield, and at times I still felt a need to retreat into it. I would sometimes go up to the roof of our building, directly above the rink and accessible via a short flight of stairs in the back hallway. Early on during the Screaming Wheels years, the music would get me wound up and vibrating in a way that was still so utterly unfamiliar it was almost narcotic or like a state of intoxication. Up on the roof, I would just stand there listening to myself breathe and to the curious night sounds that weren't human music, the sleighbelling of crickets or cicadas, the distant hum and surf of traffic, the wind rattling the flag on the courthouse lawn or stirring the trees along the boulevards, and all the other stray sounds of a typical night in Prentice. The railroad yard on the east side was still active in those days and a reliable source of a truly consoling sound: the sound of something heavy being carried away.

XII.

It's the Fourth of July, the first one I've spent in my old hometown in at least ten years. The theme of the annual Prentice Summer Fest—which takes place over Fourth of July weekend—is "Party Like It's 1999," and it's sort of a discordant kick to walk around town and hear Prince everywhere. Things have already been exploding all around me out in the neighborhoods for several days, but they've been growing in intensity all day.

Fireworks are one of the few minor growth industries in Prentice, it seems; people who are poor and beleaguered and bored love to blow stuff up. It's easy drama, I suppose, and easier spectacle. Fireworks fascinate me, but it's not a comfortable fascination. I've never had the bug, and don't understand it. They make me anxious, and in my imagination, I inevitably go to a place where explosions in the night and a sky filled with bursts of fire and light don't signal mindless fun and where a barrage of concussive sound is a regular source of real danger and terror. I imagine I'm a reporter, a war correspondent entirely unsure which side I'm on, or even which side the sides are on, but I'm certain I feel the familiar uneasiness and existential terror of the noncombatant, alone and in no real physical or personal peril yet at the mercy of all the world's racket and rancor. I, once again, recognize that I'm not made of stern stuff, and that I'm lonely.

I no longer try to feel awake.

Days like this, I miss the people who used to be my family and the people who used to be my friends, miss the old impulse to be around other people and to participate, however awkwardly, in what I guess I'll call the human community. I miss having a tribe, miss the rink, miss skating on sweltering Fourth of Julys to Russ's "AMERICA! FUCK YEAH!" mix (I wish I could find the actual cassette of the mix, but my boxes of tapes are buried in a storage space under the track; I know, though, that it included the Blasters, "American Music"; the Clash, "I'm So Bored with the U.S.A."; James Brown, "Living in America"; Creedence Clearwater Revival, "Fortunate Son"; David Bowie, "Young Americans"; Chuck Berry, "Back in the U.S.A."; Funkadelic, "One Nation Under a Groove"; and Talking Heads, "The Big Country").

The year before I moved back to Prentice, most of my contact with the outside world involved fleeting exchanges with my neighbors or random store clerks. That's really not an exaggeration. I've now been wandering around Prentice for more than a month, and I haven't run into more than a handful of people I know or remember. It's a town full—or, really, not so full—of strangers now, and even Rollie, my only remaining solid connection, has been spending a lot of time at Big Sammy's cabin somewhere up north.

A lot of people around Prentice seem to operate full-time junk sales out of their yards and garages. In some neighborhoods you get the feel of a roving flea market; these random inventories—entire lives and houses being liquidated piecemeal—provide glimpses into family histories and a community culture I couldn't have guessed at, even when I was a child spending so much time wondering about the lives of the people who surrounded me every day.

Maybe, I thought as I drifted through a bunch of these sales one day, all along there had been people like Russ (or me) in Prentice, people in the grip of some private obsession that allowed them to survive in a little universe of limited culture and sometimes oppressive conformity. At one yard sale over the weekend, I found three hardcover collections of the notebooks of Elias Canetti, a writer (and Nobel Prize laureate) I'd never read. All of these books, I've discovered, have extensive underlining. Certain quotes have been transferred to scraps of paper that were apparently used as bookmarks:

"He *sorts* the moments until they become extinguished."

"Little remains of youth's dreams. But how great is the weight of that little."

"This insatiability almost surpasses all understanding."

"They search all over for their ruins. But I am my own."

"A labyrinth made of all the paths one has taken."

". . . to tell a story in cataracts."

There's no citation provided for any of these quotes, every one of which is like a blow to my head, but I assume the words are Canetti's. I'd taken all three books over to the old man running the sale, who was seated in a lawn chair and hooked up to an oxygen tank in a patch of shade next to the garage.

"How much for these?" I asked.

"Fifty cents apiece," he said.

"That doesn't seem like enough," I said.

"It's more than enough," the man said. "If I were an honest man, I'd encourage you to steal them."

"Were these books yours?"

"They were."

"So you read them?"

"I believe I did."

"I'm curious where you found books like this in Prentice."

"I didn't find them in Prentice," he said. "If I'd had to depend on the things I could find in Prentice, I would've died of some kind of starvation a long time ago."

I thanked him and went on my way, but as I've spent the last several nights making my way through those Canetti books, I keep wondering about that guy and thinking about him as a younger man, not yet dragging around an oxygen tank, coming home from some job, having dinner with his family, then finding some private space—or maybe not even—where he could sit down and read Elias Canetti.

The experience reminds me of those index cards in the plastic pouches attached to the books and records in the library. There were often, as I've said, virgin cards, cards dated from before I was born, on which nobody but me had ever signed a name, and that was a stupid badge of pride. Other times, though, other people *would* have checked out a book or record before I had, and if, as was often the case, the particular book or record made a deep impression on me, I would study the names on the index cards. I learned things about people in Prentice I'd never met or heard of, and would never meet.

He sorts the moments until they become extinguished.

. . . to tell a story in cataracts.

XIII.

For much of my life, exhaustion has built thick, complicated screens in my skull, scrims upon which all sorts of confusing and fragmented images were projected, which felt like a fuzzed and interminable legato between night and day, sleeping and waking, and unconsciousness and consciousness. These gauzy scrims behind my eyes—and there were definitely several of them constantly flickering with static imagery—played all sorts of strange tricks with reality, or what I took for granted was reality, stretching and constricting time, producing long shadows, figments, and hallucinations, disrupting consciousness with digressions, snippets of nonsense, fragments of memory, and protracted surreal interludes. I eventually determined that each of the screens in my head drew from different pools of memory and consciousness. One of them was a pure visual and audio archive from what I'll call my actual past. Another was like a highlight reel from my subconscious, more fragmentary and slippery than the others, and more challenging; more than anything else it resembled those old recordings of radio transmissions from outer space, but there was also that channel surfing—spastic and inattentive—aspect: pre-channel surfing, actually. I once had a little transistor radio that was disguised as a can of beer (some promo item one of my uncles had given me), and late at night I used to lie in my bed or sit on the floor of my bedroom while I scrolled up and down the AM dial pulling in nothing but stray and furtive fragments of music, voices, and static that would erupt for an instant like a Roman candle and then fade or disappear just as quickly. The second screen in my head was like a cerebral version of that little radio.

I had to wrestle with every single image, voice, or snippet of music or sound that appeared on the second screen. It was—and still is—an exercise in forensic consciousness. The screen is like a whirlpool that's constantly roiling with odd words, phrases, and images, circling wildly and then disappearing below the surface. One night, for instance, the phrase "too melon tasting" uttered in an unfamiliar old woman's voice kept pacing back and forth in my brain and barging into the scrum on the second screen. For several days at least, I struggled to source this tiny and unwelcome invasion. But the more I struggled to make sense of it or locate it in my actual memory, the more persistently it looped, until it eventually became an absurd mantra—or an earworm—that I couldn't shake.

It finally came to me in the middle of the night: at some point in the recent past—it's possible, even, that it wasn't the recent past—I encountered an elderly couple tasting free samples in a liquor store, and "too melon tasting" had been the old woman's assessment of a particular drink.

There exists a third screen in my head as well. This screen, I've concluded, serves up whatever the present tosses at me: the droning voice of a teacher, the progression of voices in a conversation or a staff meeting, the music that's playing, whatever is happening in front of or around me as I'm driving, sitting at my desk, or moving about in the world—everything, in short, that isn't yet memory or past. Fragments from this "present" screen—mostly things from the peripheries of my daily experience—eventually get archived and transferred willy-nilly to the loop on the second screen. The first time I went to New York City and saw the jungle of screens in Times Square, I felt as if I was looking at a large-scale version of the insane theater in my head.

So many nights as a child, and as an adolescent, I'd find myself tracking moonlight and shadows across the floor and walls, or studying the static view outside my window as if it were a radar screen. At such times my mind would be on a very low flame, a few tired words or phrases seesawing in the silence or surfacing through the waves of static that grew louder and more erratic as the night progressed. I'd sit there barely conscious, but the moment I tried to climb into bed and close my eyes, the whole chorus would convene again with a vengeance, and all the screens would flicker and then come roaring back to life. I seemed to exist entirely in this relentless and woozy carnival of hypnagogia; I might spend what felt like hours ruminating on an outrageous pair of shoes I'd seen on a complete stranger weeks earlier.

Ultimately, toward dawn, I was always left with nothing but the barely beating heart of the world, the ceaseless surf and hum of even the quietest small town, all the invisible sleepers rolling unconscious through the slow-breaking waves of sleep. The relentless pining of the clock. The modern world on the back burner, as close as it could come to stasis. I was left with only me and what was left of the night and the puzzling snow globe that was my skull at 5:00 a.m., a snow globe that felt as if it was being slowly rolled from hand to hand by a distracted giant. I was left with the retreating darkness, the shadows receding on the walls, the cruel pinch of exhaustion, the terrible reality that I was going to have to sleepwalk through another day. *What was that they were saying about what?*

Every night I would reach a point where I couldn't fall asleep but also couldn't be truly awake. I would sense, on many, many nights, that I was drowning, that I was desperately trying to kick my way back to the surface. Or I would thrash around, grasping at the dissolving figments, stumbling through a dense and hazy subterranean no-man's-land. I would sometimes, at this impossible hour, take a walk to try to resuscitate my sanity, to get clear thoughts moving in my head again. At such times I moved in slow motion through what felt like a muslin-filtered border country, imagination and hallucination barging right up against and bleeding into reality. I might hear what sounded like chanting. The jingle of dog tags. The distant tolling of a clock or a burst of faint music sucked from a car window somewhere out in the town. I might hear a baby crying, then someone laughing, retching, a congested, inebriate laughter. A radio in a dark house. Wind chimes twisting somewhere on a backyard clothesline. The barking of a dog, answered by another on the next block.

I might think of the men over in Floyd Valley, in the slaughter-house, exhausted on their feet in the slippery dead mess, blood bubbling everywhere, breaking down animals into meat. I'd been there on several occasions in elementary school, sent there with other kids in the late darkness, to stand at the mouth of a tunnel that took the men—and in those days, they were all men—to and from the slaughterhouse and to their cars and trucks in the parking lot. We—I and the other shivering kids—would stand there just outside the weak light of the tunnel, shaking UNICEF collection cans at the blood-soaked, broken-knuckled zombies as they plodded past, blank faced and clutching their empty lunch pails, moving almost unconsciously into the bruised light that was just then creeping into the eastern sky.

Somehow, though, I made it through all those sleepless nights, managed to dress myself and stagger off to another punishing day at school. And somehow, I escaped and I got saved, and now Albert Ayler takes me across catwalks in my imagination, down fire escapes in some sleepless city in my head, and out into a landscape that's both hallucination and reality, into a city that feels utterly paralyzed yet purrs the whole night long, the whole night through; through empty streets, past other dreaming houses where there are still signs of the half life of the sleepless, glum lamplight and the blue wobble of TV screens in dark windows. I wander along a river humming with idling industry and the great under-throb of the city at 3:00 a.m., the sprawl of shifting shadows, the litter and the moonlight and the longing and the great hibernating hold-out behind and beneath every heartbreak; the silence violated in myriad and mysterious ways and the compromised twentieth-century darkness; the way light launches little sneak attacks and cameo appearances, all the creeping, sleepless things, and still that doomed saxophone rising somewhere in the night that you can never entirely banish from your bogged brain, that saxophone rising like a prayer, or, at the very least, a wish, a promise, an apology, a stirring, disjointed monologue to the Great Maybe Whatever, a beautiful loose thing made of hope and traveling like a breathing kite from a small puddle of light cradling a park bench or a forlorn mattress.

Adults in those days—or at least adults in a town like Prentice—weren't equipped to deal with such conundrums. I'm sure a teacher or two tried at various times to communicate some concern to my mother, but what was she going to do? She had her own planet to tend to. The kids at school took to calling me Zombie, but nobody really seemed to have it in for me. My real problem in childhood—and particularly in school—was in navigating the challenges of integration and interrogation. Consciously speaking—or psychologically speaking, if you prefer—I simply wasn't wired to properly interrogate anything; the questions that had clear, definite answers were of no interest to me, or, really, ever occurred to me, and whatever questions I did have I was barely able to articulate and also seemed to receive no satisfying answers to. I was a kid with no apparent interest in "why," either the question or the answer, and that made any kind of real integration virtually impossible.

Things, and people, either instantly made sense to me or they didn't, and if they didn't, I wasn't much bothered. The unfortunate thing, I guess, was that there wasn't a whole lot that instantly made sense to me, which made it difficult to make friends and tended to isolate me in my own little world.

Despite all these challenges and my complete disdain for school, I was never an obviously bad or disastrous student. Teachers regarded me as average, an overachieving underachiever. From the time I was in elementary school, my report cards included remarks such as "doesn't pay attention in class," "doesn't apply himself," or "very little participation." If my struggles in school or any of these remarks from my teachers concerned my mother, she never let on. I don't recall ever having a conversation with her about a report card, and I'm pretty sure she never went to a teacher conference at any point in my education.

Everyone stayed up late around our place. Russ would be up thumbing through the handful of magazines he either subscribed to or bought on a regular basis. Some nights he'd be out in the rink until long after midnight, buffing the floors and listening to music, vacuuming, replacing light bulbs, or sitting up in his tower making mixtapes.

Early in his marriage to my mother, I think Russ struck some kind of deal with her, because most of the time when he listened to music in the apartment, he did so with headphones on. The stereo was at the opposite end of the living room from the television, and he'd usually sit there on the floor in the corner, cross-legged and with his back to the television (and my mother). She usually hung out on the couch watching TV, talking on the phone with my aunt Tina (they talked, sometimes for hours, pretty much every night, and I had—and have—absolutely no idea what the hell they might've talked about), and reading what she called her "bullshit novels": romances and trashy horror stories, mostly, but she'd also occasionally tackle a Jane Austen novel or something like that.

It took me some time to get used to living next to the rink; we shared such close quarters in the apartment, and that big, extraordinary space next door exerted a powerful pull. In the first few months after we moved in, before I really got to know Russ and felt at home in the rink, I mostly sat alone in my bedroom, not quite sure what to do with myself. I'd never been a kid to have toys, and at the time I had few possessions of my own. Our move from my grandmother's house had involved nothing more than one of my uncles' cars and a handful of trips. The move—suddenly living right downtown and next to the rink—changed the way I thought about the night and my inability to sleep. For years I'd just retreated to my bedroom like a reasonably normal child, and spent my nights staring at the ceilings or sitting at my bedroom window looking out at the dark neighborhood and letting my head go wherever it wanted to go.

Sometimes early-morning fog would come rolling up Main Street from the river, moving as slowly and deliberately as a procession of cattle. Occasionally the fog would be thicker, more textured, and I loved to watch the way swirling strands—like scarves or streamers of crepe paper—would drift and get tangled in the dark canopies of the trees. Storms—rain or snow—were always wonderful and fascinating. Rain was relaxing. Because Prentice was built so low and the land all around it was so flat, there was a lot of sky and horizon, and when really big storms rolled in at night, the displays of thunder and lightning were spectacular. Of all natural occurrences snow most perfectly mirrored the general state of my mind at 3:00 a.m. The muffled, slow-motion, and staticky quality of a blizzard, and all the strange, bruised light that accompanied one, seemed to erase the boundary between my interior and exterior worlds almost completely.

My early vigilance was only occasionally rewarded by anything resembling action. With the exceptions of the coming and going of the fire trucks and random bursts of police sirens from elsewhere in town, very little seemed to happen in Prentice in the middle of the night. Maybe a few times a night a car, truck, or motorcycle would creep through town, even more rarely a bicycle or someone on foot. From time to time I'd see a dog, cat, or raccoon nosing around downtown.

XIV.

"Once upon a time, children, there were no malls in all the world."
Russ used to say that, and I think about it often. I was, I realize,
hopelessly forged in a time right before the sensory bombardment
of cable TV, video games, satellite dishes, computers, and multi-
plexes. In my earliest memories, there weren't more than a handful of chain restaurants or stores in Prentice, and nothing was
open twenty-four hours. We got three channels on our television,
and none of them broadcast through the night. We could pick up a
handful of radio stations during the day—all hopeless and most, if
not all, of them AM and located within maybe thirty miles of town—
and some better ones if you cared to fiddle around with the dial
in the middle of the night and could find one of the original clear-
channel stations out of Minneapolis, Chicago, Kansas City, or even
Little Rock.

We had what passed for family and community, our little local
newspaper, the magazines we got in the mail, and our music. All of
which made Russ's achievement—that huge record collection and
that passion and encyclopedic knowledge—all the more astonishing. Most of the other people around me didn't seem to have anything but their jobs and their families. I'm sure some of them had
hobbies and the usual small-town diversions—they cooked or built
stuff or worked on their cars, fucked around in their basements or
garages, and fretted over their houses and their yards; they worked,
raised children, attended church or community meetings, went to
the movies or out to eat on Friday and Saturday evenings, or maybe
drove to Floyd Valley to shop or see a play at the Summerstock
Theater.

I guess the thing for Russ—and later for me—was that there didn't
seem to be much around at that time that he considered worth
swapping for what he already had: the music, the rink, *our thing,*

as Russ called it. I suppose everyone eventually finds the thing, or things, that make life bearable, or in the really fortunate cases more than bearable. Or they don't, and they live unbearable lives.

My mother always claimed that until I came along, Russ never found anybody else who was interested in or worthy of belonging to his "little club," and maybe there was something sad in that. He'd isolated himself in Prentice, and had a bunch of obsessions that made him feel even more alien than he already felt and at the same time made him feel glumly superior, a superiority so insulated and disconnected that it was purely private. I think, though, that he needed to feel that way; he wasn't wired to be a part of a larger community in anything but an abstract way. In a big city there would always be someone who knew more or who disagreed with his taste, and his degree of certainty left no room for disagreement. He didn't want to tolerate anyone else's taste. In Prentice, he didn't have to defend his turf against anyone— there were precious few people around who would even recognize or acknowledge his turf, and I'm convinced that gave him some weird satisfaction.

Still, there were people in Prentice who quietly cultivated their own little gardens of obsessions—the man with his Elias Canetti books, for example, or Robert Carle at the library. The web of the world was certainly a whole lot smaller then, but I think those years nonetheless taught me to expect that anyone might have the capacity to surprise me. It seems like a simple and obvious thing, perhaps even trite, but you can never really know someone until you take the time, or have the opportunity, to hang out with them in their own world, watching and listening and rooting around in the little drawers and closets where they've stashed all the clues of who they really are. You would know almost nothing about Russ, for instance, if you never laid eyes on his record collection. Uncle Mooze and Aunt Tina collected dolls—they had hundreds of dolls of all types and sizes, many of them very, very old—and the real secret was that over the years, it had mostly become Mooze's hobby. He was the one who kept up the hunt long after Aunt Tina lost interest. I'm sure there were many people who considered themselves old and good friends of Mooze who had no idea he collected dolls. The doll collection was more or less hidden away in a shut-up bedroom upstairs, a bedroom that might otherwise have belonged to a child they never had.

Russ told me once that he had discovered evidence his grandfather, August, had been a lifelong nudist. When he helped clean out his grandfather's house after his death, he turned up boxes of nudist magazines, nudist colony newsletters, membership cards from organizations in Wisconsin, Pennsylvania, California, and Canada. There was also a shoebox full of Polaroids from his grandfather's visits to some of these places.

I've mentioned previously that I have a collection of notes my mother and Russ wrote to each other during their marriage. Such notes seemed to be their preferred method of communication, or perhaps the least vulnerable. I also have hundreds of notes that Russ wrote on index cards and scraps of paper—notes to himself, I assume, and mostly consisting of random thoughts, quotes from song lyrics or books, or titles of songs and albums. I can't bring myself to throw these things out, and there's really nothing overtly embarrassing or incriminating in there, but I also recognize that they were intended to be private, and I am myself so fiercely private that I get uncomfortable if I spend too much time looking at them. I long ago decided I'd just as soon let the people close to me keep their secrets. For exactly those reasons—or because I was afraid of such discoveries—I refused to pick through my mother's estate (what a ridiculous word) after her death. There were other reasons as well, but I just couldn't do it.

At the time my uncles accused me of being cowardly and said that I'd live to regret the decision. "Someday you'll wish you had those memories," Rollie told me.

"Those would be her memories," I said. "And she didn't seem to have much interest in sharing many of them with me. I have my own memories. I don't want to dig through my mom's underwear and clothes."

As I've said, I'm not sure anyone in Prentice ever really knew my mother, or if she wanted anyone to know her. As I grew older, though, the apparent blackout regarding my father confused and bothered me more. Lots of people in my life had obviously known him and had memories of his life, but all that seemed to have been privatized and packed away after his death. I suspected the silence was intended to protect me and to protect my mother, but I also at some point realized his death had been a particularly blunt trauma for his family, the sort none of them had previously experienced. As a teenager, I convinced myself that no one had known him, that he left town as a cipher and returned as somehow even more of a cipher. The boy who died in the war. Through most of my childhood I'd heard the same handful of facts or stories about my father's life—they were anecdotes, really—and not a single one gave me any kind of clear picture I could live with. I was never able to imagine or animate him in such a way that I could convince myself I knew who he was or what he looked like, the way he talked or laughed or walked or even smiled.

As I was moving into the press box, I went into my grandmother's house in search of furniture and kitchen stuff I could use, and while I was there I made my first-ever incursion into my grandmother's bedroom, where nothing seemed to have been touched since the day she died. I don't think I was consciously looking for anything, but perhaps I'm lying to myself, because I found myself on my hands and knees digging through boxes in her closet. And in one of those boxes I discovered a stash of family photos, photos I had long been told didn't exist. There weren't a ton, but there were a handful of family portraits I assumed were taken for a church directory, as well as what seemed to be school pictures of each of the kids. I knew I'd seen pictures of my father somewhere in the past, but I remembered only fleeting glimpses on each of those occasions and have no recollection of the circumstances in which I would've seen such photos, or whether I allowed myself only a glimpse or, as might have been the case, had the photographs snatched away from me. In some of the photos my father looks so much like me I could've convinced myself under other circumstances that I was in fact looking at a picture from my own childhood. In what I imagine was the last of the photos to be taken, my father is wearing his Marine Corps dress uniform, and by that point, oddly, any resemblance to me has disappeared. In not one of the photos does he smile; he either looks serious and intense or expressionless in such a flat, blank way he almost seems to have stepped completely outside himself.

It's in that absent or vacant look I can most see myself in my father.

For years people around Prentice commented on my resemblance to my father: the physical resemblance but also my detachment and aloofness seemed to remind people of him. I remember my first year in high school, when one of my teachers was taking roll call on the first day of class. He called out my name, did a brief double take, and said, "You look just like your old man." It was a strange feeling, walking around in the world and having people see you and be reminded of someone you'd never met.

Even now that I'm much older than my father was when he was killed, I'll often catch a side-eyed glimpse of myself in a mirror or window, or even when I feel as if I'm maybe a half step out of my body, and I'll experience a moment of painful self-awareness of how I must look or the ways in which I'm disturbingly absent even when I'm literally present. And in those glimpses and moments I experience the fleeting feeling that I'm seeing my father and that I knew him and know him in ways I've never been able to fully embrace or comprehend.

Shortly after I started living in the press box, Rollie came by with some boxes of stuff, including an envelope with a handful of informal snapshots of my father that I'd never seen. Every one of these pictures was as inscrutable as the little else I knew about him.

There was a picture of him in a football uniform, squinting into the sun, his head tilted back slightly in a way that could've been either accident or attitude. In two other photos, he has almost exactly the same posture and expression on his face. In one picture he's hunched, clearly uncomfortable, the squint now a scowl, the slight tilt of his head extending now to a perceptible twist of his torso, his shoulders beginning to swivel, as if he were in the process of turning away. In another photo he stands in front of a Chevy Impala, slumped against the hood with his eyes closed. And in the last of the photos, he's once again in uniform, this time surrounded by his siblings in the front yard of my grandparents' house. The others all have their arms around each other, but my father, in the middle of the portrait, has his hands in his pockets.

Most of my aunts and uncles had clearly taken after my grandfather, Big Leonard, who was an extrovert and loved people. I remember my grandfather as a giant of a man who was always smiling and laughing. My uncles Mooze and Big Leonard (II) looked just like him. Leonard was the quietest of the brothers, but he wasn't shy and had a deadpan sense of humor. He was purportedly the toughest businessman in the family, the bad cop to Mooze and Rollie's good cops. Rollie was a shorter version of my grandfather—he was probably a good four inches shorter than his father or his brothers—but more so than any of the others he inherited my grandfather's mannerisms and his gift of gab. Of my father's siblings, only Aunt Helen—who had lost her fiancé (and supposedly the only boyfriend she'd ever have) in Vietnam, two years before my father was killed—had my grandmother's joyless reserve and angular physique.

From everything I know—or what little I know—I have to assume my father was also more like my grandmother than my grandfather or any of my uncles. And I'm also, I think, forced to conclude that—at least in terms of genetics and disposition (which is probably also genetic)—I'm also more like my father and my grandmother and, of course, my mother. Yet I'm obviously not really like my father at all. Granted, he was nineteen when he was killed, and who knows what he might've been like if he'd lived as long as I have. And the really interesting question is, what would I be like now if my father had survived the war and come back home to raise me? Perhaps my mother would've been an entirely different sort of mother, and perhaps I would've become a Carnap after all, would've grown up playing sports and never discovered any of the things that made me who I am: a man, I think it's fair to say, who has puzzled his father's family and almost surely would've also puzzled his father.

Often—many, many times throughout my childhood—when my mother thought I was being too needy with Russ or maybe that I wasn't giving him enough personal space or privacy, she would say, "Why don't you leave Russ alone for a little while. He's not your father, Matt."

It was often clear to me that Russ wasn't at all sure how—or if—he should address the emotional or developmental stuff I was dealing with. I could tell that things between us were awkward and that he was holding back. I wasn't a big talker, hadn't learned to talk about emotionally perilous subjects, but on occasions when I strayed too far into some potentially fraught territory, he would say, "You should talk to your mom about that," or "That's something you should ask your uncles."

I'm sure I wanted things from Russ that he couldn't give me, and I'm also sure those were "dad things," real heart-to-heart conversations, expressions of physical affection, or—God help me—love. There were a few times early in our relationship when Russ hugged me; they felt like genuine hugs, but they were also awkward, and I'm still not sure if they were awkward because they were so uncharacteristic for him, or because he wasn't sure if he was crossing some invisible emotional boundary.

There was probably something pathetic about my relationship with Russ, for both of us. I wanted his approval, though, and I'm not sure that before he came along I'd ever been so consciously aware of that feeling, of craving approval, attention, and even affection. I never—at least until my mother left him (and took me with her)—felt as if Russ was trying to push me away or in any way resented my company.

XV.

My mother used to say I was "the boy in the bubble." I was, she claimed, more cat than boy for the first five years of my life. But she always figured that one day I would snap out of it. If I were a child today, on the doorstep of the twenty-first century, I have no doubt that I would be sent to doctors and psychologists before I even started school and diagnosed with something and given prescription drugs. In the Prentice of my early childhood, though, you didn't hear about psychiatric disorders; I'm not even sure there was a psychiatrist or psychologist in town, and when I was referred to the Cowboy as an adolescent, his modest office was in Floyd Valley. People just lived, however miserably, with whatever affliction they had. No one was bipolar, manic depressive, or whatever; they were simply crazy or nuts or not quite right in the head. And I also don't remember anyone ever being referred to as an alcoholic; people who drank too much were drunks or winos, and there were plenty of those around. The town was full of them, in fact.

I don't think I could've been more inarticulate as a child; I was almost transliterate and supposedly didn't speak until I was three years old. When I did finally speak, I used language only when it was absolutely necessary to fend off the world's attention. I was curious, but it was a free-form curiosity—wonder, more properly—and I wasn't inclined to dig into anything that sparked it or to try to get to the bottom of stuff. I just stared at things and listened, but I couldn't make sense of the things I saw and heard; I didn't yet have the language for it. The words, though, were slowly building in my head, taking shape, evolving, I suppose, from mere sounds and images. I knew this business was happening in my head—it felt, I now realize, like a small lozenge of sponge gradually swelling to fill a petri dish.

Rollie once told me I never asked questions like a normal kid. My one question, which I supposedly asked so persistently it was almost a tic, was, "What?"

I'm not smart enough to know why Russ and the power of the music and the rink penetrated the fog in a way nothing previously had, but I'm pretty sure the music somehow represented the answer to that huge, booming "what?" I've lived with since I could walk and think and talk. It reached me somehow, drilled through all the static and oriented me in a reality I could both recognize and cherish; it presented me with a life that allowed me for the first time to say, "I want this."

Maybe it was all just perfect timing: my age, the time and place, my mother's silence and sadness, the spell of the rink. I was ready to be seized.

My first years in the rink coincided with the ascendance of punk rock. The Ramones were in heavy after-hours rotation at Screaming Wheels. I don't know if those records came in the mail, or if Russ picked them up on one of his—perhaps our—trips to Minneapolis, but the first time I heard the Ramones, I went immediately apeshit. I'm pretty sure they were the first band I responded to before Russ even had a chance to make up his mind. They were markedly different from anything else in his collection, and there was really no context for them. They were exactly the kind of band a kid could instinctively love: short, sing-along songs, relentlessly paced and fueled by pure adrenaline. I skated to them before school every day for at least a month and spent countless hours sitting on the floor at night listening to them with headphones on and studying the record jackets. The band photo on the cover of the first album was everything. Russ, I realized, looked like Dee Dee, and the Ramones looked exactly like the sort of band he would've been in if he'd been in a band.

It's always been easy for me to take for granted all the incredible music I grew up with; it took me a number of years to recognize how completely immersive and out of balance it was. When I first started to make my way into the world and meet other people, I was always astonished and appalled to discover what a small part music played in other people's lives (if it played any part at all). I honestly can't tell you how disorienting it was when, years later, I would walk into someone's house or apartment and discover they had no music collection, no turntable, that the music in their life had been pared down to perhaps a few dozen CDs and a small collection of cassettes. It was almost like learning that someone you knew had no indoor plumbing or, even more literally, that they spoke an entirely different language.

I'm sure it speaks to how shallow I am, or how narrow, that even now when I visit someone else's house I immediately gravitate toward their bookshelves and music collection, and if they have few books, records, or CDs, I feel utterly lost, or at least sense that there's no way I can ever really know them.

I sometimes think about what constituted the margins of Russ's taste and my own. I'm sure there were records Russ kept around and played once in a while that weren't strictly—or at least in the long run—essential, or what he called "deathless music." Surely there were instances where he stooped a bit and embraced, however sheepishly, some confection of pure pop idiocy or gave in, however ironically, to the temporary intoxication of glorious cheese.

Russ, for instance, had a serious weakness for Christmas music. He'd sometimes pretend his collection of Christmas records—it was huge and comprehensive—was ironic, but he actually listened to those records. Every year, beginning almost immediately after Thanksgiving and running right through New Year's, Christmas music was pretty much all he played in the apartment, and he also tossed a lot of holiday records into the mix out in the rink. Some of this stuff was truly great—the Phil Spector Christmas record, for instance, and a bunch of wonderful soul, jazz, and blues stuff—but I was always puzzled by the extent to which he seemed to genuinely love those records, many of which struck me as corny and sentimental. It was so utterly uncharacteristic of him.

When I was a little older—a teenager, actually—I started to poke at him about this inexplicable weakness.

"I love Christmas," he said. "It's probably basic child psychology. As a kid it was the only really happy time of the year around our house. My parents pulled out all the stops. The rest of the year, my old man never seemed much interested in who I was or what I might want, but then Christmas would roll around, and, all of a sudden, I was being encouraged to pour all of my wishes and desires into a list for Santa Claus. And Santa always lived up to his wildest reputation around our place. It really did seem like the most improbable sort of magic. I got my first stereo, my first pair of Chuck Taylors, my first jean jacket, and my first records—the Beatles, Rolling Stones, and Bob Dylan—from Santa Claus. I believed in him for longer than I probably should've simply because I couldn't imagine either of my parents ever buying one of those things for me. I also got my first pair of skates for Christmas one year, and I didn't even ask for them or know I wanted them yet. I think Christmas was the first thing that taught me there wasn't anything wrong with dreaming and being happy."

Russ's Christmas spirit was oddly infectious, and what I most loved about the season around our apartment and the rink was its utter absence of the communal hubbub it seemed to foment everywhere else. For Russ—and for us—it was a time of quiet and mostly private rituals and pleasures. Russ had all sorts of these rituals: cutting and trimming the tree, decorating the rink, watching the same batch of movies every year, and cooking a series of meals he only made during the holidays. Other than grilling, in fact, those holiday meals represent the only times I ever remember Russ cooking at all. Unsurprisingly, I suppose, and perhaps pathetically, I inherited virtually every one of Russ's holiday rituals and his love for Christmas records. And I suppose if I were pressed for a reason why, my answer would be the same one Russ gave me all those years ago: because the season has such fierce, warm, and lucid associations with the only extended happy periods of my life.

Even now, my relationship with the records I first heard at the rink is almost talismanic; those were the first records I loved as purely physical objects. I loved everything about them, from the packaging and design to the eternally mind-blowing miracle of the way they worked, the wonderful and astonishing impossibility of the technology.

Even today, the process is almost as fascinating to me as the sound, and the symbology of the needle riding in the groove is still as good as any other I can think of for the way my mind locks into its obsessions. I loved, and love, the ritual of it—if drinking tea can be a ceremony, then surely so can listening to music. The ceremony of listening to records, the piecework aspects of it: removing the record carefully from the sleeve and placing it on the turntable, cleaning the record, putting the needle in the groove, and sitting back to study the album cover, credits, and liner notes (and lyric sheet, if provided) while you listen to the music. In this respect—as, of course, in so many others—I definitely learned from Russ and take after him. Music was never just background for him; when he played records, they were the center of his attention. This was an issue with my mother, for whom music was seldom anything more than a background and often a distraction. She refused to take anything as seriously as Russ took music, and she clearly regarded his obsession as eccentricity and, often as not, a waste of time. She didn't try to hide her disgust when I began to take an interest in Russ's record collection.

XVI.

My mother talked to me, often in long, meandering monologues that I became skilled at absorbing without ever quite listening to or processing. I seldom sensed she was looking to me for any answers, feedback, or insight. I was, after all, just a kid, and much of the time I probably couldn't grasp whatever it was she might've been trying to tell me. I had the feeling she was merely talking to herself, which I knew she did; sometimes I'd hear her talking in her bedroom or the bathroom, almost as if she were talking on the phone, but those were the days when a telephone was still a stationary object in the kitchen (on the counter at my grandmother's house) or on the table next to the sofa in the living room.

It's kind of amusing to me that I always heard myself being described—by my mother, among others—as a good listener, but I was, in fact, an excellent *nonlistener*. I've discovered that many people don't really need to believe you hear or understand what they're saying much of the time; they just want someone to absorb their stories or, lacking actual stories, their words. My mother really didn't have stories. It took her many years to learn how to actually reveal any of herself to me, and when she eventually did, I had the sense she was fighting through all sorts of layers of repression. This happened when I was perhaps old enough to hear her and when I think she'd finally decided she didn't want to hold on to everything anymore and gave herself up to a sort of willy-nilly surrendering and unburdening that I guess is fairly common when people near the ends of their lives.

Russ didn't talk much about his family or childhood, but we certainly talked about lots of other things. His father was an oddball and, I think for Russ, a source of some embarrassment; they clearly weren't close, but their relationship struck me as civil and even cordial, and I never sensed any obvious strain between them. Russ's sister, Janice, was older by a few years. Whenever she visited, she'd stay at the Road Key, a carport motel just off the old state highway outside town. Russ seemed entirely comfortable with his sister; she was outgoing, outspoken, and funny, and she was always sweet to me and her brother. She'd usually skate at the rink whenever she visited, and she and Russ would skate together after hours. They had some mock-elegant routines—almost like ballroom dancing—that involved a choreography they'd clearly worked out when they were growing up. I loved to watch them skate; they both were obviously having a good time, and I'd never seen Russ so unselfconscious. Most of their conversations involved merciless mockery of their parents.

We lived together for just over five years—Russ, my mother, and I—in that cramped apartment next to the rink. They were wonderful years for me, but I was too wrapped up in all the discoveries and changes to pay much attention to the dynamics between my mother and Russ. It was all so fresh and unusual compared to the quiet years my mother and I spent at my grandmother's and in one of Mooze's duplexes, all those years I'd spent fending for myself and tiptoeing around my mother's frequent, inexplicable squalls and prolonged silences. There had been nothing for me to do in either of those places—no one and nothing to play with, no music. The television was always on, but my mother watched programs that were meaningless to a child. We virtually never went anywhere or did anything. I used to let my grandmother and aunts drag me along to mass just to get out of the house. I spent quite a bit of time with my uncles in those days, hanging around at their houses or tagging along with them as they made their rounds. After my mother and Russ married, I spent a lot less time with my father's family; I still saw them frequently but no longer spent entire days, or even weeks, with them.

Rollie still tried to keep up our old routines, but I no longer wanted to spend my Saturday afternoons—the best and busiest day at the rink, by far—hanging around with my uncles. Once every couple weeks or so, though, he'd pick me up and we'd go to a movie or out for pizza, and in the summer, I'd still sometimes accompany him as he made the rounds among the warehouse, Misto's Tap Room, and Big Sammy's Supper Club, where we'd play pool or pinball in the game room.

There was never any question that my mother's marriage to Russ essentially cut a lot of the old ties and dependencies with the Carnaps. Before my mother met Russ, my father's entire family were hugely supportive and protective of her. We ate a lot of meals at my aunts and uncles' houses and spent all our holidays with them. Rollie and Mooze found my mother one job after another, none of which—for reasons I never understood—she managed to hang on to for long. She seldom worked directly for them; she felt, I think, that she could never win their approval, and maybe she didn't want to let them down so intimately. My grandfather was famously exacting when it came to business, and Uncle Mooze in particular was said to be a difficult and demanding boss. After she remarried, she told me several times she felt as if she'd been cut off. She still maintained a close relationship with Aunt Tina, the only other person who had married into the family—but the others all seemed to cool toward her.

A good deal of this, I'm sure, was related to the cold war that had gone on between the two families for decades. Still—and this may be projection or merely the product of my own overwhelmingly happy memories—I think my mother was at least sometimes happy in the early years of her marriage to Russ, or happier than I'd ever seen her. She admitted to me years later that she'd always been a person who liked being part of things that didn't make explicit or pressing demands on her. She liked having people around, but she chafed against communal expectations.

She certainly didn't seem to have any traditional matronly instincts and hated all stereotypes of femininity. I've mentioned that she didn't much cook and had even less patience for cleaning, laundry, or other household details. For as long as I could remember I'd done my own laundry, or one of my aunts had done it for me, and I don't think my mother ever lifted a finger to clean my room or nagged me to do so. She almost never dressed up, and favored the easiest style of tomboy clothing—jeans, T-shirts or jerseys, and tennis shoes. If they hadn't been such radically different sizes, she and Russ could've shared wardrobes. Most of the time she wore her hair either scrunched up on the top of her head or pulled back in a ponytail. She wore makeup only on the rare occasions she and Russ went out for the night, and on such occasions, she would apply lipstick so bright and uncharacteristic it shocked and secretly embarrassed me; it looked to me like she was just fooling around.

At any rate, those first few years at the rink she seemed stable and contented. She wasn't working, and she had a man in her life again. She was out from under the scrutiny and influence of my father's family (she'd always seemed particularly cowed by my grandmother). And I was happy and largely occupied and out of her hair. I was coming out of my shell in a big way, and while I think that initially relieved her, it eventually became a source of concern and even alarm.

I looked forward to coming home from school and finding the first rink rats already making their rounds and Russ at his place in the High Tower. I'm sure the rink had seen better days, at least in terms of business, but to me it felt as if we had a party in our house every day. There was a small but devoted crew of regulars who came right from school on weekdays.

I never had much to do with most of the other kids who regularly skated at the rink; they were almost all older and tended to go about their shared routines as if I were invisible. That never bothered me. I loved to skate, to move around the rink under the warm pastel globes, the disco ball, and the strings of colored lights. Much of the time it was like an out-of-body experience, the closest I came in those days to dreaming, and it was almost as if every song

Russ played was being indelibly etched in my brain, so clearly can I remember specific songs, moments, and afternoons.

People often seem incredulous when I talk about the music I listened to as a kid, but I just took it for granted. I'm sure pretty much everyone can remember the music they heard growing up, the songs and records they were exposed to at home or heard on the radio or in friends' bedrooms. It just happened I had a more intense and saturated exposure to a wider variety of music than the average small-town kid.

The music made me feel different in the best possible way, and different from all the other ways I normally felt different. I'd finally found something that interested me, something that made sense to me in a way so much else never had. It was my first real discovery and obsession, yet it was also frustrating, because there was no one my own age I could share it with as I dug deeper into it. All I had was Russ, and while he was an excellent teacher, he would never be expansive, or even effusive. He preferred short answers and explanations—he was a bullet-point guy and generally of the opinion that records should speak for themselves. Often when I pressed him for information about a particular record or artist, he would simply hand me the album cover or a stack of records by the same artist or ones of a similar style.

I don't think my mother ever put a record on the turntable of her own volition, but even she was sometimes utterly helpless to resist the power of a great song. Some of my happiest memories are of occasions when she'd smile at, sing along with, or even dance to one of Russ's records.

The music Russ listened to in the apartment was generally much different than what he played out in the rink. It tended to be mellower, more introspective, and less groove oriented. Nick Drake, for instance, or maybe Tim Buckley.

"Why can't you play any happy music?" my mother would ask.

"It's all happy music," Russ would answer.

Her own favorites, though, the records that made her smile and giggle and shimmy, were overtly happy records. I'm not sure she ever bothered to learn the names of the bands or artists behind them. She loved the Commodores and Earth, Wind & Fire. And Wilson Pickett's "Sugar, Sugar." And the Spinners' "The Rubberband Man" (my own favorite song for about six months).

Those earliest days at the rink were the happiest and most unrestrained I ever saw my mother. She and Russ had only been married for a few months, and she was showing signs of finally emerging from her cocoon. For a brief and happy period she maintained a pretty regular routine of hanging out in the rink with me after school as Russ warmed up and fine-tuned his playlist. Sometimes, before the early-evening skaters arrived, all three of us would skate together. Those nights were the most fun we ever had as a "family," and the only times I saw my mother and Russ hold hands as they skated.

I believe we all had a happy first few years or so together. Russ had spent most of his adult life alone, and he seemed grateful for the company. My mother, I'm sure, was relieved to have someone else around to pick up some of the parental slack.

At some point, however, she seemed to retreat again. Shortly after Christmas one year, she took a job at a new Sinclair station out by the freeway. I don't think money was an issue; I suspect she just felt like she needed a life away from the rink and was already getting tired of having a soundtrack for her every waking moment. Whatever her motivations, there was a marked change. She stopped skating entirely.

I'm sure Russ noticed the changes, but he had his routines, and they were unshakeable and unvarying. He and my mother still went out occasionally on a Friday or Saturday night after he'd flushed the last skaters out of the rink, and on such occasions, I usually ended up over at Mooze and Tina's, where we'd sit up late playing cards and eating popcorn. But overall, I suspect Russ had done whatever wooing he was going to do before he married my mother, and he clearly didn't have a whole lot of that sort of thing in him.

In my mother's defense, I suppose, Russ was her first serious relationship after my father's death, and she and my father had never really lived together. But if she wasn't going to pay much attention to the records Russ played, she wasn't going to get much in the way of romance.

In Russ's defense, he was what he was and never pretended to be a typical flower-and-candy sort. He'd also never lived with a romantic partner before. Near as I could discern, when it came to romantic indifference and dispassion, my mother gave as good as she got. If she had a sentimental bone in her body, she hid it along with all the other instincts or feelings she feared. It boggles my mind to think they were so young at the time—my mother was twenty-seven when she married Russ; he was twenty-six. In some ways I thought they were a perfect emotional match, but the truth is probably that they both needed someone extroverted and energetic who could coax them out of their comfort zones and preoccupations. They were certainly not as emotionally self-sufficient or tough as they might've seemed to outsiders.

When my mother was dying, she admitted to me that she "probably didn't love Russ." I couldn't fathom that and was weirdly devastated to hear her say it.

"Then why did you marry him?" I asked.

She'd shrugged. "I was bored and lonely and felt suffocated by your father's family," she said. "It happens all the time. Your dad was the only 'relationship' I'd ever had, and I suppose I can be honest with you now and tell you that it wasn't even really a relationship. I was a kid. We went on a couple clumsy dates and I got pregnant. And then basically I never saw him again. It happens all the time. When Russ came along, I thought I was ready to give it another try, but it was pretty quickly apparent that I'd made a mistake. Except you guys were so crazy about each other right from the beginning. I felt stuck."

Still, until the last year of their marriage, I never knew my mother and Russ to fight, at least not in any kind of loud and disruptive way that would've been stressful for a kid. I guess in retrospect I knew they spent a lot of time tiptoeing around each other. They were both cold warriors, and while they drifted further apart, I dug deeper into Russ's record collection and rocketed around the rink every night.

XVII.

A couple years after we had moved into the rink apartment, a guy named Leon Earle came to town and opened a hippie emporium called the Soviet Embassy, which was a combination record store, head shop, and social lounge. The name was an obvious and deliberate provocation, and everything about the place felt like a parody. Prentice had never been a hippie bastion, and the whole hippie thing had long since crested elsewhere.

Leon Earle had apparently grown up in Prentice and had drifted around the country for at least a decade before coming back to his old hometown to try his hand as a semilegitimate businessman. The Soviet Embassy sold glass pipes, bongs, rolling papers, all sorts of dated posters and T-shirts, and a small assortment of records.

Russ thought the Soviet Embassy was the funniest thing that had ever happened in Prentice, but there was a lot of loud and immediate local outrage about what was perceived to be an affront to community values. Earle wasn't even open two weeks before the *Dispatch* ran an editorial denouncing the Soviet Embassy and demanding the city take whatever measures necessary to close his business.

Earle's shop was a block and a half from the rink, on an avenue just off Main Street. Russ and I walked down there one afternoon shortly after the store had opened. I think at that point Russ still secretly hoped there would finally be a source for new records in town, but the inventory—such as it was—was a predictable letdown. It was all, or pretty much all, stuff Russ would dismiss: a bunch of Grateful Dead records (of course), as well as others by bands and artists generally associated with the same era or scene—Jefferson Airplane, the Doors, Big Brother and the Holding Company, Moby Grape, and Jimi Hendrix.

"Nothing to see here," Russ had muttered, and he laughed all the way back to the rink. "That place is genius," he said. "It's absolutely fantastic, and it won't last a year."

The truth was that Russ owned records by most of the artists represented in the Soviet Embassy bins; it was the sort of stuff he'd listened to growing up. He despised Jim Morrison and the Doors, but most of the others were okay. But a record store, he always said, shouldn't be a museum. If you couldn't go in there and discover something new or something you hadn't yet heard, it wasn't worth a damn.

Leon Earle's father, Eldon, ran an auto body shop and welding business out of a de facto junkyard on his property over on the eastern edge of downtown. He was a man who always seemed to be at war with somebody—his neighbors, the city, and all the local businesses that taped his bad checks to their cash registers and counters. He was a strange-looking man, with a tiny, bald, and perfectly round head on a big, powerfully built body; he had thick black hair on his arms and the backs of his hands. A lot of times you'd see him wandering around in the junkyard that was technically his lawn (one of the many bones of contention with his neighbors), shirtless or in a dirty, practically see-through sleeveless T-shirt, with that jet-black body hair rolling from his shoulders all the way down to his fingers and stretching across his back and chest to his neck. Other times you'd see him around town in a black shirt with a grimy white clerical collar; he called himself "the Chaplain," and claimed to be some kind of ordained minister. He'd allegedly been a military chaplain in the Korean War and had built up a small but loyal following that met on Sundays in a former bowling alley out by the municipal airport. In the summer they held services at a KOA campground fifteen miles west of town.

Leon Earle and his two sons, Greenland and Valentine, lived in Eldon's junkyard, where their accommodations consisted of a huge teepee and a houseboat that was beached on cinder blocks. Greenland Earle, the older of the two brothers, was in my grade at school. Valentine, who was in a wheelchair, was a couple years younger. Greenland was lanky, three or four inches taller than I was and skin and bones; he was alarmingly pale, almost on the verge of translucence, and he had huge green eyes like a lizard's and long, straight hair the color and consistency of broom straw. He had sucked-in cheeks, a huge overbite, and terrible posture, and he had this habit of making a fist with his right hand, jamming it into his left palm, and twisting it aggressively, as if he were tightening a bolt. Whenever he did this—which was often, and unconscious—he would screw up his face with obvious exertion and make a squeaky, grinding noise with his mouth and teeth. He had a thick, marbled callous on his left palm.

I first encountered the Earle brothers when they showed up at the rink shortly after they'd moved to town. Greenland had come up the stairs lugging his brother's wheelchair, plopped it by the skate rental counter, disappeared, then reappeared a few moments later, out of breath, with Valentine, cradling a metal globe of the moon, slung over his shoulders. I would later learn he took that globe—which had indentations to show the craters—pretty much everywhere he went.

After Greenland resettled his brother in his chair, he asked if we had any pinball machines. I told him we didn't, and he stood there for a long moment cranking away at his palm and squeaking. His brother just sat there, not saying anything, his eyes darting around and seeming to track the swirling motes from the disco ball. I asked Greenland what was wrong with his brother. "He's hungry," Greenland said.

Kids would ask Greenland what was wrong with his brother, and it was always "He's hungry" or "He's bored" or "He's tired" or "He's pissed off." I'm not sure I ever learned why Valentine was in the wheelchair or why he never spoke. Greenland hauled him everywhere he went, usually towing him behind his bike, which his grandfather had equipped with a welded hitch for the wheelchair. Greenland had a ridiculously chopped Day-Glo–green Sting-Ray bike with extended forks on the front tires, a plush banana seat, and the tallest chrome sissy bar I'd ever seen. While Valentine sat on the sidewalk with his moon in his arms, Greenland would ride wheelies up and down the block. They came by the rink most afternoons, even though Greenland never skated. They just hung around drinking pop and watching the skaters. Greenland became my first real friend, or at least the first kid I ever hung around with on a regular basis.

Every time I'd see him, Greenland would lead off with one of three phrases: "What's the plan, Stan?"; "Okay, here's the plan"; and "I've got a plan." Most of the time none of these phrases really meant anything. Before moving to Prentice, Greenland and Valentine had lived all over the place, sometimes with their father and sometimes with their mother, who I gathered lived in the Twin Cities. Right before his father assumed full custody of him and his brother and they came to Prentice, Greenland had spent six months at the Sheriff's Boys' Ranch, which was a sort of penal colony for boys too young for reform school. The Boys' Ranch was actually an impressive thing for a new kid to have on his résumé in a small town like Prentice; everybody knew about such places, and every young hooligan lived in fear of being shipped off to a boys' ranch. It got Greenland respect in some quarters and fear in others.

I'm sure everyone can remember the first kid they ever saw with a cigarette in their mouth and how shocking it seemed at the time. In my case that would be Greenland Earle, and he was smoking at least two or three years before any other kid in my grade at school. Greenland was a pioneer in so many ways in my life: He had a knack for picking locks and could break into a pop machine in under ten minutes. He was the first kid I ever heard use the word *fuck*, the first kid to explain to me what that word meant (in great and enthusiastic detail), the first kid I ever saw give anyone the finger, and the first to somehow come into possession of both dirty magazines and alcohol.

I spent a fair amount of time with Greenland and Valentine at their grandfather's crazy compound and virtually never saw Leon Earle around the place. Whenever I asked about him Greenland would say, "He's probably at the bong store," or "I think he's meditating in the teepee."

Eldon Earle had an ambiguous relationship with a woman from his congregation who helped look after the boys to some extent, but I think she spent more time and energy looking after Eldon. Her duties mostly consisted of laundry, grocery shopping, and doing her best to pick up around the place. Eldon took Greenland and Valentine to Country Kitchen for dinner several times a week, and I think the rest of the time they were pretty much on their own.

Even with the woman supposedly helping out around the place, it was an unbelievable mess; grimy from dirt, grease, and dust from the junkyard and just full of wall-to-wall clutter, including auto parts and hundreds of phone books and catalogs. "You can see we have three pianos," Greenland said the first time I visited. And it was true that they did, in fact, have three pianos, but every one of them was heaped with books, magazines, boxes, and all manner of junk.

Eldon Earle pretty much exclusively referred to the boys—and me, when I was around—as "you rats," and he seemed to spend much of his time maneuvering around them and trying to get them out of his hair. I watched him on a number of occasions go to the refrigerator and mix beer and grape soda in a big mug. Eldon also collected photographs of burning churches; he must've had at least fifty of them framed on the walls of his so-called study. It was the only room in the house with any semblance of order, or, at least, the clutter had been somewhat neatly arranged around the photos of the burning churches.

Every time I'd visit, I'd ask Greenland to take me in there to see them. As usual he had little to offer in the way of an explanation. "He likes them, I guess," he'd said when I asked him what the deal was, and it would be many years before I'd get the story from Eldon himself.

After Greenland and Valentine moved away, I'd still occasionally see their grandfather around, and as I grew older, I'd stop by to say hello when I was in town. One day I just finally came right out and asked him about the photos of the burning churches.

"It's been my hobby for many, many years," he told me. He had stumbled into it purely by accident or by luck. Years earlier he had been at an estate sale and had found an old photograph of a burning church—a big Lutheran church in Corning had caught fire in the late 1950s—and had felt compelled to buy it and hang it in his den. There was something dramatic and beautiful about it, he thought, and there truly was: the chiaroscuro of the flat blacks, grays, and silvers; the blur of the firefighters in the foreground, almost ghostly; the soft blush of the smoke and the flames rising toward the eerily backlit steeple; and beyond it all, total darkness pressing in from the fields in the background. Once he got it home and hung it on the wall in his study, he found himself drawn to it and contemplating the power it seemed to have over him. He'd gone down to the library and had done some research, and somewhere in the old newspaper microfiche he had learned that the determined cause of the fire was lightning. He was familiar, he said, with the term "act of God" as it was used to describe certain insurance calamities for which no apparent human culpability could be determined, and that got him to thinking: Why in the world would God allow— let alone cause—one of His places of worship to burn? Eldon was curious about how often church fires occurred and started poking around in the photo files of local newspapers, churches, libraries, and historical societies. And he was somewhat startled to discover that virtually every town in the area had had a church burn at some point in its history, and in some cases multiple churches.

It didn't take him long to raid the photo files of every town around Prentice, and by the time I met him, he had accumulated an extensive archival history of church fires; he had a shelf full of black-spined scrapbooks and journals, each one documenting his discoveries in as much detail as he'd been able to uncover. In addition to his own handwritten accounts, the pages were also stuffed with newspaper clippings and copies of pages from ancient books and parish histories. He also had a fat scrapbook full of picture postcards of burning churches. It was a remarkable collection, and strange, certainly, for a professed man of the cloth, even one as obviously unorthodox as Eldon Earle. There almost certainly weren't many people who'd ever seen the collection or even knew of its existence. Eldon admitted to me on more than one occasion that I was the first person who'd ever taken an interest in what he called his "hobby." I must admit I struggled to make sense of it. There was an undeniably creepy and even sinister air about it, especially when contemplated in in its entirety—virtually all of the available wall space in his study was taken up by photos of burning churches.

Many years later, when I was driving the Rubber Route, I was hanging out with Uncle Rollie at the Tender Maid. We were shooting the shit with a few other customers, including Father Reagan, who had been a priest at St. Augustine for more than forty years. Eldon Earle was in a nursing home at the time, and the assembled were discussing what an odd and contrary character he was. Father Reagan mentioned that one of his predecessors had once refused to marry Eldon back in the 1940s. Eldon hadn't been a Catholic and had stated up front that he had no intention of ever becoming one. The girl's parents had objected to the marriage as well. Father Reagan said the church had had no real choice in the matter; there was no way, under the circumstances, that Eldon could be allowed to be married at St. Augustine. It was a shame, Father Reagan said, and had certainly not ended well, at least so far as the girl's family had been concerned. Eldon had talked the girl into driving over to Floyd Valley, where they were married by a judge.

"I'll never forget the look on his face the first time I introduced myself to him," Father Reagan said. "He said he wouldn't set foot in my church for all the money in the world, and if there was a truly just God, He would burn the place to the ground."

Before the Earle brothers came along, I'd kept my distance from other kids who hung out at the rink, mostly, I think, because they usually arrived in their little cliques, and I was wrapped up in the music and more often than not sitting up in the High Tower with

Russ, watching him work and peppering him with questions. With Greenland and Valentine living just on the other side of downtown, though, I started spending more time with them outside the rink. Greenland was a great, animated talker, and he didn't have a lot of interest in the truth or even much of a command of reality. I asked him once to explain the origins of his and Valentine's names, or why his parents chose them, and he told me an angel had whispered the names in his mother's ear.

"In a dream?" I asked.

"No," he said. "At the hair store." By which I assumed he meant the hair salon, but as was so often the case with Greenland, no additional information was forthcoming. Unlike me, Greenland could sleep anytime and anywhere. He probably had narcolepsy. He used to sleep in school every day, and he'd often come to the rink and fall asleep on one of the benches along the wall.

I suppose I was eleven when I first started venturing out at night, particularly in the summer months, when it could get unbearably hot in our apartment. The rink had much higher ceilings and ceiling fans, and the huge transom windows together with the fans kept whatever breeze there was circulating. Usually at some point in the night I'd make my way from my bedroom out into the apartment. Russ would likely have gone to bed by this time, but my mother was almost always still up, or at least still camped out in the living room, half asleep in the recliner or on the couch or maybe still reading. She'd occasionally hit the thrift stores and garage sales with Russ and me and buy boxes of paperbacks and old magazines. She seemed to become more indiscriminate in her reading all the time and would blow through stacks of whatever she'd picked up—science-fiction novels, romances, cheesy pop-culture biographies of celebrities, books about UFOs and reincarnation (she was a sucker for stuff like that), self-help garbage, and even Westerns and the occasional classic; I remember she once picked up a bunch of Dickens at a garage sale and plowed her way through them. She never talked about the books she read, at least not to me, and I couldn't say what effect they had on her, other than to assuage her boredom. I'd gotten used to being one of the invisible kids; I tried hard not to do anything that would get me noticed, and I was wildly successful at this. For a number of years, I refused to wear a T-shirt or sweatshirt with any words or slogan on it; in the instant someone read the words on my shirt, they would see me. Greenland Earle was the first kid who ever seemed to look at me, and he was also the first kid to really interrogate me.

Greenland interrogated everyone, but I think he was genuinely curious about me; I was the kid who lived at the roller rink, the late-night kid, the kid who seemed to travel in the same weird orbit he did.

My aunts and uncles had always given me their pocket change. I had a giant piggy bank Aunt Helen had presented to me for my birthday one year; it was almost the same size as a real pig, and everyone in the family was interested in my progress in filling it. Also, whenever I worked the skate rental counter at the rink, Russ let me keep half the proceeds; at fifty cents a pair, I could usually make five to ten bucks a night, and I took my payment in quarters that I brought right back to my room and put in the piggy bank.

Late nights in the summer, I'd fish some quarters out of the bank and walk right past my mother in the living room—my old invisible-man routine—and make my way down the stairs and over to Eldon's, where I'd usually find Greenland hanging around with Valentine in the houseboat. Valentine slept in the lower bunk of the bed he shared with Greenland, and he had a torturous routine he'd worked out to get himself into and out of both the bed and his wheelchair. It was painful to watch, but he refused Greenland's offers of assistance.

We'd hook up Valentine's chair to the hitch on Greenland's Sting-Ray, and the three of us would ride downtown to get cold cans of pop out of the machine in front of the Standard station.

At some point in that first summer, Eldon Earle bought a dis-tressed pop-up camper and set it up out in the yard, and it quickly became Greenland's private refuge and bedroom. Valentine continued to occupy the houseboat, which had a ramp he could scoot up and down in his chair. There was a bathroom in the house and another one in the separate garage that served as Eldon's body shop. There was also a half-assed bathroom stall in the houseboat, but Eldon had removed the holding tanks and dug a huge hole directly beneath the toilet so that it functioned more as an outhouse than an actual bathroom. It was disgusting, and I think Valentine was the only person who ever used it. Every week, Greenland told me, his grandfather poured quicklime down there to keep it from stinking so bad.

I once asked Greenland where his mother was.

"She's locked up," he said.

"For what?" I asked.

"She's cuckoo," he said. On a couple other occasions, though, he claimed his mother was living in some underground religious colony in Montana.

I got in the habit of going to the Earles' after midnight in the summer—sometimes as late as two or three in the morning—and we'd hang out or ride our bikes around town. These were the first occasions I'd ever known Greenland to leave his brother behind.

"He needs his sleep and likes to be independent," Greenland said. "He's fierce." They had a pair of expensive walkie-talkies that had an incredible range, and Greenland kept his clipped to his belt at all times. Periodically, when he was separated from Valentine, he would check in on him. "Hey, V, do you copy?" he'd bark into his walkie-talkie, and from his bunk in the houseboat Valentine would press the red alert signal button, which sent back a prolonged beep. That, Greenland said, was the agreed-upon indication that everything was cool.

Greenland and I used to regularly ride our bikes all the way to the west side of town, where a fat cat local car dealer (and pal of my uncle's) who went by the name Buddy Fly had built a giant playground complex on the sprawling lawn of the newest of the

Catholic churches in town. This was one of the biggest and fanciest playgrounds I'd ever seen. Buddy Fly's playground (that's what everybody in town called it) had this huge rocket-shaped slide that must have been at least thirty feet tall, made several 360-degree circuits on its way down, and had an enclosed cupola at the top. There was also an immense green plastic dome stretched across a sandbox that featured all sorts of tunnels and chutes, kind of like those hamster colonies that were a big deal in those days. Greenland and I used to hide up in the rocket cupola or under the green dome.

It would be a year or two before people would start warning me away from Greenland, but in hindsight I'm surprised it didn't happen sooner. He seemed pretty harmless to me at the time, but he was insolent around adults and never pretended to be anything he wasn't. He asked me a lot of questions, about my life, my family, and other people in town. He intended to figure the place out, he said, and to make the most of his time in Prentice. I don't think I gave him much satisfaction. I was reticent from long practice and had learned the art of the short answer from my mother and Russ. I will say, though, that Greenland made inroads in my reserve, and his imagination intoxicated me, even if I was never really sure whether the things he told me were pure fiction or truth—or at least a kind of truth.

His own stories were—or seemed to be—digressive flights of fancy and as wild and entertaining as anything I'd ever read in a book. I asked him if Valentine ever talked, and he claimed Valentine talked all the time but only to him and when no one else was around.

"He knows more about the world than any scientist," Greenland said.

When I asked him if Valentine could get along without his wheelchair, he said his brother left his chair whenever he wanted or needed to.

"If he ever needs to run, he'll get up and run," he said. "He's conserving his energy. V needs more action than he can find in a town like this. He's used to a spy-movie life. He likes to ride motorcycles, make movies, and start fires."

I never did hear Valentine say anything, but he never made a fuss either. And Greenland tried all sorts of experiments to try to make Valentine's life more interesting. Many of these experiments involved attempts to make Valentine's wheelchair faster.

First, he was outfitted with a football helmet we painted silver with automobile primer. With Eldon's help we created a sort of waterskiing setup that allowed both Greenland and me to tow Valentine's wheelchair at the end of a long lead with a swivel socket in the middle that, at least in theory, would give the chair a big, sweeping radius. No matter how many adjustments we made, however, Valentine never traveled more than twenty feet before he'd tip over and roll into the street, usually grinning like crazy. We also built him a go-cart, but Valentine didn't have sufficient use of his hands to steer the thing, and it wasn't stable enough to stay upright on steep hills without constant corrections. He didn't seem to mind, though, and eagerly submitted to being strapped into the cart again and again for what would inevitably be yet another spectacular wipeout. One time Greenland secured Valentine's football helmet, wrapped him in carpet padding, and laid him on the sidewalk under half a sheet of plywood; Greenland then proceeded to ride over his brother several times—"Valentine Earle, the Human Ramp!"—on his bike until I begged him to stop. Once again, though, Valentine seemed to get a kick out of the experience, and when he was really happy he conveyed it with a beatific and lopsided ear-to-ear grin.

The first serious corruption of my musical taste came through my friendship with Greenland, whose own tastes were much less rarefied and obscure than my own, or at least what I'd inherited or appropriated from Russ. Greenland, as might be expected, was attracted to more widely embraced forms of music—heavy metal, hard rock, and stuff that was generally more theatrical. His extreme energy was contagious; he played a ferocious and entirely unselfconscious air guitar, complete with lip-syncing and fist thrusts.

Greenland had a portable eight-track player, and he'd haul it with him when we hung out at Buddy Fly's playground so we could listen to Black Sabbath, Nazareth, Black Oak Arkansas, and Molly Hatchet, all of which sounded just fine to me at the time.

Of course, Greenland would be a headbanger; he had the archetypal heavy-metal sensibility, even as a twelve-year-old. He had the tremendous, hyperactive energy and a constant, slow-boiling anger as pure as it was unconscious. It wasn't like he was miserable with rage or constantly lashing out and throwing tantrums. I don't even think you could say he had a typical temper. His anger was instinctual and part of his natural expression; it just flowed out of him in bursts of spontaneous and almost comic violence, incidents that seemed to give him genuine joy and pleasure. I never knew him to get into fights or to respond to antagonism with anger. But some nights, when we'd ride downtown for pop, he'd guzzle his Coke and then smash his bottle on the pavement or against a wall. He couldn't resist throwing rocks or snowballs, and when he was a little older, he started breaking windows. He was also, I think, the first graffiti vandal in Prentice and was so brazen he would paint his name—GREENLAND—in giant sloppy red letters on buildings around town. He spent most of one of his last summers in town erasing his handiwork with a wire brush and buckets of paint. This was a court-ordered punishment, and every morning Eldon would drop Greenland and Valentine off at one of the sites of Greenland's vandalism, and they would stay there all day, Valentine hunched under a big beach umbrella while Greenland worked with surprising patience and diligence. "He's thorough," Eldon would say. "Give the boy a project or a task, and he'll do it without complaining, and he'll do a good job."

Greenland seemed to like the structure, responsibility, and discipline of work. I couldn't stand it and avoided it every chance I had. My aunts and uncles constantly offered me money to mow their lawns or shovel their sidewalks, which was, and is, precisely the kind of work I despised. I admired Greenland's ability to focus, to lose himself in a project or apply himself to some goal, no matter how crazy or meaningless it might seem. Observing this trait in him, I think, allowed me to recognize its absence in my own makeup. He was a big dreamer—he was going to be a race car driver, a wrestler, a secret agent, a movie star, an alligator trapper. It changed all the time, but his dreams were always big and elaborate. And when he thought of something he wanted to do, he did it. He threw himself into his ideas and schemes.

I wasn't a daydreamer. I didn't have a single big dream, let alone practical plans or ideas. When adults asked me what I wanted to be when I grew up, it stumped me as much as a math problem. I couldn't imagine becoming something in any sort of a career sense and had a hard time grasping whatever it was most people did for jobs. I couldn't even imagine running the rink and doing all the things I was vaguely aware Russ did to keep that place operating. I could imagine, I guess, doing the things I already did: riding my bike, going for long walks, skating, sitting up in the middle of the night listening to music and reading. If I had a secret desire, it was to be able to float. Flying—or the idea of flying—frightened me, but floating seemed peaceful.

This confusion regarding reality and existence, and the world's stubborn inability to convince me of anything, was one more thing I had in common with Greenland Earle. We used to sit around trying to convince each other we weren't real. We weren't yet stoners, but it was the first flowering of that basic stoner philosophy: What if this whole thing is just a dream we haven't yet awoken from? Or, Greenland might wonder, what if you're just a space rock dreaming, and your so-called life is just some rock's own personal version of a science-fiction novel? Or what if we're all still nothing but a dream that God is having? We could waste hours trying to convince ourselves we didn't exist.

I was becoming something, if not quite yet *someone*. I was an increasingly willful punk, my oblivion or indifference giving way to a more cynical and somehow less genuine shrug. I was acquiring a sneer.

Russ was reinvigorated by punk and new wave, and those were great years for unforgettable records; they just kept coming, and Russ was making more frequent trips to the Twin Cities. I'd go from listening to eight-tracks of Kiss and Blue Oyster Cult in Greenland's pop-up camper to the constant new revelations that blasted from the speakers at the rink. Many of the great funk and R *&* B bands of the 1970s were still kicking around; Bruce Springsteen was on the cover of *Time*, Neil Young and Bob Dylan continued to be weird and relevant, rap was emerging, and artists as diverse as the Clash, Elvis Costello, Prince, the English Beat, Michael Jackson, R.E.M., the Ramones, Talking Heads, the Replacements, Afrika Bambaataa, Devo, the Blasters, Tom Tom Club, Trouble Funk, the Pretenders, George Clinton, and New Order were making their way into the rotation in the High Tower.

I still listen to most of those records, and it often seems that I've spent the years since Russ's disappearance from my life scrounging record stores in search of the music I first heard at the rink. The experience of *hearing* them, though, can never be the same. Roller-skating is, of course, by its nature interactive, and alone in my apartment or in the press box, I don't have access to Russ's energy, enthusiasm, and constant thinking-out-loud annotations and analysis. Even going out to hear live music—as transcendent as that can be—is essentially passive and can't compare to the feeling of rocketing around a rink on wheels while music blasts from speakers.

Prentice still doesn't have a record store and in its present downtrodden fin-de-siècle condition almost surely couldn't support one. I thought about opening one when my mother died and have continued to daydream about it, especially as I wander downtown and tally all the abandoned commercial spaces. I realize, though, it would be an exercise in futility.

Those years—from the time I was nine or ten until I was maybe fourteen—were mostly happy oblivion with a glorious soundtrack. Everyone outside my bubble seemed bored with their lives, bored with their jobs, bored with each other. Prentice was such a quiet town. Often it seemed as if the only real noise and action were upstairs at the rink. A lot of nights I would go down the long flight of stairs and out into the empty streets after midnight, and I would stand there listening to what felt like the entire county sleeping, all the way out of town and into the darkness of the fields, just beyond the low halo of light to the north, which was all the light and life Prentice could marshal against the darkness at that hour. There always seemed to be people out there at the edge of the halo, sleepless, crazy, drunk, bored out of their minds, travelers and trucks blowing through on their way to some interesting elsewhere.

XVIII.

In 1982, Russ took me to the Twin Cities to see the Clash, and that, I think, was the true end of my childhood. I spent the entire concert stunned, wild eyed, absolutely riveted and incredulous, with Russ ecstatic beside me, alternately thrashing along on air guitar and whooping with joy. I'd never seen or heard anything like it, and afterward we drove all the way home to Prentice, swapping exhausted and inarticulate fragments of wonder.

To this day I can remember not just all the smallest details from that concert, but the tapes we listened to on the drive up and back as well: Dylan's *Blonde on Blonde*, Big Star's *Third*, Springsteen's *Born to Run*, and, finally, something I'd never heard before that blew back the scrim in my skull. It left me feeling wide awake for the first time in years, but also more than that: there was this startling burst of clarity. Everything in the headlights seemed so precise, frozen for an instant in perfect detail. I suddenly saw everything and looked at the world in a way I couldn't recall ever having done before. We stopped at an overpass out in the country to take a piss, and I noticed, seemingly for the first time in my life, constellations of almost planetarium perfection. It's corny. The car doors were thrown open, and the music was carrying out into the dark fields. I stood there, out of my body, my head thrown back, listening to Little Willie John singing "Fever."

It felt as if the whole world was opening around me. It was both thrilling and oddly terrifying. It was as if an aluminum foil balloon was slowly inflating in my head and straining against the ceiling of my skull.

That night was, I'm pretty sure, my first experience with something I've come to think of as a variety of religious mania. I was wildly ecstatic yet at peace, and I felt this huge sense of gratitude to something I for the first time in my life regarded as God, or perhaps *some* god. I remember I extended my arms toward the windshield and turned my palms upward, a purely unconscious gesture, almost as if I were offering my gratitude to a vague deity.

What an amazing world, I thought, and perhaps even spoke the words aloud. I'd never articulated a thought like that, I knew that much. What an amazing thing it was to be alive. What a wonderful thing it was to be in that car—Russ's trashed, perfect Vista Cruiser station wagon—hurtling through the darkness and listening to Little Willie John, who might've been a creature from another planet for all I knew. I was almost literally crazy with happiness.

At some point I looked over at Russ, who was hunched over the steering wheel and drumming with his fingers. "Do you know the two questions people ask themselves most often?" he said.

I said that I didn't.

"They ask themselves 'How do I look?'" he said. "Or, 'What's wrong?'" For a minute or two he squinted out at the highway, then he said, without turning to me, "Remember this night, Matty. This is what it's all about, no matter what other sad bullshit life throws at you. But you should be prepared: your mom is going to trade me in for a bigger, safer car."

That was, of course, a strange and confusing moment, made even more confusing by the incredible moments that had preceded it.

XIX.

I was so buzzed and wound up from the concert and my strange epiphany that when we got back to the rink after one o'clock in the morning, I couldn't settle down, let alone sleep. Russ was clearly exhausted from the drive and went right to bed. I tried to lie down but my mind was still roiling. I went to my old perch at the window and saw Greenland standing down in the alley, waving a flashlight around. I crept from the apartment, across the dark rink, and down the stairs. It was a bright, cold autumn night.

"What's going on?" I said.

"I have something to show you," Greenland said. "An angel just crashed and burned a big hole in our yard."

He was his usual jittery, agitated self, but he seemed dead serious. I unlocked my bike and followed him back to his house, where he pointed the beam of his flashlight at a scorched patch of grass at the back of the yard, about twenty yards beyond the pop-up camper.

"Right there," he said, exploring the spot with the flashlight. "I saw it crash." He picked up a stick and poked around at the spot, stirring up what looked like a bunch of goose feathers. He tossed the stick, tucked the flashlight under his armpit, and commenced twisting away at his palm, squeaking and grinding his teeth and bouncing on his toes as he did. This was a sign he was really excited about something.

"I was sitting in the camper when I saw a bright light," he said. "It lit up the whole inside. You know how the lights from a passing car will jerk around on the walls late at night? This wasn't like that. It was like someone turned on a floodlight. I looked out the window, and at first I thought it was a UFO, but when it got closer I could see it was an angel tumbling around in the sky and on fire, almost like it had been shot, like a fighter plane. It crashed in the yard and then it flopped around for a minute—I could see it was a man—like it was trying to get back up and fly away. I could see right through him. One of his wings had a fire burning right along the edge, like the fuse of a firecracker, and when it reached his body, he just went completely up in flames and burned right down into the ground."

We both stood there staring at the little circle of scorched grass. "Maybe he had a fight with God," Greenland said, "or got hit by an airplane."

Like most of Greenland's stories, the tale of the burning angel was simultaneously incredible, unbelievable, and eerily convincing. It was virtually impossible to be anything but agnostic when it came to Greenland Earle; you could never be quite sure either way. For all his irrational enthusiasm and energy, he was really a deadpan character, and he never struck me as a deliberate liar. Nothing much astonished him, and something like the burning angel was likely to be forgotten the moment some more prosaic urge or idea came into his mind. In this instance he merely shrugged, shook his head, and said, "Oh well. I have to take a piss."

I don't know that I believed Greenland's story about the angel, but I also wasn't at all inclined to get to the bottom of it or even to give it much thought. I was perfectly willing to believe that wondrous and inexplicable things happened all the time and to accept them at face value.

As if to emphasize he was done with the burning angel and its disruptions, Greenland pissed right in the burnt patch of grass, then we walked downtown to get some bottles of pop. I realized I hadn't seen Valentine in a number of days, and I asked Greenland where he'd been. "He's gone," he said. "I can't say anything more about it. Top secret."

I really believe that beginning that night, my insomnia and the general state of my mind entered an entirely new stage. It was as if my brain turned the corner into true self-consciousness, the years of coiled anxiety finally bursting like fireworks in my brain. I was still too young to understand what was happening, but I was alternately amused and alarmed by all the strange new activity in my skull. Much of it, I'm sure, was triggered by the insomnia, which suddenly was no longer so passive or manageable. I eventually saw a sleep doctor and learned there was a word for all that ungovernable wee-hours traffic in my half-conscious brain: *hypnagogia,* which as I understand it is a term for the general slippery and scattered consciousness that takes place in the brain in the moments preceding sleep and, later, hypnopompic stages before waking. My mind, it seemed, would get stalled in these stages for hours at a time.

This hypnagogic torrent was becoming relentless. I was utterly helpless to manage or direct it, and my brain would lock itself down in fierce squalls of nonsense and noise, squalls that eventually erupted into full-blown storms that as often as not carried into my waking life. The screens seemed to be multiplying, and the speed at which my synapses fired fresh spools of nonsense terrified me. I could no longer pin anything down or even make sense of what was happening. Words, particularly, started to come to me in waves, unbidden and often entirely unknown to me and generally unconnected to anything resembling a real thought. Complete strangers appeared to me, impassive, like a procession of mug shots or yearbook photos. Or often these night visitors drove loud, slow buses trailing banners and bright, crackling flags; they shouted indecipherable slogans—or a single word—that seemed to be in some language I didn't speak.

I was going crazy, and I was aware of it for the first time, aware I was losing control. My head in those moments, in those interminable hours and nights, was a foreign country, another planet, a dream theater where chaos reigned, and I couldn't recognize anything as a product of my own consciousness or chemistry; none of it seemed in any way related to my actual waking life.

And yet I could never completely cut the cords of consciousness; a tiny lamp always burned in some small, distant corner of my brain, where I—or what I recognized as "I"—sat curled up and terrified in an oversized chair, watching as some other conscious-ness ran amok in the rest of the kingdom, a Bruegel or Bosch paint-ing animated by a bunch of cerebral terrorists on acid. At its worst it was a blender, or, rather, like staring into a giant blender and, amid the frenzy, trying to pick out anything recognizable. I never really got a handle on it, but in time I came to regard these storms of broken-down, pell-mell consciousness as my private Waste Land, and suspected that if I could just find a way to footnote the mess, I might eventually learn to explain myself to myself.

After what I thought of as my religious experience on the drive back to Prentice after the Clash concert, I was just in a different place. I still didn't know what to do with myself, but I had the con-stant, nagging sense—new to me—that I *should* be doing some-thing with myself. I felt I should be changed, that I should have some sudden heightened sense of purpose. It didn't work that way, though. Prentice was the same as it ever was. School remained a constant bore and a challenge.

I just wanted to get home from school every day and glide mind-lessly around the rink. Increasingly, after Russ shut the place down for the night, I'd hang around up in the tower, listening to records and making tapes. Russ now trusted me completely with his record collection and his stereo, and I'd often stay out in the dark rink well into the middle of the night, headphones on, trying desperately to play catch-up with all that music.

XX.

There were a handful of other Carnap families strung out in some of the other small towns around Prentice, all of them my father's first or second cousins, and the whole fat crew would show up for a reunion every year (I don't remember having anything to do with any of them any other time). None of the Carnaps ever seemed to have kids; some years there might've been fifty or more people at these reunions and I would be the only kid. For a few years one of the Carnap cousins had a big batch of high-strung, wild-eyed stepchildren who got dragged along, but they—along with their mother—disappeared almost as quickly as they'd come, without so much as a query from anyone on my side of the family regarding their whereabouts. The reunion was always a moderately frightening keg party to me, a long weekend affair in which everyone seemed to get drunker and louder with every passing hour.

Inclement was one of my aunt Helen's favorite words, a word that was for her wildly versatile; she might use it to mean anything from *cold, rainy, drunk, disorderly,* or *disorganized* to *in a bad mood.* Revelers at the Carnap family reunions were often extremely inclement, more inclement, in fact, than Aunt Helen would've liked. "The Corning Carnaps are much too inclement to drive home," she would pronounce to Rollie or Mooze, both of whom were likely also plenty inclement, but they would dutifully corral the party in question, confiscate their car keys, and compel them to spend the night at my grandmother's house with the rest of the inclement Carnaps.

The only reason I bring up the Carnaps' annual reunions is to make the point that none of us ever seemed to go anywhere, and even though neither my mother nor Russ were blood Carnaps, they never really went anywhere either.

There were maybe a dozen towns of varying size within twenty miles of Prentice. They were all smaller than Prentice, and most of them were very small. Despite their proximity, I never visited any of them often enough to distinguish one from another. Even well into my teenage years, I would've had a hard time naming most of them or pointing to them on a map. Every town and county around us seemed to exist as a country unto itself. I suppose people from those little towns came to Prentice to shop and eat, and perhaps even to roller-skate.

Greenland, though, was fascinated by all these other places, and he was forever trying to talk me into riding my bike a dozen or more miles in some direction to stake out new territory. I resisted these entreaties, but he succeeded in introducing me to all sorts of people and places in town that had somehow escaped my notice. After only a year or two in Prentice, he seemed to have figured out who lived in every single house and what they did with their lives. And not just what they did for a living but also their particular habits and routines, right down to peculiarities of their wardrobes and what they bought at the grocery store.

"The reason we need to explore some new places," he told me one night as we walked around town, "is because I've figured out everything there is to know about this place." He'd point to a house I'd never so much as glanced at and say, "That's where the overall whistler lives. He stays up late at night working in his garage. He's got a couple old Indian motorcycles in there, and he drinks a lot of beer. He's married, but his wife almost never comes out of the house, and when she does it's to holler at him, and it always looks like she just got out of bed. He only wears overalls, and he whistles all the time."

Greenland and I were bored teenagers in Prentice even before we were technically teenagers. We knew of other orbits of bored teenagers, constantly on the drift from one hangout to another—from the abandoned railroad on the east side to Harry's Drive-In downtown and over to the Shopping Cart parking lot out by the freeway—where they congregated after-hours like static moths under the streetlights. The teens with cars rolled up and down Main

Street and the two east–west one-ways that ran through town. The burnouts would park along Toke Road, a strip of gravel that followed the creek out into the country, hidden beneath the interstate. Or they would gather under the water tower at Tower Park, a ragged and neglected patch of grass with a basketball court and a few picnic tables.

So much was changing so fast during those years, and it wasn't simply a product of my changing perception or of growing up. The Prentice of my childhood was undergoing rapid and alarming growth and transformation. The growth, actually, was probably a chimera; what was really happening, I think, was that the town was growing up or growing into America. Or, rather, the Big Corporate America that was exploding all over the country in those days suddenly staked out new turf in the hinterlands. In a handful of years, all sorts of new businesses sprung up in Prentice and in the smaller towns around it, and many of these new businesses—all of them, actually—were national corporations and franchises, a number of which operated twenty-four hours a day. All of a sudden there were fast-food places competing with the local restaurants and drive-ins, and big corporate supermarkets and gleaming chain stores that sold everything from shoes to hardware to electronics. My childhood straddled the old America, where the closest McDonald's was in Floyd Valley, and the new version, where there was one in pretty much every town. By the time I was in high school, Prentice had a Kmart, Sears, Payless Shoesource, Perkins, Hardee's, McDonald's, Country Kitchen, Taco John's, Godfather's Pizza, Pizza Hut, Ace Hardware, and a three-screen movie theater. All these places were brightly lit, colorful, and shiny with plastic and neon. It was as if Prentice had become, almost overnight, a Podunk Vegas.

I remember one night early in this transformation. At some point I'd snuffed out my mother's cigarette in the ashtray, tucked a blanket around her on the couch, and turned down the volume on the television before retreating to my bedroom, where I took up my usual vigil at the window. Rising above the trees and the buildings a few blocks to the south was a huge, illuminated Conoco sign. I was sure the sign hadn't been there the previous night, and that word, or that name (Conoco), meant nothing to me at the time, and the sign was so huge and was so high, and its appearance so startling and unexpected, that I honestly had no idea what I was seeing. I put on my coat and boots and went to investigate. I walked past the courthouse and along the tree-lined boulevard that intersected Main Street and cut over to First Avenue, where I discovered Prentice's first twenty-four-hour convenience store. I still can't imagine where or how someone found the misguided confidence to open a twenty-four-hour gas station and convenience store in Prentice, but I was thrilled. I'd walk there almost every night, and I'm pretty sure I could count on one hand the number of customers I encountered in the middle of the night during the first year it was open.

Prentice's first-ever third-shift convenience store clerk was an apocalyptic religious zealot named Carl Franks. Every time I went in there, Carl would be reading his Bible and listening to the radio. Talk radio—Larry King, usually, whom I heard for the first time in the Conoco. Carl also chain-smoked Marlboros and claimed he drank a case of RC Cola every day. He always treated me as if we'd known each other forever and had been engaged in a long-running conversation for years. Every time I came in, he'd immediately pick up his monologue wherever he'd left off the previous night. He was, he told me, a divorced alcoholic who hadn't had a drink in four years. He'd been a compulsive shoplifter earlier in his life and been fired from every job he'd ever had. The Conoco gig, he said, was his dream job.

His dog-eared Bible was crammed with all these little religious comic books he kept trying to foist on me. I gathered from our one-sided conversations that Carl fancied the idea of both the apocalypse and hell. "The devil is winning," he used to say, always with what seemed like genuine glee. Like a lot of such characters, I suppose, he embraced all manner of extreme belief and was as predisposed to occultism, UFOlogy, and conspiracy theories as he was to religious fervor.

Carl was by this time such a regular on the talk radio programs—and this was when talk radio was quickly taking over the airwaves—that on a few occasions I managed to hear his voice on my radio in the wee hours, and I imagined him sitting alone with his Bible, chasing Marlboro puffs with sips of RC Cola under the queasy fluorescent glare of the Conoco station and quietly mulling his growing assortment of half-baked fears and fixations. I like to imagine "Carl from Minnesota" was a phrase that raised eyebrows and got heads shaking in radio control rooms all over America.

XXI.

Russ gave me my first Walkman for Christmas one year, and I've long contended—in absolute seriousness—that the Walkman is the one relatively recent invention that has had the single biggest effect on my life. Overnight it made it possible for me to more than double the time I spent listening to music. Moving around with music rolling directly into your ears definitely makes the experience more cinematic, if also more insular.

Prentice is so flat and compact; it doesn't take long to walk to the city limits in any direction. When I was young, I'd occupy myself by popping a mixtape in my Walkman and walking from the front door of the fire station straight out to the western edge of town, where the old state highway ran parallel to fields of corn and the municipal airport. From there I would walk down the highway for a couple miles to the southern edge of town, take a right, and walk the length of Tenth Avenue to the eastern outskirts (more fields, a creek, a wooded expanse), then loop back around to the north side along a winding road that made its way through most of the newer—and more prosperous—neighborhoods and developments in Prentice.

Since the town is laid out on a grid of mostly straight, numbered north–south and east–west streets, it's also possible to walk up and down every street in either direction. I could, I once discovered, walk every east–west avenue, moving from the south to the north, in under two hours. The town itself is set in the middle of fields on all sides, and those thousands of acres of farmland and brush are broken up by a meandering maze of creeks, streams, railroad tracks, and paved and gravel roads. I would walk for hours in the fields, and then, pretty much every night, I would go back to the rink and hang out and skate until Russ shut things down.

By the time I was a teenager, I knew every one of those roads for miles around. I would wander those country roads in all seasons, keeping company with farm dogs, crickets, trains, and all sorts of regular *what the fuck is this?* digressions and diversions. Since the night of the Clash concert, I'd been fascinated by the sky and had puzzled long and hard over the moon and the stars. At one time I had all the constellations mapped out and stretched across the planetarium ceiling of my skull. I knew how the sky was aligned in each season even as I had no real knowledge of how any of it worked and didn't even know the names of any of the constellations. I didn't pick up a book on astronomy until I was much older, and when I did, it still didn't make any sense to me. That kind of knowledge terrifies me, as it seems to make the world more, rather than less, mysterious.

I've quickly rediscovered the easy pleasures of that earliest version of escape. Because Prentice has been shrinking rather than expanding in the years since I've been gone, there's still all that countryside around. Almost every day I throw some CDs in a little backpack, pop one in my beat-to-shit Discman (I upgraded from the Walkman maybe five years ago), and set out to ramble in the fields. Unlike Prentice itself, the gravel roads around town are almost exactly the way I remember them. I've found I can still wander on autopilot, zigzagging for miles, and somehow still end up passing the little trailer park where I'd had that wondrous encounter with the girl and her dollhouse full of fireflies. I thought of that territory as my private refuge. I don't know anyone who lives there (and didn't as a kid), and I don't think most people who live in town ever have much cause to venture out into the country. I love the landscape, love that no matter how far I roam I can see the steeples and water towers of Prentice rising above the fields. Every time I've been out there since I've been back, I think of a Denis Johnson poem, "The Monk's Insomnia," which I discovered in an old issue of the *New Yorker* back when I was hitting up thrift stores on the Rubber Route. It's a staggering poem, and one line in particular reminds me of those gravel roads outside of Prentice: "I can see the lights / of the city I came from, / can remember how a boy sets out / like something thrown from the furnace / of a star."

While I always bring a few CDs on my walks in case I want to mix things up, I've mostly been listening to the Replacements' *Let It Be* over and over; it's one of those records that can take me right back to that last brutal stretch at the rink. Almost every time I hear "Unsatisfied" and "Sixteen Blue" especially, I feel exactly as I did when I first heard them on one of the last nights I spent with Russ in the rink. Day after day when I was working at the paper in Minneapolis, I would take the elevator down to the parking ramp, strap on my headphones, and walk to my car in the darkness as "Unsatisfied" roared in my ears. As I've been out walking the roads along the railroad tracks, I keep wishing I had a time-lapse film of all the times I've walked—in Prentice, Floyd Valley, Minneapolis, and the constellation of small towns that made up the Rubber Route—while that song played through my headphones. I remember discussing *Let It Be* with Russ during one of our last memorable conversations. I was twenty-two, and a lot of the people I'd grown up with were graduating from college, moving to interesting places all over the country, and getting real jobs.

"It's kind of pathetic," I said to Russ, "but 'Unsatisfied' kills me even more now than it did when I was fifteen."

"Trust me," Russ said. "It'll still be killing you when you're forty."

I know he was probably right, but every day lately I wake up in this ridiculous press box penthouse and experience an increasingly fleeting thrill that this is my life. I've spent much of my life dreaming of a hole in the net, and sometimes, when I'm out walking those roads, I'm convinced I've found it. I'm in exile. No one knows I'm here or what I'm up to. It's as if I've fallen off the planet and I'm living in this private space station right in the middle of my old hometown. And then I come back to the press box and stare out these big windows, and all I can see is a past and a long time-lapse series of disappearances I still can't make sense of. Where did it all go? What happened to my wheels?

One day, out of the blue, my mother announced she was taking a job at the high school library over in Floyd Valley, twenty-five miles away. Nothing really surprised me anymore, but the decision seemed out of character for her. Russ, however, was hurt by the idea; he couldn't understand what the hell she was thinking or why she'd never discussed it with him. For years he'd tried to talk her into driving to Floyd Valley with him with rare success, and now she was going to drive there every day by herself? She didn't even like to drive—was terrified of it, in fact—and what the hell was she going to do in winter when the flat, two-lane highway to Floyd Valley was constantly buffeted by blowing and drifting snow, and horrific accidents were an almost weekly occurrence?

Russ also didn't like how she'd been so sneaky about the whole thing. By the time she announced she was taking the job, she'd apparently already made several trips to Floyd Valley for job interviews that neither Russ nor I had heard a thing about. The library gig, it turned out, had been in the works for a month before she bothered to mention it.

The night my mother told Russ she was taking the job was the first time I ever heard them raise their voices with each other, and it escalated to a real, prolonged fight that lasted long into the night. To escape the drama, I went out to the rink, blasted the Ramones, and skated for hours in the dark.

I was fourteen at the time, and I'd rapidly developed an affinity for the attitude and energy of punk rock and new wave; all that loud, fast, herky-jerky stuff was skate fuel and perfect for that time in my life. Still, for an outsider White kid in a White bastion like Prentice, the old-school funk and soul was even more radical and provocative than any punk record. I could aspire to the attitude and look of the punks, but I would never be as funky, transgressive, or cool as George Clinton, Bootsy Collins, Rick James, or Prince, and no other music would ever feel as thrilling and momentous; I could feel that stuff pulsing through the soles of my skates and rattling the wheels.

XXII.

I never really expected my mother to follow through and take that job at the library in Floyd Valley. I just figured she was trying to yank Russ's chain, and it certainly worked. They continued to argue about it for a week, and I'd never seen Russ get so wound up. I'd also never known him to get drunk, but one night after he shut down the rink he stormed out of the apartment and returned a short time later with a twelve-pack of Schlitz Malt Liquor. He started out drinking alone up on the roof. By the time he came down an hour or so later, he'd polished off half of the twelve-pack and was wobbly drunk.

I was hanging out in the rink listening to records. He joined me in the High Tower and continued to drink in silence. At some point he waved me away from the turntables.

"This isn't the right medicine," he said (I was playing the Meters). He fished around in the stacks of records and put Jackson Browne's *Late for the Sky* on the turntable. I remember because I'd never heard the record before, had never even heard Jackson Browne, and was stunned that such a lightweight bummer of an album was even in Russ's collection, let alone in the almost exclusively jubilant stash of records he kept in the rink.

Russ scrambled down from the tower, strapped on his skates, removed his shorts and his shirt, and skated around the rink in his underwear to that miserable Jackson Browne record as I watched with a combination of horror and wonder. "Flip it over," he shouted after the first side was over. "More poison!" He continued to drink as he skated, and when side two played out he sat on the rink floor, pulled off his underwear, then got back up and shouted, "Hey DJ, Neil Young's *Zuma*, side two, and turn it up."

I did as I was told, and when "Stupid Girl," the first track, erupted from the speakers, Russ launched himself forward on his skates, thrashing around and playing air guitar. By this time, I was transfixed by the spectacle. I'd never seen Russ naked before, and he was roaring like he was out of his mind, whooping and scream-ing for more volume. I had the speakers cranked so high they were starting to distort, and stuff was rattling around up in the tower. At some point all the lights came on and I turned to find my mother, dressed up like a complete stranger, standing at the top of the stairs and observing Russ with a look of pure disdain. She walked across the room, climbed the steps to where I was sitting, and turned off the stereo. "Jesus Christ, Russell," she said. "Put your clothes on." And with that she grabbed me by the arm and hauled me across the rink and into the apartment. "Go to your room," she told me for the first and only time in my life.

From that single—or first—uncharacteristic decision of my moth-er's, to take that job in a town other than Prentice, followed a long season, or many seasons, *years*, of upheaval.

She started the library job in September, a couple weeks after the big fight and Russ's meltdown and just as I was starting school. By that time Russ had cooled down, even if it was obvious he was still trying to get his head around the whole idea.

My aunts and uncles couldn't understand it either, and I think they were also upset my mother hadn't bothered to discuss it with any of them. "I could've got her a job at the library here," Rollie said. "All she had to do was ask." They all tried to pump me for informa-tion, but I certainly didn't know what was going on; I also couldn't figure out what the big deal was.

I was hanging out at the liquor warehouse one day when I over-heard Rollie tell Uncle Mooze he was picking up some scuttlebutt from over in Floyd Valley.

"People love running their mouths," Mooze said. "Let them talk."

"The whole town's lousy with rumors," Rollie said. "It chaps my ass."

Mooze shrugged. "I still say let them talk," he said. "Whose busi-ness is it? And why do you care? You never liked that Vargo creep anyway."

By this time, I was getting too old to be invisible, and I saw Rollie scowl and jerk his head in my direction. I was breaking down boxes and attempting to eavesdrop. And though I still believed I never knew what anyone was talking about, it was no longer true.

I was certainly old enough to have a sense of what was going on, and I kept thinking back to Russ's comment on the drive back from the Clash concert. With each passing day—with my mother now driving off every morning for her new job in Floyd Valley, with the increasingly loud and aggressive music Russ was playing—I could sense Russ was steeling himself. Looking back, I think he recognized that he'd blown his one big chance and was helpless—or simply unable or unwilling—to do anything about it.

I've always tended to let the obvious glance right off me, to duck anything that comes close to what Russ called "the Unpleasant Truth."

Greenland, it turned out, was dealing with his own unpleasant truths. Valentine, I eventually learned, had been taken to Owatonna and placed in a foster home so he could attend a school for kids with special needs. Valentine and Greenland had been inseparable, and Greenland's devotion to his brother was one of his most endearing qualities. I'd also noticed that the Soviet Embassy had been closed for at least a month, and a *For Lease* sign had recently gone up in the front window. Leon Earle had been an elusive presence from the beginning; I probably hadn't seen him more than a handful of times since they'd moved to town, and he was never there whenever I was at the house. That particular mystery was solved when a small note appeared in the newspaper around Halloween: *Local Man Sentenced for Marijuana Distribution in Minneapolis.* I never talked to Greenland about his father, but I heard through my uncles that Leon had been living much of the time in the Twin Cities and apparently kept an apartment up there.

All of this was sad news to me and explained why Greenland had kept such a low profile for the last couple months. He seldom came downtown anymore and spent most of his time hanging out with his grandfather and helping out around the shop. He was terrified, I think, of following his brother into a foster home, or even worse, being sent to a reformatory. Most nights I would still find him sitting in his pop-up camper and smoking, huffing what he called his "spirit rag"—his name for the gasoline-soaked handkerchief he carried in his back pocket—and drinking grape soda. Sometimes he'd camp out in the back seat of his grandfather's New Yorker, listening to eight-tracks on the dashboard deck. We were sitting in the camper late one night when he asked me out of the blue what I was going to do when my mother moved out on Russ, who he referred to as my "old man."

"I can't imagine that happening, ever," I said.

Greenland said he'd heard it was a done deal. "One of the guys from my grandpa's church said your ma has another fella over in Floyd Valley. He got her that job."

I admitted I didn't know what I would do if such a thing happened and said again that I couldn't imagine it. That was the honest-to-God truth—I was absolutely incapable of imagining such a thing.

"What if your ma moves to Floyd Valley?" Greenland said.

"I couldn't leave Russ," I said. "I couldn't leave the rink. There's no way."

"But he's not your real dad," Greenland said. "Your ma wouldn't have that."

I had sensed for some time—perhaps even before the Clash concert—that my mother and Russ had problems, but I'd refused to let my mind look in that direction. And until that conversation with Greenland, I don't think I ever consciously worried about whatever was going on. I realize *consciously* is the crucial and loaded word here; all through my early childhood I'd shoved aside anything that might qualify as genuine worry or even normal anxiety. But the disintegration of my mother's marriage to Russ kicked in those sturdy doors and ushered in all the uncomfortable neuroses and anxieties of adolescence and adulthood. I don't believe anyone is born with all that baggage; I don't, of course, know what I'm talking about, but I nonetheless feel nightmares and insecurity are programmed in you by time and experience, and I was a terrific and resistant dodger for a long time.

That night after my conversation with Greenland was the first time I remember lying awake worried and filled with a vague and tangled fear my life was completely out of my control. And perhaps the most distressing thing about this new anxiety was the extent to which it somehow flipped the switch and shut down the old, whirling carnival in my head; even worse, the extent to which these new, relatively focused preoccupations were many, many more times more terrifying than the usual parade of hallucinations had ever been. This, I thought, was a true nightmare, clearly related to my actual life. I was confronting something that actually felt like a future, my future, and I sensed things were about to go horribly wrong.

In this I wasn't mistaken.

It was frustrating to watch the whole thing unfold—or dissolve, as the case may be. I was now old enough to have a real sense, however exaggerated, of what was happening. After the initial battle about my mother's new job, it became clear Russ had no intention of fighting to save his marriage. In one sense, I realized, my uncles had been right about Russ—he *was* chickenshit, far too passive and perhaps depressed to get really passionate about anything. He certainly obsessed about music and his record collection, but I can now recognize there's a distinction between obsession and genuine passion, and Russ was too terminally cool a character to be truly passionate, at least overtly, even about the things he loved. As my mother later observed, Russ needed his record collection not only to say the things he couldn't but also to simulate the things he couldn't feel.

Still, there was no getting around it: what most terrified me about the prospect of my mother leaving Russ was the thought of losing him, the rink, and his record collection all in one unfathomable stroke.

I started to feel abandoned—or at least neglected—by my mother for the first time when she took the job in Floyd Valley. I resented her. She'd leave early in the morning and often wouldn't return until seven or eight in the evening, sometimes later. She started behaving differently and changed the way she dressed and wore her hair. She barely spoke to Russ or me.

This weird new phase in my life—and in my mother and Russ's marriage—lasted for more than a year, and between Russ's "I don't know what to say" and my mother's "I don't want to talk about it," I was left almost completely in the dark. The rink, which was the one place I'd always most liked to be, was suddenly very anxious and uncomfortable.

Even though my mother seldom had much to say to me during this inscrutable and independent new stage, she had a weird confidence I'd never seen in her before, in the way she carried herself and in the tone of her voice, a toughness that displaced her old veneer of fragility. She wasn't crying on the couch or moping around the apartment anymore, and she seldom even watched TV.

My aunt Tina called one afternoon and asked me how my mother was and where she had been. I told her honestly that I didn't know—my stock answer, probably learned from my mother: "I have no idea." This phone call, perhaps even more than the gossip and vague speculation, alarmed me.

Years later, my mother claimed that the year everyone else in the family thought of as her "crisis" was actually the year she finally grew up. She told me one day that she had finally realized she didn't want to spend the rest of her life sitting around that apartment surrounded by records. Punk rock—all those loud, abrasive new records Russ kept bringing home and playing at louder and louder volumes—was more than she could stand. She'd decided she didn't want to be "bored stupid" hanging around Prentice until she was an old woman.

Every time I tried to talk with her during this time she got impatient with me and inevitably threw up her hands and said, "What's the point?" The speed and extent of her overhaul stupefied me. It was as if she had become a stranger overnight, or perhaps an even more mystifying stranger. I think both of us were changing and growing up so fast we lost track of each other.

The more I sensed Russ retreating into his own preoccupations, the more I struggled with my own issues—which, as it was increasingly apparent, *were* issues. All that winter I wrestled with full-blown insomnia, which was finally becoming a serious problem at school, or at least raising red flags. I couldn't even pretend to pay attention and often found myself nodding off in class. I'm sure I was an alarming spectacle. I wore the same clothes day after day and started skipping classes to hide out in a carrel at the library.

Winters had always been difficult for me—too much darkness, the nights were too long, and I'm sure I suffered from seasonal affective disorder—but this was different. I often felt bone-tired and wide awake. My brain just kept plodding along, refusing to surrender consciousness, pushing me down ever stranger and darker alleys until I hit some sort of wall and shut down entirely.

I've since had many occasions where I've found myself, in the middle of the night, in some place of unnecessary twenty-four-hour vigilance: truck stops, convenience stores, supermarkets, hotel lobbies, in both big cities and along dark state highways between actual cities or towns. The feeling of such places is eerily reminiscent of the way my brain felt that merciless and catastrophic winter: brightly—yet somehow fuzzily—lit, with warped, submarine acoustics and a surreal soundtrack, the most distorted possible version of reality (reality as unshakeable hallucination), every choice a bad one, every urge inexplicable, a Neanderthal urge, an animal's desire; a tableau leeched of vitality, of animation, of sense or connection. At that hour, any notion of community is absurd; everybody is an invisible man, and anything that moves registers—if it registers at all—as a peripheral blur, a nuisance to be avoided or negotiated with while expending as little consciousness as possible. When I'm at these places, I often think, *For what possible reason is this place staying open in the middle of the night? For whom—or for what—is this poor, exhausted clerk suffering?* And, of course, *What the hell am I doing here?* I'd always had a reputation of being in my own little world. Yet this was something else—it was as if I literally couldn't see myself and was oblivious to the way others might see me. I scrupulously avoided mirrors, or even reflections. It was no longer that I was in my own little world; I was completely outside it, trapped, and it was as if all my perceptions—if they could even be called that—were bouncing off a satellite before being projected in my skull.

I *was* becoming a zombie, and someone from the school called the county's Child Protective Services.

Russ's response to this news, which I learned from eavesdropping on one of their conversations, was "It's about time," which only made my mother more indignant. She was—to use one of her favorite words—*mortified*. I think she was especially pissed she'd had to take a day off work so soon after starting the library job.

My mother and I walked to the county social service offices one morning shortly after some representative got in touch about the report—that was the word that was used—someone at my school had submitted. The woman who interviewed us was soft, faux-jolly, and condescending, and had, I suppose, the stereotypical manner of someone who deals with "troubled" children and families all day. I could tell immediately she and my mother weren't going to hit it off.

After we'd gotten settled in the woman's office—which featured, I still remember, a poster that read *I Believe in God Because of Rainbows*—she went over the report: My teachers, she said, were concerned that I wasn't paying attention in class. I seemed to be sleep deprived, and there were other signs of possible neglect that she hoped to address.

At the mention of the word *neglect*, my mother became angry and defensive. "This is ridiculous," she said, and she demanded to speak to whomever had filed "this report."

The report, the woman said calmly, had been submitted by the principal, with input from a number of my teachers as well as my guidance counselor. "No one is interested in anything but the well-being of your child," she said.

"He's not a child," my mother snapped.

"I'm sorry," the woman said, becoming suddenly icy. "He is a child." She then requested permission to question me directly, "on the record." My mother demanded to know the purpose of such an inquiry, and the woman assured her she was merely interested in getting some sense of what I might be going through and why I was having difficulties at school.

My mother huffed and then waved her hand dismissively. "Go right ahead," she said.

The woman proceeded to ask me if I liked school, and I told her I didn't.

"What is it about school you don't like?" she asked.

"It's boring," I said. "It makes me tired."

"Do you get enough sleep?" she asked.

"He sleeps like a perfectly normal child," my mother interjected, much to my astonishment.

The woman ignored my mother. "How do you sleep, Matthew? Do you wake up feeling rested?"

"No," I said. "I don't sleep. I don't like to sleep."

"That's not true," my mother said.

"How would you know?" I said.

My mother had never struck me, never spanked me that I could remember, but for an instant I thought she was going to reach over and slap me.

The woman was silent for a moment, taking notes, and then she looked back up and asked, "What does your father do?"

"He runs a roller-skating rink," I said.

"That's not his father," my mother said. "His father is dead."

An expression of confused sadness flashed across the woman's face; the practiced look of forced amiability collapsed for just an instant.

"He's talking about his stepfather," my mother said. "His father died in Vietnam, before Matt was born."

"But you live with this stepfather?" the woman asked.

"Yes," I said. "At the rink. Screaming Wheels."

"You live at the rink?" the woman said. "The one just across the street?"

I nodded.

"There's an apartment in the back," my mother added.

"Are you eating okay?" the woman asked.

I shrugged. "We don't have much food at our house."

My mother threw up her hands and raised her voice in clear exasperation. "Matthew," she said, "that's simply not true!" She turned to the woman and said, "I'm so sorry. I had no idea Matt was having so many problems in school. I have a new job and we're in the process of moving. I've had so much going on. We'll get this all straightened out."

"She's never talked to me about a move," I said.

"That's between your mother and you," the woman said. "I'd feel more comfortable—and I feel sure Matthew would feel more comfortable—if we got some of this straightened out before the move. The report from the school indicates that these issues have been a concern for quite some time."

"This is the first I've heard of it," my mother said.

The woman raised her eyebrows and consulted her clipboard, rustling through the paperwork. "Well," she said, exhaling dramatically, "according to the notes from the guidance counselor's office, they've sent you several letters about these issues and concerns going back to last year."

"I didn't get them," my mother said. "Or I didn't see them."

"Surely, at the very least, you've seen Matthew's report cards?"

"I know he's not a very good student," my mother said.

"His teachers are of the opinion that he has the potential to be an excellent student," the woman said. "The issue here seems to be effort, and attention."

"I don't know what you want me to say," my mother said. "He's never liked going to school, and his stepfather is a terrible influence. I'm trying to make some changes I think will be positive all around, for Matthew and for me."

"Changes can be very difficult for a boy Matthew's age," the woman said. "Sometimes it's hard for adults to recognize when children are struggling or the ways in which they're struggling. My sense is that Matthew is struggling whether you're aware of it or not, and I think it's important that we find ways to address those struggles. I'm afraid I can't just let this slide. I have legal obligations, to the county and the school district, and I'm going to be responsible for monitoring your son's progress, his health, and his well-being. I'd like to suggest that Matthew be evaluated by a psychiatrist. We work with a very good and experienced gentleman over in Floyd Valley. He's particularly good with adolescent boys."

"Suppose I don't want my son to see a psychiatrist?" my mother said.

"I'm afraid you really don't have a choice," the woman said. "I'm asking you to do this for Matthew. I sense it would be beneficial for him to talk to a completely objective person."

My mother and I fought about that awkward meeting with the woman from the county. It was the first real fight we'd ever had; I suppose it was also my first real act of rebellion. She was furious with me for making her look like an unfit parent, and I was furious as well, furious she'd either lied outright or was so oblivious she could actually believe some of the things she'd said. I'd never really talked back to my mother, and, truth be told, she'd never made the sorts of demands or issued any rules I could refuse to comply with.

She did, though, make an appointment for me to see the Cowboy, and what the Cowboy is good at is forcing me to confront the obvious, which I've always struggled with. "I can't see that you have any choice," the Cowboy has often said to me, referring to many different situations on many different occasions.

XXIII.

I don't suppose there are many low-impact ways to break up a marriage, but I was time and again exposed to sides of my mother and Russ that I'd never seen before. After the first couple weeks there was no longer much yelling or screaming, but the level of cutting antagonism was far more subversive and harrowing to me than if they'd thrown things at each other.

One morning Russ was sitting at the kitchen table in his underwear and an old Kinks T-shirt, eating Kraft macaroni and cheese right out of the pan as my mother made coffee and prepared for work. I was already dressed for school and making a peanut butter sandwich for my lunch. As my mother grabbed her car keys off the table, she paused for a moment and fixed Russ with a withering gaze. I noticed she was wearing jewelry and stank of perfume.

"Wow, Russ," she said. "That macaroni and cheese has been sitting on the stove for at least two days." She shook her head. "What a loser. Look at yourself sometime. Some example for Matthew." And then she turned and went out the door. I'd never heard her talk to him that way, had never seen that look on her face. And I don't think I'd ever seen Russ look so defeated either. He'd just sat there eating his macaroni and cheese and thumbing through a magazine. After a couple minutes, he looked up, met my eyes, and said, "That was nice." Then he shrugged and ran his hand through his hair.

A week or so later, I flipped the lid on the garbage pail in the kitchen and saw, at the bottom of the otherwise empty bag, a photograph of my mother—a five-by-seven enlargement of a snapshot—torn into four neat pieces. I reached to the bottom of the pail, fished out the sections, and carefully rearranged them on the kitchen counter. I'd never seen the photo before. It looked like it was taken up on the roof of the rink. My mother was wearing a bikini and reclining in a lawn chair, apparently waving away the photographer with a can of beer. Her head was thrown back slightly, and her entire face was stretched as wide as I'd ever seen it in a teeth-baring, ear-to-ear grin. It was clear she was laughing, really laughing; her eyes were pencil-thin slits beneath her eyebrows. She was awkwardly flailing with her hands, hunching forward slightly from her shoulders, and it looked as if she was just on the verge of erupting from her chair.

Looking at that photograph, I felt sick to my stomach, devastated, and couldn't yet fathom the rage that would've prompted someone to tear it up and throw it in the trash.

It was December by this time, which made it all weirder. The early darkness, the cold, and the sense of captivity was a huge adjustment every year, and my father's family—the whole childless crew—were all Christmas zealots, holiday overboarders, given to holiday cheer so pitched and exaggerated it came across as lavishly desperate. It was a holiday—and it still is, for me—perfectly positioned at the nexus of sentimentality and melancholy, fraught with a fierce and nostalgic undertow and, often as not, some vague, nagging despair.

That year Russ was working overtime at milking the melancholy and despair part of the equation. I really believe deep down Russ was soft, lost in some long-gone notion of the way the world should be and feel. He couldn't show it or articulate it, but if you spent enough time around him and studied his patterns and habits, you could learn all there was to know about the sad state of his heart.

He repeated things, had a collection of banal phrases and professions of befuddlement that he recycled in lieu of actual dialogue. "I don't know what to say" was probably as close as he came to a credo or self-definition. "What is this?" was another one, part of the loop, and it seldom referred to anything specific, to any one puzzling circumstance or source of confusion. It was just one more thing he would say out loud and repeat frequently, as if to clear his head or get a grip on his emotional bearings. Many of his phrases made no sense to me, coming as they did out of nowhere and in no recognizable context. "When in doubt, turn it up," he might repeat several times while he sat at the kitchen table reading the newspaper. Other times he would mutter, over and over, "Turn it down, turn it down . . ."

One day I heard him talking on the phone with someone for what must've been close to an hour, and every thirty seconds or so, he would say, "I'm just disappointed, that's all," which would be followed by a stretch of silence into which he would eventually interject, again, "I'm just disappointed, that's all." I had no idea who he was talking to and couldn't recall hearing him have a phone conversation with anyone before. I figured, though, that this was as close to a heart-to-heart as he was capable of.

Camped out in the High Tower he would juggle records like psychotropics, swallowing truth serum one minute and a bitter pill the next. He put together playlists that mixed songs of heartache and betrayal with bursts of loud, angry punk stuff.

Since he always played whatever he was into at the time, the regular skaters had to suffer through Russ's meltdown. There were a number of holiday parties that month and a lot of pissed-off skaters who didn't appreciate having to endure an entire side of Bob Dylan's *Blood on the Tracks*, or the Faces' "Glad and Sorry" three times in one session. Their patience might be rewarded by the Ronettes' "Sleigh Ride," but such a tease would be followed by Neil Young's "Stupid Girl" played at disturbing volume. It wasn't a happy Christmas at Screaming Wheels.

At some point I went—against my will—to stay with Mooze and Tina for a few days.

I remember there were nights when Russ unrolled a sleeping bag up in the High Tower and slept in the rink. Some mornings before I went to school I would make a sweep of the place, picking up beer cans. My mother seemed, if not exactly happy, resolved somehow, determined. About what there was no telling.

"All of a sudden it seems like she's got her shit together," I heard Russ tell someone on the phone one night. "And that scares the shit out of me." I felt pretty much the same way. I'd never seen her like that before. Every day she got up early, got herself ready and made coffee, and left for work at exactly the same time, which was several hours earlier than she used to get up most mornings. She was evidently doing some shopping over in Floyd Valley as well, as she was suddenly dressing in new and uncharacteristic clothes.

During this time, I was dealing with full-blown, wide-awake, anxiety-pacing-in-big-iron-boots-all-night-in-my-brain insomnia. The stuff going on in my head was slowed way down, a procession of big, actual, and unavoidable thoughts, and my body was more or less paralyzed and idling at a postmidnight red light all the way through to morning. I was so exhausted I would drift in and out of a light slumber, the distinctions between awake and asleep all but erased as I tiptoed along a border as narrow as dental floss.

I also, more and more often, experienced complete shutdowns in the daytime, making me increasingly incapable of staying afloat in the normal stream of consciousness. They now seem to have words for everything, and what I was experiencing, day after muddled day, was daytime parahypnagogia (DPH), which the literature of sleep—of sleeplessness—says is "more likely to occur when one is tired, bored, suffering from attention fatigue, and/or engaged in a passive activity." Check. Check. Check. Check.

Over the years, I've acquired a huge collection of books, pamphlets, and articles on sleep and insomnia. The first time I stumbled across a journal article on parahypnagogia, I felt a huge sense of both relief and blank wonder. There were, apparently, other people like me. "Individuals describe DPH as a transient and fleeting episode that is dissociative, trance-like, dreamlike, uncanny, and often pleasurable," the article claimed. "But, unlike a daydream, it is not self-directed. A DPH episode is spontaneous and may consist of a flash image, thought, and/or creative insight that is quickly forgotten. However, the individual remains aware of having had a DPH experience."

This description felt mostly spot-on to me, except that these episodes weren't fleeting in my case, and they weren't often pleasurable. One of the frustrating things about all the various hypnagogic episodes I experienced was that I *would* frequently have flashes of what I thought were "creative insights"—often they felt like genuine revelations, even life-changing ones—but they would slip away from me. In the midst of these trances, I got in the habit of jotting notes on index cards, phrases that seemed significant or even profound. I have, in fact, done this for years, and I still have shoeboxes full of these index cards. So many times I would emerge from one of my trance states and immediately reach for the stack of index cards, eager to retrieve my latest epiphany only to discover some squib of inscrutable nonsense—*To be a planet, without clothes,* for instance. Or, *Baby Jesus was nothing but a doll. Who do you think you're fooling?* Or, *How come I don't have any trophies?*

There were nights my mother never came home, and if Russ knew where she was, he didn't pass that information along to me. He just kept plodding through his normal routines, even though he was often drunk and his behavior in the rink grew erratic. One night, he forced the skaters to listen to an Andy Williams Christmas record in its entirety. I'm sure there were various groups—Job's Daughters, the Boy Scouts, the Jaycees, and the Rotarians—who had their Christmas parties at Screaming Wheels that year and told stories about Russ's strange behavior for years afterward.

Some nights it seemed he wasn't fully conscious that there were paying customers in the rink. Often, he just stayed up in the tower playing records long after everyone had left. Before this awkward interlude I'd never really seen him drink, but now he was drinking every day. He wasn't a loud or raging drunk, just a stereotypical sad drinker, sloppy, unsteady, and unconsciously funny.

One night I went out and sat with him in the dark. He was listening to Nick Drake, and that didn't seem like a good thing.

Greenland had been in a funk—a sulk, his grandfather called it— ever since Valentine got shipped off to Owatonna. Junior high was hard on him; kids were suddenly meaner, crueler, more intolerant of eccentricity. He—and I, to a lesser extent—had been given a sort of free pass for several years while the other kids jockeyed for positions within the various high school cliques; now, however, that they had figured out where they belonged—picked teams, as Russ put it—they had safety in numbers, and could start to really zero in on the kids who found themselves without a seat in the cakewalk circle of adolescence. I was definitely part of that loose and disconnected group on the outside, but much of my old invisibility still seemed to work for me. I knew how not to get noticed. Greenland, on the other hand, was almost compulsively noticeable, an expert at attracting negative attention. He was helplessly different and couldn't help asserting that difference. And there was nothing a pack of so-called normal kids detested more than deliberate, assertive abnormality, and poor Greenland ran the gauntlet every day. He wouldn't back down from a beating, and I didn't have the courage to defend him. Soon, in an act of despicable cowardice and an attempt at self-preservation, I went out of my way to avoid him at school.

I have no computer here in the press box. Still, two or three (or four, or five) times a week, I find myself at the library, checking my Hotmail account on one of the computers there. And every single time, helplessly, I pull up Yahoo and type Russ's name into the search box, and he's not there. He's vanished.

My mother went out on our last New Year's Eve at the rink; she said she was going to some kind of party with her coworkers in Floyd Valley. She'd apparently gotten her hands on a Younkers charge card and was all dressed up in some of her fancy new clothes. She'd also started wearing jewelry, all sorts of earrings, necklaces, and rings that were unfamiliar to me. Throughout their marriage neither she nor Russ had ever worn wedding rings.

Before she went out that night, I sensed the tension ratcheting up in the apartment, and I retreated to my bedroom. Russ had been sitting at the kitchen table, flipping through his latest batch of music magazines. He'd always been thin and an indifferent dresser, but lately he was losing weight and had lost all interest in his appearance, or even basic hygiene. Every day he seemed to wake up and pull on the same pair of jeans, the same long-sleeved T-shirt, and the same hooded sweatshirt. I remember he was looking particularly ragged that night. At one point I heard my mother's heels click briskly across the kitchen floor. She said something I couldn't hear, then I heard Russ say, "He's *your* kid. Why don't you at least act like you recognize that fact once in a while? You think he doesn't notice you're never around? It's not my job to raise the poor little bastard."

My mother snapped off some response, but I still couldn't make out her words. I was really listening now, though, and had opened my bedroom door a crack.

"I've done enough babysitting," Russ said. "Raise your own damn child."

My mother must've turned to face him at this point, because I could now hear her crystal clear. "I carried him around inside me for nine months," she said. "And I spent another couple years lugging him everywhere, breastfeeding him, and changing his diapers. Can you imagine that? There's absolutely no way in hell you can begin to imagine that, Russell. No sacrifice you will ever make for anyone will ever come close to that."

"What the hell does that have to do with anything?" Russ said. "It doesn't have a fucking thing to do with me, that's for sure. Blame biology. Blame yourself for getting knocked up. By someone who wasn't me, in case you've forgotten. I know for damn sure there's a whole lot more to being a mother than carrying a kid around for nine months."

"I haven't asked much of you, Russ," my mother said. "The least you can do for me is keep your eye on Matt when I'm not around. He likes you better than me, anyway."

"Don't talk such horseshit," Russ said, his voice getting louder. "You think he doesn't pick up on how you feel or what's going on? He's a kid, for fuck's sake. You can go right ahead and ignore me for weeks at a time, don't bother to let me know where you're going or what you're doing. I can take it. But it's just plain cruel to give Matt the same treatment. This is your child, and you're fucking him up just as surely as your mother and father fucked you up. What are you going to do when I'm out of the picture?"

In an instant they were shouting over each other, interrupting and being cruel in a way that didn't seem to come natural to either of them. It was a graceless cruelty, blunt as a fat carnival hammer. They were both unaccustomed to having to talk as fast as they thought or felt.

Russ unconsciously—or perhaps it was a gesture of helplessness—went to the stereo and put on a record; it was an Elvis Costello record, completely inappropriate for the situation but apparently already on the turntable.

"Turn off that fucking music," my mother shouted. "What the hell is wrong with you that you can't stand even five minutes of silence?"

"You call this silence?" Russ said. "I'm trying to drown you out."

"You're trying to drown out the world," my mother said.

My mother must've gone to the stereo and turned off the power, because there was suddenly this long moment of silence. I could hear myself breathing. I was terrified in the only way I knew how to be terrified: paralyzed, unthinking, unfeeling, my brain in full lockdown.

I sat up listening to *Led Zeppelin IV*, loud, on my Walkman, and replayed "When the Levee Breaks" several times in succession, thrilled by the ferocious squall and John Bonham's thunderous drumming.

I'm trying to figure out how old Russ would've been that last New Year's Eve at the rink. If I was a couple months away from turning fifteen, then he would've been maybe thirty-two. He seemed so much older than that in my memory. That last year or so it was like he'd shrunk, or at least folded into himself, becoming an apostrophe. He still had that shaggy mop of hair, but he was so pale, sallow on his really bad days, and his face was becoming increasingly gaunt, with sharp angles and shrunken cheeks like Iggy Pop.

Uncle Rollie showed up on New Year's Day around noon. Russ was still slumped behind his turntables, and I was skating alone to Neil Young's *Trans*, which Russ was blasting at ear-splitting volume. Russ didn't even look up to acknowledge Rollie's appearance or greeting, other than to drag *Trans* off the turntable and replace it with Hüsker Dü's *New Day Rising*.

"Ditch the wheels, Bubby," Rollie said to me. "We're going out to celebrate the new year."

Rollie seemed to be expanding as Russ was shrinking. He'd always been a big guy, broad and barrel-chested, but he was putting on serious weight, particularly around his midsection. He favored loud Sansabelt slacks with an expanding waistline and tight, expansive v-neck sweaters, and had the gait—equal parts waddle and swagger—of already big men who continue to put on weight.

My father's family was supposed to be some combination of German, Austrian, and Swiss, but my grandfather and all my uncles looked to me like stereotypical Italian gangsters. Rollie in particular had that look and that sort of attitude and profile. He had a head full of thick black hair that he kept combed back with Brylcreem, and a lot of jet-black hair on his arms and on the back of his hands and neck.

That afternoon we headed to Misto's, where most of the usual crowd was in the middle of a poker game. The place was full of smoke, and I could tell the game was intense; there was a lot of money on the table, and most of the guys barely acknowledged our entrance. I'd reached the age where I'd mostly lost fascination with the cases of gag gifts and novelties and the general *Naked City* vibe of the place. At that point, whenever I came around there, someone would jerk their head in my direction and everybody would clam up.

Rollie and I didn't have much to talk about anymore. We'd never, in fact, had a lot to talk about, but I was suddenly hyperaware of the long, awkward silences and Rollie's clumsy, fumbling attempts to make conversation with me. I think he realized he'd lost me, that he had no idea who I was or who I was becoming, and I couldn't tell if he saw much of my father in me anymore.

I'm sure you could chalk up a lot of the awkwardness to the onslaught of adolescence, but I also think the years with Russ had driven a wedge between my father's family and me. I didn't have people telling me I looked and acted like my father anymore, and it wasn't until much later that I learned this was because the similarities were becoming more alarming than charming.

We hung around Misto's for maybe an hour that New Year's Day. Rollie didn't join the card game, and the mood was more subdued than usual; there was little of the good-natured but occasionally barbed banter I was accustomed to.

After we left Misto's we drove to Big Sammy's Supper Club. A polka band was entertaining an older crowd in the "party lounge," and Rollie and I had hamburgers and onion rings while we played air hockey and pinball in the game room.

Rollie, it turned out, had been given the responsibility of breaking the news to me that my mother was leaving Russ. It had obviously been in the works for quite some time, and though I'd sensed something bad was coming, I still couldn't admit it to myself. Everyone else had apparently known the details for a couple months, including Russ, but nobody wanted to break it to me until everything was sorted out on paper.

I could never forgive my mother for passing off such a dirty job to Rollie. Granted, Rollie was the guy in the family who was generally tasked with responsibility in times of crisis, but I was as pissed off as I'd ever been.

After all the old folks cleared out, we hung around while Big Sammy rang out the till and did the books. I played Pac-Man while Rollie and Big Sammy had a beer and shot the shit at the bar. Rollie came and got me when Sammy was ready to lock up. At our car in the parking lot, Big Sammy gave Rollie a hug and swatted me playfully upside the head. As we were pulling out of the lot, Rollie turned to me, pinched me on the chin, and said, "Tough luck, Bub. Your ma's found herself a new clown. That's just the way it goes."

It was classic Rollie, his blunt, bizarre version of a heart-to-heart talk. I'd heard him all my life; he was notorious for his tributes and toasts at weddings, banquets, birthdays, and family gatherings, for his clumsy pep talks and what he called his "big game" monologues, and for his discomfiting—and generally discomforting—attempts at comforting the distressed or grieving. People still talked about the rambling eulogy he gave at my grandfather's funeral, a eulogy that touched on Big Leonard's "strong wrists" and his apparent parallel parking skills. As far as anyone could remember, Rollie's eulogy represented the first and only time anyone ever uttered the term "ballbuster" in the church. He had also—and my grandmother never forgave him for this—stepped out from behind the lectern at one point to demonstrate, or rather imitate, my grandfather's unique gait when intoxicated.

It was a perfect imitation, I remember that. Inebriated, Big Leonard almost looked like he was waltzing, or maybe tangoing, with some unseen partner. He would place his left hand, fingers splayed, directly over his crotch, with his thumb resting on his belt buckle; his right hand, fingers poised as if above a keyboard, would be placed at the top of his right buttock, and it would look like he was trying with great effort to hold himself perfectly erect. Then, with a look of intense but unfocused concentration on his face, he would push his body along in quick, tiny, flat-footed steps, inter-rupted at regular intervals by these wobbly, unsteady pauses, like a man trying to cross a tightrope in a stiff breeze.

After we left Big Sammy's, and after he dropped the bombshell on me, I was treated to one of Rollie's classic monologues. I had a pretty good idea what he'd meant when he said my mother had found "a new clown," but Rollie nonetheless proceeded to elaborate.

"Your ma's had a tough go of it," he said. "She's a little wiggy, you know that. We've tried to look after the both of you, and none of us have ever asked much of her. We've pretty much let her do her own thing, even when some of your aunts and uncles thought we should cut her off. You know how she sulks. She cut off all her hair one time when you were still a baby, right down to the scalp. Your grand-mother almost had a heart attack. You probably never knew how many times your uncles and me had to go around town making nice on all the rubber checks she used to write; I still have no idea what she does with her money, but she gets checks from the military and we put money in her account, but she always seems to be broke."

I told Rollie I didn't want to talk about it.

"I know you don't, Bubby," he said, "but you're going to have to deal with this. Listen, we all know you like this screwball your mother's been married to. The rest of us never hit it off with him much, but that's okay, and it's not your problem. Anyway, now she's got a new thing, and we gotta let her go. I think she wants out from under all the old family baggage here in Prentice, and she's met some new doorknob in Floyd Valley. You're an odd duck too, Bubs, but you're a bright kid, and this is just one more thing you're gonna have to figure out."

It was an unseasonably warm night and a thick, wet fog had settled over everything, and there was something pleasant and appropriate about that. Snow had come in regular bursts since Thanksgiving, and now it was melting and settling and evaporat-ing in the seemingly endless and unbroken fields. I loved moving through fog, liked feeling enveloped and slightly lost, and it struck me as sad and beautiful the way the fog trapped and broke down light, fuzzed and smeared and ultimately defeated it. You'd drive through these strange and grainy bursts of light, amid limited visibility, and suddenly a brief window would open to reveal a farmyard or driveway or intersection, and just as quickly the window would close, and we'd be back to flying in the clouds. For the most part the headlights of Rollie's car didn't penetrate or reveal much beyond the fog we were driving through. The whole time Rollie played a Neil Sedaka eight-track. I found myself listening intently to each song, marveling at the slick, antiseptic arrangements and the corny lyrics. Rollie—whenever his monologue ran out of steam—hummed to the music and drummed on the steering wheel with his thumbs.

I must've been processing what he'd said to me, because at some point I shouted, "I'm not moving!"

Rollie actually laughed out loud. "My God, Bubby," he said. "I think that's the first time I ever heard you raise your voice."

I was surprised as well, surprised by how much anger I suddenly felt, how strange it was, and how it seemed to flood my brain and override the old defenses I usually called on to keep it at bay. All those months of confusion and fear that had been building inside me became something else, morphed into real anger, and I had no idea what to do with it or what would become of it. It was as if it had been simmering quietly on some back burner and had finally boiled over, kicking up all sorts of unfamiliar feelings. I was mad at my mother and Russ for not having the guts to give me the news themselves, and I was terrified about what was going to happen to me. I honestly couldn't believe my mother would tear me away from Russ and the rink and move me to Floyd Valley.

I was also worried about Russ. Who was this "doorknob" Rollie was talking about, and how come I'd never met him or even heard my mother mention him? Was this really how adults did things, just walked out one door and through another?

I had just reached a point where I was starting to feel at home in the world and learning to process all the things I'd gleaned from my years with Russ. Now I was expected to just start all over in a new place? It was inconceivable.

It was late, and I just wanted to go home and listen to music. I told Rollie as much, and he drove me back into town and walked me to the door of the rink. He gave me a big bear hug that lifted me off my feet, then he said, "You're a tough kid, just like your old man. Things are gonna work out all right, scout's honor. We'll look after you just like we always have."

When I got to the top of the stairs, the rink was completely dark except for the odd splashes and shards of outside light scattered along the walls and resting in shimmering streaks and pools around the gleaming hardwood floor. Russ was slumped in the High Tower, bathed in a weird green glow from the stereo console. His chin was cupped in his hands, and his eyes appeared to be closed. He gave no indication he'd heard me come up the stairs or was aware of my presence. He was playing Joni Mitchell's *Blue*, a record I can no longer listen to because every song now recalls that night and that time in my life. I couldn't tell you what any of the songs are about, or even what most of them are trying to say, but I know how it *feels*, what it felt like then.

After the last song had finished, there was a moment of silence as the arm floated back to its cradle, then Russ played the last song again. I tried to listen closely to the words, but I was exhausted, and my head already in full hypnagogic flight. I'd taken a seat along the back wall, from which I could watch Russ through the darkness. He stood up in the middle of the song and stretched, raising his arms above his head and opening his mouth in a silent scream, a black hole in the bottom of his green, stereo-lit face. He then hugged himself, wrapped his skinny arms around his shoulders and shuddered, hopping maniacally as he did so. For some reason this was one of the saddest, most disturbing things I'd ever seen. I could hear his sobs over the music; they were wrenching, almost asthmatic gasps he was clearly trying to control.

I was stunned, sitting there watching an intensely private moment, and it was almost unbearable. That last song, which Russ played three times in succession, was called "The Last Time I Saw Richard." Years later, I would find a copy of *Blue* at a thrift store, and I remember opening the gatefold with trepidation to study the lyrics to "The Last Time I Saw Richard." Reading them in the middle of a thrift store in a Minneapolis suburb, I felt queasy and flushed with embarrassment, almost as if I were snooping in Russ's journal. There were lines about disillusionment and cynicism—"pretty lies, just pretty lies"—and one line that sounded like something my mother might've said to Russ or included in a note if she wrote poetry: "It's just that now you're romanticizing some pain that's in your head / You got tombs in your eyes but the songs you punched are dreaming."

I'm not sure how long I sat there watching Russ, but even through the hours of exhaustion, I seldom took my eyes from him. I was increasingly aware that at some point, probably as a necessary survival tool, I had—or my subconscious brain had—constructed a tower above the chaos, an overlord chamber, from which a consciousness that functioned much like an air traffic controller could sort things out and direct my attention. I could isolate one part of the swirling chaos in my brain and puzzle over it for hours.

The next morning at the rink, as the world took its first plodding steps out of the holidays and into the bleak backstretch of the new year, my brain rolled like a lysergic time-lapse film. One strange moment folded into another, but there was no proper sense of continuity or chronology. I sat slumped on the bench just inside the entryway, in the shadows by the skate rental counter, virtually all night. The light changed, drifted by degrees through subtle variations of darkness, the shadows deepening and shifting in the corners, the stray fragments and angles of outside light from the transom windows moving slowly around the room, expanding and shrinking until they disappeared entirely or were folded into the first wash of daylight.

There was a soundtrack all night. Russ kept playing records, moving stuff on and off the turntable. I lost track sometimes; some of the songs didn't fully register or penetrate, or they rolled straight through to one of the lower frequency bands in my brain. A lot of the records were unfamiliar to me, and there didn't seem to be any theme or cohesion. It certainly wasn't all melancholy or heartbreak. At times it seemed as if Russ was just yanking records out of the racks at random. He may have been looking for a specific mood or feeling, but I couldn't figure out what it was. Somewhere in the middle of the night he drifted through a procession of soul 45s, mostly up-tempo songs I couldn't remember hearing before. At one point Russ stood up, pulled his sweatshirt over his head, and tossed it into the middle of the rink. His jeans were baggy, and because he had absolutely no hips or ass, they kept slipping down, with or without a belt. He leaned back into the turntable and replaced a Muddy Waters record with the Clash's *Sandinista!*, and he proceeded to listen to all six sides of that album, every song in order. Later—several years later, in fact—he admitted to me that that morning was possibly the *only* time he'd ever listened to that record in its entirety.

During a number of songs, he actually seemed to be dancing up in the High Tower, doing a pretty amazing impersonation of a fucked-up guy doing a fucked-up impersonation of Mick Jagger. He played air guitar and even held an imaginary microphone to his mouth from time to time.

I went to the bathroom at some point, and when I returned dawn was barging in through the transom windows, and the light in the rink was at its most bruised and aquatic. Russ had strapped on his skates and was gliding around to some piece of music that sounded like opera.

That was one of the most indelible moments of my life. Both of us had been up all night. I'd kept my silent vigil for hours and still received no indication Russ was aware of my presence. I watched him skate around the rink in the first murky light of the second murky morning of another year. He was still shirtless and skated as if he were asleep on his feet and dreaming, nothing fancy, just going around and around, almost as if the wind was sweeping him along. At times he seemed to move in slow motion.

I'd never heard classical music of any sort played in either the apartment or rink; in fact I had had no exposure to it at all. I thought such music was fancy stuff for people who were a lot different from us. In the context of that morning, though, with Russ sailing around the rink like a kite, a narcoleptic figure skater, a wheel zombie (his term for people who got seemingly possessed on their skates), whatever record he was listening to was the most beautiful music I'd ever heard. I remember being half awake and being briefly transported by a voice or voices singing in a language I couldn't understand. It felt good, almost narcotic.

I finally got up from the bench, walked across the rink, and climbed the steps to the tower. The record sleeve lay next to the turntable. It had almost psychedelic artwork and lettering; it could've been a Jefferson Airplane record. *Mahler*, the lettering read, *Das Lied von der Erde*. I turned the jacket over in my hands. *Song of the Earth* it said in smaller letters under the original title. I looked at the record as it spun on the turntable; the last side was playing. A woman was singing as if her heart was breaking, or already broken.

Russ was moving so slowly around the rink by this time he was practically plodding (that was his word for it)—no longer properly gliding but just picking up his skates and putting them down. He was the best skater I've ever seen, hands down, but shirtless, with his jeans hanging halfway down his ass and his hair in his eyes, he was reduced to just another fucked-up plodder, a roundy-roundy, grinding along with his head down and his eyes closed.

The music was full of stops and starts and dark, droning bursts of sound that would drop back into quieter and prettier interludes. The woman would disappear for long stretches, during which things got very dreary, as if a big storm was brewing and as if the woman was slowly and excruciatingly having her heart removed by a garden spade, and when her voice emerged again it sounded like her heart was in her hands, and then she was easing it up into the dark sky like a broken Mylar balloon and watching it disappear into the clouds.

After the song faded away and the turntable arm had settled in its cradle, Russ finally looked up and acknowledged me in the High Tower. "Play something," he said.

"What do you want me to play?" I asked.

He shook his head and chuckled. "Play whatever you want," he said. "You know the drill. Play something I can skate to. Show me what you've got."

We were both exhausted. My mind suddenly raced again. Russ was sitting in the middle of the rink, or maybe crouched over his skates, staring up at me with this slack, disturbing smirk. "I'm waiting," he said. "Come on, Matt, my wheels are cooling off."

I had no idea what to play and was rifling through the records looking for familiar covers. I knew how Russ worked and was trying to imitate him; I'd watched him so many times I had his mannerisms down pat. I knew he would line up a huge stack of records before he played a single one. He spent a lot of time every day making and organizing these stacks, and I always sensed a clear strategy was involved. I was being forced to work quickly and on the fly, so I started by pulling albums I recognized and liked: James Brown's *The Payback*, The Spinners' *Pick of the Litter*, Sweet's *Desolation Boulevard*, and Earth, Wind & Fire's *That's The Way of the World*. Eventually, when I had a substantial stack of records to choose from—and a nice balance between LPs and 45s—I started putting stuff on the turntable.

I learned right away how difficult it was to sustain a good, cohesive groove, to find a mix that locked into a certain pace or mood and kept it rolling. I'd absorbed a lot of Russ's philosophy regarding the art of the mix, geared specifically as his was to the rhythmic demands of roller-skating. Russ liked what he called "bursts" or "high runs"—a series of records that shared a basic energy level or beat and could sustain a pace for ten or fifteen minutes. "Waves," he would say. "You're building waves, and if you could chart the energy level of the skaters, it should ideally look like a heart monitor hooked up to a giant with an erratic heartbeat—a nice, sustained pause at the top of the arc followed by a plunge, a relaxed stretch in third gear, then a gradual climb back to the top. You have to imagine you've got your foot on the gas pedal that's propelling these skaters around the track. You want to hold them steady at cruising speed—say seventy miles an hour—and then take them down to fifty, then thirty, before you put the pedal down and take them back up to seventy. This isn't dancing, or even running; you have more speed potential on skates, and more endurance, so you can push the energy level a lot higher and keep it there longer. When you stall out for too long at thirty or jerk it up and down too much, that's when people take a break and sit down. And when people are sitting out too many songs, that's when you know you've fucked up the mix."

I don't remember much about the songs I played for Russ that morning—I regret that I didn't enter them in the tower logbook and that I would never acquire Russ's habit of documenting everything I listened to—but I know I was feeling pretty good. Russ skated through it all without complaint and with only the occasional whoop of pleasure and other gestures of approval.

I must've played records for two or three hours that morning. Russ didn't do anything fancy on his skates. Most of the time he moved in a slow, head-down trance broken by stretches where he would work up alarming speed. Because of the rink's small size, when you really got rolling, it was as if you were being sucked into a whirlpool. I never understood science, but I do remember monkeying around with some kind of centrifuge in school once, and when you'd get up to maximum speed at Screaming Wheels, it felt how I imagined it would feel to be trapped in one of those things. I got dizzy trying to track Russ as he rocketed around on the rink beneath me; at times he seemed to break up before my eyes, an asteroid burning out of control.

Occasionally he'd slow down and coast for a time, gliding along in long, smooth strides, his hands clasped behind his back and his head bowed, like an ice-skater, or a speed skater warming up. He was still shirtless, and his torso gleamed with sweat. Several times between records he'd pass the tower and shout, "Surprise me."

I know I played Booker T. & the MG's' "Green Onions" (my favorite song of all time) and Archie Bell & the Drells' "Tighten Up." I'm also pretty sure I played Neil Young's "Sedan Delivery"—I'd listened to *Rust Never Sleeps* over and over since I'd received a copy as a birthday gift. When I followed up War's "Why Can't We Be Friends?" with Talking Heads' "The Great Curve," Russ let out a sustained howl and turned to me with a look of wild-eyed glee. I think that was the first time I ever felt a sense of command and power in the High Tower. It was such an ecstatic experience to play music designed to make someone else move or feel something, and I'd had a run there at the end where it seemed as if Russ was wired directly to the music I was playing.

I remember that the last song I played that morning was The Who's "Squeeze Box," at the conclusion of which Russ collapsed on the floor in maniacal laughter. "I'm crying uncle," he said. "Outstanding job, Matty. I've never felt prouder. You conjured up some seriously good chemistry."

XXIV.

There's a certain time every night—usually about a three-hour window—when I can stand up in the press box and watch lights going out all over town, a rolling blackout stretching all the way east and into the countryside. I used to love to be out walking and counting the house and porch lights as they were extinguished along my route. Watching them from this vantage, though, watching Prentice grow progressively darker as people shut things down and go looking for sleep, is a different feeling. It's loneliness, I suppose, like watching a hillside of fireflies slowly go dark.

Earlier in the evening, I walked downtown to a community talent show at the high school auditorium. It was wrenching and weirdly inspiring, all those clumsy dreamers with their fiercest hopes still as far away as undiscovered planets, yet there they were, still plugging away to the world's huge and howling indifference. A few performers—mostly kids—had modest talent, but most were hopeless, graceless, pumped full of a desire to be something they cannot and never will be. The hope, though, is the thing that gets you: the inexplicable confidence to get up there and bare their dreams to a room full of friends, neighbors, and strangers. And what really struck me, and gutted me in the end, was my sense that so many of the performers—particularly the older ones—had somehow succeeded in imagining themselves as the very things, and the sorts of people, they wanted to be, transcending the world's favor and opinion and the painful, wondrous spectacle of how they appeared to others.

XXV.

I know what things sound like, or, more accurately, I associate a soundtrack with virtually every experience, environment, encounter, and memory. Certain songs and records are hopelessly entwined with my feelings and memories; I have to go through the music to access them, and the music opens up or enhances things I can't otherwise access. Much, I suppose, as some people can look through an album of photographs and recreate memories of particular moments or even entire chapters of their lives, I can hear a song, a record, an old mixtape and be immediately transported to a different time, place, or feeling. This often feels like the only way I can remember, and I have no way of knowing whether my memories are accurate or not. It feels as if I've assembled this massive soundtrack, and I'm trying to build a movie—or reimagine a life—around it.

At the moment, though, I feel as if my brain has been shackled to an old bank safe and pitched from a foundering boat into rolling seas.

With my mother's new job, there were an increasing number of days that winter—particularly if there was a snowstorm—that she stayed in Floyd Valley with her new boyfriend, who I still hadn't met well into the new year. I hadn't even so much as heard my mother, or anyone else, utter his name. Her marriage, though, which had settled into a silent game of keep-away I couldn't understand, clearly wasn't over. We still lived in the rink apartment even as my mother spent more time in Floyd Valley, and during this strange interlude—it would be almost three months before my mother forced her hand with me—we never broached the subject of any new arrangements. I later learned (from her) that she was waiting for the divorce to be finalized before making the official move—she'd worried about scandalizing my father's family and her new boyfriend's colleagues.

I sensed we were biding our time and of course secretly held out hope for some miracle that would allow me to stay in Prentice with Russ. Business tended to pick up at the rink during the winter, when everyone developed cabin fever and there was not much else to do, particularly on the weekends. After the holiday meltdowns Russ seemed to settle back into something approximating his normal groove in the High Tower. He was still in a deep funk around the apartment and clearly preoccupied as he went about his usual opening and closing routines at the rink. But for the most part his playlists settled back into their usual satisfying and consistently surprising rhythms.

Art Vargo started making regular appearances at the rink, which was unusual. In all my years there I don't think he showed up more than a handful of times. That winter he was zipping around town on a new snowmobile and would show up at the rink bundled up in what looked like an expensive racing outfit, complete with a Darth Vader–like helmet. I came home from school one day and found Russ and his father wandering around the rink, engaged in what looked like a serious and intense discussion. When I sat in the tower and started to strap on my skates, Russ asked me to give them a few minutes of privacy. Most of the subsequent visits were similar; the two of them would retreat to some corner or to the little office off the skate rental counter, and when Art left, Russ would be in a gloomy mood. These visits especially puzzled me because I'd never known Russ and his father to engage in anything resembling an actual conversation. Most of the encounters I'd witnessed involved the smallest of talk—Art would enthuse about some new and inexplicable hobbyhorse, and Russ would make a few droll comments or ask a couple of bemused questions.

During my first appointment with the Cowboy, we talked about my mother and the impending move to Floyd Valley. Early on he asked me if I believed my mother to be a nurturer.

"What does that mean?" I asked.

"Do you think she's been a good mother?"

"She's the only mother I have," I said.

"That doesn't require her to be a good mother," the Cowboy said. "Do you love her?"

"I should," I said.

"Again, that's not a requirement. If you were to say you loved your mother, what would you mean by that?"

I thought about this question but couldn't come up with an answer. Perhaps I was distracted by the turquoise rings the Cowboy wore on many of his fingers. They were big rings, distracting rings.

"I think you need to learn to answer that question," he said. "As it pertains to your mother but also to other people and things in your life. It's a critical question, really. Hard to get along in this world without some understanding of love and what it means to you."

I asked the Cowboy what love meant to him.

He smiled and spread his arms wide, as if to say, "*This.* All of this." Then he thrust out a leg, nudged a huge dictionary off a shelf with the heel of his cowboy boot, and kicked it across the floor to me. "Look up the word," he said. "A dictionary is a good thing to learn to use. I've consistently discovered there are words to name or describe things that might otherwise seem elusive or confusing to me. It's helpful to know all the possible things words can mean— if only to others."

I picked up the dictionary and thumbed through it. I found the definition of love on page 707 and stared uncomprehendingly at a bunch of confusing italicized words, random acronyms, and paren-thetical abbreviations. I had a paperback dictionary in my bedroom that I used all the time to look up words, but I'd never bothered with all the minutiae.

"Here," the Cowboy said. "Throw it over here. You'll learn."

I tossed him the book. "It's on page 707," I said.

He crossed the room and crouched down next to my chair with the dictionary open in his hands. "This first business is like an operator's manual," he said, running his long, skinny finger over the text. "It's the nuts and bolts: how you pronounce the word, what class of words, or grammar, it belongs to—that little *n* means it's a noun—and where it comes from, its etymology. You can usually skip all that unless you're really curious, but it says here the word *love* has evolved from the Old English *lufa*, which was related to both *luba* in Old High German, *leof* in Old English, and *lubere* or *libere* in Latin—*love, dear*, and *to please*, in other words. Beyond that are all the things we now agree *love* means to English-speaking people: 'Strong affection for another arising out of kinship or personal ties; attraction based on sexual desire: affection and tenderness felt by lovers; affection based on admiration, benevolence, or common interests; warm attachment, enthusiasm, or devotion; unselfish loyal and benevolent concern for the good of another; the fatherly concern of God for humankind; the sexual embrace; a score of zero (as in tennis); to hold dear, cherish.' It's a versatile word, you see? Like many words it can mean many things to many different people."

"I asked what it meant to you," I said.

"It means all those things," the Cowboy said. "Or most of them."

"What do you love?" I asked.

Again, he spread his hands apart. "I love my family and friends," he said. "I love my children and my dog. I love to cook and eat. I love music and books. I love the wide-open space of the West, which is where I grew up. I love the world, love waking up every morning and expecting to be surprised."

"Do you love your wife?" I asked.

"I'm no longer married," he said. "But I did love her once. Very much. Love can change over time. People change. It happens. But I did love her, and I suppose I still feel a different kind of love for her. We had wonderful years together and raised three beautiful children. Yet even the love I feel for them can be complicated."

"Do you love your mother?"

He laughed. "That range of definitions provides lots of wiggle room," he said. "My love for my mother would need to be qualified, but, yes, I love her, though it hasn't been easy at times. Love is a loaded and perhaps overused word, but I suspect the people who manage to be happy in this world tend to use it liberally. Passion isn't the same thing as love, but it's often a portal or an expression of love." He closed the dictionary, returned to his chair, and then abruptly changed the subject. "Do you ever imagine what your relationship with your father would've been like had he lived? Do you have a sense of who he was?"

"Not really," I said. "No one really talks about him."

"Do you know how he died?"

"He died in the war," I said. "He was a soldier."

The Cowboy raised his hands above his head and cracked his knuckles. "That's established. But do you wonder who your father was?" he asked. "Or what his life was like or what he might have experienced in the war?"

"I don't think so," I said.

"Come on," the Cowboy said. "You're allowed to feel things. You're allowed to think things and wonder about things. You don't need anyone's permission to do any of that. So, tell me, in your own words: Who was your father?"

"I really don't have any idea."

"Who *would* he be, if you could somehow bring him back and he was sitting right here with us now? Use your imagination."

"I think he would be different than he was," I said. "And I probably wouldn't like him."

"And how do you think he was?" the Cowboy asked.

"Silent," I said. "And sad. Nobody and nothing."

The Cowboy raised his eyebrows. "Is that how you see your dad, or how you see yourself?"

"It's both of us," I said. "I'm just like him."

"According to whom?"

"According to everyone. According to me."

"Well," he said, "we can work on that. You have a significant advantage over your father: You're alive. You can still change."

The Cowboy left me that day with a couple assignments: to try to sort out the feelings I had for my mother and to come up with a list of people and things I loved, or at the very least liked a lot. He would continue to insist over our time together that I needed to find words to communicate the things I thought and felt. "The music," he said, "allows you to feel, but you need to figure out how to translate those feelings, how to speak."

He'd start sentences with words like "I feel," "I think," "I wish," and "I want," and then ask me to finish them. Often in those early days he would sit for long stretches in silence, waiting me out. The Cowboy was a very patient man.

I realized during this time that the word part of my brain was seriously undeveloped, despite the fact that I'd been a pretty passionate reader since early childhood. I tended to think in images and sounds, or at least those generally took precedence in my consciousness. I looked and I listened, but the things I looked at and listened to often didn't translate into words. The feelings they aroused in me—and I'm pretty sure they *were* feelings—were more inchoate, impressionistic, chemical changes in the way I felt: stimulants, perhaps. Russ used to say music could change the way blood moved through his body and was sometimes the only thing that could make him actually move. "All this sediment settles in you," he said, "and music is like the spoon that stirs it up. It's an emotional laxative."

The Cowboy encouraged me to sit quietly with a notebook each night and try to catch whatever words, thoughts, or feelings crossed my mind. I'd been doing something like this for at least a couple years, but the things I was writing down weren't original. They were, I recognized, merely cryptic and confounding fragments I snatched from the sprawling babel that had grown up in the foothills where I spent most of my nights, and the habit of making notes was nothing more than a feeble attempt to parse all that traffic and noise.

I tried to do as the Cowboy suggested, but initially I found myself sitting in the darkness of my room, waiting impatiently for a train of words and staring for hours down desolate tracks. All the Cowboy's prompts—*I feel*, *I think*, *I wish*, *I want*—were dutifully written in the notebook on my lap, false starts I couldn't push any further. I kept losing my way in my mind. Slowly, though, words started to come. I would stare off across the roofs of downtown and suddenly start writing about Mr. Tollefson, the old man who lived above the flower shop on Main Street. He was one of Prentice's sidewalk drunks, and because he was always trembling and unsteady, the kids all called him Shakey. The hippie girls who ran the flower shop called him Shivaree. Mr. Tollefson spent most days at the public library, sitting at a table in the back with papers strewn all over the place. Every one of the papers was covered with what looked like math equations scrawled in microscopic handwriting. I felt sorry for him. You could tell he'd once been handsome, and there was still something distinguished-looking about him. He always wore a suit jacket and tie. His glasses were so smudged and dusted with dandruff it was clear he could barely see out of them, and as a result he developed a tic that involved opening his mouth wide and craning his long neck in an attempt to peer over the top of his glasses. One time I was standing behind him at the Conoco as he tried to count out change; it was like he was rolling dice, and when he finally managed to cough up his payment, the change exploded from his hand and bounced all over the place.

I wrote about Mr. Tollefson, a list of impressions and memories, and on my next visit I presented this list to the Cowboy.

The Cowboy studied the list for a few minutes and then said, "This is an interesting collection of observations. What draws you to Mr. Tollefson?"

I told him that when I sit at my bedroom window looking out over Prentice, I sometimes get visual snapshots of memories associated with some of the people and places I've encountered.

"And what do you think about this particular man? You've obviously spent some time observing him."

"I feel sorry for him," I said.

"Have you ever spoken to him?"

"No."

"Why not?" the Cowboy asked. "Maybe he's lonely. Maybe he's sick. Maybe sitting in the library doing his math equations gives him pleasure. It's a good and virtuous thing to notice people like Mr. Tollefson, to *see* them—that's an important form of acknowledgment, and I'm sure there are many people who don't pay him any mind or give him a thought. But I'm sure he, too, has a story and a voice, and he might be eager to share that with someone. If you knew a bit more about him, perhaps you wouldn't feel so sorry for him. Or perhaps you would feel even more sorry for him."

"There are a lot of people like Mr. Tollefson in Prentice," I said.

"I'm sure there are a lot of people like Mr. Tollefson in almost any town," the Cowboy said. "But I'm also sure each of these people is unique and has their own story. When your teachers observed you in class and presented those observations—which they translated into concerns—to the social worker, how well do you think they knew you? Were those random observations an accurate portrait of you and what you were struggling with? Did they in any way tell your story?"

"No," I said.

"No," the Cowboy said. "How can any one of us know what someone else is going through, or who they are and what they love and how they're struggling, unless we ask them, or they tell us?"

"It's hard to ask," I said.

"It's not that hard. It's even harder to tell if no one asks. Communication has to start somewhere. What if you created a little encyclopedia of all the people and things in Prentice that are of some interest to you? You could start with yourself, with your family: Who really are you? Who are these other people? What's their story? How did they get from their own childhoods to where they are now? And what happened to them along the way? Isn't that essentially what you're now trying to figure out?"

That winter was especially relentless. It had rolled in with a ferocious blizzard the first week of November and would keep its lead foot on the pedal well into February. Once the snow came and the temperature sunk below thirty degrees there was hardly a single respite, no warm spell all winter. It seemed like every time the temperature crept toward freezing we'd get some kind of sleet or ice storm. The ice was everywhere, thick and yellow as the nail on a little toe, and it kept getting thicker and more slippery and more impossible all the time. Just when I'd think it couldn't get any worse, it got worse—we'd get another eight inches of snow, followed by more freezing rain just to put a thorough glaze over everything. People gave up on shoveling, surrendered the sidewalks entirely. The town apparently blew through its annual plowing budget; the streets were squeezed to one narrow and heavily rutted lane, with ice and snow banked high on all sides and on every corner.

March limped along like an ancient and heartsick tortoise with no signs whatsoever that winter would abate. The whole city felt bruised and hungover, and everything looked as if it had been shot in poor lighting with expired Super 8 film; it was as if my own life was composed of home movies from somebody else's long-ago disastrous life. I had no real soundtrack for days such as those, but if I could've come up with one—if I knew then what I know now—it would have to be suitably awful and unbearable: thrift store organ records from the 1950s and 1960s, maybe, or schlock pop/religious choirs—the kinds of small-town choirs that held car washes and candy sales so they could make some terrible record inspired by Up with People, *Jesus Christ Superstar,* or *Hair.* Just plain dark or brooding would be inappropriate; no, it would have to be music that *mocks* the darkness you feel, that taunts you and doesn't just complement your misery but aggravates it and takes it completely over the top.

It really was hard to be human when you were forced to live like that, like this, for almost six months of the year. It was, it is, hard to be anything but grim and self-involved. All those human stories the Cowboy was goading me to imagine and tell were mostly inaccessible to me during the winter months. Everyone in Prentice seemed to be in hibernation, and who wants to socialize with a bunch of people who do nothing but sit around and bitch about the weather? Even worse were those who tried to put on a happy face and offer pathetic displays of hearty optimism that were so plainly false, forced, and unconvincing that any sane human being would rather sit home nursing an ear infection and reading Revelations.

I came home from school one day in the middle of March and the rink was silent as I climbed the stairs, a very rare occurrence. A small wall of shipping boxes was stacked against the skate rental counter, and my mother emerged from the apartment pushing a dolly loaded with more boxes. I stood with my backpack dangling from my hand, watching her come toward me across the rink floor.

"What's this?" I said.

She set the dolly down at my feet, took my face in her hands, and tried to look me in the eye. "I'm sorry, Matt," she said, and I squirmed away from her. She sat on one of the benches and said again, "I'm sorry, Matt. I'm so sorry, but this is my life too. Please sit down and talk to me."

"Where's Russ?" I asked.

She shook her head and shrugged. "He's not here," she said. "This is hard for him. It's hard for all of us."

"Where are we going?" I asked.

"You know where we're going, Matt," she said. "I've put this off long enough. For you. To give you time. But we can't put it off any longer. I need you with me."

"Then stay here," I said. "I still don't even know where we're going."

"I've told you we're going to Floyd Valley," she said. "That's where I work, and that's where we're going to live now. I've tried to talk to you about this, but you've refused to listen. We'll have a big house. You'll have lots of space of your own."

"I have lots of space of my own here," I said.

"This isn't a home, Matt," she said. "It's a roller-skating rink, and it's not healthy. When you're older you can do whatever you want, but right now you're my child, and you have to come with me."

I'm sure I cried when I was an infant or a toddler, but I can count the number of times I can actually remember crying on both hands and still have a couple fingers to spare. But I cried then, a raging, bawling meltdown. I stalked away to the apartment. My bedroom was empty except for the bed, the nightstand, and the dresser. The rest of the apartment looked almost exactly as it had always looked, the same shelves and piles of books and records, the same magazines on the coffee table, the same overwhelming presence of Russ everywhere. It was his apartment, his stuff, his home. It was as if my mother and I had never lived there. I had talked with the Cowboy about the impending move, but nothing could've prepared me for it.

"There's a certain helplessness and a forfeit of will that comes with being a child," he had said to me. "You don't get to make most of the big decisions, and lots of times you're going to be a hostage to inevitability. That's not to say the adults in your life don't take your wishes and feelings into account, but ultimately, they call the shots. You have to look at it as a training period; you're learning how the world works, and what you want and don't want, so when you finally get to make your own decisions, you know who you are."

The Cowboy had sympathized with me, but he'd also encouraged me to keep an open mind about the move. "Think about when you first moved into the rink," he said. "Surely you had no way of knowing what sort of adventure you were in for. You didn't yet know your stepfather or what a huge influence he would be for you. You didn't know anything about music and really had no reason to even suspect that this huge and interesting world you discovered in the rink existed. Every life change has the potential to expose you to new discoveries, about yourself and the world. Who knows? Floyd Valley is a much bigger city, and you're at an age where you're starting to be independent enough to really explore this place. I think there are things you'll find interesting, and there will be many, many more kids your own age, and maybe you'll connect with some of them."

The whole thing was so anticlimactic; I wasn't even given a chance to say good-bye to anyone—to Russ, to Greenland Earle, to my aunts and uncles. I was furious with all of them for letting my mother just haul me away. At some point I just shut down and helped my mother carry our boxes down the stairs to the car. It was a Friday, I remember, and our school's spring break would begin on Monday. I'd been looking forward to the week off, but clearly my mother had planned the move to coincide with the break. Floyd Valley was a twenty-five-minute drive from Prentice, and that particular drive was the longest twenty-five minutes of my life.

We drove in almost complete silence. Just as we got on the highway headed south out of Prentice, my mother said, "I think you'll like my new friend, Matty. He loves music too."

"Your *new friend?*" I said.

We didn't exchange another word until we pulled up to the house, a split-level with a long driveway, big front yard, and lots of windows. It appeared to be part of a newish development—the house was more modern than most of the houses in Prentice—and the only trees on the street were a bunch of tiny specimens arranged in perfectly symmetric rows along the boulevard.

We pulled into the driveway and stepped out of the car, and this character—the new man in my mother's life, her "new friend"—emerged from the front door and scurried toward us. There were still patches of icy crust here and there, and he took tiny, exaggerated steps, his arms thrown out and paddling dramatically, as if he were already falling. He was also making this "oh-oh-oh" sound—I think it was intended to convey excitement—as he clattered in our direction. He was babbling, really, shouting our names and other clearly affected jollities. When he finally skidded to a stop in front of us he attempted to pull me into a clumsy bear hug—"Oh, Matthew, how splendid to finally meet you!" I wasn't particularly tall for my age—probably about five eight at the time—but I already had a couple inches on this man, and he was wearing shiny new Dingo boots. He and my mother both clucked and half gasped with nervous energy, and I guess introductions were made. I don't think I said a word. I did learn, though, that the man's name was Baron Peterson, and he proceeded to hustle me up the front sidewalk and into the house. He was gripping the front sleeve of my jacket and my mother was shoving me from behind; it was as if they were extricating an injured man from a traffic accident.

I immediately noticed the entryway walls and ceiling were covered with mirrored tiles. Baron threw out his arms in an abracadabra gesture and shouted, "Welcome to *chez moi!*"

This guy—and I never learned to think of him as Baron, or even Barry (which was, I later learned, his real name), and God forbid I ever thought of him as my stepfather—couldn't seem to keep his hands off my mother. He kept putting his arm around her and wrenching her in tight. She was at least four inches taller than him and half as wide. The displays of affection between my mother and Russ were rare, and here was this ridiculous-looking guy who couldn't stop touching her. She seemed to love it, and the whole thing creeped me out.

This was where we were apparently going to live—in this house and with this guy—and as they gave me a tour of the place, I had a kind of out-of-body experience.

There was virtually nothing in the front room but a huge grand piano placed in full view of the picture window that looked out on the street. Lest passersby miss the sight of Baron Peterson hunched over his piano, there was a bank of track lighting with all six bulbs trained on the piano bench. It didn't take me long to learn that Baron's ridiculous "private" recitals were a source of enduring amusement in the neighborhood. He taught music and drama at the high school, and kids used to cruise by the house regularly to laugh at him, honk their horns, and toss the occasional egg.

On first pass the only merciful thing about this new arrangement was the fact that my bedroom was in the basement, and near as I could tell, the basement afforded the only privacy in the entire house. It looked, in fact, like I would not only have my own bathroom as well but essentially my own efficiency apartment—there was a small living room off the bedroom, just at the bottom of the stairs, and a set of sliding glass doors that opened onto a little patio. It wouldn't take me long to learn I could come and go without ever actually going upstairs. This was all very convenient, not to mention a huge relief, as it was pretty quickly made clear that most of the stuff upstairs was off-limits to me.

In one of his pathetic early attempts to pal up to me and make a positive impression, Baron described himself as "a fellow music buff." He had a RadioShack stereo, and his collection of records was heavy on schlock pianists (Ferrante & Teicher, Peter Nero, guys like that), Rod McKuen, and, unsurprisingly, a huge assortment of Broadway cast recordings. There was also, of course, no shortage of lame White jazz (Doc Severinsen, Maynard Ferguson, Chuck Mangione, etc.). When Baron was trying really hard to impress me, he would break out his ELO or Cat Stevens records.

Life around that house quickly broke down into an upstairs/downstairs version of reality. Upstairs was the exclusive province of the grown-ups, antiseptic, with wall-to-wall white shag carpeting, a leather couch and matching chairs, and a bunch of framed Broadway posters and bad Picasso reproductions. The "master bedroom," as Baron referred to it, was dominated by a king-size waterbed. The whole house was full of mirrors, or at least the upstairs was, which was reason enough for me to avoid it. There were, in fact, all sorts of reasons for me to avoid it.

Downstairs is where I slowly carved out my own small and increasingly unhappy private world. The adults virtually never ventured downstairs; if they needed anything from me, they simply shouted from the top of the stairs. It was as if they were both afraid of me, afraid my needs and unhappiness would spoil their newfound bliss.

There was no getting around the fact that my mother was an entirely different person around this guy and that this whole transformation had resulted in a level of happiness that baffled me. I hate to think I resented my mother her happiness or—God forgive me—her *love*, but it was disconcerting that her fulfillment seemed so completely indifferent and unrelated to my own.

I missed Russ and the rink. I was in serious withdrawal from the wheels, the music, the feeling of being swept along. I didn't have anything, really, but a small collection of books, most of which I had long outgrown, and several boxes of mixtapes I'd made at the rink. I went from having access to thousands of records to owning maybe a dozen actual physical albums of my own.

I had that week of spring break to at least try to get my head around the notion that I would be resuming classes at an entirely different school. There had been maybe a hundred students in my grade back in Prentice, and I'd had a hard time fitting in and meeting other kids there. I had absolutely no idea what awaited me in Floyd Valley.

Everyone in Prentice thought of Floyd Valley as a big city; Minneapolis and St. Paul were "the Cities," but Floyd Valley was "the City." People headed there would say they were going "into town." I don't suppose the population was more than forty thousand in those days, maybe nowhere near that, but it was the closest decent-sized town and the place Prentice residents were most likely to go for Christmas shopping, furniture, appliances, back-to-school supplies, or a nice dinner out. Even so, and even though it was less than a half hour from Prentice, I'd never spent much time there. Russ hated the place, and until my mother got a job there, she could seldom be bothered to leave Prentice.

During those first brutal days in Floyd Valley, I mostly felt like a befuddled spectator in my mother's new life. She and Baron always seemed to be cuddled up on the huge leather couch, and I just skulked around on the peripheries of their adoration. They both seemed content and mostly oblivious to the fact that I was drifting around the house at all hours, the last, lingering ghost of my mother's old life.

A few nights into my stay in Barry "Baron" Peterson's basement, as I paced back and forth in the darkness listening to "London Calling" at almost subliminal levels on my crappy cassette player, it occurred to me that I was, quite literally, free to go. The glass sliding doors in my little living room opened into the backyard, and the backyard ran down a slight incline, perhaps thirty yards, to the frozen Floyd River. That river, I discovered, was the slickest and quickest road into the heart of town.

The first night I ventured out it was strictly an exploratory mission; I was just getting the lay of the land. Floyd Valley still struck me as an almost unimaginably large town, and I couldn't yet conceive of wandering around and exploring it freely on my own. The truth, though, was that it wasn't really a big city at all; it was just a bigger and slightly more sprawling version of Prentice, also almost entirely White but with perhaps a larger population of white-collar, upper-middle-class residents. It didn't take me long to learn there wasn't a whole lot more going on there than there had been in Prentice.

I ventured down to the river and cautiously tested the ice with my boot; it seemed solid enough, and the snow cover was packed down enough that I could walk right down the middle of the river on top of the crust. From there I could see the lights of the city sprawled out maybe a half mile to the south.

That river suggested some glimmer of possibility, of escape. I'd noticed that Baron had a canoe up on sawhorses on the patio, and a pair of snowshoes hung on a peg next to the sliding doors. That back door off the basement, I realized, was my escape hatch, and I was going to get to know that river.

In the meantime, though, and almost from the beginning, my life in Floyd Valley settled into a fierce battle of wills with Baron. "I can't tolerate this" became his standard response to pretty much every one of my personality traits and behaviors, however unconscious. He "couldn't tolerate" the way I dressed or wore my hair, my posture, my responses to his questions. He constantly complained about what he called my aloofness and accused me of disrespecting both him and my mother. He didn't like the music I listened to—he didn't even have to hear it; the album covers were enough to make him raise his eyebrows or shudder dramatically—or the things I was interested in. Even more galling, apparently, were the things I *wasn't* interested in. He also decided within the first few months that "we" needed to address my nocturnal tendencies. It was, he announced one day at the kitchen table, time for me to learn to sleep "like a normal person."

Every day seemed to bring some new stern pronouncement from Baron Peterson. "There are going to be some changes," he'd say. I needed to learn to live a more structured and disciplined life. I needed to get involved with extracurricular activities at school, needed to learn how to make friends, even though my biggest obstacle to meeting new people at school was my perceived relationship with Baron Peterson. He was the music and theater pooh-bah and the source of near universal ridicule. Other than the small group of pompous and outrageously affected music and drama goofballs, everybody else regarded him as a pretentious dick and a buffoon. I think Baron regarded himself, or fancied himself, as Floyd Valley High's resident Bohemian. He wore things like bright and baggy Guatemalan smocks, or leather vests with silk scarves. His bell-bottom jeans, which hadn't been in style for at least a decade, were always creased and were apparently replaced the instant they began to fade. Most of the time he wore those clunky fucking Dingo boots, but, weather permitting, he would also break out a pair of big, preposterous sandals that looked like props from some Sunday school play.

Baron taught his classes in the school's old theater, a dark half bowl with rows of seats rising from the stage and dead-ending at a wraparound series of booths—booths for sound and lighting and a booth for the Impresario's office (that's what the sign on the door said: IMPRESSARIO [sic]). The office had two curved glass windows that looked directly down on the theater.

It was a large office, full of props and theater posters, as well as photographs of Barry in his glory days as a small-fry summer stock thespian—there he was hamming it up in *Fiddler on the Roof* or *South Pacific* or some other dud I'd never heard of. He'd also written a hopelessly corny one-act play in which he played a lonely and despairing old country preacher who has a crisis of faith brought on by the death of his wife and the loss of much of his congregation. One Christmas Eve, as he sits down alone for his forlorn dinner, having just delivered a dispirited sermon to a small gathering of indifferent parishioners, he is visited by—surprise, surprise!—a choir of carolers made up of people whose lives he has touched over the years. Heartfelt tributes and a big, festive party ensue. Tears flow.

Much of this "play" was written in attempted rhyme, and it was the corniest and most excruciating thing I'd ever seen. Baron had been staging it every Christmas for years; it was something of a local holiday tradition, and they'd bus people in from every rest home in the area.

For the remainder of my adolescence, that miserable play was the traumatic lowlight of every Christmas season. My mother thought it was the most charming thing she'd ever seen. Every year, Baron added some wretched new wrinkle to the production—the appearance of a Salvation Army band, a stray dog, or a hungry waif straight out of Dickens. "Just trying to keep things interesting," he'd say, oblivious to the impossibility of that proposition.

The play was called *An Angel Unawares*, and Baron always played the lead, Reverend Hopewell. He would outfit himself in a pair of wool knickers, a burlap smock, and a long, bright-red stocking cap; he'd stroll about the stage with a long-stemmed pipe, and despite occasional references to twentieth-century events, he looked like nothing so much as a French voyageur or a Tyrolean eccentric. For much of the play Reverend Hopewell would just sit on a stool in the middle of the stage, staring into a fake cardboard fireplace and trapped under a bright spotlight, sweating visibly and reciting the awful monologue, which was inexplicably delivered in the third person. He projected so forcefully that a shower of spit constantly bloomed and dissipated like fireworks directly in front of his powdered face, which would be streaked with sweat trails.

It was almost more than I could bear, seeing him made up like a clown and waddling around the stage like a fat little penguin, bellowing like a fool. I would spend the entire performance hot-faced with shame, certain any nonconscripted audience members were there strictly for yuks. It was, as I've said, a campy and unfathomable holiday tradition for many families, but for the right sort of high school student—the pot smokers, especially—there was no better or cheaper entertainment to be had in southern Minnesota in those days.

If my mother's relationship with Russ had confused me, watching this new man in her life annually take his dignity to a place from which it could never return forced me to recognize how completely and essentially unknowable my mother was to me. What could she possibly see in this fraudulent character? Watching him muddle through his performance as Reverend Hopewell—Reverend Hungwell, the stoners referred to him as—how could she be anything but wholly, utterly appalled? What could Russ possibly have done to drive her into the stubby arms of a man like Baron Peterson? I would never be able to fathom it.

When my mother started working at Floyd Valley High everything about her changed, maybe from a more objective standpoint for the better, but fifteen years old is a terrible time for a kid to have to adjust to his mother becoming an entirely different person.

As I got a bit older, I honestly felt bad for how much I despised Baron, because as far as my mother was concerned, he turned out to be pretty much the real deal. He and I never learned to stand each other, but I suppose he was good to my mother. He spoiled and coddled her and somehow managed to draw her out of her shell or to burst her bubble of oblivion. I think she deserved her nine years of happiness—she *was* happy, I'm pretty sure, and they were together until she died—but her relationship with Baron drove me away almost from the moment we moved into that house, and I still can't help feeling that was exactly what he wanted. One of the hazards of such remembering is that it only aggravates the most pressing and debilitating of my psychological problems, the very avoidance of introspection—and perhaps reality—that has driven me further and further into music, the imaginary diversion of books, and what has often felt like a permanent and terminal isolation.

The Cowboy was probably a lifesaver in that regard. During those early years in Floyd Valley I resisted seeing him—I didn't want to answer his questions, didn't want to talk, didn't want to feel anything—but to my mother's credit, she kept pushing me to go see the man. Which was funny, really, since I don't think she ever talked herself into seeing a therapist. I know that in time she came to regret that, and that regret was a big reason she kept encouraging me to see the Cowboy. "What if it saves you years of silent suffering and confusion?" she would say to me. "Maybe we all just need someone to ask us the clear, tough questions most of us would never dream of asking each other. Do you know that for the first thirty-five years of my life, no one ever asked me if I was happy? Or asked me what I was going through? You never know, Matt. Maybe you'll get one positive thing out of it or learn one thing about yourself you need to know to live in your skin. All sorts of stuff we might initially turn up our noses at has the possibility to change our lives."

Perhaps because my mother was so happy in her new life, she was more aware of my unhappiness. Or maybe my misery was so apparent that there was no way she could miss it. Baron would come home every night and play his shitty records while he cooked dinner (not surprisingly, I suppose, he fancied himself a gourmand) and sang or hummed along in his affected Robert Goulet baritone. He owned—and regularly played—a Seals and

Crofts record, and every time I heard it I wanted to run away and go back to the rink.

There was a relatively new record store downtown called Turn It Up!, and it had a surprisingly decent selection. I was ecstatic when I discovered it, but also distraught; I didn't have access to any money of my own or a stereo to play records. I nonetheless started stopping there almost every day after school, and I was eventually emboldened to shoplift a copy of Neil Young's *Decade* one afternoon when the clerk momentarily disappeared into the back room. It was so easy, and so oddly thrilling, that I began to steal one or two records a week and sneak them into the house in my backpack.

I usually drove to school in the morning with my mother and Baron, but this meant I would arrive at least a half hour before the other students. I told my mother I wanted to start taking the bus, a ruse that allowed me to skip school and stay home listening to my growing collection of stolen records on Baron's stereo.

This would have been a glorious arrangement if it weren't for the fact that both my mother and Baron worked at the school. In hindsight, I'm surprised it took three days for them to catch me—or for someone to rat me out. Baron was furious and told me I was grounded, which was laughable given that I never left the house other than to go to school. My mother was surprisingly calm about the whole thing. After Baron and I had a blowout in the kitchen, she came downstairs and sat with me in my bedroom. She calmly asked where I got the records, and I told her the truth. I really didn't know how to lie and had always tried to be honest with her.

"Why can't you listen to Baron's records?" she asked.

"Because they're terrible," I said. "And he doesn't want me to use his stereo."

"I'll get you a stereo for your room," she said. "And I suppose I can give you an allowance so you don't have to steal records. I'm ashamed of you, Matty. You know better. How do you think Russ would feel if you stole some of his records? I know you think music makes your life better, or maybe more bearable, but near as I can tell it hasn't really changed your life in a whole lot of years. It hasn't made you happier or helped you make friends or do better in school. Honestly, you're going to end up just like Russ."

"That would be fine with me," I said.

My mother just shook her head. "Please don't say that, Matt."

Russ probably would've agreed with my mother about much of that. He used to say that if something really changes your life, it only does so one time. Maybe it was possible to have your life changed several times, or even many times, but the real life changers did permanent work—permanent damage, Russ said, but I knew that was just his rock 'n' roll persona talking. At any rate, there was no getting around the fact that music really did change my life, or at least it changed the way I felt about life—about my life—and provided me with a new set of expectations. I don't think it was a one-time deal; it kept changing me in smaller ways, perhaps, but there were always new directions and discoveries that opened up other places and prospects. It was like a series of aftershocks. You'd bring home a new record and it had the potential to change the way you thought about and listened to music, and this would happen again and again and again. You were constantly revising and rewriting your own personal version of musical history. It was as if you went to bed one night and when you woke up and went outside the next morning, there were all these beautiful, strange new buildings you'd never seen before. Even now, every time I go into a record store, there is always some record—or dozens, or hundreds of records—that I don't have and should have, records that inevitably cause me to rethink or reevaluate more familiar records, to listen to them in another context or from another perspective.

I discussed this latest episode—and my conversation with my mother—with the Cowboy. "I might have to agree with your mother," he said. "I know you love music, and I don't in any way want to dismiss its importance to you, but it doesn't seem to draw

you out into the world. It's one function of a great passion to introduce you to yourself—it's an act of self-discovery—but one of its
other important functions is to serve as a kind of calling card in
your relationships with others, to help you introduce yourself and
connect with others. I'm still not sure you could tell me what you
believe, or believe *in*. I'm talking about a belief that connects you
to a community of others. Music is inherently social, communal—
people form bands, they venture out to see and hear music and to
dance. Music wouldn't have survived this long and evolved without that communal aspect. You know, surely, that this community
exists? When you're sitting alone listening to your records there are
probably many, many others out there in just this one city who are
engaged in the same activity. That's not to say you're not unique, or
that your experience isn't unique to you, but there are others like
you. I can guarantee you that."

I'm sure the Cowboy was right about everything, and he only
seemed to get righter the further along I went with him. I figured it
must be terribly boring being a therapist after a while; if you did it
long enough, there surely couldn't be anything terribly surprising
or original about the human psyche. For my part, I suppose there
was some comfort—but also some disappointment—in knowing
that the things that were wrong with me were so readily apparent to
a complete stranger. It probably didn't take the Cowboy more than
two or three hours to figure me out.

I tried to never blame my mother or point fingers, and I never
once—at least out loud—blamed her for any part of my failure to
engage with other kids, for my awkwardness in dealing with even
the immediate members of my family. I don't know if the Cowboy
blamed my mother, but he was clearly trying to encourage me to
be as unlike her as possible. He also surmised, very early on, that I
didn't have "a good communicative relationship" with my mother.
"Who do you blame for that?" he asked.

I said I never thought in those terms; I didn't suppose it was anyone's fault, or, more precisely, that anyone was to blame.

He retreated a bit. He had taken the wrong tack, he admitted; he didn't mean to assign blame or create bad feelings where perhaps none existed. He was, he said, simply trying to understand my "isolationist tendencies" and my struggles with communication.

"We inherit things from our parents, unconsciously," he said. "Things that are maybe hindering. We may inherit some of their habits or tendencies in isolation, without some of their other, offsetting qualities, if you see what I mean—their strengths, maybe, the compensatory things."

I told him that, on the one hand, I didn't understand what he was saying. On the other hand, it seemed obvious: I was just like my mother.

"That's not what I'm trying to say," the Cowboy said. "It may not be as obvious as you think, or as obvious as many people *like* to think. So many people are eager to blame their problems or behaviors on their parents, very often unfairly. At a certain point you're responsible for your own life. Perhaps if we use the terms *ascribe* or *trace* to discuss the way in which these inheritances appear in our lives, it will seem less punitive or contentious. Do you see traces of your mother in the person you're becoming? Or let me ask you this: Did your mother take an active interest in your day-to-day life when you were young? Did she make frequent inquiries or often initiate casual conversations?"

The answer to those questions, of course, was no.

"How about your sleep issues?" the Cowboy asked. "Did you ever discuss them with your mother? Or did she ever express any concern about your sleep patterns?"

The answer, once again, was no.

"And regarding your father: you've said you know very little, that neither your mother nor your family—your father's family—ever has much to say about him."

"So, you're trying to say I have a bad mother," I said.

"That's not what I'm trying to say," the Cowboy said. "I'm just trying to point out that the problems you have communicating, or the extent to which you seem uncomfortable talking about things that are maybe difficult, are some of the inheritances I mentioned earlier. It's a family issue and not unique to you. You've said that no one in your family takes photographs or keeps any kind of a photographic record of their lives, or your life, together. That's a bit unusual, and I think it's telling. Photography embodies shared memories and captured moments from a communal past—it's a form of shorthand communication, as well as a trigger for conversation and reminiscences. Photographs are a way to learn about our past—who we are and where we come from and where we've been—without a whole lot of exposition. It sounds like real communication is difficult for everyone in your family. Some of your aunts and uncles are apparently great talkers, but that's not the same as being great communicators. The fact that none of them have children might also have something to do with it; it takes a special kind of acquired patience and condescension to really communicate with children. The upshot of all this is that you've never learned how to truly engage in communication. It's an acquired skill and takes practice. It's as if you've spent much of your life in a private glass observatory."

"I don't have anything to say," I said. "I've never had anything to say."

"I don't believe that's true," the Cowboy said. "You have to start somewhere. You should reach out to people. Call your uncles, reach out to Russ, talk to your mother, tell her what you want and need and how you feel. Tell people you're having a hard time, you're angry, you're lonely. There's no crime in any of that. Everyone can relate to it. Tell me one thing that you feel right now, or one thing that you want."

"I want a stereo," I said.

"Then get a stereo," the Cowboy said. "Let's figure out how to get you a stereo and then maybe we can get you back on track."

There were two phones in Baron's house—one in the master bedroom, and one in the living room—and I didn't feel comfortable using either of them. I actually didn't feel comfortable talking on a phone, period. I'm not sure that at that point in my life I'd ever answered a ringing phone. The phone in our apartment at the rink often rang when we were all home and no one would move to answer it. We didn't have an answering machine, so there were times when the phone would ring and ring and ring. There *was* an answering machine out in the rink, precisely, I think, so Russ wouldn't have to answer the phone. The message provided the rink's address and hours, and that was it.

I did, though, think about calling Russ or Rollie almost every night, but I didn't want to talk to either of them with Baron or my mother eavesdropping, and I was also insecure. That's still an issue; I worry that if I call someone I'll be interrupting something, or that the ensuing conversation will be awkward (it almost always is) and full of uncomfortable silences (it almost always is).

Rollie and Mooze came over one night to take us all to dinner and to meet Baron for the first time. They were both clearly uncomfortable, and I think it was awkward for all of us, with the exception of Baron, who was so pompous and full of weird self-confidence that he prattled away throughout the dinner, barging into every pocket of dead air and obviously trying to impress my uncles with self-absorbed monologues about his theater career, his culinary expertise (the place Rollie chose, Baron proclaimed, did not show off Floyd Valley's "generally excellent restaurant scene in a good light"), and the "surprising cultural vibrancy of this *truly extraordinary* town in the middle of nowhere."

After dinner we dropped Baron and my mother off back at home, and Rollie and Mooze took me bowling.

"How about that guy?" Rollie said as we pulled out of the driveway.

"Tough pill to swallow, eh, Bubby?" Mooze said.

"Is he good to you and your ma?" Rollie asked.

"I hate him," I said.

"You're just gonna have to try to grin and bear it," Rollie said. "Maybe it'll get better. You're still just feeling each other out. At any rate, you'll be out from under him in no time at all."

Mooze let out a whistle and shook his head. "Talk about an overcorrection," he said. "Can you imagine that guy in the same room with Russ Vargo?"

"Russ would hate his guts," I said.

"I'm pretty sure the feeling would be mutual," Rollie said.

At the bowling alley, Rollie and Mooze presented me with a savings book from the Floyd Valley State Bank. "Your grandpa opened this account for you right after you were born," Rollie said. "We've all been kicking in a little every year, and we were going to save it until you graduated from high school, but we figured you could probably use a little running-around money right about now."

"Hell, kid," Mooze said. "You're loaded. Don't go wild with it."

I opened the little blue book and stared at the balance. There was almost $50,000 in the account.

"This is mine?" I said.

"Yeah, it's yours," Rollie said. "But you gotta make it last. That might seem like a lot now, but it ain't gonna go very far when you're living on your own."

I had very little experience with money. I was a kid who never really wanted or bought anything beyond the occasional candy bar or can of pop. For years I'd coasted on the money in the giant piggy bank that had been my sole inheritance from my grandmother, as well as my aunts' and uncles' spare change.

Rollie had to explain to me how the savings account worked, and I was astonished to learn I could simply go to the bank branch downtown and withdraw or deposit money at any time. No adult permission was needed. "Your ma don't even have to know about it," Mooze said.

Rollie did a double take and gave Mooze a swat upside the head. "What the hell are you saying? Matty don't have to keep secrets from his ma. You want to get us all in trouble?"

Mooze shrugged. "Whatever you think," he said. "But that's yours, Matty. Keep it safe and don't let your ma or the actor take it away from you."

"I want to buy a stereo for my bedroom," I said. "That's the only thing I really want right now."

Rollie offered to come over the next day to take me out to buy a stereo. "We'll go shopping and get you set up," he said. "I'll call your ma and tell her it was my idea."

He was waiting in the driveway when I got home from school the next day, and we drove out to the Sound World at the mall. As we pulled into the parking lot I realized I needed to go the bank. "Nah, I got this one, Bubby," Rollie said. "You save that money."

I wanted a good stereo, I knew that much, and I knew I had to have separate components. I couldn't stand those shitty all-in-one consoles. I also wanted power. Russ's rink model, of course, was my ideal. Rollie also had pretty expensive tastes; his own stereo, I knew, was top of the line. I ended up with a much better stereo than I even realized at the time, and a much better stereo than I needed for my basement bedroom. Rollie basically told the guy at Sound World we wanted really good, solid, and reliable stuff, and we walked out with a turntable, amplifier, cassette deck, and a huge pair of JBL speakers I still have today.

That was probably the happiest day in all my miserable years in Floyd Valley, and I'm not sure I'll ever feel the thrill I experienced when we got that stereo home and Rollie helped me set it up in my room. My mother seemed genuinely happy for me and grateful to Rollie, but I could tell Baron was pissed.

"I don't remember discussing this," he said when Rollie and I hauled the stuff in from the car.

"What's to discuss?" Rollie said.

Baron hovered and huffed as we set it up. It was clearly a much better stereo than his own RadioShack setup.

"I really hope this isn't going to be an issue around here," he said.

"Why don't you both try to not make it an issue," Rollie said, "and we'll get Matty some headphones."

As thrilled as I was, I was in serious withdrawal from Russ's record collection, and I became even more preoccupied with building a collection of my own.

The high school in Floyd Valley was a lot bigger than my old school in Prentice. The classes were often two or three times the size, which made it even easier to be invisible and to sleepwalk through the school day.

There weren't a lot of pleasant surprises in that stretch of my life, but I was excited to discover that Greenland and Valentine Earle had been reunited and now lived with an aunt in Floyd Valley. Greenland had pretty much disappeared from my life over the last year, and I don't think I was ever happier to see someone.

Greenland and Valentine were living in a trailer park not far from Baron's house. We drove right by it, in fact, on our way into town every day. It was this big, sprawling cluster of trailers and trucks and junked cars and clotheslines. It looked like a much bigger version of their grandfather's junkyard in Prentice.

I quickly figured out that the river behind the house—I would never learn to think of it as my house, or even *our* house—would take you right past the Keystone Trailer Park, and in time the river would become the corridor Greenland and I used to sneak back and forth late at night. The first day I saw Greenland, though, he was sitting alone in the back seat of the school bus and banging on the seat in front of him with what appeared to be a huge cow bone. I heard the banging but didn't notice Greenland until the bus driver admonished him to be quiet.

It turned out he was trying to get my attention. After he stopped banging, he commenced whining in a high-pitched voice, "Corn Dog! Corn Dog!" That was the inexplicable name he called me whenever he wanted to get on my nerves.

I was instantly dragged back into Greenland's strange world. He carried that bone with him for months, rattling it off lockers and tossing it around like a drumstick or a baton; he insisted it was a dinosaur bone.

The first time Greenland hiked along the river and trudged up the slope to bang on my window at one o'clock in the morning, he said, "Your mother left Russ for a guy with a gazebo? How weak is that? He must have a big old boner for her."

I'd never much noticed the gazebo and didn't have any idea what it was. The thing was perched at the edge of the backyard overlooking the river. In time that white gazebo would become one more of Baron's embarrassments. He kept an upright piano in the garage, and in the summer, he would pay guys to move it out to the gazebo. Most nights he would go out there for what he called his "dusk recitals." Some of his friends and people from the neighborhood would actually drag lawn chairs and blankets over to the yard, and they'd all sit around drinking wine and egging him on. Many nights some of his favorite students would come over to sing with him or play violins and cellos. Baron would dress up for these recitals as if he were appearing in a concert hall or some shitty cocktail lounge.

I couldn't handle any of this. He would actually sit there playing the piano in his gazebo while my mother or I mowed the lawn. I never saw the guy lift a finger around the place. Before we came along, he had a housekeeper and paid someone to take care of his lawn. One day, after he'd covered his piano and trundled back across the yard, he wiped his brow with a handkerchief as I was finishing up with the mowing. "Whew," he said, looking at me and raising his eyebrows. "Mastering an art form is incredibly hard work. I'm still not quite there, but I continue to make baby steps." I couldn't muster anything but a blank stare. I don't think I ever smiled or laughed in that man's presence.

One time early in our difficult years together, that man I would never learn to call my stepfather stuck his head down the stairs and bellowed my name dramatically—he was the only person in my life who unfailingly called me by my full name: "MATH-HEW!" (invariably shouted or hissed.) Though I quickly learned not to be so responsive, I left my room to see what he wanted. As I said, this was early in the deal, and he was still maybe trying to make some minimal and condescending effort to win me over or, God forbid, "bond with me."

From the top of the stairs he waggled a copy of Eric Clapton's *Timepieces*—some greatest-hits package, I think—and did this jumpy eyebrow thing he did when he thought he was being playful. "*Sloooowhand*," he mock-whispered, as if he were offering me something illicit—this was the DJ voice he used when he was trying to sound really hip or knowing, and it made my skin crawl. "Wanna have a listen?"

I, of course, declined and told him I was working on some stuff for school, which was a lie. I didn't yet know him well enough to be a truly willful dick; if anything, I was still in that early awkward stage where I was just bashful and painfully uncomfortable around him. I did, though, recognize the *Slowhand* ruse for exactly what it was. He wouldn't, it turned out, make these sorts of gestures often, or for much longer. I think he quickly figured out the whole buddy part of stepparenting wasn't his bag. I also don't think he liked me, and truth be told I didn't give him many reasons to. Maybe if I'd been a different kind of kid, things would've been different. Remembering the *Slowhand* incident now, I can almost feel sorry for him. Suppose he bought that record—conferred with a clerk and painfully deliberated over his selection—merely in an attempt to please me? Maybe it was my fault. Maybe all of it was my fault.

I was already disgracefully self-conscious when I met Baron, but being around him all the time and brooding over his behavior and affectations made me self-conscious in a whole new way. Who the hell did Baron think he was? What did he think people saw when they looked at him? Were these even things he considered?

You cannot, of course, ever see yourself as others see you. You can't begin to imagine, and absolutely don't want to imagine, how others see you, or what they think when they see you, or what ideas and images go through their heads when they think of you. Surely even someone as seemingly self-confident as Baron would be seriously wounded if he really knew how and what I thought of him, and what other kids at school thought about him.

You can suspect—rightly, wrongly—all sorts of things about how you're perceived. You can cultivate and project some self-image, and some people are obviously really good at this, and they more or less succeed in becoming the person they pretend to be. But how many of them aren't, at least to some extent, acting? How many truly authentic people are there? I don't know why I waste time with questions like that, but I do. And I also suspect many other people get carried away with trying to get their heads around such ideas, with trying to figure out not just who they are but who other people think they are.

Maybe you look in the mirror first thing in the morning or when you're in the bathroom at a gas station, or maybe you're on a first date or at a business meeting that's going poorly, and you sort of squint at your reflection and turn your head back and forth, appraising, trying to look at yourself from some remove, as gauzy and filtered as possible, but you can't stand it, can't do it, don't have it in you to really see yourself, let alone to see the person the rest of the world sees when they look at you. At some point you maybe learn to recognize you're not that guy the world sees, that you're something less, or something more, or just something else. And maybe life is learning to make your peace with that.

In my longest, darkest nights I like to think I know who I am, or at least that I know how much fractious company I keep, how crowded it is. I know I contain multitudes. I also know it would be the greatest and most crippling of misfortunes to have even the briefest, punishing glimpse into how I'm truly seen by other people—a cruel remark overheard from the next room, a retributive slip of brutal honesty, a vengeful snipe from a complete stranger on a crowded sidewalk. I don't believe I could bear that sort of knowledge, and I'm sure that has a lot to do with why I've always been so hesitant to allow other people to know me. The Cowboy and I, of course, spent a lot of time over the years going back and forth on this subject.

"With few exceptions," he said, "the rest of the world probably isn't going to know you in a truly meaningful sense, and what they're going to surmise is likely to be based on whatever it is you project, and/or their own superficial preconceptions and personalities. Who you believe yourself to be, though, that's different! And it's a very important difference."

I knew the Cowboy was right about that, or perhaps I just supposed he was right. And I spent a lot of time wrestling with that question. Who was I? Who did I intend to be? Or *what* (the question that was pressed on me all the time)? And my best answer to all of those questions was *this*. I'm sure I thought I was somehow being authentic, or at least that's what I was shooting for. I wanted to accept that I was what I helplessly was. Perhaps I couldn't articulate it any better than that, but all the Cowboy's prodding was effective in a way, in that it always drove me back to that same blank certainty: this is who I am, this is who I have been, this is who I will be, and this is who I want to be. If it wasn't, why wouldn't I choose to be someone else?

There were problems with this line of thinking as well, as the Cowboy pointed out. Specifically, what was *this*? "A human being and its personality and identity aren't simply something you can point to and say, 'That is Matthew Carnap' and be done with it. You're not a ball, or a pencil. Do you see what I'm saying? There are all sorts of things you or I could point to and identify with the same certainty we possessed when we were toddlers. Our ideas about such things don't change much; if I ask you to bring me a pencil or a ball, you'll know what I'm talking about."

"How would I know what kind of ball you wanted?" I said.

"Okay," the Cowboy said. "See? How do I know what kind of ball you are? What do I, or what do you, learn when you persist in saying, 'I am this, this is me'? You need to learn to define those terms, if only for yourself."

"I don't know how," I said.

"Yes, you do," the Cowboy said. "It doesn't have to be like a dictionary definition, but you should be able to say what you believe in or stand for. Whether you recognize it or not, the core principles that will shape the rest of your life are being built inside you. You *are* becoming someone, and for a good long time you're still going to be in the process of becoming someone else, someone other than who you precisely are at this moment. And understanding who you precisely are at this moment beyond just a defiant 'I' is important to that change. The world and circumstances beyond your control are going to dictate what happens to some extent, but you're also going to have to make choices. You're going to come to fork after fork in the road, and it's going to be up to you to decide which paths you choose. Granted, you'll encounter plenty of people who just allow themselves to be carried along, but if you have a strong and well-developed concept of who you are and what you want, you're going to be in a much better position to make choices that are consistent with the life you imagine for yourself. If you know where you're going, or where you want to go, doesn't it stand to reason you're more likely to get there?"

The Floyd Valley years passed in a slow-motion, almost time-lapse, muddle. After maybe six months Baron more or less gave up on me. His surrender coincided with his marriage to my mother—they were married in a stupid little ceremony in the gazebo, over Labor Day weekend. He still routinely bitched about my music, but I never got the impression I was being uniquely persecuted, and I generally ignored him.

I was relatively free to do whatever I wanted in my basement bunker, and I didn't interact with either Baron or my mother enough to feel like I was being scrutinized. I had plenty of time alone and often had the house to myself and could blast my stereo as loud as I wanted. I think in retrospect that the years from fourteen to sixteen were the most boring and challenging of all. I was absolutely done with childhood, I knew that much, but I didn't yet have the full liberties of a teenager, let alone an adult.

Russ got back in touch with me a few months after the move, but I only saw him a handful of times those first couple years. Usually we got together when he was in Floyd Valley, and we'd make the rounds of the record and thrift stores and maybe get a pizza. These encounters were awkward for both of us. He was clearly depressed, and whenever he left I would feel a lingering sadness for days. I missed him and the rink like crazy, and I recognized that outside the rink he was painfully out of his element. It had always been this way with him, of course; the rink was his context, the world away from the rink an endless series of agonizing and awkward confrontations. He never asked about my mother. I tried to talk to him about Baron, but he'd get gloomy whenever I did. It was still too sore a subject, for both of us, really. I remember one time I tried to describe Baron's gazebo recitals to him (this after telling him the *Slowhand* story). He was silent for a moment and then said, with a completely straight face, "I'd kill him. What you're describing is psychological warfare."

For the most part I seldom touched the money in my bank account, but one time I drove up to the Twin Cities with Rollie to see a baseball game, on the condition that he would take me to a couple record stores. Before we left, I stopped off at the bank and withdrew $200, which seemed wildly extravagant at the time, but I was determined to come back with some of the music—it didn't really matter what—that I remembered from the rink.

This was one of the first years the Twins were playing in the thoroughly crummy Metrodome, so it was probably 1985 or '86. Rollie thought that ridiculous dump was one of the most incredible things he'd ever seen. It was an afternoon game, I remember, and I couldn't wait for the damn thing to end so we could go record shopping. As the game dragged on and on, and as Rollie schmoozed with his liquor-industry pals who had hooked us up with the expensive seats, I fretted that the record stores would be closed before we could get to them. Late in the game, when I expressed this concern to Rollie, he said, "Relax, Bubby, this ain't Prentice or Floyd Valley. Stuff stays open late."

We eventually made it to Northern Lights downtown and Positively Fourth Street by the University of Minnesota. I'd been in both on a handful of occasions with Russ, and they were almost otherworldly places to me. All the Minneapolis independent record stores in those days were fantastic—the Electric Fetus, Northern Lights, Oar Folkjokeopus, Positively Fourth Street, Wax Museum, Sursumcorda, and probably several others I'm forgetting—and every time I walked into one of them I experienced a surge of joy and expectation. There was a level of anxiety—or perhaps panic—in these visits as well; I never knew where to start, and I always felt rushed. I could've easily spent all day in most of the stores, and there were so many tantalizing and unfamiliar records. That day, though, I was focused on finding the familiar, and I had no problem spending all $200. The challenge was in not spending it all at Northern Lights.

I wished Russ had been there to point me toward some of the newer stuff. I was happy, though, with my purchases. Ecstatic, actually. I spent the drive home shuffling through the pile of records on my lap and studying the photos and notes. For the next three or four years my trips to the Twin Cities to buy records would be the highlights of an otherwise boring life. At the very least I know that when I look back on my high school years, I think of the music I listened to and the trips to those record stores, most of which are long gone.

I was also spending a lot of time with Greenland Earle those days, and our time together mostly consisted of trying to find ways to amuse ourselves.

The trailer Greenland and Valentine lived in with their aunt was owned by their grandfather on their mother's side. The grandfather, an old biker, was the caretaker at the trailer park. They'd built a wheelchair ramp up to the door of the trailer as well as a deck around the front, so Valentine could sit out there in his chair. Greenland and I had absolutely no social network beyond each other. We were like Stone Age teenagers. We fucked around on the river, built rafts out of whatever scrap materials we could find. Threw rocks and snowballs and blew shit up whenever we managed to get our hands on fireworks. Sometimes we hung out in the little park downtown. Greenland smoked all the time back then, openly, and some nights when he'd come up the river and tap on the patio door outside my bedroom, he would have liquor he'd stolen from somewhere. One time he showed up with a gym bag full of those little airplane bottles of vodka, whiskey, and rum. We had built a fort just up the riverbank from Baron's house, a bunker made of scavenged cinder blocks, plywood, and two-by-fours. Our hideaway was well hidden, and over time we kept excavating further and further into the bank until we had enough room for a couple old chairs we fished out of a landfill. The dirt floor was covered with several layers of carpet remnant, and the ceiling was reinforced with studs and plywood and covered with more carpeting, sod, and rocks. We spent a lot of time in there, working at becoming burnouts; Greenland, I suppose, was already there, but I was entering new territory all the time.

Greenland kept coming up the river with more and more liquor. We had cases of beer, a growing collection of cheap wine, and, eventually, hundreds of those tiny airline bottles of hard liquor. Greenland refused to tell me where he got all this stuff, but I had a hard time believing either his grandfather or his aunt wouldn't notice the disappearance of so much booze. I never knew Greenland to have contact with any other kids besides Valentine and me, and I had no idea what he got up to when we weren't together.

By the summer after our sophomore year, he was getting his hands on pot as well as an assortment of pipes and bongs. I had to be initiated into each step of my descent into full burnout status; Greenland had to explain what we were doing, how we did it, and why we were doing it. Even today I wonder who the hell initiated him or how he came by his own knowledge of these things, let alone the things themselves.

I discovered I loved almost any mind-altering substance. Why wouldn't I? The alcohol and pot didn't affect me the way they did Greenland, whose responses were more stereotypical—he'd become more animated and talkative and impulsive when he drank, funnier and more contemplative when he was stoned. Both alcohol and pot had pretty much the same effect on me: they were relaxing, profoundly so. Pot in particular had the ability to shift my brain into neutral, where I could idle pleasantly for hours at a time. At a certain point I would shut down entirely; I think for the first time in my life there were stretches when my brain ceased operating, as if a circuit breaker had been tripped. I started experiencing brief periods of actual sleep. I would go out to the river in the middle of the night to smoke pot alone, and when I came back to my room, I would have to lie down to keep from falling over. In the last two or three hours before the sun made its appearance, I would roll around in the shallowest waters of sleep, lulled by the murmuring tide of the world. Still, it was a fitful sleep at best, I suppose— I don't ever recall waking and feeling refreshed or even rested.

It didn't take me long to get tired of alcohol and pot. I'd inherited an almost inhuman tolerance from my father's side of the family, and pretty quickly I learned it didn't really make much difference if I drank or smoked more—the results were essentially the same: I merely shut down. Part of the problem I'm sure was that there wasn't anything active or social about these activities. It was usually just Greenland and me alone in our fort or wandering in a stupor along the river. My challenge had always been boredom, and though I found the feeling of being drunk or stoned pleasant enough, this period of experimentation was ultimately just another exercise in boredom and only served to aggravate my worst tendencies. I probably couldn't have articulated it as such at the time, but I was desperate for more feeling instead of less. I was becoming thoroughly stupid, and I was aware of this and disgusted by it.

I felt like I was letting the Cowboy down, and letting myself down. I saw "normal" kids at school and around town, and I was increasingly aware that I wasn't like them and, further, that they mostly had things—social skills, energy, enthusiasm, friends—that I didn't have and wanted, even if I had no idea how I might get them or where they came from. I also sensed that Greenland was wired in a way I could never truly be, and I already knew he was destined for serious trouble I wanted no part of.

Greenland didn't have any money, and it was plenty obvious his family didn't have any either. He'd mentioned his aunt was on welfare, and he'd occasionally have a wad of food stamps. I'm pretty sure, though, that he stole those from his aunt or his grandfather. I'm also sure he stole stuff from all over town, but he didn't talk or brag about it. I suspect stealing was just one of his many survival skills, and though I learned from harrowing experience that he was a masterful shoplifter—we'd go into a store, then later he'd produce all sorts of stuff he'd clearly lifted without my knowledge while we were there—his more public stealing was brazen, almost heedless. I knew he'd steal stuff off trucks or out of cars, from garages and yards. This, of course, was before the days of ubiquitous surveillance cameras and sophisticated inventory systems, but a lot of what Greenland was stealing was stuff whose absence people would surely notice and report, and Floyd Valley wasn't a big enough town that you could get away with that sort of thing for long.

Greenland was one of the smartest and most canny people I've ever known. I could never figure out how he knew all the things he knew—big words, world history, geography, and all sorts of practical skills I would never be able to master. But he seemed to have zero regard for his own intelligence, no interest in school, no ambition, no real passion beyond his desire to do whatever he wanted. He couldn't stand anyone telling him what to do, and that hardwired rebellious streak made him, I suppose, essentially immoral, or perhaps amoral. Given a different set of circumstances and a different family, he might've become one of those guys who goes off to the wilderness to live off the land.

He did eventually get caught. And once he got caught it snowballed—people all over town started fingering him whenever stuff went missing. It turned out the liquor he was stealing was mostly from my uncles. Their distribution trucks serviced many of the bars and liquor stores in Floyd Valley and usually made deliveries through back entrances accessible from alleys. While the driver dollied in cases of beer, Greenland would climb into the truck, grab what he could, and make his getaway. A neighbor who lived across the alley from one of the liquor stores saw him making off with a case of beer one day and called the police. When the police ran him down, he was riding a stolen bike and sitting awkwardly on top of the case of beer, which was balanced on the bike seat.

I wasn't, strictly speaking, an accomplice to Greenland's crimes. I don't know, maybe I was. Surely, people would say to me all the time, I knew about his stealing. Baron and my mother grilled me. My uncles grilled me. I was called in and questioned by the high school's police liaison officer in the principal's office. I told the truth, carefully, perhaps selectively: Sure, I *suspected* Greenland was stealing, but there was no collusion. I didn't steal anything myself and had never had any discussion with him about the subject.

I refused to rat Greenland out. I also never mentioned our fort or offered any specifics. I wasn't present when he was questioned, but he apparently kept me out of it as well. Still, as far as everyone was concerned, I was clearly guilty by association, and I was warned repeatedly that I was no longer to have anything to do with him.

I ultimately would have no say in the matter. Greenland was already in plenty of trouble, but after a couple weeks of investigations and interrogations he was finally persuaded—or coerced—to confess to a series of break-ins of several homes and trailers around Floyd Valley. It was a huge scandal, especially at the high school, where anyone who had been paying attention at all knew I was pretty much his only friend. Greenland had put me on the radar, and not in a good way. I suddenly had a bad reputation, but the new attention, although unwelcome, was weirdly respectful. People kept their distance.

My mother was appalled, and Baron was furious. They grounded me, ineffectively, of course—I could still get in and out of the house after they fell asleep. I was a marked man, though, and suddenly felt conspicuous wherever I went. After being questioned three or four times at great length by various authorities, I was paranoid.

I had no contact with Greenland, but he was scheduled to appear in juvenile court, and I received a summons to testify. I was terrified, and for two weeks I worried constantly about what I would be asked and what I would say. My mother was certain I was lying to her and seemed convinced I was Greenland's full partner in his criminal activities. Nothing I said could persuade her otherwise. Baron hired a lawyer to talk me through the process and accompany me to the hearing. This guy—he couldn't have been thirty yet—also clearly believed I was lying and kept advising me not to say anything to incriminate myself. "As of right now, you're not charged with anything," he said. "And we need to make sure it stays that way. When in doubt, plead ignorance. 'I don't know' is a perfectly good answer to any question."

The experience shook me up, but I wasn't afraid for myself. I was, though, terrified for Greenland. The lawyer tried to convince me that Greenland had everything to lose and was likely to say anything to save his ass. I hadn't seen or spoken to him since a couple days before he was arrested, and we both had to wait almost three weeks before the hearing. I continued to go to school during this time, but Greenland was absent. I could tell people were talking about us, but nobody at school said a word to me about any of it.

Baron and my mother insisted on taking me to Younkers to buy me a suit and tie for Greenland's hearing, which was ridiculous. I wasn't charged with anything.

The day of the hearing was an awful anticlimax. Greenland was sitting in the front row of the small courtroom next to his lawyer and his grandfather Eldon, who was hooked up to an oxygen tank. Greenland waved and smiled when I entered the room. I felt foolish in my suit, and was accompanied by my mother, Baron, Uncle Rollie, and the lawyer. Greenland was dressed exactly as he would've been dressed on any other day: jeans, sweatshirt, and tennis shoes.

The hearing didn't last long. There were no real dramatics, no witnesses or cross-examinations. It was nothing like TV. The judge did most of the talking and asked most of the questions.

Greenland answered every question honestly and matter-of-factly. He didn't deny anything. The judge asked him if he had any explanations for his behavior, and Greenland merely shrugged and answered, "I was bored." He was asked if he had had accomplices, or if anyone had been in any way involved in, or aware of, his crimes.

"It was just me," Greenland said.

His lawyer spent some time quietly conferring with the judge, who then turned his attention to me.

"How do you know Mr. Earle?" he asked.

"Greenland?" I said, and the judge smiled and nodded. "He's my best friend, I suppose," I said.

"And how long have you known each other?"

"Maybe three or four years," I said.

"And in those years of your friendship were you at any time aware that Mr. Earle was engaged in any of the activities of which he is accused?"

"Not really," I said. "He never said anything about it to me."

"He never enlisted your assistance in breaking into people's cars or homes?"

"No," I said.

The judge asked Greenland if I was telling the truth.

"He always tells the truth," Greenland said. "We both do."

The judge then read off a long list of the crimes Greenland was charged with and asked him if he had in fact committed each of them.

"Yes," Greenland said. "I think so. I don't remember specific addresses."

"But you understand the charges and are prepared to plead guilty?"

"Yes," Greenland said.

"And you understand the consequences?"

"I never understand the consequences," Greenland said.

"But you're prepared to accept them?"

Greenland shrugged. "I guess so. I don't suppose I have much choice."

This was not, of course, the first time Greenland had been in trouble. There had apparently been several previous incidents in Prentice involving theft and vandalism. And there was his time at the Sheriff's Boys' Ranch before I met him, although I never learned what he did to get sent there. I didn't understand trouble then, had no real conception of consequences, and certainly couldn't imagine being in the spot that Greenland was in. As I sat there in the courtroom trying to grasp what was happening and studying Greenland—he was so cool, betrayed no anxiety, no anger, no feelings at all—I was in awe of his bravery and secretiveness. I knew I wasn't capable of either, didn't know how to be furtive, brazen, or dangerous. There was no way I could break into a stranger's house in the middle of the night. I wished then that I'd made a greater effort to talk to Greenland about these things, pried a little harder, not because I wanted to know how to do the stuff he'd done, but because I was curious about how he did it and why. Clearly there was a lot about him I didn't know and hadn't tried to understand.

His lawyer outlined a brief, pathetic history of Greenland's life: all the bouncing around he and Valentine had done, his responsibility for and devotion to Valentine, his lack of proper adult supervision, the criminal history of both his parents. He mentioned a family history of mental illness and a childhood of "profound dysfunction," and said that according to Greenland's school records, his intelligence was "off the charts." He argued that Greenland hadn't been given a chance; his life, he said, was a textbook history of deprivation and neglect, and if he were given a stable environment, proper attention, encouragement, structure, and discipline, there was every reason to expect that he would thrive.

"The system has failed this young man," the lawyer concluded. "He doesn't understand consequences precisely because he has never been treated as a consequential human being."

The judge was clearly unmoved. He offered Greenland one last chance to speak for himself, and Greenland merely shrugged and said, "I don't have anything else to say."

There was a break in the proceedings, and our overdressed little party retreated to the lobby of the courthouse, where Baron immediately turned to me and said, "What in God's name is wrong with you? It's a miracle you're not in exactly the same mess as that miserable little criminal. It's only a matter of time before he kills someone."

My mother not only made no attempt to defend me but piped in as well. "I'm so disappointed in you, Matthew," she said. "Such poor judgment. You should know better than to get mixed up in a mess like this. I don't for one second believe you didn't know exactly what was going on."

I didn't want to listen to either of them, and in that moment I resolved to never listen to anything either of them said to me ever again. In all the time I'd known Greenland, my mother had never so much as met or spoken to him. Granted, the majority of the time I spent with Greenland was as far from the world of adults as we could get, but she knew he was my friend, and if she'd paid attention, she would've known he was my *only* friend. I had instinctively known neither she nor Baron would approve of Greenland, just as I had known neither of them would ever try to really know him.

Russ had met him, though, and would try to engage him when Greenland came around the rink. I think Russ got a kick out of him. "He's a curious little dude," he once said to me. Russ was also super sweet to Valentine, would bend down next to the wheelchair and speak to him exactly as he would speak to anyone else. I used to marvel at his ability to make Valentine smile and even laugh his gurgling little laugh. I was proud both Greenland and Valentine were so comfortable at the rink and that Russ was always welcoming to them, even though they never spent a penny in the place and I never once succeeded in getting Greenland to strap on a pair of skates. And actually it's not true that they never spent money at the rink, because every time they came to hang out with me, Russ would give us all rolls of quarters for the soda, chips, and candy machines. That was really the only pack I ever belonged to, and those memories are mostly what I think of when I think of my childhood.

I was still a few years away from really being able to open up, but I felt a huge sadness that day. I think I understood that that chapter of my life was ending. It had been ending since the day my mother and I drove out of Prentice and out of Russ's life. When I reconnected with Greenland in Floyd Valley, it had felt like a reprieve from my grieving, like I was given an unexpected and merciful extension of my childhood.

That day would in fact be the official end. The judge sent Greenland to the juvenile reformatory in Red Wing, where he would be locked away until he turned eighteen. We all sat there for a while in silence after Greenland was led away. He turned and gave me one last wave as he disappeared out a side door, and I felt certain I was seeing him for the last time.

My academic performance that first year in Floyd Valley—I think it was my sophomore year (I was never a kid who bought year-books or kept any paper trail related to school)—was abysmal. At some point the Cowboy procured me a prescription for Ritalin, and in many ways it proved to be a very effective and even pleasurable drug for me. It did nothing for my sleep, but it dissipated the fog in the morning, sharpened my focus and concentration, and gave me an energy I'd never found anywhere else outside of the rink. I actually felt engaged by some of my classes—most notably English, American history, social studies, and psychology—and I managed, somewhat miraculously, to become a pretty decent student.

At the very least I credit Ritalin—and the Cowboy—with getting me the rest of the way through high school. I graduated, and for a long time that had seemed like an impossible goal. School would never, though, be pleasant, and there were too many early and agonizing experiences for me to ever regard it as anything but an ordeal. My last year of high school was an endurance test. I had no social life, avoided both Baron and my mother, and was just count-ing the days until I could be done with the whole boring racket. I'd already talked to my uncles about going to work in the family busi-ness. I didn't care in what capacity; I was simply determined to do anything possible to avoid going to college. In hindsight, I'm sur-prised I got so little pushback about this decision from my fam-ily. But maybe I shouldn't be; none of them went to college, and they didn't have any real perspective on the subject. I also sus-pect they were all so astonished and relieved I'd managed to gradu-ate from high school that the idea of college was too exhausting to contemplate. Perhaps unsurprisingly, the only person who made a real push to persuade me to go—or at the very least to enroll in some classes at Floyd Valley Junior College—was the Cowboy.

"The world out there beyond Floyd Valley is radically different from the world your aunts and uncles—or even your mother—grew up in," he told me. "It's different than the world they live in now. This world. A college degree, a college education, opens up so many possibilities that don't exist in a lot of places like this. I have a hard time imagining you being happy spending your life in Floyd Valley or Prentice. Maybe you still don't know what you want, or at least aren't prepared to admit it, but I would hate to think that when you eventually figure it out, you find out you don't have the qualifications. So many interesting jobs now require a college degree."

"I can't imagine going to school again," I said.

"Then what is it you *can* imagine?" the Cowboy asked.

"I'm not sure," I said. "I'm working on it."

"You better be," the Cowboy said. "The meter is officially running. This is your life now. There's going to come a point in the near future where whatever frustrations and failures you experience are going to be yours and yours alone."

I now recognize that, in many ways, I was a pretty spoiled kid. But I never got a lot of what I'll call keen attention during my childhood or adolescence. Because I had so few actual friends and engaged in none of the organized activities that occupied so many other kids' childhoods, I didn't experience much in the way of peer influence. The only kid I could point to as having any influence on me was Greenland, but unlike with Russ, Greenland's peculiar personality didn't rub off on me. I admired him and found him entertaining, was grateful for his friendship, but I could never be like him, and I didn't try. I also knew that, left to my own devices, I never would've tried to befriend him. Even now I can't figure out what it was I got from him. I suppose he expanded my imagination; he certainly had no problem imagining things, and he had a way of making the dreams he regularly talked about vivid to me. He often talked, for instance, about the two of us going to New York City, or of his dream of hopping trains and traveling out west to the mountains, or of traveling down the Mississippi to New Orleans.

I was never sure how or where Greenland learned the things he knew, but I can see now that was because I was a kid and not paying proper attention—I hung out at the library all the time, and Greenland sometimes tagged along with me.

I was drawn to stories and the music room and routinely checked out piles of books and records. Though I don't remember Greenland ever checking anything out—I'm not even sure he had a library card—I now recall he used to sit at one of the long white tables in the art section, just outside the record room, with stacks of art and photography books that he would make his way through, turning the pages slowly and intently studying the images. Before this moment, I would've sworn I somehow discovered all those photo books on my own, but it was Greenland who discovered them and who called my attention to them.

"Look at this," he'd say, drawing me away from the records, and I'd sit beside him at the white table, and together we would stare into the photographs of Walker Evans, William Eggleston, Robert Frank, and Diane Arbus. "This is all America," Greenland would say, whispering excitedly in a rare display of respect for decorum. "We need a car, Corn Dog. We have to go out there and see some of this stuff and some of these people. This is where all your music comes from."

Those books, and those pictures, are still inextricably linked to most of my romanticized notions of the United States and its seemingly endless wonders. It was rare to find a picture in those books that looked anything like the world we'd grown up in. I hadn't traveled much, but Greenland had; throughout his early childhood his parents had crisscrossed the country several times, mainly moving from the West Coast to Minnesota on a couple occasions, but there were also brief stints in Vermont and upstate New York.

"We went wherever there were hippies," Greenland told me. "I don't remember most of it, but when we were driving around, I remember seeing stuff that looked just like some of this stuff in these books. It was like a movie." We were both drawn to photos of big cities—New York, primarily—but the pictures of the South and the desolate, wide-open spaces of the West also had an allure.

The Prentice Library had a remarkable collection of photography monographs, every bit as improbable as its record collection, and much of it I would later learn came from the same source. The oldest son of the man who was president of the appliance factory when I was a kid died of leukemia in his early thirties, and his family donated his books and records to the library. Every one of the photo books had a bookplate in the front with his name—Steven Capp—and almost everything I discovered in that library seemed to come from either his collection or from the cutout bins at Lansing Drug.

At some point I dug around in the library's microfiche to try to learn a little more about Steven Capp. I found out he had graduated from Prentice High School, gone off to the University of Chicago to study classics, and then been accepted to the Iowa Writer's Workshop, where he worked at becoming a poet. Somewhere I have a folder full of his poems, poems I spent years tracking down in mostly obscure literary journals. I remember the poems as difficult, but I have no idea if they were any good.

I learned to believe that, as Greenland had said, the world in those photographs was where the music I loved came from. I started to associate my favorite albums and songs with particular photographers and images. In a weird way, spending so much time looking through those books—usually while listening to music on my Walkman—expanded my imagination in a way all the books I read growing up never did. I could study the people and places in the pictures and feel as if I'd been someplace else. Those books were also an education in looking, in how to really see the world around me. It seems obvious now, but I think I went through life looking straight ahead and trying to pay attention to what the world wanted me to pay attention to, and I noticed that most of the photos that really fascinated me were of things in the margins or peripheries, things you had to actually look *around* to see.

This development delighted the Cowboy. He asked me to bring in some of the books I found particularly interesting so we could look at photographs together. One week I brought in the library's copy of William Eggleston's *Guide*—one of my favorites—and the Cowboy was as fascinated by it as I was.

"What do you make of this?" he said.

"It's like songs," I said. "And sometimes it's like nothing."

"Or maybe not nothing," the Cowboy said, flipping slowly through the book in his lap. "But I know what you mean. It's like the kind of thing you might look at a hundred times a day to the point you no longer even process it. Glimpses into things that become so familiar that when you actually see them, they seem exotic and out of place. How are they like music to you?"

"I'm not sure," I said. "Maybe it's that songs make me really see them. Or they're like the things in your life that music helps you escape. They're so quiet."

"They are quiet," he said. "That's the thing about photographs. If you really look at them hard enough and long enough, your imagination or your memory starts to animate them. You hear voices, traffic, dogs barking, a door slam. The world of that moment was moving. Other things were going on outside the frame of each individual picture. An instant earlier or later, and you'd be looking at a different picture. Things were happening when the photographer froze these moments. They're a part of something, right? A life, an experience, a place in time. If a song is like a little stretch of a river, a photograph is more like a boat tied off at a dock, but your imagination and your memory can untie the boat and put it back in the river, make it move. You can take it down the river or back up the river."

That conversation, which carried on for many months, was probably my one true breakthrough with the Cowboy. Perhaps because it really felt like a conversation, and he seemed as energized by it as I was. Together we would *interrogate* (to use the Cowboy's word) the photographs, posing questions, making an inventory of details and speculations. "This is forensics," he said. "First, we'll treat every photograph as a crime scene, then we'll gradually try to move in less cool or clinical directions. We'll try to be both tough and compassionate. What's the first question that comes to your mind when you look at a picture?"

"What's going on?" I said.

"Exactly. What else?"

"Where is this? Who's this person?"

"Right," the Cowboy said. "Who's this person? Who are these people? What are they doing? Where are we? When was this? What is this thing, and why is it worthy of attention? What was going on here before this picture was taken, and what happened next? A lot of these pictures might be stories in and of themselves. Some of them could be entire novels. Others might be a brief chapter of a story or a poem."

"Or a song," I said.

"Absolutely," he said. "You can try to figure out what song. The more time I spend looking at these photographs, the more details I notice, and from those details I can surmise—or maybe just imagine—things about these places and people. Their taste, for instance. How they dress. The way they furnish their homes. Whether they look happy or sad, rich or poor. What kinds of cars they drive, and the houses they live in, and the condition of their lawns."

We looked at the portraits taken by August Sander and Diane Arbus. "In many ways," the Cowboy said, "for someone in my line of work, these are even more interesting and challenging than the Eggleston or Evans photos. They're complex, and both more and less ambiguous. We've talked about this quite a bit—who, or what, does the world see when it looks at us? How much can anyone really know from a portrait of us? If I took a hundred pictures of you, you would definitely recognize every one of them was 'you,' but how many would really represent either the way you see yourself or the way you want to be seen?"

"None," I said. "I hate pictures of myself."

"Maybe so," the Cowboy said. "But when we look at these portraits and try to pose the same questions we did of the other, very different photos, it's a much trickier investigation. We're liable to be wrong, and these would be mistakes with consequences. We're judging, really."

"The captions tell you what they are," I said.

"In a way," the Cowboy said. "Sander, especially, tells you something about these people, mostly what they do for a living, or some kind of label, but he can't tell you *who* they are. Still, we can try to see them, to recognize them. It's an act of empathy to try to understand who these people are, what they've been through, and what they might be up against. But they lived in a different time and probably spoke a different language. Probably the only things we can really know about them are the essentials, the things we might've felt or experienced ourselves. As long as we're feeling something, though, rather than merely engaging in cold speculation or stereotyping, we can learn something, if only about ourselves. The hope is that if you can learn to see and feel this way, eventually that current of compassion can flow both ways."

Years later, the Cowboy told me that the time we spent looking at and talking about photographs had perhaps benefitted him even more than me. He said it changed the way he thought about his work and proved effective with many of his other clients as well. "It continues to amaze me how much I can learn from someone based on their responses to some of these pictures," he said. "You can find out all sorts of telling things about where they're at and how they see themselves and the world. Whether they have a healthy capacity for empathy, for instance, whether they're open and curious or closed off. How functional their imagination is. And whether or not they're a narcissist, or even a psychopath."

One afternoon he presented me with a Polaroid camera and five boxes of film and asked me to take pictures of things that told a little story, or a series of brief stories, about my life. "You're still not very comfortable telling," he said. "Let's see how you do if you just concentrate on showing."

He also took a series of photos of me sitting in his office and asked me to write about each of them, approaching the assignment exactly as we'd approached the other photos we'd looked at. "Step as far outside yourself as you possibly can," he said, "and describe this person as if he were someone you've just seen for the first time. And then tell me exactly what *you* see. Look at yourself and imagine what other people see, or *who* other people see."

By the time I was a senior in high school, I knew only that I wanted life to be interesting. The Ritalin—and later the Adderall—allowed me to see things more clearly. I'll always be a channel surfer, but I learned how to zero in on the stuff that interested me instead of flitting mindlessly from one thing to the next. Attention deficit disorder is a conundrum—it has no tolerance for boredom, but in its most extreme manifestations is the ultimate boredom. You can't focus on any one thing, so you're bored and frustrated all the time.

I did as much as I needed to do to get by and to get Baron and my mother off my back, but I don't really believe I learned much of anything in school. The extent to which any class engaged me was generally in pointing me toward tangential stuff I had to explore on my own. I understood that the things I really wanted to know or learn were somewhere else.

XXVI.

I stand here at the long bank of windows in the press box and there's a cold, harsh glare of sunlight reflecting off everything in every direction—the football field buried in snow, the exposed bits of metal in the grandstands and along the edges of the scoreboard and sparking all around the wire fences that enclose the entire compound. You can tell by the way the smoke and steam dawdle above the houses and the desolate strip mall beyond, trapped beneath the low canopy of unbroken gray sky, that it's cold as shit out there.

Less than a week until Thanksgiving and Prentice already feels like Stalingrad. Almost nothing moves anywhere, and the cars and trucks that are moving all spew exhaust—more dawdling smoke and steam—and lurch, fishtailing, in fits and starts along the ice-crusted roads.

I've never in my life had a better vantage—or perhaps, on such days, a more clear-eyed and discouraging vantage. If I'd sat down and tried to dream up a perfect living space, I couldn't have imagined anything quite so perfect or spectacular as my press box penthouse. It's like a swanky tree house—the Swiss Family Robinson does Manhattan—and most of the things I've always believed mattered to me are stylishly arranged around me here. The *things*, though. Part of me understands how misguided I've been, and am. At some point I desperately wanted every one of these things, and most of the time, I *still* want them. For better or worse they are who I am, or who I've become. Most of the time—pretty much all the time—I can't imagine living without them. But I now know why so many of Russ's old favorite records made him so wrenchingly sad.

The weekly paper I worked for in Minneapolis had giant Dell desktops. I had almost no experience with computers at the time I took that job, and I used to stick around after hours trying desperately to figure out what this new monkey business was all about. I realized almost immediately that the World Wide Web was going to be the most destructive thing to ever happen to me. The type of brain I had would be useless against it. Instant gratification would replace delayed gratification, and I suddenly understood that delayed gratification had been precisely what kept me going all those years, the implicit hope that one day, if I kept looking and digging, I would find the things—and the answers—I was looking for.

Still, while I knew I couldn't possibly live in the Library of Babel, there was initially a lazy, idiot thrill to the whole free-for-all, even if I couldn't imagine it supplanting the joy of happily mucking around at the library and making new discoveries.

I'd completely lost touch with Russ by then, heard nothing from him in nearly seven years, in fact. The rink was gone by that time; the city had forced Russ out, torn down the entire block of buildings, and broken ground on a new fire station and municipal office complex.

He came to my high school graduation. When he showed up he looked as sad as I'd ever seen him. My mother, Baron, and my aunts and uncles were all crowded together in one of the front rows of the school auditorium, while Russ sat alone way in the back. He ducked into the aisle and gave me a quick hug as my class filed out, then disappeared. I invited him to join us for dinner at some local steakhouse, but I knew he wouldn't show.

I'd gone to Prentice the weekend before they tore down the rink building. Russ was reluctant to call Baron's house, and since he never answered his own phone anymore, I'd had a hard time getting in touch with him since we'd moved. I received the news the rink was closing from Rollie, my usual source of Prentice news. I was, of course, devastated. Rollie had come by on a Saturday afternoon to take me to dinner, and when I went out to the driveway and got in his car, he handed me a copy of the *Dispatch*. "Tough news, Bubby," he said. "It's all over but the shouting." I looked at the headline with disbelief: "Armory Building, Home of Fire Station,

Scheduled for Demolition." The brief article beneath the headline said Art Vargo had reached a deal with the city for the property, and the fire department would be temporarily relocated to the city maintenance building and garage on the east side. The entire block, including Misto's Tap, had also been acquired and was slated for demolition. The city planned to break ground on a new municipal complex in early spring. Screaming Wheels received only a two-sentence mention: "Also included in the acquisition is Vargo's Screaming Wheels, a roller-skating rink that has been in business since 1971. The rink was operated by Russell Vargo and had recently fallen on hard times."

Rollie and I went out for pizza, and we had even less to say to each other than usual.

"Your guy's gonna be all right," Rollie did tell me. "His old man got a boatload of cash for that building, and he's been selling off most of the family properties in town. I gotta believe Russ is going to come into some serious money. His family's always been loaded, and now they're really cashing in."

"What's he going to do?" I asked.

"Who knows," Rollie said. "What would a guy like that do with a shit ton of money?"

"That rink was his life," I said. "I can't imagine what else he would do."

Rollie shrugged. "Then I guess you'll have to ask him."

"I hardly ever talk to him anymore," I said, "and I haven't seen him for probably six months."

"You should stay in touch," Rollie said. "You guys are two peas in a pod."

When Rollie dropped me off back at the house, I asked him to tell Russ I was trying to get a hold of him and wanted to see the rink one more time before it was gone.

A couple days later Rollie called me. He had stopped by the rink to talk to Russ, and Russ had suggested I come by the following weekend to help him pack things up. I'd just gotten my driver's license, but neither Baron nor my mother seemed enthusiastic about letting me use their cars. I no longer felt comfortable even asking them for a ride to Prentice. My mother clearly wanted nothing to do with the place—I'm not sure she'd been back since the day we moved—and Baron regarded Prentice as beneath attention, and though he'd never met Russ, he'd made up his mind about him and wasn't bashful about saying he was a bad influence on me.

I came home from school one day in the middle of the week and Rollie and Mooze were waiting for me in the driveway. Even my uncles now seemed reluctant to come to the door and engage with Baron.

"It's time we got you a car, Bubby," Rollie said. "I don't mind schlepping you around, but you need some getaway wheels of your own." Rollie and Mooze had a pal who ran a dealership in Floyd Valley, one of those big car carnivals with hundreds of vehicles in the lot and plastic streamers strung all over the place, rattling in the wind.

We went into the showroom and sat around for a while, eating popcorn while my uncles shot the shit with their friends. They seemed to know all of the salesmen.

A guy named Louie Sack, who I'd known since I was a little kid and who had been part of the old Misto's gang, was the point man on the transaction. "What are we looking for today?" he asked.

"It's the kid's first car," Mooze said. "He needs something that screams 'Freedom.'"

"Absolutely," Rollie said. "The kind of car he could live in."

"He's going to live in this car?" Louie said.

"He just might," Mooze said.

"What do you think, kid?" Louie asked.

I shrugged. "I want a car with a stereo," I said. "A car that runs."

"They all run, numbnuts," Louie said. "You want something sporty that can go like hell?"

"He's not a sporty guy," Rollie said. "Solid and practical and maybe a little funky. Right, Bubs?"

I nodded.

"I think I have just the car," Louie said, and he led us out into the lot to a chestnut-brown station wagon. It was a 1984 Buick Skyhawk, built long and low, with 69,000 miles on the odometer and a skylight. "Four doors, plus the hatch," Louie said. "It's got eighty-four horsepower, five-speed manual transmission, and front-wheel drive. Body and interior are both in great shape, and the previous owner installed a nice Pioneer cassette deck with what I'm told are some very powerful speakers."

Rollie and I took the Skyhawk for a spin, and I felt a weird and uncharacteristic surge of what I think was ecstasy. I'd always been indifferent to cars and hadn't even been in much of a hurry to get my driver's license. Despite the fact that so much of the music I loved extolled the virtues of automobiles and the freedom they provided, they were still an abstraction back then, purely practical and entirely mysterious. I'd never spent time driving around in cars with other kids, and in my family, cars were little more than a means of getting from point A to point B. I'd never so much as entertained the notion of having a car of my own before. But as I drove around in that station wagon with Rollie, I had a sudden vision of all the ways a car would change my life.

Rollie had yanked the Boz Scaggs cassette from his own car and inserted it in the deck of the Skyhawk. That wouldn't have been my first choice, but it sounded magnificent, and as Rollie nudged the volume higher it was like being immersed in the music, a whole new experience, and even better than headphones. I'd loved listening to music in Russ's truck as a kid, but this was different. His truck only had two speakers down around the floor mats, nothing like the power of the ones in the Skyhawk, which had two speakers up front, two more in the passenger doors in the back seat, and two huge, booming speakers in the far back on each side of the hatch. It was one of those car stereos that could make the whole vehicle shake, and it sounded almost as good as the system at the rink.

"What do you think, Bubby?" Rollie said.

"I love it," I said, and I'm sure I was wide eyed and grinning ear to ear.

"You think this is the ticket?" he said.

"This is definitely the ticket," I said. "How much does it cost?"

"Don't worry, we'll take care of that," Rollie said. "Louie owes us some money. And I can add you and the car to the company policy. It'll be up to you to keep it running, which means you'll be on the hook for gas, oil changes, and all the basic maintenance. That'll be the deal. You fuck it up or run it into the ground, I'm going to be pissed and take it away. Is that a deal?"

"That's a deal," I said.

"It also means I now expect to see you more often," he said. "You're going to get your own ass over to Prentice to see your aunts and uncles. We miss you."

"Does my mom know about this?" I asked.

"She will soon enough," Rollie said. "It'll be a nice little surprise for her and that troll."

I loved that Skyhawk from the beginning. The back seat folded down, leaving enough horizontal space for two people to sleep comfortably. It was the perfect car for me, and I drove it the entire time I was working the Rubber Route, babied it and spent thousands keeping it running long past the point anybody else would've given it up for dead. When it finally broke down for good, I was in Escanaba, in the Upper Peninsula of Michigan, and I was devastated.

My mother and Baron were furious with my uncles—and me— about the car. Baron felt Rollie and Mooze had "usurped" his "authority." And my mother was upset that none of us had consulted her. "We're still your parents," she said, "and all this sneaking around behind our backs is disrespectful. We should have a say in big decisions like this. I'm the one who's going to have to sit here and wonder where you are and what you're up to when you're out driving around."

"You've never even offered to let me drive your cars," I said.

"You still haven't earned our trust," Baron said. "And we're the ones who are going to have to deal with any problems you have with that car. A car is an expensive thing to keep running, and you can't expect any handouts from us."

"I don't expect any handouts from you," I said. "It's my car, and I'll deal with it myself."

"It's *our* car," Baron said. "For as long as you live under this roof, we're a family. The same rules will apply to that car that apply to the other cars, and anything else, for that matter. You will not drive that car anywhere under any circumstances without our permission."

"It's my car," I said. "And I'll drive it whenever and wherever I want. You have nothing to do with it."

"You're going to give us the keys to that car right now," Baron said. "I'm not going to stand for this insolence in my house."

"No way," I said. "If you so much as lay a finger on that car or try to take the keys, I will smash your piano into a thousand pieces."

"Don't you dare threaten us, Matthew," my mother said. "Give us the keys."

I shoved the keys in the pocket of my jeans, dashed off down the stairs, and locked myself in my bedroom.

Rollie later told me that my mother called him that night and chewed him out. He said she'd never so much as raised her voice with him before, and he was startled by how angry she was. "I got her to calm down after a while," he said. "I reminded her what it was like to be seventeen, and I told her that if she didn't ease up she was going to lose you. I also said that if things were too rough around your place, you could come and live with me. I think that did the trick."

The next Saturday I drove to Prentice on my own for the first time. I was excited to see Russ and show him my new car—which was stupid and naïve—and I expected to have one last chance to skate at Screaming Wheels. I hadn't been on my skates since we moved; I don't think I consciously avoided the rink, but I suppose there was an unconscious avoidance on my part, and almost certainly on Russ's. On the rare occasions we'd gotten together it had been on neutral territory, like some restaurant in Floyd Valley. Then we'd drive around hitting up record and thrift stores and trying to do the other things we'd done so effortlessly during our years together.

I wasn't prepared for the scene I encountered when I reached the top of the rink stairs. There were boxes everywhere. All the rental skates were gone, along with the vending machines. All the ceiling lights had been removed, or at least the stringers and big colored globes had, and the bare, dangling bulbs were both feeble and glaring. The once-romantic atmosphere of the room had been obliterated, and the place now had the vibe of an abandoned sweatshop. Even more distressing, the stereo and records were gone, and the High Tower—that privileged perch where I'd spent some of the happiest days of my childhood—had been dismantled, reduced to a ragged pile of busted-up wood and threadbare carpeting.

I could hardly believe what I was seeing, and I could hardly stand it. Russ wasn't in the rink, so I made my way back into the apartment, where I found him on his knees in the living room, taking records from the wall of shelves and putting them in crates. He looked at me over his shoulder when I entered the room, then went right back to what he was doing. I stood behind him for several long moments, during which neither of us spoke a word. It was hot in the apartment, and stuffy, and Russ had sweated through his T-shirt. I briefly wandered through the other rooms, almost all of them empty or piled with boxes and black, bulging garbage bags. The place felt so tiny. It was a wonder, I thought, that the three of us had lived there together for so long.

When I finally made my way back to the living room, Russ continued to ignore me, even when I asked if there was something I could do to help. "Are you mad at me?" I finally asked, speaking to his back.

"Yes," he said. "I'm mad at everyone. And everything."

"I'm sorry," I said.

He turned then to face me, still on his knees, and said, "This is the most fucked-up thing I've ever had to deal with, Matt. I'm a seriously miserable human being right now."

I started to cry—maybe the second or third time I could remember really crying—and then Russ started to cry. I'd never seen him cry like that—there'd been that one other time, in the early stages of his breakup with my mother, but he'd essentially been alone on that occasion, slumped in the middle of the rink, and I'd merely watched him from a distance—and that only made me cry harder. I collapsed on the floor, and Russ crawled across the room and took me in his skinny arms. We sat there for what seemed like a long time, rocking gently and crying together.

That was unquestionably an uncharacteristic moment for both of us, but there was nothing self-conscious or awkward about it, at least for the first few moments. Then Russ pulled himself together, rolled away from me, and collapsed flat on his back on the floor.

"All right," he said. "We got that over with and it was probably good for both of us, but now let's pretend it never happened. We're both sad and we love each other, but the world is out of our control. Okay? I've missed you, Matt, probably more than I've missed your mother. But I don't call the shots, and you're not my kid. You've got my fingerprints all over you, and I'm not sure that's such a good thing, but I'm proud all the same. I hope like hell I didn't ruin your life."

"You haven't ruined my life," I said.

"Then I hope like hell you didn't ruin mine," he said.

"So do I," I said.

Russ shrugged. "Well," he said. "I got some things off my chest. Now you can help me tear down what's left of this dream."

"It sucks," I said.

"It does suck," he said. "But I was supposed to be out of here a week ago, and the fuckers are itching to roll in the wrecking ball. There's a big dumpster in the alley out back. Everything that's in a garbage bag can be chucked in there."

"What's in the garbage bags?" I asked.

"Garbage."

"What happened to all the skates?"

"Don't worry, buddy, I didn't get rid of the skates. I packed 'em all up and put them in a storage unit, along with anything else that was salvageable."

I hauled all the garbage bags to the dumpster and then helped Russ carry the boxes of records and other stuff down the stairs to a rental truck. After maybe four or five hours, we'd pretty much emptied the place out.

Before we locked the doors for the last time, Russ climbed up on a ladder and unscrewed the sign above the entryway—*The spirit of the living creatures was in the wheels.* He handed it down to me from the ladder and said, "That's yours."

I still have that sign here in the press box, above my desk. It's one of my prized possessions.

One early afternoon I was standing at the press box windows, drinking my one daily cup of coffee and girding myself for a trip to the grocery store, when I saw two dogs, unaccompanied by any human I could see, frolicking in the snow that blanketed the acres of practice fields and baseball diamonds. They chased each other in wider and wider circles and occasionally paused to wrestle before resuming their chase. Very quickly they'd succeeded in carving a series of troughs and trails through the snow, and I was mesmerized by the increasingly elaborate patterns they left behind. It almost looked as if they were working in tandem to spell out some message, and I was so simultaneously buzzed and exhausted that I stood there for quite some time, squinting, trying to see if I could translate their calligraphy.

The skies had cleared, and a bright sun was just beginning its climb. I got bundled up for my slog downtown to fetch my car from my grandmother's garage, and by the time I emerged from the press box to begin my descent of the bleachers, Rollie's crew had arrived at the football field with their plows, blowers, and shovels. I followed the path they'd plowed and went around the track to the main entrance, which led out to the parking lot. I had to fumble with my confounding key ring to find the one that fit the front door. There was a master key that worked on most of the stadium locks, but I could never figure out which one it was, and I usually ended up trying every key until I found the right one.

As I stepped into the bright sun and the parking lot, I saw a woman had joined the dogs. She was darting around in the snow, alternately chasing them and being chased. One of the dogs saw me and broke away to charge in my direction as I was walking down the driveway. He was a big mutt, a hound mix, and as he bounded toward me the woman clapped her hands and shouted for him to return. He ignored her entreaties and kept coming. I crouched down to greet him, and as he threw himself at me, he was squirming and electric with excitement.

The woman plodded over to corral him. "I'm so sorry," she said. "They love the snow, and they've been going stir crazy all day." As she spoke the expression on her face changed, and I could tell she was studying my face. "I think I know you," she said. "Or knew you. Are you Matt?"

Improbable, and seemingly impossible, but there standing in front of me was the firefly girl of my old fairy tale.

"Veronica?" I said.

She smiled and said, "You remember that night?"

"Of course I remember," I said. "I remember *you*. That experience has been pretty hard to forget."

"How funny," she said.

"Yeah," I said. "Funny, I guess. And unbelievable."

"Do you still live here? In Prentice?"

"It's kind of a long story," I said. "But, yes, I live right here"— I gestured behind me at the football field—"up in that press box."

Her eyes followed my hand. "That's weird," she said.

"It's not quite as pathetic as it might sound," I said. "I mean, it *is* very weird, but it's also a really beautiful and surreal setup. Probably temporary. How about you? Are you in Prentice?"

"Yes," she said. "I came back in August. I teach ESL at the elementary school just up the street. I was in Mankato for much of the time since I left here. That's where I went to college."

I have never been smooth with women, particularly women I find fascinating, and this unexpected encounter was making me gulpy and rattled. Veronica looked almost exactly as I remembered her from that night in her bedroom with the dollhouse and the fireflies and her curtain trick. I think I'd spent years unconsciously expecting her to reappear. I would, I'd always felt sure, recognize her anywhere. I remembered that I'd made a mixtape for her once upon a time, but she'd disappeared before I'd had a chance to hand it to her in the hallways at school.

Almost as if she were reading my mind, she said, "You look pretty much the same. Taller, I suppose, but you look like the same boy."

"I'm still the same boy," I said. "Probably more than I'm comfortable admitting."

She stared at me with the same open smile she'd had as a girl. "I feel like we have things to talk about," she said.

"I'm sure we do," I said. "Maybe we could get together sometime?"

"Let's," Veronica said.

I told her I was on my way to get groceries but promised to get in touch. We exchanged phone numbers, she gave me an assertive hug, then I watched as she dashed away across the field with her dogs.

Growing up I understood, of course, that my mother suffered and that she had suffered in the past. I knew she could cry and sulk and throw the occasional understated tantrum. But I also knew she had a hard time talking about her problems or herself. She could talk *around* her feelings and issues and would move in tighter and tighter circles until she got close enough to what was really bothering her that you could at least draw your own conclusions. I didn't have that ability back then. I preferred not to talk about things, period. I preferred, in fact, not to *think* about the sorts of questions the woman at social services had raised or the questions the Cowboy asked. Before my mother's breakup with Russ, I'm quite sure I'd never sensed any real anger or anything I could call suffering in myself. My response to their dissolution was initially a more elevated version of my old confusion, then a more passionate version, and eventually an anguished one. I had to learn to recognize I was suffering, and through these stages I slowly worked my way to clearer, more genuine emotions.

I nonetheless continued to repress whatever it was I might've felt, or should've felt, right up until my mother's death, when I was confronted with so much anxiety, sadness, and helplessness I could no longer pretend everything was okay. It took a while for the reality of the situation to sink in—I'd never watched anyone die, never spent time in hospitals, never had to navigate the grim bureaucracy of sickness and death, and nothing I'd experienced could've prepared me for it. There were seventeen months between the time my mother was diagnosed with breast cancer and her death, and they passed in a panicked, incredulous blur. For the first six months or so my mother was in and out of the hospital and depressed, uncooperative, and absolutely unwilling to fight. Baron was useless, a blubbering, inconsolable wreck from the first day to the last. His anxiety was unmanageable and seemingly infectious. He broke out in some terrifying combination of eczema and acne, had a minor stroke from untreated high blood pressure, and was so overly medicated he was generally shaky and incoherent. After the initial round of procedures and treatments there was a brief glimmer of hope, and my mother returned home for several months. Baron, however, couldn't pull himself together enough to deal with or take care of her, and she practically begged me to spend more time with her. She never suggested I be a caregiver but insisted it was a comfort to have me there.

I dutifully started taking up regular weekend residencies in my old basement bedroom, and in retrospect I'm glad I did. We had a lot of good talks in the last eight months of her life—more real communication than we'd had in all the other years of our lives combined. We were finally able to talk to each other as adults, and she was obviously dying, so there were long stretches of uncharacteristic stocktaking and unburdening. She was also heavily medicated much of the time, and I'm sure that helped loosen her up. At any rate, I do feel as if I finally got to know her in that last year, to understand all the things she'd dealt with in her life *and* the grief and depression she was up against through the early years of my childhood.

I understood she was a complicated and atypical person and mother, but I had never—to myself or anyone else—acknowledged the effect her unhappiness and emotional distance had had on me. Through most of the years of her marriage to Baron, I had drifted further and further from her. Throughout my adolescence it seemed like there were days and weeks when we wouldn't exchange so much as a word. Some of that, surely, was my fault, or at least fairly typical of adolescence. But I was aware she didn't seek me out, seemed to actively avoid me, in fact, and it was a lingering source of resentment. Those years were ostensibly her happy and contented years, and I couldn't understand why I seemed to play a role in neither her happiness nor her contentment. By the time I started to drive the Rubber Route we seldom communicated with each other, and I regarded her as a stranger.

In the last several days of my mother's life, she went downhill alarmingly fast. I wasn't at all prepared for a death that seemed so sudden; she'd been dying, of course, I knew that, but she seemed comfortable and mostly at peace right up until those last few days. But then she became agitated and irritable. She reached a point where the pain meds were no longer doing their work.

We spoke for the last time a day before she died. I'd been sitting quietly at her bedside reading Raymond Carver when she turned her head slowly to stare at me. "I don't know anything about love, Matthew," she said. "It's a mystery to me. I'm sure I love you, but I never learned to express or show it, and I can't love the way you do."

"That's not true," I said.

"It is," she said. "I could depend on you, even though I didn't want to. The way you loved Russ and his music and the rink? I never knew that feeling in my life. I never even had a hobby, let alone a passion. It kind of disgusts me, and I'm sorry. I hope I didn't kill all your dreams. I don't just want you to be okay—I want you to be happy."

"I'll be okay," I said, then I kissed her on the lips for the first time since I was a child.

My mother's death hit me harder than anything had ever hit me, and I felt a desperate pain I'd never felt before. I remember walking out of that hospital in a state of shock; it was August and steamy, and I wandered around Floyd Valley for a couple hours, listening to the swelling of the cicadas and feeling as if I was trapped in the closing credits of some heartbreaking movie that deserved a happier ending. At some point I accompanied Baron, Rollie, and Mooze to a funeral home and went through the awful, blank stuff such a visit entails. The actual funeral was so small I felt angry and offended through the entire service; Baron tried to read some shitty poem but couldn't get through it, and I remember Rollie getting up and saying, "All right, come on," and herding him away from the podium. My aunt Tina spoke as well, as did some minister I'm certain my mother would not have wanted involved with any of the proceedings.

That was it. She was cremated, and Baron, inconsolable, carried her urn around through the entire reception and then, I assume, took her home and put her on his fireplace mantle under his Broadway posters.

In a sense I was really just getting to know my mother when she died, and we were both breaking down all the walls that had made our relationship so distant and difficult for as long as I could remember. We were, it turned out, more alike than I'd ever been willing to admit to myself.

"When you were a baby and really young, I tried to do the mom thing," she told me a month or so before her death. "But I'll be the first to admit I wasn't a natural; I loved you, of course, and I experienced a lot of things you're supposed to experience—I was stunned every day when I'd look at you that I'd somehow managed to bring this amazing little human into the world. But there was something essentially unlovable about you. That sounds terrible, and I don't mean it the way it sounds, but it was almost as if you recognized that I was damaged goods and you couldn't depend on me. You were never fussy or needy, and you couldn't stand to be babied or cuddled. You didn't seem to want or need comfort, and only tolerated being held because it seemed like what was expected of you. I assumed I was doing something wrong; it was as if all the things I was denied as a child, things I probably wanted and needed, you were determined to deny yourself. Or maybe I just didn't understand how to do them properly. I was selfish, and so young, and there was a part of me that was relieved to be let off the hook. You were so easy and self-sufficient all the way through childhood, and that made it easy for me to retreat into my own garbage. It often seemed like I barely had to feed you. Your aunts were around to help too, and I realize now they did so much of the heavy lifting in those early years. I don't know; maybe it was a too-many-cooks scenario, and we never properly bonded. By the time Russ came along, you were already your own little man, and I just handed you off to him. I saw right away how you latched on to him—and how he latched on to you—and I guess I thought it was a guy thing, you know, that you were desperate for a father figure or whatever, so I let you go. I'm really so sorry, Matt; it seems like I just constantly passed you off to anybody who was around. I wasn't enough of a mom to you. I was so certain I'd messed you up that I refused to have another child. Both Russ and Baron tried to talk me around on that, but I couldn't imagine putting another kid through what I put you through."

It was nice to have that opportunity to clear the air, even if I still couldn't bring myself to voice any real grievances; she was the only mom I had, and she'd done what she could—but it was too late for either of us to really make any fundamental changes. Right up until the end there were no emotional breakdowns, no touchy-feely stuff.

Maybe if she'd been an entirely different woman and had had a different childhood of her own, things would've been different between us. Or if my father had lived. That isn't the way it was, though, and I never wasted time trying to imagine a different childhood or set of circumstances. I couldn't even imagine—and can't imagine—what it might've been like if I'd had siblings. The childhood I'd had made such things impossible. I was an only child in a family where children—or at least the child I was—seemed to be regarded as a puzzling disruption of the natural order of things. I don't think I ever felt truly neglected by anyone in the family, but I also don't think I ever felt like a proper child. Even when I *was* a child, but especially now, when I see depictions of childhood and family life in ads, books, movies, or TV shows, they always confuse me. They're like messages from an alternative world whose rituals and dynamics are, and have always been, unrecognizable to me.

I've been back in Prentice for almost six months now. In all that time I haven't, for the most part, been living in the present tense.

Everything seems to be a memory now: every record, book, and object around me—the entire town of Prentice, really—is an artifact in the museum of my past. I've been lost in that museum.

Rollie stops by a couple times a week to check up on me and see that everything is in order here at the football complex. And every time he's had to let himself in at the gate, lumber up the track, and climb the steps of the bleachers to get to me, he's out of breath and bitching because I never answer my phone. "You're alive," he always says. "Thank God."

Rollie and I have been through a lot together, particularly over the last five years. Since I've been living in the press box, I've realized that, more than anyone else I can think of, I've depended on him my entire life. Through all those early years after my father's death, he was pretty much the only guardian my mother and I had. I also recognize that I've been guilty of taking his generosity for granted. I'm always grateful to see him these days. The old awkwardness and long silences of the past have given way to a much more comfortable and expansive relationship. I think all that death brought us closer together, and as an adult I've developed a more clear-eyed understanding of how tough and tender and resilient he is and how hard he's had to work—and still works—to keep the sprawling Carnap empire afloat, particularly since he's been going it alone. I can see he's getting old, and I worry about his health. Rollie's always carried too much weight, but in his younger days he carried it effortlessly. I can see it's much harder on him now. He had a knee replaced a few years ago and has a chronically bad back that's slowed him down. He also apparently has sleep apnea and has to sleep hooked up to one of those CPAP machines. Yet he seems, despite it all, indefatigable, and I can't recall a single time I've seen him in a bad mood. I sometimes think he's the one person in my life who's loved me with absolutely no strings attached. He's the only man who's ever kissed me, and he still seldom says good-bye without a huge bear hug and a kiss on the cheek. "Okay, precious," he's said to me on hundreds of occasions. "Don't you worry about a thing." It's his way of saying good-bye.

Since I've been back in Prentice, Rollie has been my main source of human contact until that encounter with Veronica, and the day after running into her and her dogs, this realization led me to screw up my nerve and dial her number.

She answered on the second ring, as I was still working out what I might say to her.

"Hello, Veronica," I said. "It's Matt Carnap. I thought maybe you'd be at work."

"It's Sunday."

"Nice," I said. "So it is. I guess I heard the St. Augustine bells earlier."

"They're big with the bells," she said. "Near as I can tell it's not just a Sunday thing. What are you up to? Did you get your provisions?"

"Provisions?"

"I believe you were on your way to the grocery store yesterday."

"Oh, yeah. That's right. I did get my provisions. That's one of the challenges of this place. Getting groceries back up here is an expedition, especially in the winter. Other than that, I'm not up to much. How about you?"

"I've just been sitting around waiting for you to call and invite me to see your press box," she said. "I'm sort of joking, but sort of not. I'm honestly not trying to be forward, but I'm dying to see this place."

"You can see it now," I said. "I mean, if you don't have anything else going on."

"That would be swell," she said. "I'll head over. How do I get in there?"

"I'll have to come down and let you in. I'll meet you at the front gate by the ticket window."

"How exciting! See you in ten minutes."

I put on my coat and boots and went down to the track. Once I hit the ground at the bottom of the bleacher steps, I broke into a sprint and ran as hard as I could all the way to the front gate, where I paused to catch my breath. I popped the padlock, swung the gate open, and stood in the middle of the massive arch, watching Veronica walk up the long driveway.

"There's the king in his castle," she said when she got closer. "What a gentleman. You really should have a horse."

I closed the gate behind us and we strolled along the track. Darkness was just beginning to settle, but the light still had that beautiful, crepuscular transparency of a Midwestern winter.

"What exactly is your arrangement here?" Veronica asked.

"It's complicated," I said.

"It would have to be," she said.

"The short version is my family donated the land for this thing, and one of my uncles put up the money to build the stadium. When the high school was consolidated, there wasn't a football team to play here anymore, and my uncle assumed the upkeep. When my life kind of fell apart up in Minneapolis, my uncle talked me into moving back here by turning this press box into an apartment."

"What was wrong with a regular apartment?" she asked.

"Nothing," I said. "It was my uncle's idea. We were out here one day and had a funny conversation that I didn't at all take seriously, but he apparently did. And one thing led to another."

We climbed the bleacher steps and I opened the door for her. Until that day, nobody other than Rollie had ever visited me in the press box. Veronica stopped maybe five feet inside the door and gasped.

"I know," I said. "It's ridiculous."

"It's magnificent!" she said. "I've never seen anything like it. How lucky are you?" She started wandering around, taking things in. "My God. Truly, Matt, this is magical. Look at all these books and records. I'm envious. And look at the view! You can see my house. You can see all the way across town. I'd just stand at these windows all day."

"Sometimes I do," I said. "Which house is yours?"

"Just across the street from where you saw me with my dogs," she said. "Right on the corner. The little white house that used to be an Ankeny's market."

I knew the house, remembered the little neighborhood market from my childhood.

I offered her a seat on the couch, and she plopped down and smiled at me. It was a dazzling smile, and, no shit, she followed it by saying, "I'm dazzled!"

We sat around talking for five hours. I never once put a record on the turntable. I told her more about my life than I'd ever told anyone, with the possible exception of the Cowboy. Veronica struck me as the happiest person I'd ever met. She also had been raised without a father, but her mother, she said, was her best friend and hero. "She's an enchantress," she said. "Seriously, I still think of her as a magician. I loved childhood so much, and I owe that all to her. She had to work her ass off at backbreaking jobs, and I learned to be really independent, but when she'd come home we were a little troop of two—actors, comedians, naturalists, chefs, art cooperative. We created a newspaper of our own little world. My mom taught wonder, and from the time I was in high school I knew I wanted to work with kids. Because at an early age most kids are still capable of real curiosity and spontaneous joy, you know? And they share a universal physical language of exuberance and improvisation. They run, jump, do handstands and cartwheels. They have amazing imaginations and are just learning to dream, and they're instinctively drawn to all the colors in the jumbo box of crayons. And it's incredible, because they have all these keys, these massive key rings, that they can use to unlock things in the world and in themselves. And then as they get older most of them forget what all the keys are for, and then they start losing or discarding keys altogether. That's one of the things I really love about this place of yours and all this stuff. You still have a great big key ring."

We eventually walked downtown and got a pizza, and then I walked Veronica back to her house and kissed her good-night.

As I turned to walk back to the press box she called out to me.

"Thanks so much, Matt," she said. "I had a lovely time. It's thrilling to see your lights up there at night and know you're up there dreaming. Maybe next time we can dance."

The next morning Rollie showed up at the press box and banged on the windows until he woke me up. He'd driven over at such an unreasonably early hour to deliver the news that Art Vargo had died at the St. Mark's hospice.

My first thought after Rollie delivered the news was that maybe Russ would surface. He had no other family in town, but like my uncles, Russ's father had had a large, longstanding presence in Prentice. The Vargos, in fact, had been around even longer than the Carnaps had. Their empire may have started to crumble with the death of Russ's grandfather, and by the time Art died he'd presumably liquidated most of their holdings; nonetheless, his death was big news in Prentice, and surely someone must've found a way to track down Russ. There were all sorts of complicated reasons why he would've drifted out of touch with me, but I couldn't believe he would cut off all contact with his family. And I knew that if he was out there and somehow unaware of his father's death, he would be devastated.

The possibility that Russ was in town and had perhaps been in town while his father was dying, entered my mind shortly after Rollie left. *At the very least,* I thought, *his sister is likely in Prentice.*

I keep my car in a stall in my grandmother's old garage, which is about six blocks from the press box. I walk pretty much everywhere in Prentice, or ride a bike, but when I need to use the car, I have to walk down the bleachers, along the track, and out across the practice fields to get to the street. It's a punishing exercise in the winter, having to make that trek of three or four hundred yards, particularly when it involves wading through snow in frigid temperatures. But Art Vargo's death, and the possibility that Russ would be in town, was a compelling reason, so I made my way to Second Avenue, got my car, and drove to Art Vargo's house on the edge of town.

The place was snowed in. There was a minivan in the driveway, but it was buried in snow and had clearly been there for a while. There was no sign—no car tracks or footprints—to indicate anyone had been there for at least several days.

I drove back into town, picked up a newspaper, and stopped at Country Kitchen to eat breakfast. *Arthur Vargo, Prentice Pillar, Dead at 83* was the front-page headline. The article, however, was more of a tribute to August Vargo and the mark he'd made on the community than it was a celebration of Art's life. That, really, was who Art was, at least according to his death notice: a great man's son. "It was a credit to him that he stayed in Prentice to look after his father's legacy," the mayor was quoted as saying. The article also mentioned Art's love of track and field. "A competitive athlete and runner well into old age," it noted, "Vargo completed numerous marathons and other races and installed a track and field complex at his home in Prentice." At the end of the article it said, "Vargo is survived by a daughter, Janice Werner, of Phoenix, Arizona, and a son, Russell Vargo, who ran the family's roller-skating rink in Prentice for many years. Funeral arrangements are pending."

I went to the pay phone at Country Kitchen, looked up Art's number in the phone book, and dialed it. The phone rang for what seemed like a long time and then went to the answering machine. "I'm probably around somewhere," Art's voice said. "Leave me a message and I'll get back to you eventually."

I left a long and stammering message for Russ and Janice, expressed my condolences, told them I was living in town, and asked them to call me if they had a chance. I don't know why, but I felt anxious, as if I were leaving a message for an old girlfriend from whom I'd been long and bitterly estranged. I had, of course, been estranged from Russ for a long time, but I didn't believe there was any enmity or lingering grievances between us, and there was certainly no loss of affection on my part. I'd thought about Russ, wondered where he was, and worried about him constantly in the years since we'd last talked. During all that time, though, I also worried that I had said or done something to hurt him or piss him off. But I couldn't come up with anything that explained the long silence and separation other than the personality defects we shared.

I suppose I was afraid the connection we'd once had—powerful, but essentially awkward—would be lost. Or that the years we'd been out of touch would've driven us both so far into ourselves we would no longer recognize each other or remember the way our relationship worked or the shared and often unspoken language that bonded us. The dynamic had clearly changed even before we'd drifted out of touch. I was no longer a mute little kid who studied Russ's every move and hung on to his every word. Once I wasn't with him every day and didn't have constant access to his record collection and his opinions, I'd had to sort things out for myself and develop some taste of my own. Still, there's never been a time that I discovered something new I loved and haven't wondered what Russ would make of it.

Russ would be forty-six now. He and my mother were married almost twenty years ago. How is that possible? How is it possible we've now spent more time apart than together? Maybe we have absolutely nothing left to say to each other.

Often over the years I've had occasion to ponder Russ's "Hole Theory," which was formulated, I'm pretty sure, to justify his music obsession and his record collection, but I've found it useful as a general operating principle for life. Russ's theory, which he articulated to me in different ways and at different times, boiled down to this: If you lost one person, passion, or thing in your life, how big of a hole would you be looking at? And how likely is it that you could find anything else big enough to fill that hole?

By the time I took up my hermitage in the press box, my life had been blown full of holes, and though every one was proving impossible to fill, some were more gaping and preoccupying than others. But, pathetic as it maybe was, Russ felt like the biggest hole of all, precisely because I'd spent the intervening years constantly staring into that hole and trying to live my life around it, addressing it, interrogating it, and sifting through its piles of marginal dirt. And the older I got, the more I actually went into the hole and perhaps even inhabited the hole, spending more and more time excavating in the darkness and trying to drill through to the pockets of light I knew were there. Russ's absence nagged at me. I couldn't shake it, couldn't stop feeling that I hadn't done enough to communicate to him how much our time together meant to me, how much he meant to me, how thoroughly he shaped me. What I was dealing with, as the Cowboy had insisted since the day my mother and I moved out of the rink, was grief. At the time I didn't know grief, had never truly experienced or felt it, and I resisted the idea. It seemed dramatic, and neither Russ nor I were comfortable with drama.

"To admit you're grieving means to acknowledge you're feeling something," the Cowboy had told me. "Something painful and hard to sort out. And you're still reluctant to admit to any complicated feelings at all. You don't even like to own up to the simplest, most universal feelings. It's a kind of crutch or survival mechanism—as long as you don't acknowledge any feelings, you can pretend you don't feel anything. And if you don't feel anything, you can't get hurt. This doesn't make you unique, unfortunately, but it's a developmental problem, and people who don't figure it out at some point tend to lead very unhappy, emotionally isolated lives. We've now looked at enough photographs to understand that life's not about what you see but *how* you see."

Whatever ideas I had about family, however inchoate and perhaps dysfunctional, were shattered by the death of my mother and by all the other deaths that followed in such rapid and alarming succession. I was suddenly an orphan, and I felt those losses keenly. There had never been a lot of architecture or structure to my life, but what little was there was bound up with all these dying people, and our shared history, and the simple rituals and routines that had made us unmistakably a family.

I realized I'd never had a notion of home rooted in a specific house or place. My home had been wherever I, my mother, my grandparents, and my aunts and uncles were. The sole exception had been the rink and our little apartment. That felt like home to me, and it still feels like home to me. It wasn't just the place and the instant thrill and sense of contentment I felt when I walked into that rink for the first time; it was something more. For a time, at least,

I'd felt like my mother, Russ, and I were an actual family. We had a shared life and space for five and a half years and in all the years before that I'd never, I realized, known stability, or had a place that was truly my own, or had the same pleasant and reliable routines day after day. For years now when people ask me about my home and my family, I tell them I grew up in a roller-skating rink. That's just my first, unconscious instinct, and it's the truth. Those were the years, and that was the place, where I finally experienced the enchantment so many people associate with childhood and where the world and its possibilities came alive for me. I now realized, though, that something was pretty obviously missing, and what it was was still a hard thing for me to admit, let alone get my head around. As a child hadn't I ever wanted to hold someone or to be held? To be comforted? Didn't I crave those universal signs of love and affection that the rest of the world seemed to take for granted? I must have. That's the only honest conclusion. Yet I still longed mostly for what I'd had. I remember, during my time on the Rubber Route, sitting up late in motel rooms with maps spread out before me and blindly tracing highways and roads with my fingers, searching, I'm quite certain, for the land beyond that dark hallway that ran from our apartment into the now vanished rink. Out there somewhere, I always figured, would be the new world, a place where that heavy curtain would be swept aside and I'd once again feel at home.

But it's one thing to have someone you love die—you can learn to live with that, with the knowledge they made their mark and a door has closed. Estrangement is a different and more hectoring kind of grief; it's a lingering form of torture and torment to carry the knowledge that someone essential to you is alive and somewhere out in the world carrying on without you. Even if you try to shove that awareness aside, it's still there. You don't feel like the conversation is finished or the connection is hopelessly lost. And with Russ, because so much of my life is, or at least feels like, such a fun-house mirror image of the life he led when he was the age I am now, the conversation has continued over all the years of our separation, albeit as a series of one-sided monologues and interrogations. I long ago recognized that when I talk to myself (as I often do), I'm just continuing my old conversations with Russ.

Mostly, though, I find myself constantly wondering what he's up to and where he is; wondering whether he's okay or even, given all the recent death in my life, whether he's alive. Maybe, I think, he's remarried and has children of his own, and has finally moved out from under the years he spent with my mother and me.

After I drove to Art Vargo's dark, snowed-in house, I made my way back to the press box and drank myself sick while staring out across the desolate moonscape of Prentice and listening to old, sad records that made me feel like a lovelorn teenager.

The next day, four days before Art Vargo's funeral, I got a phone call from Russ's sister, Janice. She was in town and staying at the Days Inn out by the freeway rather than at Art's house, which she said was too cold—she didn't know how to work the furnace, and Art hadn't lived there for more than a year. "I don't think anyone's been in there since he first went into the hospital," she said. "I blame myself. I should've come back at some point and dealt with it, but I never had a relationship with my dad, and now it's a horror show and I can't deal with it. The refrigerator is full of rotten stuff, there are squirrels—I think they're squirrels; I hope they're squirrels—coming in and out through the roof, and they've shredded shit all over the house. It feels like a place that hasn't been lived in for fifty years."

She was obviously distraught, but her most pressing concern was that she hadn't been able to track down Russ. She said she didn't have any idea where he was or even where to begin looking. "What a terrible sister I am," she said. "It's like he disappeared and we all just let him go. I assumed he'd never stray far from Prentice, and that if he did, he'd keep in touch with at least one person in this town. I didn't really worry about him until you told me you had lost touch, and I've been terrified ever since. There's no way we can have this funeral until I've gotten a hold of him. He'd never forgive me."

I reiterated to her what I knew, which was that the last I'd heard from Russ he'd been working at small AM radio stations in northern Iowa. Like Janice, I hadn't tried very hard to track him down, but I once called the station where he'd been working when I last had news of him, and the woman I'd talked to was a newer employee and hadn't heard of Russ. The station, she told me, along with most of the others in the region, had been purchased by some large media corporation and consolidated into a network of automated formats. Based on my late years on the Rubber Route, I assumed all of the stations in the part of Iowa where Russ had worked were now either conservative talk radio, Christian, or contemporary country. There was no way Russ would've stuck around and wasted his time with such formats. I was pissed at myself. All those times I'd been down in places like Mason City, Cedar Rapids, and Davenport on the Rubber Route and I'd never made any real attempt to see if I could find Russ. He'd worked at stations around there for at least five years; people would've heard his shows or seen him around town. Surely, he would've made friends, and there would be people who remembered him. A guy couldn't just disappear without a trace in northern Iowa. Until I lost touch with him, to the best of my knowledge, Russ had never been more than a couple hundred miles from Prentice.

I told Janice I would drive to Mason City—which was, I was pretty sure, the first stop on Russ's radio odyssey—to see if I could turn up any news about his whereabouts. Mason City was about an hour south of Prentice, and I'd probably made that trip at least fifty times during my years on the Rubber Route. I called Veronica to cancel a pizza date and briefly fill her in on the new developments, and then I got in my car and drove.

In the winter, the drive south out of Prentice and into Iowa could be a white-knuckle affair on even a relatively clear day. The only road to Mason City is an old two-lane state highway that had once upon a time been carved through the absolutely flat farm country of southern Minnesota and northern Iowa. The wind blew out there pretty much all the time, the blowing and drifting snow was a constant challenge, and it didn't take much to create white-out conditions.

It was snowing when I left Prentice, and by the time I got out in the country, maybe twenty miles out of town, it was really coming down. Visibility was diminishing by the mile, and the combination of the snow and the wind bursts buffeting my car made for very slow going. I was accustomed to driving in such conditions, and there was something about it I found simultaneously nerve-racking and oddly relaxing. It required complete concentration, but you also had the sense you were in a bubble; it felt like piloting a plane through clouds or bursts of turbulence, or steering a boat through choppy waves and fog. You couldn't see other vehicles on the road until you ran right up on them or they burst into view in the opposite lane.

I crept along, listening to Otis Redding and making constant steering adjustments to keep the car on the road. For a long time, it really did feel as if I was flying. The last half hour of my approach to Mason City I didn't encounter any other cars and couldn't make out road signs or even lane markers. At some point I just popped down out of the clouds, the wind abated, and I entered the outskirts of the city, which began emerging in steady increments as if a series of scrims was being lifted one after another.

I drove around town until I found the radio station, a modest cinder-block building huddled under the signal tower along the southern edge of the city. There were several unplowed parking spaces in front of the station, only one of which was occupied. Through the tiny vestibule I could see the lobby was dark, but I tried the front door and it was open. Inside was a reception desk and a couple cluttered cubicles off the control room, where a guy who couldn't have been much older than I am sat huddled over the control board and shuffled through papers under the bulb of a solitary desk lamp.

From the ceiling speakers in the dark lobby I could hear some typical Top 40 contemporary country hit. That was one of the relatively few music genres I paid absolutely no attention to, but it was so ubiquitous in the blank Midwest—you heard it in gas stations, grocery stores, pizza parlors, and bars—that the song was vaguely familiar. There was a big sign above the abandoned front desk that read, "Mason City is 1530 COUNTRY." The clock on the wall indicated that it was 1:40, and it seemed strange to me that the place was so dark and abandoned. I realized, though, that it was a Sunday afternoon.

The DJ's voice broke in on the speaker above my head. "That's snow you're seeing out there," he said, "and the National Weather Service says there's more where that came from. A lot more, apparently. We're looking at six to ten inches by the time it lets up tomorrow morning, and a blizzard warning is in effect until 10:00 a.m. It's hazardous out there on the roads, so it's probably a good idea to stay put, cook yourself a big pot of chili, work your way through the beer in the fridge, and stay tuned to 1530, your home for country in Mason City." He punched some buttons and a national news update lurched into the speakers, too loud and a couple of seconds too late.

I tapped on the glass and the guy bolted from his chair in obvious terror. I'm sure I was just a dark apparition on the other side of the window, but he nonetheless came out from behind the control board and swung the door open. "Jesus," he said. "You scared the living shit out of me. Was the front door unlocked?"

"It was," I said. "I waltzed right in."

He shook his head. "My bad," he said. "That's how people get killed."

"Do a lot of people get killed in your line of work?" I asked.

"People get killed in every line of work," he said. "You wouldn't believe the shit people say to me on the phone. Please assure me you're not an angry listener."

"I'm not an angry listener," I said. "I'm trying to find a guy who used to work here."

"Who's that?" he said.

"A guy named Russ Vargo," I said.

"How long ago was this?"

"A long time ago," I said. "Maybe eight years ago?"

"Oh, shit," the guy said. "That's ancient history. I haven't even been here five years, but we've probably gone through ten formats and a couple different owners since then. Hang on a minute." He scuttled back behind the board, put his headphones on, and, after reading something from a laminated sheet of paper, inserted a cartridge.

He removed his headphones. "Who was this guy again?" he said.

"His name was Russ Vargo," I said. "He was here for a couple years, I think. Worked nights."

The guy shrugged. "Way, way before my time," he said. "There's one old guy around who was probably here at the same time. He's been here forever. Granny Hicks. The sports guy."

"Granny?" I said.

"His real name is Granville, I think. He's a drunk, but he's also a local institution. We can't get rid of him."

"Any chance you could put me in touch with him?" I asked.

"Sure," he said. "I don't think he'd mind." He flipped through a Rolodex next to the console, scribbled a number down on a scrap of paper, and handed it to me. "Why are you looking for this Vargo guy?" he asked.

"He was my stepfather," I said. "His dad died, and we're trying to get in touch with him."

"That's a bummer," the guy said. "And you're looking for him in a place he worked ten years ago?"

"We lost touch with him," I said.

"I'd say. This line of work, he could be anywhere by now."

"Yeah," I said. "That's what I'm afraid of." I asked if I could use the phone at the front desk.

"It's all yours," he said, waving his hand. "Good luck."

I sat at the reception desk in the dark lobby and dialed Granny Hicks's number. The voice that answered on the third ring was frail and congested and sounded like it belonged to a ninety-year-old woman. "I'm looking for Granny Hicks," I said.

"Speaking. Who's this?"

"My name is Matthew Carnap," I said, "and I'm out at the radio station right now. I'm trying to find a guy who used to work here a number of years ago. Russ Vargo?"

Hicks croaked out a rattling laugh. "The Cheese," he said. "Sure. What did he do now?"

"The Cheese?" I said.

"That was his handle at the station," Hicks said. "Jergie 'the Cheese' Bergen. Claimed he was descended from some Norwegian king. He was full of shit, but a funny guy."

"He was my stepfather," I said. "We have a family emergency and we've been trying to find him. I was hoping somebody down here might have a lead."

"Oh boy," Hicks said. "If he's still working in radio, I'd eat my hat. I know he was at another station after he left here, but I don't recall where. He was one of those old-school characters, a pirate. Didn't like playlists or coloring within the lines. He had good bits, though, and some of the kids around here loved him. Program directors and station managers were another story. He got in trouble for playing too much noisy shit and getting political."

"Do you think anybody else at the station might have contact info for him?" I asked.

"I think I'm the only person still at the station who was around when he was here," Hicks said. "But I'm not sure. Maybe Margret Gunderson, who sells ads and used to do our payroll, worked with the Cheese. She's been around for a long time. I can give her a shout and get back to you. Are you on the front desk phone?"

I told him I was.

"Okay then," Hicks said. "Stay put and answer the phone if it rings."

I sat at the desk for maybe five minutes. I heard ads for a local car dealership, a pizza chain, and a funeral parlor. The control room guy prattled on about the snow, which I could see was still falling outside the windows. The ringing of the phone startled me, and I wasn't sure how I should answer it. I went pro: "1530 Country," I said.

There was a chuckle on the other end of the line. "You're pretty good," a woman's voice said.

"I'm just trying to make myself useful," I said.

"This is Margret Gunderson," she said. "I just got off the phone with Granny Hicks, and he said you were looking for information about Russ Vargo."

"I am," I said. "Thanks for calling me back."

"No problem at all," she said. "I remember Russ very well. We worked together on some dances and promotions at a record store in town. He's a wonderful guy. What are you looking for?"

"Him," I said. "He was my stepfather once upon a time, and we were very close. His father has died back in my hometown and none of us have been able to track Russ down. I sort of lost his trail after he left here."

"Oh, lord," Margret said. "I'm so sorry to hear that. I ran into Russ a few months ago, purely by chance. He showed up for the funeral of the guy who used to run the record store. At the time he was driving a cab in Waterloo. I'd guess he's still down there. He worked at a station in Waterloo for a while after he left here, but he said he was out of the radio business."

I thanked Margret for her help and told her I would try to track Russ down in Waterloo.

"I hope you're not planning on driving there today," she said. "The roads are dreadful."

"Yes," I said. "I had a rough go of it from Prentice to Mason City, and it doesn't seem to be improving. I'll probably get a room here in town and see how it looks in the morning."

"Well, be careful," she said. "And I hope you find Russ. When you do, please tell him I said hello and send condolences."

I assured her I would and thanked her again, and we hung up. I sat there in the dark warren of cubicles and felt a weird sense of desperation, maybe even panic. What the hell was I supposed to do? The DJ poked his head out of the control room. "Any luck?" he asked.

"No luck," I said.

"Bummer."

I asked him if he knew anyone in Waterloo.

"Not a soul," he said. "Why?"

"That's where Margret Gunderson thinks he's living now."

"Working in radio?"

"No," I said. "Driving a cab. Or that's what Margret believes."

"It would be a bitch to get to Waterloo today," he said. "Anyway, I don't want to rush you out of here, but I need to get back on the air, and I want to lock that door when you leave."

"I'm on my way," I said.

He walked me to the door and wished me luck, and I stumbled back out into the storm. The snow on the ground was wet and heavy, and the wind was blowing so hard I had to duck my head as I picked my way across the parking lot to my car.

I sat there for maybe five minutes, waiting for the defroster to kick in. I'd had a lot of treacherous winter trips on the Rubber Route, and though there'd never been any urgency in getting from one place to another, I'd always prided myself on plodding along, whatever the driving conditions. This did feel urgent, however, and it would be just as risky trying to get back to Prentice as it would to plow ahead to Waterloo, and I would be heading back defeated.

It was almost 2:30, and Waterloo was maybe ninety minutes away under ideal driving conditions. From past experience I knew it might well take me two or three times that in the blizzard. I realized I was doing my basketball thing as I was sitting there, shooting imaginary free throws and whispering the word *magic* with each shot. Though I'd never really played basketball, this was an unconscious incantation I'd been doing since I was a little kid, and over the years I'd come to regard it as strangely efficacious.

I finally steeled myself, put a cassette of Bob Dylan's *Highway 61 Revisited* in the deck, and eased the car out of the lot. Immediately I was fishtailing along a street that ran right through town, and every time I corrected, the back end of the car swung the other way. There were almost no other cars on the streets, but it spooked me all the same, so I pulled into a gas station to fill the tank and get a big jug of cold, caffeinated soda. I also went to the pay phone near the bathrooms, dug my calling card out of my wallet, and called Rollie to check in. No one answered at the warehouse, so I tried him at home, and he picked up on the first ring.

"Where the hell are you, kid?"

"I'm in Mason City," I said. "Trying to track down Russ."

"Oh, Christ, Matty, in this weather?" he said. "Listen, that's nuts. I just heard from Vargo's sister, and she's been in touch with Russ. He's around here somewhere."

"Around Prentice?"

"That's what I gather," Rollie said. "At any rate, he knows about the old man."

"Where is he?" I asked.

"How the hell do I know?" he said. "I don't keep tabs on the guy. I just know he's around town somewhere. He and his sister are probably already divvying up Art's money. I don't know what you're doing driving around in a freaking snowstorm, but turn around and get your ass back here in one piece. You can sort it out yourself when you get back."

I somehow made it back to Prentice. I drove through the storm on muddled autopilot, contending with the exterior whiteout as it dueled with the interior blackout. At times I crept along the highway at maybe fifteen miles an hour. I couldn't believe how nervous I felt. My mind was simultaneously racing and blank. I couldn't form a clear thought, and I'm certain I was a hazard. I remember passing dozens of cars and trucks in the ditch, but my Honda Civic—never the ideal vehicle for such conditions—kept plowing through the drifts and clinging to the one lane that continuously disappeared and reemerged like a phantom.

By the time I pulled up to my grandmother's house it was almost nine o'clock. After putting my car in the garage, I walked back to the press box, slogging through wet snow that was frequently up to my knees. I felt a surge of the old wonder as I struggled across the practice fields toward the stadium, which loomed like an impressionist cathedral in the beautiful poststorm murk. I'd left a couple lights on in the press box, and the effect—those points of fuzzed light suspended in the darkness—was ethereal. Up there, behind that long bank of windows, was where I lived now, and for the first time since I'd moved back to Prentice, I felt like I was home.

Once I'd settled in and changed into dry clothes, I collapsed in a chair and tried to figure out my next move. I was anxious to see Russ, but I also wanted to respect the circumstances—his father had died, he hadn't seen his sister in a number of years, and I'm sure he had all kinds of Prentice baggage he wasn't keen to face. We hadn't been in touch for almost a decade, and I felt guilty about that, but I also realized I had some inchoate resentment toward Russ. I thought about the things I'd been through since we'd last talked, about the loss I'd endured and all the changes in my life, and though I'd never really examined that resentment or let it preoccupy me, the questions were always there: Where was he? And why wasn't he in touch? Whatever his lingering hostilities toward my mom, how could he not have felt *something*? Why couldn't he at least reach out to me?

I was as guilty of playing keep-away as he was, of course. I still could never understand what stopped me from trying to get in touch with him when I was driving the Rubber Route and still had some idea where he was. I think of those nights I'd sit in motel rooms and listen to his late-night program on the Mason City station (or was it Davenport?).

I now suppose I was afraid of rejection, afraid he'd washed his hands of that time in his life. I had a kid's happy memories, after all, and he had his adult disappointments. He was so young when I'd met him, twenty-six, younger than I am now. I could imagine him regarding that time as nothing more than a phase he went through on his way to becoming something else.

I had to steel myself for the possibility he wouldn't be much interested in seeing me and catching up on old times. But I was nonetheless excited about the prospects for a reunion, however awkward or brief.

It was getting late by Prentice standards—9:45—but I nonetheless called Janice at the Days Inn. She was awake and immediately apologetic. "I'm so sorry for sending you on a wild goose chase," she said. "Particularly in this weather."

"It was an adventure, to say the least," I said. "So Russ has surfaced?"

"I have reliable sources and some physical evidence that indicates he has," she said.

"What does that mean?" I asked. "You haven't seen him?"

"No, nor have I talked with him, which is strange. But apparently he went and saw Dad at the funeral home yesterday afternoon. And he left a note for me at the front desk of the motel. It was kind of classic Russ. All it said was, *Here. Talk soon.*"

"That *is* classic Russ," I said. "But it's also weird. Who tracked him down?"

"I have no idea, but I ran into someone I went to high school with who said they'd bumped into him in town a couple weeks ago."

"A couple weeks ago?" I said. "Again, weird."

"He's still a puzzle to me," Janice said. "At any rate, I didn't want to finalize the funeral arrangements until I got in touch with him, and now we're up against Thanksgiving. I don't expect it will be a big service, but I put it off until next Monday. The only other option at this point would be Wednesday, and that would only give us a couple days to pull something together. Supposing we actually *can* manage to pull something together. Dad left a note about funeral arrangements, which he absurdly had notarized and attached to his will. *Burn me*, it said. *No particular desire to be strewn about anywhere. As for the rest, I suppose the usual mumbo jumbo will suffice. If anyone has something to say, let them say it. What do I care? I'll be dead.*" With that she let loose a skreeing, full-throated laugh that unspooled in waves of increasingly higher pitches. I instantly remembered that intoxicating laugh from her visits to Screaming Wheels.

I laughed along with her. "He was an interesting character," I said.

"Oh, God, was he ever. Imagine having him for a father. I'm sure I'll never meet a weirder man."

"I didn't really get to know him," I said. "He almost never came around the rink. But from everything I heard from Russ he was fascinating, that's for damn sure."

"Not so much," Janice said. "Trust me. He was just weird as hell for as long as I can remember, and he got weirder as he got older."

We chatted for a bit longer, then I asked her to tell Russ I was in town when she finally spoke to him and to pass along my phone number. "I'm really eager to see him," I said.

"So am I," she said. "I'm just hoping like hell he hasn't gone down the Art road. He definitely got the old man's weirdo genes. Cross your fingers."

"That's what I love about Russ," I said. "The weirdo genes. I think he somehow passed some of them to me. I'm a little terrified he's become normal."

"Not a fucking chance!" Janice said, and she unleashed that laugh again.

XXVII.

I stayed up much of the night, pacing and listening to records and staring out across the rooftops of Prentice, which, from my vantage, had been transformed into an idyllic snow globe by the storm. I watched as the first ineffectual light of Monday morning came sweeping into the town from the east. Thanksgiving was only a few days away, which felt strange; it had completely snuck up on me. If Janice hadn't mentioned it, I would likely have remained oblivious, so completely disconnected and out of time were my days in Prentice. Just as in the previous year, Rollie likely would call me at some point on Wednesday and insist I join him at Big Sammy's Supper Club for a private dinner with his dwindling circle of Prentice bachelors.

There had been a message from Rollie on my machine when I got home: "Please let me know you're alive. My guys will come and blow the snow in the morning."

I tried to sleep shortly after the sun came up, but I was too restless. I kept trying different records—Brian Eno's *Music for Airports*, Van Morrison's *Inarticulate Speech of the Heart*, Nick Drake, Brahms—that I hoped would help me calm down, but nothing worked. I finally put on Earth, Wind & Fire's *That's the Way of the World* and danced deliriously.

Rollie was an early riser, so I called him at 7:30 to let him know I'd made it home safe. He was relieved to hear from me, but seemed agitated. "I'm dealing with a fuckup here, Bubby. I know the roads are still shit, but I need a favor."

"Sure," I said. "What's up?"

"I sat around the warehouse all day Friday and Saturday waiting for an important delivery, and it turned out some dipshit in the Cities put the wrong zip code on there and it got dumped at the post office in Hollandale. I can't lift boxes for shit anymore, so if you could take one of the vans over there and pick the stuff up, I'd owe you."

I told him it was no problem and agreed to meet him at the warehouse in a few hours. I couldn't, of course, say no to Rollie, but I was anxious about the possibility Russ might call while I was out. Hollandale was only fifteen miles away, a straight shot on the interstate, but I had no idea what Rollie's errand entailed or how long it would take.

I was as wound up as I'd been in years, couldn't sit still, and every one of my tics was triggering in manic, uncontrollable bursts. I paced and danced and ran in place, shot imaginary baskets, and played furious air guitar. I spent about fifteen minutes changing the greeting on my answering machine, re-recording it over and over, trying to make it sound breezy and nonchalant. Mostly, though, I wanted to make it clear that I was around and available. I eventually settled on "Hey, it's Matt. I probably haven't strayed too far. Leave me a message and I'll get right back to you."

I called Veronica, and she and her dogs met me outside the stadium and walked with me downtown to fetch my car from my grandmother's house. Then I drove to the Carnap warehouse on the east side of town and found Rollie sorting through papers at his desk.

"Hey, Bubby," he said. He looked up at me and squinted. "What's going on in that head of yours?"

"I'm pretty good," I said.

"What? You're wound up like a top," Rollie said. "It's all over you. Didn't you sleep?"

"Not much," I said. "Have you seen Russ or heard from him?"

"Not a peep, and I wouldn't expect to. We were never exactly cozy. You're bound to run into him eventually, though. He's supposed to be around here somewhere."

"I'm kind of nervous about seeing him," I said.

"Oh, hell, Bubs. It'll be fine. You guys have a thing. Say, is the heat working up there in the box?"

"It seems to be," I said. "It's plenty warm."

"Make sure you keep those defrosters on, or those windows will ice over."

"I got it, Rollie. We went through this a dozen times last year. Are you going to tell me about this job?"

"Just take one of the vans and drive out to Hollandale to the post office," he said. "There's just one old guy who works at the place. He'll know what's what. There should be a bunch of boxes you'll need to bring back in the van."

XXVIII.

Hollandale was the first little town off the interstate heading west out of Prentice and right off the highway. The population wasn't more than a couple hundred people, but there were farms scattered around the countryside stretching between there and Prentice, and Hollandale somehow managed to sustain both a shiny new bank and a funeral home.

The post office was in a corrugated-tin one-story building. The postmaster was playing solitaire at the counter when I came in. He was an old fellow, with a dirty dress shirt and baggy suspenders, straight out of central casting. I told him I was there to pick up some boxes for Roland Carnap over in Prentice.

He looked at me over the tops of his glasses and said, "You're Matthew Carnap?"

"Yes," I said.

He handed me a slip of paper and said, "I'll just need you to sign this. The boxes are right up the street, 167 Maple. There are a bunch of them. And there's this as well." He slid a padded envelope, addressed to me, across the counter. I tore it open and removed a ring with four keys attached.

"What are these?" I asked.

"They look like keys," he said. "I assume you'll need those to get in there for your boxes."

Before I'd finished signing the paperwork the old guy had turned his attention back to his card game.

Maple Street, the main drag in Hollandale, was only about five blocks long running south to north. I checked the street addresses and trolled along looking for 167.

At the northern edge of town, perched at the edge of fields of shattered corn, was the old Gene's United Skates. I hadn't been there since the Screaming Wheels days and was taken aback to see that huge old Quonset barn still sitting there, set way back on a large plot of land and surrounded by unplowed parking lots. The place appeared to be out of business, but I pulled around the corner and parked. At the end of the driveway I saw a rusty mailbox with fading laminate sticker numbers: 167.

I trudged through the snow until I was close enough to read the words painted on the whitewashed façade. I stood there for several moments staring up at that sign. The paint job looked recent, and in a swirling font similar to the original Coca-Cola logo were the words—two feet high and rendered in bright red—*The Spirit of the Living Creatures*. Directly above the entryway on a green awning, in another stylish script, were white letters that read, *The Rolling Revival. Your Skate Escape—Till the Wheels Fall Off.*

I tried the front door and, as expected, it was locked. I put my face to the glass and tried to see inside, but it was too dark, and the glare of the sun off the glass made it impossible to make out anything. I'd put the keys from the padded envelope in my coat pocket, and I fished them out and fumbled with the door lock. My hands, I realized, were shaking, and I was actually queasy. I felt like I was hallucinating or dreaming, literally, and it was increasingly frightening.

The second key I tried tripped the lock, and I stepped inside. It took a moment for my eyes to adjust, and I was more unsteady by the second, but the light inside was eerily familiar. The building was huge, maybe five times as big as Screaming Wheels, and the rink was a classic oval, almost as large, it seemed, as a football field. The ceiling seemed to be far away, and there were glass block windows stretching around the entire rink just beneath the trusses, and through every one of those windows fractured sunlight rolled like moving water into the interior darkness.

The wood of the rink floor was burnished, and patches of shifting light moved there as well. I took another few steps and took the whole thing in as best I could. There, along the western wall, and perched well above the rink floor, was an almost exact replica of the

High Tower. Just up a few carpeted steps to my left was a lounge area lined with benches. Beyond that was an alcove, separated from the main room by a counter and filled with racks of skates. And along the adjacent wall, flanked by the bathrooms, were orderly stacks of boxes.

A note was taped to the top of a box sitting on the skate rental counter: "Here. Talk soon. Handle with care!" I took a key and broke the tape seal on the box: records. And a typed playlist, faded and weathered, with a handwritten note at the top—*Screaming Wheels: The Gold Standard.*

I poked into a few other boxes. Every one of them was full of records.

I wandered around in there for at least a half hour, poking around and alternately laughing and crying. I flipped every light switch I could find, and each time some new detail emerged that made me laugh and cry even harder. The disco ball was up there, suspended from the ceiling. There were actually three of them, one huge one in the middle and smaller ones at opposite ends of the rink. The pastel-colored globes I remembered from Screaming Wheels were up there as well, or at least uncanny replicas of them. The whole room was lit up like a dream carnival at dusk.

I eventually made my way up to the High Tower. It was even higher than the old one, and instead of one modest set of five carpeted steps there was a circular iron staircase that took you up through a hole in the middle of the tower floor. The stereo setup was truly awe-inspiring. Besides the turntables and amplifier, there were a bunch of other daunting pieces of immense hardware and a mixing board. I was too intimidated to touch any of it.

Rollie had had a mobile phone for a couple years—it was this ugly little Nokia thing that looked like a toy—and had been badgering me to get one so we could track each other down, but the idea terrified me. I'd only recently started seeing people talking on mobile phones around Prentice, and many of my old Minneapolis friends had also been early adopters. I had zero interest in talking with anyone on a mobile phone; I didn't even really want to talk to anyone on a landline, but at least landlines were avoidable; I didn't have to answer, and a caller had no way of knowing I wasn't home. I hated my answering machine, providing as it did an awkward and unwelcome acknowledgement that I had, in fact, *received* a call.

As I wandered around that rink, though, I wished for the first time that I had a mobile phone. I wanted to call Rollie, or Veronica, wanted to get to the bottom of this incredible business. I wanted an explanation.

The phone at the admission booth by the front door had no dial tone; ditto for the one on the wall behind the skate rental counter. In a nook off the front of the rink was an arcade—a bunch of pinball and video games, and a photo booth—with a phone booth back in the corner. I picked up the receiver and was thrilled to hear a dial tone. I fished in my pockets for a quarter, but I had no change at all. Nonetheless, I was determined, so I trudged back through the snow of the parking lot to my car and checked the ashtray, the floorboards, under the seats and floormats, in the creases of the seats, cursing the whole while. I, who had once driven all over the Midwest with a trunk full of quarters, now couldn't turn up a single one. As I walked back across the lot to the rink, I noticed tracks—both foot and car—around the front door; someone, obviously, had come and gone since the snow had fallen.

I went back into the rink and walked around the place some more, checking things out and turning off lights. After I'd turned out the last of them, I noticed a beam of sunlight splashing off a windowpane high above the rink in the back corner. I flipped a light switch again and my eyes followed the sunbeam. Maybe thirty feet above the rink was what looked like an enclosed opera box—or a press box—with three windows. I found a door in the northwest corner of the rink, and it led to a short vestibule and an exit. On one side of this vestibule was a narrow circular stairway, much like the one leading to the High Tower. I followed it up and at the top was another door. I knocked several times and, after receiving no answer, tried the handle. The door opened into a small, tidy loft apartment: one high-ceilinged room with a bedroom and living room on one side, a bathroom in the corner, a little kitchen, and a bank of windows that looked out over the rink. It smelled new, like sawdust and fresh paint. On the bedstand sat a splayed copy of Philip K. Dick's *The Man in the High Castle*. A little strip of peeling masking tape with the word *Tower* written on it covered the word *Castle*. I'd given Russ that book many years ago and had put the tape there myself. Tucked in the pages of the book was my uncle Rollie's business card.

On the refrigerator door, Russ had reconstructed the curious gallery that had hung on the refrigerator in our old apartment: There was the familiar postcard photo of Richard Nixon and Elvis Presley, a photo of Dean Martin, and a Kim Fowley quote I'd puzzled over a hundred times: *The world owes you a living—flaming creatures. Go wild until you get it.* There was also a snapshot I'd never seen of Russ, my mother, and me sitting at a picnic table somewhere, a stack of records and an old portable phonograph on the table between us. All of us were smiling, maybe even laughing. We looked happy.

I found a scrap of paper, scrawled a note, and left it on the bed: *Here. Talk soon.*

On the trip back to Prentice I drove in silence, but it was a loud silence. My head roared with questions, excitement, terror, exhilaration, disbelief. At one point I glanced at the speedometer and realized I was going almost a hundred miles an hour.

When I pulled the van into the warehouse parking lot, I still hadn't formulated a single clear thought or question. Rollie was on the phone when I walked into his office, and he only looked up at me briefly and raised his eyebrows. I stood there staring at him as he talked, but I don't remember a thing he said. I was studying him like a chess piece, but he wasn't giving anything away.

He hung up the phone eventually and stared back at me. "Well," he said. "How'd that go? You have my stuff?"

"Your *stuff*, Rollie? Seriously, what the fuck?" This, I realized, was shouted.

"What's gotten into you, Bubby? I sent you on a little errand. Was that too much to ask?"

"Jesus, Rollie! Come on! What the hell is going on? I seriously think I'm going crazy."

For the first time I saw a smirk creep across his face. He shuffled some papers on his desk and then looked back up at me and smiled. "It's pretty nice, eh?"

"What?" I said. "Define *it*. I have no fucking idea. Honest to God, Rollie. What is it?"

"The whole shebang," Rollie said. "You're a smart fella. I assume you figured out how to get in there and had a chance to eyeball things."

"I went there to pick up a delivery for you," I said. "And then what happened?"

"And then what happened?"

"You know damn well what happened, Rollie," I said. "I feel like I've been set up."

"You have been set up, Bubby. It was all a setup."

"A really elaborate, crazy setup," I said. "How'd that happen? Whose big idea was this?"

"It's not a big idea, Bubs. Let's be honest, you've never had an idea in your life. You're a dreamer. It's not the easiest way to get along in this world, but there's nothing wrong with it."

"Okay," I said. "Whose dream is it, then?"

Rollie smiled and shrugged. "It sure as hell isn't mine. Look, you're going to have to hash this out with your buddy."

"Russ?" I said. "He's not my buddy."

"What is he, then?"

I hesitated. "I don't know what he is."

"Well, whatever the hell he is, you two can sit down and take it from here."

"Where is he?"

Rollie laughed, then let out a big sigh. "He's in town, Matty. He was in here earlier looking for you. If I had to guess, I'd say he's probably out at the football field, waiting to pounce. You're both fucking nuts."

"Fuck, Rollie," I said. "How much of this is you and how much of it is Russ?"

"Talk to Vargo," he said. He came out from behind his desk and pulled me into a bear hug. "Relax, Bubby," he said. "It's okay to let yourself be happy. Between you and Russ, you have enough money to buy an island somewhere and live out your days. You can do whatever the hell you want if this doesn't work. And you know what your grandfather would say about all of it? You remember? 'This is happiness,' Big Leonard would say every time we were all together. 'This is a blessing. Honor it.' Besides, I'm not going to live forever. It's time for you to find your tribe."

XXIX.

Russ was indeed waiting for me back at the football field. As I walked up Second Avenue from my grandmother's house to the stadium, I saw him pacing in front of the ticket office. When he saw me coming up the driveway, he stopped pacing and watched my approach.

He was taller than I remembered, a couple inches taller than me, and still skinny. His hair was shaggy but short and flecked with gray. As I got closer, he broke out his biggest shit-eating grin. "There you are," he said. "We're here. This is excellent. If we'd waited a few more years, we'd have been able to track each other through the microchips they're going to implant in all of us. Wow, look at you, Matt. Damn, man. You actually grew up."

He threw open his arms and I moved into his embrace. We stood there for several minutes, just holding on to each other. I was blubbering.

"I'm sorry," I said, over and over again.

"So am I," he said. "But whatever. Be here now, motherfucker. Come on, I need to see this pad of yours."

I unlocked the gate and we strolled to the press box. "How long have you been around?" I said.

"I've been living out in Hollandale on and off for five months," he said. "I came back when my dad first started really fading, maybe a year ago, and I've been here full time and laying low since the end of August." He threw up his hands. "I got nowhere else to go!"

"Did you know I was here?"

"Not initially," he said. "But I finally got up the courage to talk to your uncle when I was back here in late July, and he told me. He also told me the old Gene's United Skates was for sale. He gave me your phone number and encouraged me to call you, but I wasn't ready. Maybe a month after I first talked to Rollie, he called and told me there was a potential buyer for the rink who was going to tear it down and build on the lot, so he went ahead and bought the fucking thing. He was willing to sell me a fifty percent stake if I'd agree to be partners." He shrugged. "One thing led to another. It was too good to pass up, and your uncle, you know, he has all these connections, and once we started really talking, he went hog wild. We both agreed to keep it on the down low until we were pretty much ready to roll."

"Why didn't anyone tell me?" I said.

Russ laughed. "Duh, Matty. It was supposed to be a surprise. Rollie didn't know if you'd be game or not, and he wasn't entirely sure you were committed to hanging around Prentice. It was his idea to spring it on you. He got a serious kick out of the whole thing. He's a funny guy, you know? I had no idea. It just kept snow-balling. And he finally couldn't wait any longer and he came up with the whole post office charade last week."

"I'm still completely stunned," I said.

"I have to admit it's been unreal fun," Russ said. "I've been dreaming some version of this dream for years, but I never allowed myself to think of it in concrete terms, and eventually I wasn't sure I had it in me anymore."

We'd climbed the steps of the bleachers, and as I unlocked the press box door I said, "This is pretty nuts. I feel kind of sheepish about it."

As I pushed open the door and we stepped inside, Russ erupted in wild, suffocating laughter. "Holy. Fucking. Shit," he kept saying. "Jesus, Matt. This is science fiction. Talk about the High Tower. We should've just replaced the football field with a rink. My God, I'd never leave here. You know, I've driven by here probably a hundred times, and at night I could see your lights. It was pretty dreamy, and I had to resist the urge to bum-rush you, but this is beyond my wildest imagination."

"It's beyond my wildest imagination," I said. "I still feel like it's going to evaporate. I feel the same way about the amazing shit I saw over there in Hollandale today. It felt so much like Screaming

Wheels, but on this gargantuan Hollywood scale. I went into what I assume is your apartment, and it had a lot of this vibe on a cozier scale."

"That's all Rollie," Russ said. "Who knew your uncle had such a swanky imagination? I think the same guys who did this also did all the work at the rink. And there was this amazing young architect who was working some shit job in town when your uncle found him. All of his plans were a marvel. If he'd had his way, that rink apartment would've been ten times the size, but I wanted to keep it small."

As we were talking, Russ of course gravitated to the record racks. He was running his index finger along the spines, pulling out the occasional record for additional investigation. "I'm impressed, Matty; you've built an incredible collection. "

"Not as incredible as yours," I said. "But I've spent years trying to replicate it. I was afraid you'd gotten rid of your records."

"Never even considered it," Russ said. "I did get tired of moving them around, but what would be left of me if I sold my records? I've still never bought a CD player."

"As you can see, I'm not that pure," I said. "I gave in when new stuff started coming out only on CD."

"Yeah, well, we'll obviously have to get a CD player for the tower. It's unavoidable at this point." He turned, plopped down on the couch, and said, "So you get the drill, right, Matty? Maybe it can't be just like the old times, and maybe we'll drive each other batshit, but are you willing to do this with me? Or at least give it a shot?"

"I'm in," I said. "Of course. I can't, though, claim this is anything that ever entered my mind when I moved back here. It actually never entered my mind, period. And it's probably crazy stupid timing. Everywhere I went on the Rubber Route I saw rinks that were out of business."

"That is the elephant in the room," Russ said. "So let's be honest with ourselves: neither of us needs to make a living. I've talked about this with Rollie. He doesn't care about money. My old man never really cared about money. Somehow or another, both of our families managed to become rich as fuck in this dinky, dying town. I was staggered when I found out how much money my dad had. It's obscene, really. I never in my life asked him for anything, but he left everything to Janice and me. Rollie ragged him for selling all his properties and cashing in, but I think for once in his life, Art was actually thinking about his kids. He didn't want us to have to spend the rest of our lives sorting out his estate. And your uncles lived like average, small-town guys, but they were always loaded. Surely you knew that. The bottom line is, we aren't going to have to worry about any bottom line; we don't even have to pretend we're businessmen. In my mind, we're going into public service. That's not to say we can't be creative. The time will come, very soon, when we can market the rink as retro entertainment. We can run shuttle buses just like Gene used to do back in the day, but we can be even more ambitious. We can do events and try to entice people over from Floyd Valley and down from the Cities with party buses. Or we can do nothing whatsoever and listen to music and skate and hang out."

"I think we can get people to skate," I said. "There's a whole generation of young people who have no idea what they missed."

"Exactly, and with the fucking internet we're supposedly going to have all these new ways of reaching people. I'm counting on you for that."

"I don't know shit about the internet," I said. "I don't even own a computer."

"Okay, so we'll figure it out as we go," Russ said. "And who knows? If all this Y2K hysteria is legit, it may all come crashing down in a month or so. I really don't care if I never send or receive an email in my life, just as long as we can still get enough power for the rink."

"It's a hoax," I said. "I'm not worried about it."

"Neither am I." He was still wandering around, taking things in.

"You need to get in touch with Janice," I said. "She's been worried sick about you."

"I know she has. I love my sister, but I just haven't had the energy to deal with her and the arrangements. I'm supposed to be meeting her right about now, though, so I need to scram and take care of it. Before I go, though, I want you to know how devastated I was to hear your mom died. It was like a bomb went off. For so many years I was bitter about Screaming Wheels. I seriously and stupidly thought I'd found my calling and would be there spinning records the rest of my life. I was so focused on the loss of the rink, it took me awhile to realize I was also—and perhaps especially—grieving for that period that you, your mom, and I spent together in that place. The whole package gutted me. I never had it better."

"I was hurt I never heard from you," I said. "I thought maybe you didn't get the news."

"Oh, I heard," Russ said. "My dad gave me occasional updates and called me when Jean died. I tried getting in touch with you when I heard she was really sick, left messages on that nutjob's answering machine in Floyd Valley, and when I heard nothing back after a few weeks, I just assumed you were in a dark place and had probably moved on with your life."

"You left messages at Baron's house?"

"Yes, a lot of them. I spoke to him once. I told him how sorry I was, and I practically begged him to have you call me. I was going to drive down for the funeral, but I worried it would be a distraction or a shit show. Ultimately, though, I was chickenshit. And I'm really, really sorry about that. Rollie told me it was brutal."

"It *was* brutal," I said. "That whole period was hell. As she was dying, though, my mother and I talked a lot about those years at the rink, and she was heartbroken you and I weren't in touch. She had a lot of her own regrets about that time."

The phone rang and I let it go to the answering machine. It was Janice: "Hi, Matt. It's Janice. If my brother happens to be there, would you please tell that asshole I've been sitting here at the Oak Grill for half an hour waiting for him? He should know better than to piss me off."

"Oh fuck," Russ said. "Okay, I'm on my way. I feel really embarrassed about this"—he fished a mobile phone out of his pocket—"but your uncle insisted I had to get this thing so he could track me down when his guys needed to get in and out of the rink. Anyway, here's the number. The rink lines won't be hooked up until next week." He jotted the number down on a copy of the *Dispatch* that included his father's obituary, gave me another hug, and dashed out the door. I watched him go down the bleacher steps and amble off around the track. He still moved like he was on skates.

XXX.

I couldn't sit still, and I had the urge to drive back out to the rink and skate off some of my manic energy. I rustled around in my pockets for Veronica's phone number and called her. She answered on the second ring.

"Hey," I said.

"Who's this?" she said.

"Matt," I said. "The guy over at the football field."

"Oh, *that* Matt. Sure, now it's coming back to me. Kidding. I was hoping I'd hear from you. What's going on?"

"I've had an unbelievable day," I said. "And I was hoping you were free to talk. I have a weird proposition for you."

"Already with the weird propositions," she said. "Oh, boy."

"I promise it's no weirder than your proposition out by the railroad tracks," I said.

"I don't know that I'd call that a proposition," she said.

"I certainly would."

"Suit yourself. I just finished grading some papers, so it's good timing. Where are you?"

"I'm at the press box," I said. I went to the window and could see her lights. "I see you," I said.

"No, you don't," Veronica said. "The curtains are drawn. Now, though, you can see me. I'm waving."

I saw the curtains part and could just make out a figure behind the glass.

"Wow," I said. "Creepy. That reminds me of those curtains at your mother's house."

"Oh, God," she said. "You have quite a memory."

"Where do you want to meet?" I said.

"I'll start walking over."

"I'll come down to meet you," I said.

We met up in the driveway outside the gates, and Veronica took my hand like it was the most natural thing in the world.

"So tell me about this unbelievable day," she said.

"I'd really like to show you rather than tell you."

"Does this involve fireflies and a dollhouse?" she asked.

"In a way," I said. "I'd say it's comparable, at the very least."

"I'm intrigued," she said. "What does it involve?"

"It involves a short drive," I said. "And I promise you I'm not a creep."

"How reassuring," she said. "I'm game. It's a school night, though, so you can't keep me out late."

"That's fine. We'll have to walk up to my grandmother's house to get my car, though," I said.

"We can take my car if it's easier," she said.

"That's a good idea," I said. "I'd be a serious hazard behind the wheel right now."

"You're not drunk, are you?"

"No," I said. "Just sleep deprived and really wired. And nervous."

"What are you nervous about?"

"It's good nervousness," I said. "Trust me."

As we walked to her house, Veronica asked where we were going.

"I'd rather not say," I said. "It's a surprise."

"Can I take my dogs?" she said.

"I don't see why not."

She went up the steps of her house, opened the door, and the dogs came bounding out and swarmed me. "Be nice," she said to them. "Want to go for a car ride?" Both dogs immediately rushed to her Subaru station wagon.

"They know that phrase," I said.

"They know lots of phrases," she said. "And they live for car rides."

After we'd all piled into the car, I told Veronica to head west on the interstate. "We're going to Hollandale," I said.

"Never heard of it. How far?"

"Fifteen miles, maybe. Not far."

"I now have some indication that you like music," she said. "A very strong indication that I must confess kind of intimidates me. But there are a bunch of CDs in that box at your feet if you want to see if I have anything that passes muster."

I've tried hard in my adult life not to judge other people's musical tastes. But I also have to confess that I've never been very successful. This seemed like a test, and I hated myself for that. *At least, I thought, music is enough a part of her life that she keeps a box of CDs in her car.* I pulled the box onto my lap, and as I did, I could feel her watching me out of the corner of her eyes and waiting for my reaction.

"Watch the road," I said.

There were maybe twenty-five discs in the shoebox. I scanned the titles, then went back and ran through them again, grading them in my mind. Prince's *Sign o' the Times* and *Purple Rain*. Greatest hits packages by Billie Holiday and James Brown. Toni Braxton, Mariah Carey, Janet Jackson, Alanis Morissette, and a couple different R.E.M. albums. Joni Mitchell's *Blue* and Bob Dylan's *Blood on the Tracks*. Van Morrison's *Into the Music*. The Beatles' *Rubber Soul*. Neil Young's *Harvest Moon*. Dusty Springfield's *Dusty in Memphis*. Beth Orton's *Trailer Park*. A couple different Lucinda Williams records—*Sweet Old World* and *Car Wheels on a Gravel Road*—and a handful of records I hadn't heard yet but knew of, including PJ Harvey's *Is This Desire?* and Everything but the Girl's *Temperamental*.

"The suspense is killing me," she said.

"I might cry," I said.

"Oh, God. Why?"

"I'm really not a crier," I said. "Honest to God. But I've been crying all day."

"Why?"

"I'm not sure. But they've all been happy tears."

"My taste makes you want to cry happy tears?"

"Yes," I said. "You have a bunch of stuff I love, a bunch I don't know, and some I've never even heard of. That's fantastic."

"Yeah? Are there any you hate? Because if you say Prince or Joni Mitchell, I'm gonna have to stop the car and make you walk home."

"Nope," I said. "I love them both. And I'm not just being nice. I take this stuff way too seriously."

"Put something on," she said.

I looked through the discs again and chose Van Morrison's *Into the Music*.

"This is the nicest surprise," I said. "It's one of my really special records. I played it over and over when my mother died. But it's not at all a bummer to me. There's an uplift to the whole thing."

"It's my spring record," Veronica said. "'When the Healing Has Begun' is the song I listen to over and over every cruel April, when I'm just dying for May."

"I totally get that. That was one of the songs that really pulled me through my grief."

The dogs were both already sound asleep in the back seat by the time I told Veronica to take the Hollandale turnoff. We drove slowly down Maple Street, past the post office and the bright lights and clattering American flags of the bank and the funeral home. "Next driveway on the right," I said, just as we were about to plunge back into the darkness of the countryside.

The parking lot had been plowed since I was there earlier, and we pulled right up to the front door. "Here we are," I said.

As we got out of the car and Veronica turned the dogs loose, I saw her already taking in the signs on the building, which were illuminated by a couple floodlights. "What is this?" she said. "Please tell me you're not taking me to some church."

I shrugged. "You never know. But yeah, kind of."

"'Spirit of the Living Creatures'?" she said.

"It's from Ezekiel."

"Are you a religious guy?" she said.

"I could be. I for sure believe what this place teaches, though. Wholeheartedly."

I thought maybe Russ would be back, but there were no other cars in the parking lot. After I unlocked the front door, Veronica called for the dogs, and we all moved into the vestibule near the ticket counter.

"Please don't look until I tell you," I said, and she covered her eyes.

I found a couple switch plates and turned on the main lights, then I scurried across the room with both dogs tagging along, flipping all the other switches I could find. It was too bright. I remembered that the dimmer switches at Screaming Wheels, as well as the controls for the disco balls and ceiling lights, were in the High Tower.

"Keep your eyes closed," I said, and I climbed the staircase to the tower. The switches were right where I expected them, and I dimmed the lights until the effect was that of the gloaming vibe I associated with the best rinks. I tapped a couple buttons next to the dimmer switches, and the pastel orbs came on and the disco balls began to swivel. I wished I knew how to operate the sound system, but that would have to wait for Russ.

"Okay," I shouted. "You can come on in."

When I emerged at the bottom of the staircase, the dogs were scampering around the rink and chasing disco ball shadows. Veronica was turning slow circles in the middle of the rink floor with her arms stretched out and her head thrown back, as if she were trying to catch snowflakes with her tongue.

"Have you ever been here?" I asked.

"Are you kidding?" she said. "Where is here? Where am I? And what are we doing here?"

"This is the old Gene's United Skates," I said. "It was the big skating rink around here when I was a kid. I think it was the biggest roller-skating rink in Minnesota. I spent every day during those years when I first met you skating and listening to music, and this place was our big competitor. This vibe is kind of what I was looking for when I came back to Prentice."

I couldn't help myself. I was getting emotional. Veronica came over and hugged me. "So why are we here?" she said. "Is this where you start dreaming again?"

"It's a really, really long story," I said. "But, yes, I hope so. I came here this afternoon on a sham errand for my uncle. All those signs out front are new—they're all a sort of coded language only Russ and I understand—and everything in here is more or less new but also a seriously uncanny recreation of the old rink. I hadn't been out here in at least fifteen years. It turns out this place was closed and for sale, and my uncle and Russ bought it, and Russ had an apartment built up there in the corner"—I pointed. "He's going to live here and I'm going to run it with him. Does that sound crazy?"

"Yes," Veronica said. "It all sounds crazy. But it also sounds wonderful. This place totally feels like it belongs to you."

"You can't experience the full effect until the music is blasting and you're rolling and out of your body," I said. "Are you a skater?"

"I grew up in southern Minnesota in the seventies and eighties," she said. "What do you think? Of course I'm a skater. In Mankato we had Patton's Roller Garden. I don't think I've skated since probably my freshman year of high school, but I used to have some moves."

The dogs heard Russ at the door before we did, and they ran, barking, in that direction. When he emerged from the vestibule, he looked genuinely startled. "Jesus, man, you scared the shit out of me," he said. "Where did these dogs come from?"

"This is Veronica," I said. "They're hers."

She'd managed to get a hold of both their collars and was trying to wrangle them. "This is Louis," she said, indicating the bigger of the pair, a hound mix. "And this is Wardell. They're both pound mutts. Wardell's got some husky in him, and maybe some retriever. He's a diabetic. Neither of them would hurt a fly, and they're the apples of my eye."

"Veronica, this is Russ," I said.

"Pleased to meet you," Russ said. He looked at me and raised his eyebrows, and then kissed Veronica's hand. "What do you think?"

"I'm enchanted," Veronica said.

"How do you guys know each other?"

"We've been friends for fifteen years," Veronica said. "Sort of."

I asked Russ if we could show Veronica the apartment. "Sure," he said. "I haven't really had a chance to make it unpresentable yet."

He led us across the rink and out into the hallway, where we followed him up the stairs. It looked even more surreal with nothing but the lights from the rink splashing around in there.

"I feel like I'm inside an aquarium," Veronica said. "Or an old steamship. It's like a more compact version of the press box."

"Exactly," Russ said. "Same architect. It doesn't have quite the same sweeping vista or length, but I like it. I wanted it to be like the captain's quarters on top of a big boat."

I led Veronica to the refrigerator and pointed out the family picture. "That's my mother and me with Russ, back in the Screaming Wheels days."

"Your mother is drop-dead gorgeous," Veronica said.

"Your uncle gave me that picture," Russ said. "I'd never seen it before. When Rollie brought that by was when I really started to come around on the guy."

We sat around talking while the dogs made themselves at home on Russ's bed, and then we went back downstairs and took Veronica to see the High Tower.

"This system is a killer," Russ said. "I'm not shitting you, Matty. We're going to be able to rattle the windows."

"I was too afraid to touch it," I said. "It looks way out of my league."

"You'll learn. Why don't you guys strap on some skates? I haven't broken this thing in yet. You'll be my first skaters."

"What do you think?" I asked Veronica. "Are you game?"

"Are you crazy? Of course, let's skate."

Russ followed us to the rental counter. "You guys help yourselves," he said. "I gotta haul some more of these records up to the tower." He picked up a box and started to carry it across the rink. After he'd traveled maybe fifteen feet, he turned back and said, "You know what's in here, Matty?"

"I peeked," I said. "It's the Gold Standard."

Veronica and I picked out skates and went to one of the benches to change out of our shoes.

"Hey, Matt," Russ shouted from the High Tower. "I've got your old Screaming Wheels skates. They're under the counter. I'm pissed you left them behind. Also, you still have the sign?"

"I do," I said. "It's in the press box."

"I want it back."

"Of course."

"What's the sign say?" Veronica said.

"*The spirit of the living creatures was in the wheels.*"

Russ climbed back down from the tower, fished around in a cooler near the door, and walked back over to us with a couple beers. "Okay, this is important business," he said. "We need to huddle about this. What's the first song going to be?"

"It always used to be 'Ring of Fire,'" I said.

"That was just an icebreaker."

"It's a good one," I said.

"It's a *really* good one," Veronica said. "That's one of the first records I remember."

Russ shrugged. "What else? I'm out of practice. You have a playlist in mind?"

"You're the master," I said. "You always told me to trust the feel and honor the groove. Remember? The customers are here to skate, and your job is to keep them on the floor and moving."

"Oh, right," Russ said. "Jesus, this is pressure. I'm actually nervous. Veronica, any requests?"

"Surprise me," she said.

Back in the High Tower he fired up the sound system and started barking into a microphone—a new wrinkle. "Who's ready for the twenty-first century?" he shouted.

"Not me," I shouted back.

"Me either," Veronica said.

"Viva the twentieth century!" Russ said. "The spirit of the living creatures is in the wheels forever and ever, or until the wheels fall off! Free your mind and your ass will follow! Who's ready to get turned inside out? Who's ready to vibrate and levitate? Who's ready to roll?"

Veronica and I both threw our heads back and whooped.

The horn intro to "Ring of Fire" erupted from the ceiling speakers, crystal clear and seemingly coming from everywhere, and Veronica and I simultaneously launched ourselves out onto the floor. She was a few steps ahead of me, whooping for the dogs, and they came bounding after her, slipping and sliding and running in wild circles. I paused for a moment, watched the wondrous spectacle of them rocketing across the floor, then I skated in pursuit. As Veronica rounded the first turn she executed a perfect heel pivot, shouted my name, and reached for my hand. When I took it she swept me along, howling with laughter as the dogs skidded and leapt around us. We kept picking up velocity, leaning into the curves, and I felt that beautiful and familiar throbbing in the soles of my skates, and my heart felt full to the point of bursting, and somewhere beyond the motion and the music, I was aware of Russ in the High Tower bouncing up and down and thrusting a fist in the air and shouting, "Yes! Yes! Yes! Yes! Yes!"

For Allison Locey, for shining so bright for so many.

Acknowledgments

With huge love and gratitude: Kate McGuire and Lily and Reed Hoffmann, for everything, but especially for showing me I wasn't done with my changes and for accommodating my late nights and noise. Sladjana Dirakovic and John Wareham. Chrissie and Bob Dunlap. Steve Horwitz and Stu Abraham. Chris Fischbach. Jim Baker. Geoff Garton. Mike Cummings. Chris Hesler. Burl Gilyard. David Rathman. Alec Soth. Tim Carpenter. Jason Vaughn. Raymond and Adam Meeks. David Small. Mike McGuire. Tim O'Connell. Peter Schilling. Andy Sturdevant. Anne and Torstein Hansen. Kristin Henning and Tom Bartel. Jimmy Gaines. Inna Valin. Beth Popalisky. Carrie Thompson and Goma Carchedi. Everybody at the Murray Hotel in Livingston, Montana. Jennifer Thompson and Nathan Vogt at Nordlyset. Anitra Budd and all the terrific Coffee House people. The VMM. The Rollercade and the Roller Garden. My amazing family, for plumbing my heart. Sheila Kennedy, for taking off my training wheels. My beloved guide dogs—Chula, Willis, Wendell, and Winsor—for getting me dressed and feeding me light. And to Greenland Earle, wherever you are.

Coffee House Press began as a small letterpress operation in 1972 and has grown into an internationally renowned nonprofit publisher of literary fiction, essay, poetry, and other work that doesn't fit neatly into genre categories.

Coffee House is both a publisher and an arts organization. Through our *Books in Action* program and publications, we've become interdisciplinary collaborators and incubators for new work and audience experiences. Our vision for the future is one where a publisher is a catalyst and connector.

LITERATURE
is not the same thing as
PUBLISHING

Funder Acknowledgments

Coffee House Press is an internationally renowned independent book publisher and arts nonprofit based in Minneapolis, MN; through its literary publications and *Books in Action* program, Coffee House acts as a catalyst and connector—between authors and readers, ideas and resources, creativity and community, inspiration and action.

Coffee House Press books are made possible through the generous support of grants and donations from corporations, state and federal grant programs, family foundations, and the many individuals who believe in the transformational power of literature. This activity is made possible by the voters of Minnesota through a Minnesota State Arts Board Operating Support grant, thanks to the legislative appropriation from the Arts and Cultural Heritage Fund. Coffee House also receives major operating support from the Amazon Literary Partnership, Jerome Foundation, McKnight Foundation, Target Foundation, and the National Endowment for the Arts (NEA). To find out more about how NEA grants impact individuals and communities, visit www.arts.gov.

Coffee House Press receives additional support from Bookmobile; Dorsey & Whitney LLP; Elmer L. & Eleanor J. Andersen Foundation; Fredrikson & Byron, P.A.; the Matching Grant Program Fund of the Minneapolis Foundation; Mr. Pancks' Fund in memory of Graham Kimpton; the Schwab Charitable Fund; and the U.S. Bank Foundation.

The Publisher's Circle of Coffee House Press

Publisher's Circle members make significant contributions to Coffee House Press's annual giving campaign. Understanding that a strong financial base is necessary for the press to meet the challenges and opportunities that arise each year, this group plays a crucial part in the success of Coffee House's mission.

Recent Publisher's Circle members include many anonymous donors, Patricia A. Beithon, Anitra Budd, Andrew Brantingham, Dave & Kelli Cloutier, Mary Ebert & Paul Stembler, Jocelyn Hale & Glenn Miller, the Rehael Fund-Roger Hale/Nor Hall of the Minneapolis Foundation, Randy Hartten & Ron Lotz, Dylan Hicks & Nina Hale, William Hardacker, Kenneth & Susan Kahn, Stephen & Isabel Keating, the Kenneth Koch Literary Estate, Cinda Kornblum, Jennifer Kwon Dobbs & Stefan Liess, the Lambert Family Foundation, the Lenfestey Family Foundation, Sarah Lutman & Rob Rudolph, the Carol & Aaron Mack Charitable Fund of the Minneapolis Foundation, Gillian McCain, Malcolm S. McDermid & Katie Windle, Mary & Malcolm McDermid, Daniel N. Smith III & Maureen Millea Smith, Peter Nelson & Jennifer Swenson, Enrique & Jennifer Olivarez, Alan Polsky, Robin Preble, Jeffrey Sugerman & Sarah Schultz, Nan G. Swid, Grant Wood, and Margaret Wurtele.

For more information about the Publisher's Circle and other ways to support Coffee House Press books, authors, and activities, please visit www.coffeehousepress.org/pages/donate or contact us at info@coffeehousepress.org.

Brad Zellar has worked as a writer and editor for daily and weekly newspapers, as well as for regional and national magazines. A former senior editor at *City Pages*, *The Rake*, and *Utne Reader*, Zellar is also the author of *Suburban World: The Norling Photos, Conductors of the Moving World, House of Coates*, and *Driftless*. He has frequently collaborated with the photographer Alec Soth, and together they produced seven editions of *The LBM Dispatch*, chronicling American community life in the twenty-first century. Zellar's work has been featured in the *New York Times Magazine*, *The Believer*, *Paris Review*, *Vice*, *Guernica*, *Aperture*, and Russian *Esquire*. He spent fifteen years working in bookstores and was a co-owner of Rag & Bone Books in Minneapolis. He currently lives in Saint Paul.

Till the Wheels Fall Off was designed by
Bookmobile Design & Digital Publisher Services.
Text is set in Alegreya Regular.